Praise for *USA TODAY* bestselling author
RaeAnne Thayne

"If you're going to read only one book this
season, make it *Blackberry Summer*."
—Debbie Macomber, #1 *New York Times*
bestselling author

"A warm, wise story with
emotionally complex and intriguing characters."
—*RT Book Reviews* on *The Daddy Makeover* (4 ½ stars)

"Well-developed characters, plus plenty of raw
emotion—and humor—add up to one of the
author's finest books."
—*RT Book Reviews* on
His Second-Chance Family (4 ½ stars, Top Pick)

"Thayne is a gifted storyteller, whose realistic characters
and absorbing dialogue weave a mesmerizing tale."
—*WordWeaving.com*

RAEANNE THAYNE

finds inspiration in the beautiful northern Utah mountains, where she lives with her husband and three children. Her books have won numerous honors, including three RITA® Award nominations from the Romance Writers of America and a Career Achievement Award from *RT Book Reviews* magazine.

RaeAnne loves to hear from readers and can be reached through her website at www.raeannethayne.com.

USA TODAY Bestselling Author

RaeAnne Thayne

BRAMBLEBERRY SHORES

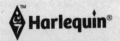 **Harlequin**®

TORONTO NEW YORK LONDON
AMSTERDAM PARIS SYDNEY HAMBURG
STOCKHOLM ATHENS TOKYO MILAN MADRID
PRAGUE WARSAW BUDAPEST AUCKLAND

Recycling programs
for this product may
not exist in your area.

ISBN-13: 978-0-373-68836-4

BRAMBLEBERRY SHORES
Copyright © 2011 by Harlequin Books S.A.

The publisher acknowledges the copyright holder
of the individual works as follows:

THE DADDY MAKEOVER
Copyright © 2007 by RaeAnne Thayne

HIS SECOND-CHANCE FAMILY
Copyright © 2008 by RaeAnne Thayne

CONTENTS

THE DADDY MAKEOVER

Chapter 1

On a scale of one to ten, Sage Benedetto would probably rate the concept of jogging before sunrise every day somewhere around a negative twenty.

While she highly doubted she would ever evolve enough that she could wholly enjoy these runs, after a month, she had at least grown to tolerate the activity. Her gut didn't automatically cramp at just the idea of throwing on her running shoes and her muscles no longer started to spasm after the first few steps.

She supposed that was a good thing.

This would probably never be her favorite thing to do, but she *had* promised, she reminded herself. And while she had many faults—all of which somehow seemed more glaringly obvious in the pale light of early morning—breaking her word was not among them.

Despite the random muscle aches and her inherent dislike of just about any activity that involved sending her heart rate into heavy exertion mode, she had even come to discover an ethereal beauty in these quiet early-morning runs.

The towering sea stacks offshore glowed pink in the first, hesitant rays of the sun; this wide, gorgeous stretch of Oregon beach was empty, at least for a little while longer.

Soon the beach would be crowded with treasure hunters looking for shells or colored glass or any other gift the sea surrendered during the night. But for now it was hers.

Hers and Conan's, anyway.

A huge red beast emerged from behind a cluster of rocks and shuffled to her, scaring up a seagull.

She sighed. This was the reason she was here before sunrise, her thigh muscles burning and her breath sawing raggedly. This rangy, melancholy creature was her responsibility, her curse, her unexpected legacy.

"There you are. You can't keep slipping off your leash or we won't do this anymore."

Abigail's big mutt, rescued from the pound right around the time Abigail rescued Sage, cocked his head and gazed at Sage out of doleful eyes the murky dark green of the sea in a November storm.

Some days these jogs along the shore seemed to lift his spirits—the only reason she carried on with them when she would much rather be home in bed for another hour.

This apparently wouldn't be one of those days.

"I know," she murmured, rubbing his chin as she slipped the leash back on. "She loved these kind of mornings, didn't she? With the air clear and cool and sweet and the day just waiting to explode with possibilities. Anything-can-happen days, that's what she called them."

Conan whined a little and lowered himself to the sand, his head sagging to his forepaws as if he were entirely too exhausted to move.

"You've got to snap out of it, bud. We both do."

She tried to swallow down the lump of grief that had taken up permanent residence in her throat during the past month. Her eyes burned and she wondered when these raw moments of sorrow would stop taking her by surprise.

She blinked away the tears. "Come on, dude. I'll race you home."

He gave her a long, considering look, then heaved to his feet and shuffled off in the direction of Brambleberry House, still a mile down the beach. Even at his most ponderous pace, Conan could outrun her. A pretty sad state of affairs, she decided, and tried to pick up her speed.

Focusing on the sand in front of her, she had only made it a few hundred yards down the beach, when she heard a sharp bark. She turned in the direction of the sound; Conan was at the end of his long retractable leash, sitting with a small figure above the high-tide mark in the sand.

The figure was a young girl, one she wasn't even sure was old enough to be considered a tween. A young girl who was wearing only a pale green nightgown and what looked to be seashell-pink flip-flops on her feet.

To Sage's deep surprise, Conan's tail wagged and he nudged at the girl's hand in a blatant invitation to pet him. She hadn't seen Conan greet *anyone* with this kind of friendly enthusiasm for the better part of a month.

Sage scanned the beach looking in vain for the girl's companion. She checked her watch and saw it was barely 6:00 a.m. What on earth was a young girl doing out here alone on an empty stretch of beach at such an hour, and in nightclothes at that?

"Morning," she called out.

The girl waved. "Is this your dog?" she called to Sage with a big smile. "She's so pretty!"

Conan would just love being called pretty. When he wasn't grieving and morose, the beast had more prickly pride than a hedgehog with an attitude. "*She's* a *he*. And, yeah, I guess you could say he's mine."

Partly hers, anyway. Technically, she shared custody of the dog and ownership of Brambleberry House. But she wasn't about to let thoughts of Anna Galvez ruin one of Abigail's anything-can-happen days.

"His name is Conan," she said instead. "I'm Sage."

"Hi, Conan and Sage. My name's Chloe Elizabeth Spencer."

The girl had short, wavy dark hair, intense green eyes and delicate elfin features. If she'd been in a more whimsical mood, Sage might have thought her a water sprite delivered by the sea.

A cold, wet breeze blew off the Pacific and the girl shivered suddenly, drawing Sage's attention back to her thin nightgown and her nearly bare feet. "Chloe, what are you doing out here by yourself so early?"

She shrugged her narrow shoulders with a winsome smile. "Looking for sand dollars. I found four yesterday but they were all broken so I thought if I came out early enough, the tide might leave some good ones and I could get them before anybody else. I promised my friend Henry I'd bring one back to him and I can't break a promise. He lives in the apartment next door. He's only seven and won't be eight until December. I've been eight for two whole months."

"Where's your mom or dad? Do they know you left?"

"My mom's dead." She said the words in a matter-of-fact way that Sage was only too familiar with. "She died when I was six."

"What about your dad, then?"

"I'm not sure. He's probably still asleep. He got mad at me last night because I wanted to find more sand dollars so I decided to come by myself this morning."

Sage looked around at the few isolated cottages and guesthouses on this stretch of beach. "Are you staying close by? I thought I knew all the eight-year-olds in town."

"Every one?" With a lift of her dark eyebrow, the girl somehow managed to look skeptical and intrigued at the same time.

"I do," Sage assured her. "The ones who live here year-round, anyway. I'm sure I don't remember meeting you."

Cannon Beach's population was only a couple thousand year-round. In the summer, those numbers swelled as tourists flocked to the Oregon shore, but they were still a week or so away from the big crowds.

"We're only here for a few days. Maybe a week. But if it's longer, then my dad says he'll have to send me to stay with Mrs. Strictland so he can get some work done. She's my dad's assistant and she hates me. I don't like going to her house."

Though she knew it was unfair to make snap judgments about a man she had not even met, a clear image of the girl's father formed in Sage's mind—a man too busy to hunt for sand dollars with his motherless child and eager to foist her on his minions so he could return to conquering the world.

She fought down her instinctive urge to take Chloe home with her and watch over her like a sandpiper guarding her nest.

"Do you remember where you're staying, sweetheart?"

Chloe pointed vaguely north. "I think it's that way." She frowned and squinted in the opposite direction. "Or maybe that way. I'm not sure."

"Are you in a hotel or a condo?"

The girl shook her head. "It's a house, right on the beach. My dad would have liked to stay at The Sea Urchin but Mr. Wu said they were all booked. He didn't look very happy when he said it. I think he doesn't like my dad very much."

No wonder she had always considered Stanley Wu an excellent judge of character. She hadn't even met Chloe's father and already she disliked him.

"But what I don't get," the girl went on, "is if he doesn't like my dad, why is he going to sell him his hotel?"

Sage blinked at that unexpected bit of information. She hadn't heard Stanley and Jade Wu were considering selling The Sea Urchin. They had been fixtures in Cannon Beach for decades, their elegant boutique hotel of twenty or so guest rooms consistently named among the best accommodations along the coast.

"Do you know if your rental is close to The Sea Urchin?"

Chloe screwed up her features. "Pretty close, but I think it's on the other side. I didn't walk past it this morning, I don't think."

Though she seemed remarkably unconcerned about standing on wet sand in only her nightgown and flip-flops, she shivered a little and pulled Conan closer.

Sage sighed, bidding a regretful goodbye to any hopes

she might have entertained of enjoying a quiet moment for breakfast before heading to work. She couldn't leave this girl alone here, not when she apparently didn't have the first clue how to find her way home.

She shrugged out of her hooded sweatshirt and tucked it around Chloe's small shoulders, immediately shivering herself as the cool ocean breeze danced over her perspiration-dampened skin.

"Come on. I'll help you find where you're staying. Your dad will be worried."

Conan barked—whether in agreement with the plan or skepticism about the level of concern of Chloe's father, she wasn't sure. Whatever the reason, the dog led the way up the beach toward downtown with more enthusiasm than he'd shown for the ocean-side run. Chloe and Sage followed with the girl chatting the entire way.

In no time, Sage knew all about Chloe's best friend, Henry, her favorite TV show and her distant, work-obsessed father. She had also helped Chloe find a half-dozen pristine sand dollars the gulls hadn't picked at yet, as well as a couple of pieces of driftwood and a gorgeous piece of translucent orange agate.

"How do you know so much about shells and birds and stuff?" Chloe asked after Sage pointed out a surf scoter and a grebe.

She smiled at Chloe's obvious awe. "It's my job to know it. I'm a naturalist. Do you know what that is?"

"Somebody who studies nature?"

"Excellent! That's exactly what I do. I work for an organization that teaches people more about the world around them. When I'm not working on research, I get to show people the plants and animals that live here on the Oregon Coast. I even teach classes to kids. In fact, our first nature camp of the summer starts today. That's how I know so many of the local children, because most of them have been my campers at some time or another."

"Really? That's so cool!"

She smiled back, charmed by the funny little creature. "Yeah, I think so, too."

"Can I come to your camp?" The girl didn't wait for an answer. "My dad has another hotel in Carmel. That's in California, too, like San Francisco where we live. Once I went with him there and my nanny took me to see the tide pools. We saw starfish and anemones and everything. It was *super*cool."

Her nanny, again. Did the girl's father even acknowledge she existed?

"Did you at least tell your nanny where you were going this morning?" she asked.

Chloe stopped to pick up a chipped shell to add to the burgeoning collection in her nightgown pockets. "Don't have one. Señora Marcos quit two days ago. That's why my dad had to bring me here, too, to Cannon Beach, because he didn't know what else to do with me and it was too late for him to cancel his trip. But Señora Marcos wasn't the nanny that who took me to see the tide pools anyway. That was Jamie. She quit, too. And the one after that was Ms. Ludwig. She had bad breath and eyes like a mean pig. You know what? I was *glad* when she said she couldn't stand another minute of me. I didn't like her, either."

She said this with such nonchalance the words nearly broke Sage's heart. It sounded like a very lonely existence—a self-involved father and a string of humorless nannies unwilling to exert any effort to reach one energetic little girl.

The story had a bitterly familiar ring to it, one that left her with sick anger balled up in her stomach.

None of her business, she reminded herself. She was a stranger and didn't know the dynamics between Chloe and her father. Her own experience was apropos of nothing.

"Does any of this look familiar?" she asked. "Do you think your beach house is close by?"

The girl frowned. "I'm not sure. It's a brown house made out of wood. I remember that."

Sage sighed. *Brown* and *made of wood* might be helpful information if it didn't describe most of the houses in Cannon Beach. The town had strict zoning laws dictating the style and aesthetics of all construction, ensuring the beachside charm remained.

They walked a little farther, past weathered cedar houses and shops. Sage was beginning to wonder if perhaps she ought to call in Bill Rich, the local police chief, when Chloe suddenly squealed with excitement, which prompted Conan to answer with a bark.

"There it is! Right there." Chloe pointed to a house with an unobstructed view of the ocean and the sea stacks. Sage had always loved the place, with its quaint widow's walk and steep gables.

"Are you sure?" she asked.

Chloe nodded. "I remember the fish windchimes. I heard them when I was going to sleep and it sounded like angels singing. And I remember the house next door had those big balls that look like ginormous Christmas ornaments."

Sage shifted her gaze to take in the collection of Japanese glass fishing floats that adorned Blair and Kristine Saunders' landscape.

"Do you have a key?" she asked the girl.

Chloe held tight to Conan's collar. "No. My dad didn't give me one. But I climbed out the window of my room. I can just go back that way."

Sage was tempted to let her. A quick glance at her watch told her it was now twenty minutes to seven and she had exactly forty minutes to change and make it in to work. Her life would certainly be easier if she let Chloe sneak into her rental house, but it wouldn't be right, she knew. She needed to make sure the girl's father knew what Chloe had been up to.

"We'd better make sure your dad knows you're safe."

"I bet he didn't even know I was gone," Chloe muttered. "He's going to be mad when he finds out."

"You can't just sneak out on your own, Chloe. It's not safe. Anything could have happened to you out on the beach by yourself. I have to tell your dad. I'm sorry."

She rang the doorbell, then felt like the worst sort of weasel when Chloe glared at her.

Before she could defend her action, the door opened and she forgot everything she intended to say—as well as her own name and how to put two words together.

Chloe neglected to mention the little fact that her father was gorgeous. Sage swallowed hard. The odd trembling in her thighs had nothing to do with her earlier run.

He had rugged, commanding features, with high cheekbones, a square, firm jaw and green eyes a shade darker than his daughter's. It was obvious he'd just stepped out of the shower. His hair was wet, his chest bare and he wore only a pair of gray trousers and an unbuttoned blue dress shirt.

Sage swallowed again. Why did she have to meet a

man like him *today* when she smelled like wet dog and four miles of sweat? And she already disliked him, she reminded herself.

"Can I help you?" he asked. She didn't mistake the shadow of irritation on those rugged features.

She blinked and tugged Chloe forward.

"Chloe?" he stared at his daughter, baffled concern replacing annoyance. "What's going on? I thought you were still sound asleep in your bed. What are you doing out here in your nightgown?"

She didn't answer for a moment then she shrugged. "Nothing. I just went for a walk to get some more sand dollars. I found a ton. Well, Sage helped me. Look." She thrust her armload at her father.

He didn't take them, gazing at his daughter's hard-won treasure with little visible reaction. Or so Sage thought, until she happened to catch the storm clouds scudding across his green eyes like a winter squall stirring up seafoam.

"What do you mean, you went for a walk? It's barely six-thirty in the morning!"

Chloe shrugged. "I woke up early but you were still sleeping and I didn't want to wake you up. I was just going to be gone for a minute, but…then I couldn't remember how to get back."

"You are in serious trouble, young lady."

His voice was suddenly as hard as a sea stack and Sage was automatically seven years old again, trying desperately to understand how her world could change with such sudden cruelty.

"I am?" Chloe's fingers seemed to tighten on Conan's collar but the dog didn't so much as whimper.

"You know you're not supposed to leave the house

alone. You *know* that. *Any* house, whether our own or a
temporary one."

"But Daddy—

"You promised me, Chloe. Do you remember that?
I knew bringing you along on this trip would be a huge
mistake but you promised you would behave yourself,
for once. Do you call running off down the beach by
yourself behaving?"

He didn't raise his voice one single decibel but muscles inside Sage's stomach clenched and she hated it,
hated it. The terrible thing was, she couldn't blame the
man. Not really. She could imagine any parent would
be upset to discover a child had wandered away in an
unknown setting.

She knew it was a normal reaction, but still this particular situation had an entirely too-familiar ring to it.

"But I wasn't alone for very long," Chloe insisted. "I
made two new friends, Daddy. This is Sage and her dog's
name is Conan. She lives here and she knows all kinds of
things about birds and shells and fish. She's a naturist."

"Naturalist," Sage corrected.

"Right. A naturalist. She teaches summer camp and
tells kids about shells and birds and stuff like that."

For the first time since she rang the doorbell, the man
shifted his gaze to her.

"I'm Sage Benedetto," she said, hoping her cool voice
masked the nerves still jumping in her stomach. Though
she wanted to yell and scream and ask him what the hell
he thought he was doing trying to quash this sweet little
girl's spirit, the words tangled in her throat.

"I live down the coast about a half mile in the big
Victorian," she said instead.

He stared at her for a long second, an odd, arrested

look in his eyes. She didn't know how long he might have stared at her if Conan hadn't barked. The man blinked a little then closed his fingers around hers.

She was quite certain she imagined the odd little sizzle when their fingers touched. She *didn't* imagine the slightly disconcerted expression that crossed his features.

"Eben Spencer. Thank you for taking the time to bring my daughter home."

"You're welcome," she said in that same cool voice. "You might want to keep a closer eye on her."

"Easier said than done, Ms. Benedetto. But thank you for the advice."

"No problem."

She forced a tight smile for him, then a more genuine one for his daughter. "Bye, Chloe. You need to rinse those sand dollars in fresh water until the water runs clear, then soak them in bleach and water for five or ten minutes. That way they'll be hard enough for you to take them home without breaking. Remember, Henry's counting on you."

The girl giggled as Sage called to Conan, who barked at her, nuzzled Chloe, then bounded off ahead as they headed back toward Brambleberry House.

He watched her jog down the beach, the strange woman with the wild mane of honey-colored hair and thinly veiled disdain in her haunting amber-flecked brown eyes.

She didn't like him. That much was obvious. He hadn't missed the coldness in her expression nor the way she clipped off the ends of her words when she spoke to him.

He wasn't sure why that bothered him so much. Plenty of people disliked him. Constantly striving to win approval from others simply for the sake of their approval wasn't in his nature and he had long ago learned some measure of unpopularity was one of the prices one paid for success.

He was damn good at what he did, had taken his family's faltering hotel business and through careful management, a shrewd business plan and attention to detail turned it into a formidable force in the luxury hotel business.

Over the years, he had bumped up against plenty of affronted egos and prickly psyches. But seeing the disdain in Sage Benedetto's unsettling eyes annoyed him. And the very fact that he was bothered by it only irked him more.

What did he care what some wind-tousled stranger with a massive, ungainly mutt for a dog thought of him?

She stopped at a huge, cheerful yellow Victorian with incongruent lavender trim some distance down the beach. He watched her go inside and couldn't stop thinking about that odd jolt when their hands had touched.

It was completely crazy but he could swear some kind of strange, shimmery connection had arced between them and he had almost felt as if something inside him recognized her.

Foolish. Completely unlike him. He wasn't the sort to let his imagination run wild—nor was he the kind of man to be attracted to a woman who so clearly did not share his interest.

"She's nice. I like her. And I *love* her dog. Conan is so cute," Chloe chirped from inside the room and Eben realized with considerable dismay that he still stood at the window looking after her in the early-morning light

He jerked his attention away from thoughts of Sage Benedetto and focused on his daughter. Chloe had spread her treasures on the coffee table in their temporary living room, leaving who knew what kind of sand and grime on the polished mahogany.

He sighed, shut the door and advanced on her. "All right, young lady. Let's hear it."

He did his best to be firm, his tone the same one he would use with a recalcitrant employee.

These were the kind of moments that reminded him all too painfully that he didn't have the first idea how to correctly discipline a child. God knows, he had no childhood experience to draw from. He and his sister had virtually raised each other, caught in a hellish no-man's-land between two people who had had no business reproducing.

Between their mother's tantrums and violent moods and their father's shameless self-indulgence, it was a wonder either he or his sister could function as adults.

Cami had found happiness. As for him, he was doing the best he could not to repeat the mistakes of his parents.

"You know the rules about leaving the house by yourself. What do you have to say for yourself?"

Chloe shifted her gaze to the sand dollars in front of her and he hated himself when he saw the animation fade from her eyes. "I'm sorry, Daddy. I promise I won't do it again."

Eben sighed. "You say that every time, but then you find some other way to cause trouble."

"I don't mean to." Her voice was small, sad, and he found himself wishing fiercely that he were better at this.

"I try to be good but it's so *hard*."

He had to agree with her. Nothing was as hard as trying to do the right thing all the time. Even right now, some wild part of him wanted to call up Stanley and Jade Wu and tell them to go to hell, that he didn't want their stupid hotel if they were going to make him work this hard for it.

That same wild corner of his psyche wanted to toss Chloe onto his shoulders and run out into the surf with her in his bare feet, to feel the sand squishing between his toes and the cold water sluicing over his skin and her squeals of laughter ringing in his ears.

He tamped it down, containing it deep inside. "Try a little harder, okay?" he said sternly. "This deal is important to me, Chloe. I've told you that. You've got to be on your best behavior. I can't afford any distractions. It's only for a few more days, then I promise when we get back to San Francisco, we'll find a new nanny."

She nodded, her little mouth set in a tight line that told him clearly she was just as annoyed with him as Sage Benedetto had been.

"I'm supposed to have meetings with Mr. and Mrs. Wu most of the day so I've made arrangements for a caregiver through an agency here. All I'm asking is for you to behave. Can you try for a few hours?"

She looked up at him through her lashes. "When you're done with your meeting, can we buy a kite and fly it on the beach? Sage said Cannon Beach is the perfect place to fly kites because it's always windy and because there's lots of room so you don't run into people."

"If you promise to be on your best behavior, we can talk about it after my meetings."

She ran to him and threw her arms around his waist. "I'll be so good, Daddy, I promise, I promise, I *promise*."

He returned her embrace, his heart a heavy weight in his chest. He hated thinking of her going to boarding school at the end of the summer. But in the two years since Brooke died, Chloe had run through six nannies with her headstrong behavior. Some sort of record, he was certain. He couldn't do this by himself and he was running out of options.

"Maybe Sage and Conan can help us fly the kite," Chloe exclaimed. "Can they, Daddy?"

The very last thing he wanted to do was spend more time with Sage Benedetto of the judgmental eyes and the luscious mouth.

"We'll have to see," he said. He could only hope a day of trying to be on her best behavior would exhaust Chloe sufficiently that she would forget all about their temporary neighbor and her gargantuan canine.

Chapter 2

"Sorry, Conan. You've got to stay here."

Sage muscled her bike around Anna's minivan and wheeled it out of the small garage, trying to ignore the soulful eyes gazing back at her through the flowers on the other side of the low wrought-iron fence circling the house. "You'll be all right. I'll come back at lunchtime to throw a ball with you for awhile, okay?"

Conan didn't look convinced. He added a morose whine, his head cocked to one side and his chin tucked into his chest. She blew out a frustrated breath. They had been through this routine just about every day for the past month and the dog didn't seem to be adjusting.

She couldn't really blame the poor thing for not wanting to be alone. He was used to having Abigail's company all day.

The two of them had been inseparable from the moment Abigail had brought him home from the pound.

Conan would ride along with Abigail to the shops, his head hanging out the backseat window of her big Buick, tongue lolling. He would patiently wait for her on the porch of her friends' houses when she would make her regular round of visits, would sniff through the yard while Abigail tended her flowers, would curl up every evening beside her favorite chair in front of the huge bay windows overlooking the ocean.

Conan was lonely and Sage could certainly empathize with that. "I'm sorry, bud," she said again. "I'll be back before you know it."

The dog suddenly barked, his ears perking up like twin mountain peaks. He barreled to the front porch just as the door opened. From her place on the other side of the fence, Sage watched Anna Galvez—trim and proper in a navy blazer and gray slacks—set down her briefcase to greet the dog with a smile and a scratch under his chin.

Anna murmured something to the dog but Sage was too far away to hear. She wasn't too far to see Anna's warm smile for Conan trickle away when she straightened and saw Sage on the other side of the wrought-iron.

She brushed hair off her slacks and picked up her briefcase, then walked to the gate.

"Good morning. I thought I heard you come down the stairs some time ago. I figured you had already left."

Sage straddled her bike, not at all in the mood for conversation. Her fault for sticking around when she heard the door open. If she'd left then, she could have been halfway to town by now. But that would have been rude and she couldn't seem to shake the feeling Abigail wanted her to at least pretend politeness with Anna.

"I couldn't walk out in the middle of his guiltfest."

"He's good at that, isn't he?" Anna frowned at the

dog. "I expected him to be past this phase by now. It's been a month. Don't you think he should already be accustomed to the changes in his life?"

Sage shrugged. "I guess some of us need a little more time than others to grieve."

Anna's mouth tightened and Sage immediately regretted the low comment. So much for politeness. She wanted to apologize but couldn't seem to form the words.

"I wish I could take him with me to work," Anna said after an awkward moment.

Sage gave the other woman a disbelieving look. Anna couldn't possibly want a big, gangly dog wreaking havoc with the tchotchkes and whatnot in her book and gift shop in town. Conan would bankrupt her in less than an hour.

"I've been coming home for lunch to keep him company for awhile. Throw a ball, give him a treat. That kind of thing. For now, that's the best I can do."

For an instant, guilt flickered in Anna's brown eyes but she blinked it away. "I'm sorry. I should have realized you were doing so much. I'm a little preoccupied with some things at the store right now but it's only right that I do my share. Abigail left him to both of us, which means he's my responsibility as well. I'm sorry," she said again.

"Don't worry about it."

"I'm afraid I can't come back to the house today," she said with a frown. "But I'll try to arrange my schedule so I can take a few hours to be here with him tomorrow."

"I'm sure he would enjoy that," Sage said. As always, she regretted the awkwardness between her and Anna. She knew Abigail had wanted them to be friends but

Sage doubted it was possible. They were simply too different.

Anna was brisk and efficient, her world centered on By-The-Wind, the shop she had purchased from Abigail two years earlier after having managed it for a year before that. Sage didn't believe Anna had even the tiniest morsel of a sense of humor—or if she did, it was buried so deeply beneath spreadsheets and deposit slips that Sage had never seen sign of it.

After two weeks of sharing the same house, though in different apartments, Anna was still a stranger to Sage. Tightly wound and tense, Anna never seemed to relax.

Sage figured they were as different as it was possible for two women to be, one quirky and independent-minded, the other staid and responsible. Yet Abigail had loved them both.

When she was being brutally honest with herself, she could admit *that* was at least part of the reason for her natural reserve with Anna Galvez—small-minded, petty jealousy.

A weird kind of sibling rivalry, even.

Abigail had loved Anna—enough to leave her half of Brambleberry House and all its contents. Sage knew she was being selfish but she couldn't help resenting it. Not the house—she couldn't care less about that—but Abigail's affection.

"I'd better get going," Sage said.

"Uh, would you like a ride since we're both going the same way?"

She shook her head. "I'm good. Thanks anyway. If you give me a ride, I won't be able to come home at lunch."

"Oh. Right. I'll see you later then."

Sage stuffed her bag in the wicker basket of her one-speed bike and headed off to town. A moment later, Anna pulled past in her white minivan, moving at a cautious speed on the curving road.

Sage knew the roomy van was a practical choice since Anna probably had to transport things for the store, but she couldn't help thinking how the vehicle seemed to perfectly mirror Anna's personality: bland and business-like and boring.

Somebody had certainly climbed out of bed on the bitchy side, she chided herself, resolving that she would think only pleasant thoughts about Anna Galvez today, if she thought of her at all.

The same went for little sea sprites she had met on the beach and their entirely too-gorgeous fathers. She had too much to do today with all the chaos and con-fusion of her first day of camp to spend time thinking about Chloe and Eben Spencer.

The road roughly followed the shore here. Through the heavy pines, she could catch a glimpse of the sea stacks and hear the low murmur of the waves. Three houses down, she waved at a neighbor pulling out of his driveway in a large pickup truck with Garrett Car-pentry on the side.

He was heading the other direction toward Manza-nita but Will Garrett pulled up alongside her and rolled down his passenger-side window. "Morning, Sage."

She straddled her bike. "Hey, Will."

"Sorry I haven't made it over to look at the work you want done on the house. Been a busy week."

She stared. "Work? What work?"

"Anna called me last week. Said she wanted me to give her a bid for a possible remodel of the kitchen and bath-room on the second-floor apartment. She also wanted me to check the feasibility of knocking out a couple walls in Abigail's apartment to open up the floor plan a little."

"Oh, did she?"

Anger swept over her, hot and bright. Any warmth she might have been trying to force herself into feeling toward Anna seeped out into the dirt.

How dare she?

They had agreed to discuss any matters pertaining to the house and come to a consensus on them, but Anna hadn't said a single word about any of this.

Abigail had left the house to both of them, which meant they *both* should make minor little decisions like knocking out walls and remodeling kitchens. Yet Anna hadn't bothered to bring this up, even when they were talking a few moments ago.

Was her opinion so insignificant?

She knew her anger was overblown—irrational, even—but she couldn't help it. It was too soon. She wasn't ready to go knocking down walls and remodeling kitchens, erasing any sign of the crumbling old house Abigail had loved so dearly.

"She didn't talk to you about it?"

"Not yet," she said grimly.

Something in her tone of voice—or maybe the smoke curling out of her ears—had tipped him off that she wasn't pleased. His expression turned wary. "Well, uh, if you talk to her, let her know I'm going to try to come by this evening to check things out, if that's still okay. Seven or so. One of you can give me a buzz if that's a problem."

He looked eager to escape. She sighed—she shouldn't vent her frustration on Will. It certainly wasn't his fault Anna Galvez was a bossy, managing, stiff-necked pencil-pusher who seemed to believe she knew what was best for the whole bloody world.

She forced a smile. "I'm sure it will be fine. See you tonight."

Though he didn't smile in return—Will rarely smiled anymore—he nodded and put his truck in gear, then headed down the road.

She watched after him for only a moment, then continued pedaling her way toward town.

She still simmered with anger toward Anna's high-handedness, but it was tempered by her usual ache of sorrow for Will. So much pain in the world. Sometimes she couldn't bear it.

She tried her best to leave the world a better place than when she found it. But riding a bike to work and volunteering with Meals on Wheels seemed exercises in futility when she couldn't do a darn thing to ease the burden of those she cared about.

Will was another of Abigail's lost sheep—Sage's affectionate term for the little band of creatures her friend had watched over with her endless supply of love. Abigail seemed to collect people in need and gathered them toward her. The lonely, the forgotten, the grieving. Will had been right there with the rest of them.

No, that wasn't exactly true. Will had belonged to Abigail long before he had ever needed watching over. He had grown up in the same house where he now lived and he and his wife Robin had both known and loved Abigail all their lives.

Sage had lived at Brambleberry House long enough to remember him when he was a handsome charmer, with a teasing grin for everyone. He used to charge into

Abigail's parlor and sweep her off her feet, twirling her around and around.

He always had a funny story to tell and he had invariably been the first one on the scene whenever anyone needed help—whether it was moving a piano or spreading a dump-truckload of gravel on a driveway or pumping out a flooded basement.

When Sage moved in upstairs at Brambleberry, Will had become like a big brother to her, offering her the same warm affection he poured out on everyone else in town. Robin had been just as bighearted—lovely and generous and open.

When Robin discovered Sage didn't having a dining room table yet, she had put her husband to work on one and Will had crafted a beautiful round piece of art as a housewarming present.

Sage had soaked it all in, had reveled in the miracle that she had finally found a place to belong among these wonderful people who had opened their lives to her.

If Abigail had been the heart of her circle of friends, Will had been the sturdy, reliable backbone and Robin the nerve center. Their little pigtailed toddler Cara had just been everyone's joy.

Then in the blink of an eye, everything changed.

So much pain.

She let out a breath as she gave a hand signal and turned onto the street toward work. Robin and Will had been crazy about each other. She had walked in on them once in a corner of Abigail's yard at a Fourth of July barbecue. They hadn't been kissing, had just been holding each other, but even from several yards away Sage could feel the love vibrating between them, a strong, tangible connection.

She couldn't imagine the depth of Will's pain at knowing that kind of love and losing it.

Oddly, the mental meanderings made her think of Eben Spencer, sweet little Chloe's abrupt, unfriendly father. The girl had said her mother was dead. Did Eben mourn her loss as deeply as Will did Robin and little Cara, killed two years ago by a drunk driver as they were walking across the street not far from here?

She pulled up to the center and looped her bike lock through the rack out front, determined to put Eben and Chloe Spencer out of her head.

She didn't want to think about either of them. She had learned early in her time at Cannon Beach not to pay much mind to the tourists. Like the fragile summer, they disappeared too soon.

Her resolve was tested even before lunchtime. Since the weather held through the morning, she and her dozen new campers gathered at a picnic table under the spreading boughs of a pine tree outside the center.

She was showing them intertidal zone specimens in aquarium display cases collected earlier that morning by center staffers when she heard a familiar voice call her name.

She turned to find her new friend from the morning barreling toward her, eyes wide, her gamine face animated.

Moving at a slower pace came Eben Spencer, his silk, undoubtedly expensive tie off-center and his hair slightly messed. He did *not* look as if he were having a great day.

Of course, when Sage was having a lousy day, she ended up with circles under her eyes, stress lines cutting through her face and a pounding headache she could swear was visible for miles around.

Eben Spencer just looked slightly rumpled in an entirely too-sexy way.

Heedless of the other children in the class, Chloe rushed to her and threw her arms around Sage's waist.

"It's not my fault this time, I promise."

Under other circumstances, she might have been annoyed at the interruption to her class but she couldn't ignore Chloe's distress—or the frustration stamped on Eben's features.

"Lindsey, can you take over for a minute?" she asked her assistant camp director.

"Of course." The college student who had worked for the nature center every summer since high school stepped forward and Sage led Eben and Chloe away from the interested campers.

"What's not your fault? What's going on?"

"I didn't do *anything*, I swear. It's not my fault at *all* that she was so mean."

Sage looked to Eben for elucidation.

"The caregiver the agency in Portland sent over was…unacceptable." Eben raked a hand through his wavy hair, messing it even more.

"She was mean to me," Chloe said. "She wouldn't let me walk out to the beach, even when I told her my dad said it was okay. She didn't believe me so I called my dad and she got mad at me and pulled my hair and said I was a bad word."

From that explanation, she gathered the caregiver hadn't appreciated an eight-year-old going over her head.

"Oh, dear. A bad word, huh?"

Chloe nodded. "She called me a spoiled little poop, only she didn't say poop."

"I'm sorry," Sage said, trying to figure out exactly what part she played in this unfolding drama.

"I didn't care about the name but I didn't like that she pulled my hair. She didn't have to be so mean. I think she was a *big* poop."

"Chloe," her father said sternly.

"Well, I do. So I called my dad again and told him what she did and he came right over from The Sea Urchin and told her to leave right now. He said a bad word, too, but I think she deserved it."

She gave a quick glance at her father, then mouthed H-E-L-L.

Sage had to fight a smile. "I see," she said. She found it admirably unexpected that Eben would rush to his daughter's defense.

"And now the place that sent her doesn't have anybody else to take care of me."

Sage raised her eyebrows and glanced at Eben. "I suppose the temp pool is probably pretty shallow right now since the tourist season is heading into full gear."

"I'm figuring that out," he answered. "The agency says it will be at least tomorrow or the next day before they can find someone else. In the meantime, I've got conference calls scheduled all day."

Sage waited to hear what all of this had to do with her, though she was beginning to guess. Her speculation was confirmed by his next words.

"I can't expect Chloe to entertain herself in a strange place while I'm occupied. I remembered you mentioning a summer camp and hoped that you might have room for one more."

"Oh, I'm sorry. We're completely full."

The center had always maintained a strict limit of

twelve campers per session to ensure an adequate adult-to-student ratio. Beyond that, she had her hands full this year. Three of the children had learning disabilities and she had already figured out after the first few hours that two more might be on their way to becoming behavior problems if she couldn't figure out how to channel their energy.

Even as she thought of the trouble to her staff if she added another camper, her mind raced trying to figure out how to accommodate Eben and his daughter.

"I was afraid you would say that." He smiled stiffly. "Thank you for your time anyway. We'll try to figure something else out."

He looked resigned but accepting. His daughter, on the other hand, appeared close to tears. Her shoulders slumped and her chin quivered.

"But I really wanted to come to camp with Sage," she wailed. "It sounded super, super fun! I don't want to stay in a boring house all day long while you talk on the phone!"

"Chloe, that's enough. If the camp doesn't have room for you, that's the way it is."

"You think I'm a little poop, too, don't you?" Chloe's chin was definitely quivering now. "That's why you don't want me in your camp. You don't like me, either."

"Oh, honey, that's not true. We just have rules about how many children we can have in our camp."

"I would be really good. You wouldn't even know I'm here. Oh, please, Sage!"

She studied them both—Chloe so dejected and her father resigned. She had to wonder how much pride he had forced himself to swallow for his daughter's sake to bring her here and ask Sage for a favor.

How could she disappoint them?

"We're at capacity," she finally said, "but I think we can probably find room to squeeze in one more."

"You mean it? Really?" The girl looked afraid to hope.

Sage nodded and Chloe squealed with delight and hugged her again. "Yes! Thank you, thank you, thank you!"

Sage hugged her in return. "You're welcome. You're going to have to work hard and listen to me and the other grown-ups, though."

"I will. I'll be super super good."

Sage glanced up to meet Eben's gaze and found him watching her with that same odd, slightly thunderstruck expression she had seen him wear earlier that morning. She didn't fathom it—nor did she quite understand why it made her insides tremble.

"I'm busy with the class out here," she spoke briskly to hide her reaction, "but if you go inside the center, Amy can provide you with the registration information. Tell her I said we could make an exception this once and add one more camper beyond our usual limit."

"Thank you, Ms. Benedetto." One corner of his mouth lifted into a relieved smile and the trembling in her stomach seemed to go into hyperdrive, much like the Harder twins after a little sugar.

Somehow that slight smile made him look even more attractive and her reaction to it alarmed her.

"Amy will give you a list of supplies you will need to provide for Chloe." Annoyance at herself sharpened her voice. "She's going to need waterproof boots and a warmer jacket this afternoon when we go out to Haystack, though we can probably scrounge something for her today."

"Thank you."

"May I go with the other children?" Chloe asked, her green eyes gleaming with eagerness.

"Sure," Sage said. She and Eben watched Chloe race to the picnic table and squeeze into a spot between two girls of similar ages, who slid over to make room for her.

She turned back to Eben. "Our class ends at four, whether your conference calls are done or not."

He sent her a swift look. "I'll be sure to hang up on my attorneys if they run long. I wouldn't want to keep you waiting."

"It's not me you would be letting down. It's Chloe."

His mouth tightened with clear irritation but she watched in fascination as he carefully pushed it away and resumed a polite expression. "Thank you again for accommodating Chloe. I know you're stretching the rules for her and I do appreciate it."

Without waiting for an answer, he turned around and walked toward the center. She watched him go, that fast, take-no-prisoners stride eating up the beach.

What a disagreeable man. He ought to have a British accent for all the stuffy reserve in his voice.

She sighed. Too bad he had to be gorgeous. Someone with his uptight personality ought to have the looks to match, tight, thin lips, a honker of a nose, and squinty pale eyes set too close together.

Instead, Eben Spencer had been blessed with stunning green eyes, wavy dark hair and lean, chiseled features.

Didn't matter, she told herself. In her book, personality mattered far more than looks and by all indications Eben Spencer scored a big fat zero in that department.

"Ms. B, Ms. B.! What's this one? Lindsey doesn't know."

She turned back to the picnic table. She had work to do, she reminded herself sternly. She needed to keep her attention tightly focused on her day camp and the thirteen children in it—not on particularly gorgeous hotel magnates with all the charm of a spiny urchin.

Chapter 3

"Your daughter will just *love* the day camp." The bubbly receptionist inside the office delivered a thousand-watt smile out of white teeth in perfect alignment as she handed him the papers.

"It's one of our most popular summer activities," she went on. "People come from all over to bring their children to learn about the rocky shore and the kids just eat it up. And our camp director is just wonderful. The children all adore her. Sometimes I think she's just a big kid herself."

He raised an eyebrow, his mind on Sage Benedetto, and her honey-blond curls, lush curves and all that blatant sensuality.

"Is that right?" he murmured.

The receptionist either didn't catch his dry tone or chose to ignore him. He voted for the former.

"You should see her when they're tide-pooling, in her

big old boots and a grin as big as the Haystack. Sage knows everything about the coastal ecosystem. She can identify every creature in a tide pool in an instant and can tell you what they eat, how they reproduce and who their biggest predator might be. She's just amazing."

He didn't want to hear the receptionist gush about Sage Benedetto. He really preferred to know as little about her as possible. He had already spent the morning trying to shake thoughts of her out of his head so he could focus on business.

He smiled politely. "That's good to hear. I'm relieved Chloe will be in competent hands."

"Oh, you won't find better hands anywhere on the coast, I promise," she assured him.

For a brief second, he had a wickedly inappropriate reaction to that bit of information, but with determined effort, he managed to channel his attention back to the registration papers in front of them.

He quickly read over and signed every document required—just a little more paperwork than he usually faced when purchasing a new hotel.

He didn't mind the somewhat exorbitant fee or the tacked-on late-registration penalty. If not for Sage and her summer camp, his options would have been severely limited.

He didn't have high hopes that the agency in Portland would find someone quickly, which would probably mean he would have to cancel the entire trip and abandon the conference calls scheduled for the week or fly in his assistant to keep an eye on Chloe, something neither Chloe nor Betsy would appreciate.

No, Sage Benedetto had quite likely saved a deal that was fiercely important to Spencer Hotels.

He would have liked to surrender Chloe to someone a little more…restrained…but he wasn't going to quibble.

"All right. She's all set, registered for the entire week. Now, you know you're going to need to provide your daughter with a pair of muck boots and rain-gear, right?"

"Ms. Benedetto already informed me of that. I'll be sure Chloe is equipped with everything she needs tomorrow."

"Here's the rest of the list of what you need."

"Thank you."

He took it from her with a quick glance at his watch. He was supposed to be talking to his advertising team in New York in twenty minutes and he wasn't sure he was going to make it.

Outside, steely clouds had begun to gather with the capriciousness of seaside weather. Even with them, the view was stunning, with dramatic sea stacks offshore and a wide sandy beach that seemed to stretch for miles.

He shifted his gaze to the group of children still gathered around the picnic table. Chloe looked as if she had settled right in. As she chattered to one of the other girls, her eyes were bright and happy in a way he hadn't seen in a long time.

He was vastly relieved, grateful to see her natural energy directed toward something educational and fun instead of toward getting into as much trouble as humanly possible for an eight-year-old girl.

This next few days promised to be difficult with all the new conditions Stanley Wu was imposing on the sale of his hotel. Having a good place for Chloe to go during the day would ease his path considerably.

His attention twisted to the woman standing at the head of the table. In khaki slacks and a navy-blue knit shirt, Sage Benedetto should have looked stern and official. But she was laughing at something one of the children said, her blond curls escaping a loose braid.

With her olive-toned skin and blonde hair, she looked exotic and sensual. Raw desire tightened his gut but he forced himself to ignore it as he walked the short distance to the cluster of children.

Chloe barely looked up when he approached. "I'm leaving," he told her. "I'll be back this afternoon to pick you up."

"Okay. Bye, Daddy," she chirped, then immediately turned her attention back to the other girls and their activity as if she had already forgotten his presence.

He stood by the table for a moment, feeling awkward and wishing he were better at this whole parenting thing. His love for his daughter was as vast and tumultuous as the ocean and most of the time it scared the hell out of him.

He looked up and found Sage watching him, a warmth in her eyes that hadn't been there earlier. Sunlight slanted beneath the clouds, turning the hair escaping her braid to a riotous halo of curls around her face.

She looked like something from an old master painting, lush and earthy, and when her features lightened into a smile, lust tightened inside him again.

"Don't worry, Mr. Spencer. We'll take good care of Chloe."

He nodded, angry again at this instinctive reaction to her. The only thing for it was to leave the situation, he decided, to avoid contact with her as much as possible.

"I have no doubts you will. Excuse me. I've got to return to work."

At his abrupt tone, the warmth slid away from her features. "Right. Your empire-building awaits."

He almost preferred her light mockery to that momentary flicker of warmth. It certainly made it easier for him to keep his inappropriate responses under control.

"I'll be back for Chloe at four."

He started to walk away, then paused, feeling churlish and ungrateful. She was doing him a huge favor and he couldn't return that favor with curt rudeness.

"Uh, thank you again for finding space for her. I appreciate it."

Her smile was much cooler this time. "I have no doubts you do," she murmured.

He studied her for a moment, then matched the temperature of his own smile to hers and walked to the nature center's parking lot where his rented Jaguar waited.

His mind was still on Sage Benedetto as he drove through town, stopping at a crosswalk for a trio of gray-haired shoppers to make their slow way across the road, then two mothers pushing strollers.

He forced himself to curb his impatience as he waited. Even though it was early June, the tourist season on the Oregon Coast seemed to be in full swing, something that boded favorably for someone in the hotel business.

He had learned that the season never really ended here, unlike some other resort areas. There was certainly a high season and a low season but people came to the coast year-round.

In the summer, families came to play in the sand and enjoy the natural beauty; winter brought storm watchers and beachcombers to the wide public beaches.

Though his ultimate destination was his temporary quarters, he automatically slowed as he approached The Sea Urchin. He could see it set back among Sitka spruce and pine: the graceful, elegant architecture, the weathered gray-stone facade, the extravagant flower gardens already blooming with vibrant color.

He wanted it, as he hadn't coveted anything in a long, long time. In the four months since he had first seen the hotel on a trip down the coast to scout possible property locations, he had become obsessed with owning it.

His original plan had been to build a new hotel somewhere along the coast, possibly farther south in the Newport area.

But the moment he caught sight of The Sea Urchin— and Cannon Beach—the place called to him in a way he couldn't begin to explain.

He had no idea why it affected him so strongly. He wasn't one for capricious business moves, heaven knows. In the dozen years since he'd taken over his family company at the ripe age of twenty-four, he had tried to make each decision with a cool head and a sharp eye for the bottom line.

Building a new property made better business sense—everything was custom designed and there were more modern amenities. That would have been a far more lucrative choice for Spencer Hotels and was the option his people had been pushing.

But when he saw The Sea Urchin, with its clean lines and incredible views of the coast, his much-vaunted business acumen seemed to drift away with the tide.

It had been rainy and dismal that February day, a cold, dank wind whistling off the Pacific. He had been calling himself all kinds of fool for coming here in the first place, for packing his schedule so tightly when he was supposed to be leaving for the United Kingdom in only a few days.

But on the recommendation of a local woman, he had driven past The Sea Urchin and seen it silhouetted against the sea, warm, welcoming lights in all the windows, and he had wanted it.

He had never known this sense of *rightness* before, but somehow he couldn't shake the odd sense that he could make this small hotel with its twenty guest rooms the glimmering crown jewel of Spencer Hotels.

He sighed and forced himself to drive past the hotel. *He* might be certain his destiny and The Sea Urchin's were somehow intertwined, but Stanley and Jade Wu were proving a little harder to convince.

Renewed frustration simmered through him. A week ago, this sale was supposed to be a done deal. All the parties involved had finally agreed on an asking price— a quarter million dollars more than Eben had planned to pay when he and the Wus first discussed the sale in February.

He thought all the legalities had been worked out with his advance team before he flew to Portland. The only thing left was for Stanley and Jade to sign the papers, but they had been putting him off for two days.

He could feel the property slipping through his fingers and for the first time in his business life, he didn't know how the hell to grab hold of something he wanted.

He understood their ambivalence. They had run The Sea Urchin for thirty-five years, had built it through skill and hard work and shrewd business sense into a stylishly beautiful hotel. Surrendering the family business to a stranger—seeing it folded into the *empire* Sage Benedetto had mocked with such disdain—could only be difficult for them.

He understood all that, Eben thought again as he pulled into the driveway and climbed out of the car, but his patience was trickling away rapidly.

He fiercely wanted The Sea Urchin and he wasn't sure how he would cope with his disappointment if the deal fell through. And in the meantime, he still had a company of a hundred hotels to run.

Oh, she was tired.

Right now the idea of sliding into a hot bath with a good book sounded like a slice of heaven. In the gathering twilight, Sage pedaled home with a steady drizzle soaking her to the skin.

So much for the weather forecasters' prediction of sunshine for the next three days. Having lived in Oregon for five years now, she ought to know better. The weather was fickle and erratic. She had learned to live with it and even enjoyed it for the most part.

She tried to always be prepared for any eventuality. Of course, this was the day she had forgotten to pack her rain slicker in her bike basket.

She blamed her negligence on her distraction that morning with Eben and Chloe Spencer, though maybe that was only because she was approaching their beach house.

She wiped rain out of her eyes as she passed it. A sleek silver Jaguar was sprawled arrogantly in the driveway.

Of course. What else would she expect?

Against her will, her eyes were drawn to the wide bay window in front. The blinds were open and she thought she saw a dark shadow move around inside before she quickly jerked her attention back to the road.

Wouldn't it be just like her to have a wipeout right in front of his house, with him watching out the window?

She stubbornly worked to put them both out of her head as she rode the half mile to Brambleberry House. The house came into view as she rounded the last corner and some of her exhaustion faded away in the sweet, welcome comfort of coming home.

She loved this old place with its turrets and gables and graceful old personality, though some of the usual joy she felt returning to it had been missing since Abigail's death.

As she pedaled into the driveway, Conan barked a halfhearted greeting from the front porch.

Stubborn thing. He should be waiting inside where it was warm and dry. Instead, he insisted on waiting on the front porch—for her or for Anna or for Abigail, she didn't know. She got the sense Conan kept expecting Abigail to drive her big Buick home any moment now.

Conan loped out into the rain to greet her by the fence and she ached at the sadness in his big eyes. "Let me put my bike away, okay? Then you can tell me about your day while I change into dry clothes."

She opened the garage door and as she parked her bike, she heard Conan bark again and the sound of a vehicle outside. She glanced out the wide garage door to see Will Garrett's pickup truck pulling into the driveway.

Rats. She'd forgotten all about their conversation that morning. So much for her dreams of a long soak.

He climbed out into the rain—though he was at least smart enough to wear a Gore-Tex jacket.

"Hi, Will. Anna's not here yet."

"I'm sure she'll be here soon. I'm a little early."

"I never told her you were coming. I'm sorry, Will. I knew there was something I forgot to do today. I honestly don't have any idea when she'll be home."

The man she had met five years ago when she first moved here would have grinned and teased her about her bubbleheaded moment. But the solemn stranger he had become since the death of his wife and baby girl only nodded. "I can come back later. Not a problem."

Guilt was a miserable companion on a rainy night. "No. Come in. You're here, you might as well get started, at least in the empty apartment. Without Anna here, I don't feel right about taking you into Abigail's apartment to see what to do there, since it's her territory now. But I have a key to the second floor. I just need to run up and get it."

"Better change into something dry while you're up there. Wouldn't do for you to catch pneumonia."

His solemn concern absurdly made her want to cry. She hadn't had anybody to fuss over her since Abigail's death.

"I'll hurry," she assured him, and dripped her way up the stairs, leaving him behind with Conan.

She returned five minutes later in dry jeans, a sweatshirt and toweled-dry hair. She hurried down the stairs to the second-floor landing, where Will must have climbed with Conan. The two of them sat on the top step and the dog had his chin on Will's knee.

"Sorry to leave you waiting." She pulled out a key and fitted it in the keyhole.

Will rose. "Not a problem. Conan's been telling me about his day."

"He's quite the uncanny conversationalist, isn't he?"

He managed half a smile and followed her into the apartment.

The rooms here, their furnishings blanketed in dust covers, had a vaguely forlorn feeling to them. Unlike the rest of the house, the air was stale and close. Whenever she came in here, Sage thought the apartment seemed to be waiting for something, silly as that seemed.

Abigail had rented the second floor only twice in the

five years Sage had lived at Brambleberry House. Each time had been on a temporary basis, the apartment becoming a transitional home for Abigail's strays for just a few months at a time.

The place should be lived in. It was comfortable and roomy, with three bedrooms, a huge living room and a fairly good-sized kitchen.

The plumbing was in terrible shape and the vinyl tiles in the kitchen and bathroom were peeling and outdated, in definite need of replacement. The appliances and cabinets in the kitchen were ancient, too, and the whole place could use new paint and some repairs to the crumbling lathe and plaster walls.

Despite the battle scars, the apartment had big windows all around that let light throughout the rooms and the living room enjoyed a particularly breathtaking view of the sea. Not as nice as the one from her third-floor apartment, but lovely still.

She wandered to the window now and realized she had a perfect view of Eben and Chloe Spencer's place, the lights still beating back the darkness.

"Hey Sage, can you come hold the end of the tape measure?"

She jerked out of her reverie and followed his voice to the bathroom. For the next few minutes she assisted while Will studied, measured, measured again and finally jotted figures on his clipboard.

They were in the kitchen when through the open doorway she saw Conan suddenly lift his head from his morose study of the peeling wallpaper. A moment later, she heard the squeak of the front door and reminded herself to add WD-40 to her shopping list.

Conan scrambled up, nosed open the door and galloped for the stairs. A moment later he was back, with Anna not far behind him.

"Hey, Will. I saw your van out front. I didn't realize you were coming tonight."

Sage fought down her guilt. She wasn't the one in the wrong here. Anna had no business arranging all this without talking to her.

"I meant to call you but the day slipped away from me," she said. "I bumped into Will this morning on the way to work and he told me he was coming out tonight to give us a bid on the work we apparently want him to do."

Anna didn't miss her tight tone. Sage thought she saw color creep over her dusky cheekbones. "I figured there was no harm having him come out to take a look. Information is always a good thing. We need to know what our initial capital outlay might be to renovate the apartment so we can accurately determine whether it's cost-effective to rent it out."

Sage really hated that prim, business tone. Did any personality at all lurk under Anna's stiff facade? It had to. She knew it must. Abigail had cared about her, had respected her enough to sell her the gift shop and to leave her half of Brambleberry House.

Sage had seen little sign of it, though. She figured Anna probably fell asleep at night dreaming of her portfolio allocation.

She didn't want to battle this out tonight. She was too darn tired after wrestling thirteen energetic kids all day.

Instead, she reached into her pocket for the dog treat she had grabbed upstairs when she had changed her clothes. She palmed it and held it casually at thigh level.

Conan was a sucker for the bacon treats. Just as she intended, the dog instantly left Anna's side and sidled over to her. Anna tried to hide her quick flicker of hurt but she wasn't quite quick enough.

"Dirty trick," Will murmured from behind her.

Having a witness to her sneakiness made her feel petty and small. She wasn't fit company for anyone tonight. She let out a breath and resolved to try harder to be kind.

"I think we're done up here," Will said. "Should I take a look at the first floor now?"

Anna nodded and led the way down the stairs. Sage thought about escaping to her apartment and indulging in that warm bath that had been calling her name all evening, but she knew it would be cowardly, especially after Will had witnessed her subversive bribery of Conan.

She followed them down the stairs to Abigail's apartment. With some trepidation, Sage stood in the doorway. She hadn't been here since Anna moved her things in two weeks ago. She couldn't help expecting to see Abigail bustle out of the kitchen with her tea tray and a plateful of Pepperidge Farm Raspberry Milanos.

All three of them—four, counting Conan—paused inside the living room. Shared grief for the woman they had all loved twisted around them like thorny vines.

Anna was the first to break the charged moment as she briskly moved into the room. "Sorry about the mess. If I'd had warning, I might have had time to straighten up a little."

Sage couldn't see much mess, just a newspaper spread out on the coffee table and a blanket jumbled in a heap on the couch, but she figured those few items slightly out of place probably affected Anna as much as if a hurricane had blown through.

"What I would like to do is knock down the wall between the kitchen and the dining room to make the kitchen bigger. And then I was wondering about the feasibility of taking out the wall between the two smaller bedrooms to make that a big master."

Abigail's presence was so strong here. While Will and Anna were busy in the kitchen, Sage stood in the middle of the living room and closed her eyes, her throat tight. She could still smell her here, that soft scent of freesia.

Abigail wouldn't have wanted her to wallow in this wrenching grief, she knew, but she couldn't seem to fight it back.

For one odd second, the scent of freesia seemed stronger and she could swear she felt a soft, papery hand on her cheek.

To distract herself from the weird sensation, she glanced around the rooms and through the open doorway to one of the bedrooms and suddenly caught sight of Abigail's vast doll collection.

Collecting dolls had always seemed too ordinary a hobby for Abigail, given her friend's other eccentricities, but Abigail had loved each piece in the room.

She moved to the doorway and flipped on the light switch, enjoying as always that first burst of amazement at the floor-to-ceiling display cases crammed full of thousands of dolls. There was her favorite, a mischievous-looking senior citizen wearing a tie-dyed shirt and a peace medallion. Golden Flower Child. She was certain the artist had handcrafted it specifically for Abigail.

"You should take some of them up to your apartment."

Sage quickly dropped her hand from the doll's familiar smile to find Anna watching her.

"They're part of the contents of the house, which she

left jointly to both of us," Anna went on. "Half of them are yours."

She glanced at the aging hippie doll with longing, then shook her head. "They belong together. I'm not sure we should split up the collection."

After a long pause, Anna's expression turned serious. "Why don't you take them all upstairs with you, then?"

She had a feeling the offer had not been an easy one for Anna to make. It touched her somewhere deep inside. The lump in her throat swelled and she felt even more guilty for the dog-treat trick.

"We don't have to decide anything like that today. For now, we can leave them where they are, as long as you don't mind."

Before Anna could voice the arguments Sage could see brewing in her dark eyes, Will joined them. "You want the good news or the bad?"

"Good news," Anna said instantly. Sage would have saved the best for last. Good news after bad always made the worst seem a little more palatable.

"None of the walls you want to take out are weight-bearing, so we should be okay that way."

"What's the bad?" Anna asked.

"We're going to have to reroute some plumbing. It's going to cost you."

He gave a figure that staggered Sage, though Anna didn't seem at all surprised.

"Well, there's no rush on this floor. What about the work upstairs?"

Those figures were no less stunning. "That's more than reasonable," Anna said. "Are you positive that will cover your entire overhead? I don't want you skimping your profit."

"It's fair."

Anna gave him a careful look, then smiled. "It *will* be fair when we tack back on the twenty percent you cut off the labor costs."

"I give my friends a deal."

"Not these friends. We'll pay your going rate or we'll find somebody else to do the work."

Anna's insistence surprised Sage as much as the numbers. She would have expected the other woman to pinch pennies wherever she could and she had to admit she was impressed that she refused to take advantage of Will's generosity.

"You'll take a discount and that's final," he said firmly. "You'll never find another contractor who will treat Brambleberry House with the same loving care."

"You guys can hash this out better without me," Sage announced. She wasn't sure she could spend any more time in Abigail's apartment without breaking into tears. "I'm tired and I'm hungry. Right now all I want to do is fix some dinner and take a long, hot soak in the tub with a glass of wine. You can give me the details tomorrow."

"I'll walk Conan tonight. It's my turn," Anna said.

She nodded her agreement and headed up the stairs to her veggie burger and silence.

Chapter 4

This was the reason he wanted The Sea Urchin so desperately.

Eben leaned his elbows on the deck railing off the back of their beach house watching dawn spread out across the Pacific the next morning, fingers of pink and lavender and orange slicing through the wisps of fog left from the rains of the night before.

The air smelled of the sea, salty and sharp; gulls wheeled and dived looking for breakfast.

He was the only human in sight—a rare occurrence for him. He wasn't used to solitude and quiet, not with chattering Chloe around all the time. He wasn't completely sure he liked it—but he knew that if he could package this kind of morning for all his properties, Spencer Hotels would never have a vacancy again.

Normal people—people very much unlike uptight Californian businessmen—would eat this whole relaxation thing up. The Sea Urchin would be busy year-round, with people booking their suites months, even years, in advance.

He sipped his coffee and tried to force the tension from his shoulders. Another few days of this and he would be a certifiable beach bum, ready to chuck the stress of life in San Francisco for a quiet stretch of shoreline and a good cup of coffee.

Or maybe not.

He had never been one to sit still for long, not with so much to do. He'd been up since four taking a conference call with Tokyo in preparation for a series of meetings there next week and in two hours he would have to drive the ninety minutes to Portland to meet with his attorneys.

Despite the calm and beauty of the morning, his mind raced with his lengthy to-do list.

In the distance he saw a jogger running up the beach toward town and envy poked him. He would give his coffee and a whole lot more to be the one running along the hard-packed sand close to the surf, working off these restless edges.

Others found calm and peace in the soothing sound of the sea. For Eben, a good, hard run usually did the trick. But with Chloe asleep inside, that was impossible. He couldn't leave her alone in a strange place, even if he left a note and took his cell phone so she could reach him.

The jogger drew closer and recognition clicked in at exactly the same moment he heard a bark of greeting. A moment later, Sage Benedetto's big gangly red dog loped into view.

The dog barked again, changed directions and headed

straight toward him. After an odd hesitation, the big dog's owner waved briefly and followed her animal.

Though he knew it was foolish, anticipation curled through him like those tendrils of fog on the water.

She was still some distance away when the dog nuzzled his head under Eben's hand, looking for attention. He had never had a pet and wasn't very used to animals, but he scratched the dog's chin and was rewarded by the dog nudging his hand for more.

When Sage approached, he saw she was wearing bike shorts and a hooded sweatshirt with an emblem that read Portland Saturday Market across the front.

She looked soft and sensual in the early morning light, like some kind of lush fertility goddess. Her exotic features were flushed and her hair was in a wild ponytail.

She looked as if she had just climbed out of bed after making love all night long.

His insides burned with sudden hunger but he hid his reaction behind a casual smile. "Great morning for a run."

She raised an eyebrow. "You think?"

"I was just now pondering how much I'd love to be out there doing the same thing if only Chloe weren't asleep inside."

She gave a sudden delighted smile that made him feel as if the sun had just climbed directly above his beach house. Before he could catch his breath, she grabbed the coffee mug straight out of his hand and sipped it, pressing her mouth exactly where his own lips had been.

"Problem solved. I'll stay here in case Chloe wakes up and you can take Conan."

She made a shooing gesture with the hand not holding his coffee. "You two boys go on and run to your little hearts' content and I'll go back to sleep for a few moments."

She slid into one of the wide, plump rockers on the deck and closed her eyes, his mug still cradled in her hands.

She was completely serious, Eben realized, not quite sure whether to be amused or annoyed. But with a sudden anticipation zinging through him, he couldn't help but smile. "At least come inside where it's warm while I throw on some jogging shoes."

She opened her eyes and her gaze flashed down to his bare toes then back at him with an inscrutable expression on her features. "I'm fine out here, but if you would feel better having me inside in case Chloe wakes up, I have no problem with that, either."

She followed him inside to the living room with its floor-to-ceiling windows overlooking the shore.

"Nice," she murmured.

He was intensely aware of her, more than he had been of any woman in a long, long time.

He was also cognizant of the fact that they were virtually alone, with only his daughter sleeping on the other side of the house, something he *didn't* want to think about.

"Give me five minutes to grab my shoes."

She was already nestling into the comfortable leather couch that faced the windows, her eyes already closing, her muscles going slack. "No problem. Take your time. This is perfect. Absolutely perfect."

He threw on his shoes quickly and hurried back to the family room. She gave all appearances of being asleep. He watched her for only a moment, entranced by the wisp of honey-colored hair curling over her cheekbone.

When he realized he was gazing at her like some kind of Peeping Tom, he hurried out the door to the deck and whistled to Conan, who was busy marking every support of the deck.

The dog stopped mid-pee, barked with an eagerness that matched Eben's and the two of them set off down the beach.

With a sense of freedom he hadn't known in a long time, he ran on the hard-packed sand, dodging waves and the occasional long, ragged clump of kelp. The dog raced right along with him, easily matching his stride to Eben's and in no time they had a comfortable rhythm.

By the time they reached the headlands on the north end of the beach, he felt loose and liberated, as if the jog had chased all the cobwebs from his mind.

He paused for a moment to enjoy the full splendor of the sunrise slanting out across the water while the dog chased a couple of seagulls pecking at something in the sand.

After some time, Eben checked his watch with some regret. "We'd better hustle back. Some of us need to go to work," he told the dog, who tilted his head with a quizzical look then barked as if he understood exactly what Eben had said. The dog turned and charged back down the beach the way they'd come.

The beach had been largely empty on their way north but on the run back, they passed several other joggers and beachcombers, all of whom greeted him with friendly smiles—or at least offered smiles to Conan.

Several called the dog by name and gave them curious looks that Eben deflected with a wave. All the locals were probably wondering who was running with Sage Benedetto's dog but he didn't have the breath to enlighten any of them, even if he'd wanted to.

"Wait out here," he ordered the sandy dog when they

reached the beach house, his breath still coming fast and hard. Conan flopped onto the deck and curled his head in his paws, apparently content to rest.

He let himself into the house and found Sage exactly where he'd left her, sound asleep on his couch.

A quick peek into Chloe's room showed him she was still asleep as well, the blankets jumbled around her feet.

He closed her door with gentle care and returned to the family room. Okay, so he hadn't worked all the restlessness out of his system, apparently. Some of it still simmered through him, especially as he watched Sage sleep on his couch. She looked rumpled and sexy, her lashes fluttering against the olive skin of her high cheekbones and the slightest of smiles playing over those lush lips.

What was she dreaming about? he wondered, hunger tightening his insides.

Maybe it was a reaction to the blood still pumping through him from the good, hard run—or, he admitted honestly, probably just the delectable woman in front of him—but Eben wanted her more than he could remember ever wanting a woman.

He cleared his throat, again fighting back his heretofore unknown voyeuristic tendencies. "Uh, Ms. Benedetto. Time to go. The run's over."

Her mouth twitched a little in sleep but her eyes remained stubbornly closed. She made a little sleepy sound and rolled over, presenting her back to him, looking for all the world as if she were settling in to nap the morning away.

Now what was he supposed to do?

"Sage?" he said again.

When she still didn't respond, he sighed and reached

a hand out to her shoulder. "Sage, wake up. You have to go to work, remember? We both do."

After a moment, she heaved a long sigh and turned over again. She blinked her eyes open and gazed at him in confusion for a moment before he saw consciousness slowly return like the tide coming in.

She sat up, gave a yawn and stretched her arms above her head. Eben swallowed and did his best to remember how to breathe.

"I have to say, that had to be just about the best jog I've had in a month," she murmured with a sleepy, sexy smile.

She rose, stretching again with graceful limbs, and Eben stared at her a long moment—at the becoming flush on her features, at the wild tangle of her hair, at her slightly parted lips.

He sensed exactly the instant his control slipped out the window—when she smiled at him again, her head canted to one side. With a groan, he surrendered the battle and reached for her.

She was soft and warm and smelled of the leather sofa where she had been sleeping and an exotic spicy-sweet flowery scent that had to be purely Sage.

He told himself he would stop with just a tiny taste. He had taken her dog out running, after all. Didn't she owe him something for that? Stealing a little morning kiss seemed like small recompense.

He didn't expect her mouth to taste of coffee and mint and he certainly didn't expect, after one shocked second, for her to make a low, aroused sound in her throat then wrap her arms around his neck as if she couldn't bear the idea of letting him go.

From that point on, he lost all sense of time and space

and reason. His foolish idea of giving into the heat for only an instant with one little taste went out the window along with the rest of his control.

The only thing he could focus on was the woman in his arms—her intoxicating scent and taste, the texture of her sweatshirt under his hands, the soft curves pressing against him.

He needed to stop, for a million reasons. He barely knew the woman. She barely knew him. Chloe could wake and come out of her room any moment. He had just jogged three miles down the beach and back and probably smelled like a locker room.

All these thoughts flickered through his mind but he couldn't quite catch hold of any of them. The blood singing through him and the wild hunger burning up his insides were the only things that seemed to matter.

He deepened the kiss and she sighed against his mouth. He was intensely aware of her soft fingers in his hair, of the other hand curving around his neck. Even with the heat scorching him, the wonder of feeling her hands on him absurdly drew a lump to his throat.

How long had it been since he'd known a woman's touch? Brooke's shockingly sudden death from an aneurysm had been two years ago and he hadn't been with anyone since then. Even for months before her death, things had been rocky between them. He knew he had failed her in many, many ways.

The specter of his disastrous marriage finally helped him regain some small measure of control.

He stilled, then opened his eyes as the sensation of being watched prickled down his spine.

Not Chloe, he hoped, and swept the room with a glance. No, he realized. Sage's big red dog watched them through the wide windows leading to the deck. And if Conan had been human, Eben would have sworn he was grinning at them.

Though he ached at the effort, Eben forced himself to break the kiss and step back, his breathing uneven and his thoughts a tangled mess.

"Well. That was…unexpected," she murmured.

Her color was high but she didn't look upset by their heated embrace, only surprised.

He, on the other hand, was stunned to his core.

What the hell was he thinking? This kind of thing was not at all like him. He was known in all circles— social, business and otherwise—for his cool head and detached calm.

He had spent his life working hard to keep himself in check. Oh, he knew himself well enough to understand it was a survival mechanism from his childhood—if he couldn't control his parents' tumultuous natures, their wild outbursts, their screaming fights, and substance abuse, at least he could contain his own behavior.

Those habits had carried into adulthood and into his marriage. In the heat of anger, Brooke used to call him a machine, accusing him of having no heart, no feeling. She *had* to have an affair, she told him, if only to know what it was like to be with a man who had blood instead of antifreeze running through his veins.

This new, urgent heat for an exotic, wild-haired nature girl sent him way, *way* out of his comfort zone.

"My apologies," he said, his voice stiff. "I'm not quite sure what happened there."

"Aren't you?"

He sent her a swift look and saw the corner of her

mouth lift. He didn't like the feeling she was laughing at him.

"You can be certain it won't happen again."

A strange light flickered in the depths of her dark eyes. "Okay. Good to know."

She studied him for a moment, then smiled. He wanted to think the expression looked a little strained but he thought that was possibly his imagination.

"Thank you for taking Conan jogging for me. I admit, I'm not crazy about the whole morning exercise thing. I'm trying to warm up to it but it's been slow going so far. I thought after a month I would enjoy it more, but what are you going to do? It seems to cheer him up a little, though, so I guess I'll stick with it."

He couldn't seem to make his brain work but he managed to catch hold of a few of the pieces of what she said.

"You're telling me your dog is depressed?" he asked, feeling supremely stupid for even posing the question.

"You could say that." She glanced out the window where Conan still watched them and lowered her voice as if the dog could hear them through the glass. "He misses his human companion. She died a month ago."

The dog's *human companion* had died a month ago and Sage had been jogging with Conan for a month. Even in his current disordered state, he figured the two events had to be connected.

"She left you her dog?"

"That and a whole lot of other problems. It's a long story." One she obviously had no intention of sharing with him, he realized as she headed for the door.

"I'd better go. I've got thirteen eager young campers who'll be ready to explore the coastline with me in just an hour. I'm sure you've got things to do, people to see, worlds to conquer and all that."

His mouth tightened at the faint echo of derision in her voice, but before he could defend himself from her obviously harsh view of his life, she opened the door and walked out into the cool morning air, to be greeted with enthusiasm by the dog, who jumped around as if he hadn't seen her in months.

Just now the animal looked far from the bereft, grieving animal she had described. She patted his sides, which had the dog's eyes rolling back in his head. Eben couldn't say he blamed him.

"Thanks again for exercising Conan," she called back.

"No problem. I enjoyed it."

Stepping outside, he decided he wasn't going to think about anything else he might have enjoyed about the morning.

"The run was good for me," he said instead. "Helps keep my brain sharp while I'm swindling retirees and gullible widows out of their life savings."

Her mouth quirked a little at that but she only shook her wild mane of hair and took off down the stairs of his deck and across the beach, the dog close on her heels.

Chapter 5

She tried to tell herself that heated kiss was just a one-shot deal, some weird anomaly of fate and circumstance that would never, ever, *ever* be repeated.

She and Eben were two vastly different people with different values, different tax brackets. Their lives should never have intersected in the first place—and their mouths certainly shouldn't have either.

But as she showered and dressed for work, Sage couldn't shake the odd, jittery feeling that something momentous had just happened to her, something life-changing and substantial.

It was silly, she knew, but she couldn't shake the feeling that her life had just turned a corner down a route she was not at all sure she was prepared to follow.

Just a kiss, she repeated in a stern mantra as she gave Conan one last morning scratch, pulled her bike out of the garage and cycled through the strands of morning fog that hadn't yet burned off. Two people reacting to their unlikely attraction to each other in the usual fashion. One never-to-be-repeated kiss certainly was not about to alter the rest of her life, for heaven's sake.

She was still working hard to convince herself of that when she arrived at the nature center and let herself into her office. She was answering e-mail from a school group interested in arranging a field trip between her camp sessions when Lindsey poked her head into her office.

"So the weirdest thing happened this morning," Lindsey said without preamble.

Sage raised an eyebrow. "Good morning to you, too."

Her assistant director grinned. "Yeah, yeah. Hello, how are you, great to see you and all that. I've been up at the bakery since four already helping my dad so it feels more like lunchtime to me by this time. But back to my weird morning."

She pushed away the lingering memory of Eben and that stunning kiss and tried to focus on Lindsey's story. "Don't tell me you had another creepy dream about old Mr. Delarosa walking down Hemlock Street in a Speedo again."

Lindsey screwed up her face. "No! Ew. Thanks for putting that visual in my head again. I just spent the last three months in intensive therapy trying to purge it."

Sage fought a smile. "Sorry. What happened this morning?"

"I was making the usual morning deliveries of muffins to The Sea Urchin and suddenly this huge dog comes running at me out of nowhere. Scared the bejabbers out of me."

"Yeah?"

"It was Conan, of course."

"Of course. He is the only dog in Cannon Beach, after all."

"Well, maybe not, but you have to admit he's pretty distinctive-looking. There's no mistaking him for anyone else. So when I couldn't see you or Anna anywhere, I thought maybe Conan broke out of your place and was running loose. I was trying to grab hold of his collar so I could take him back to Brambleberry House when suddenly, who should show up but this extremely sexy guy who looked familiar in an odd sort of way?"

Sage didn't even want to think about just how extremely sexy *she* found Eben Spencer.

"He whistled to Conan and the two of them just kept running down the beach."

"That *is* strange," Sage murmured.

"I couldn't help but wonder what on earth our newest little camper's father was doing running with your dog at six in the morning. That *was* Chloe Spencer's hottie of a dad, wasn't it?"

Sage could feel warmth soak her cheeks. She could only be grateful the coloring she inherited from the Italian side of her family hid her blushing.

"It was. Conan and I bumped into Eben this morning on our daily jog and he, uh, graciously offered to exercise Conan for me."

Lindsey raised an eyebrow—the one with the diamond stud in it. "You sure that's all there is to the story? I'm sensing more. Come on, give me all the juice."

She would *not* allow anything resembling a guilty expression to cross her features, she vowed. They shared one kiss, that's all, and she was absolutely not going to share that information with anyone else—especially not Lindsey, who had a vivid imagination and would be spinning this whole thing way out of control.

"What juice?" she said. "You think I spent the night ripping up the sheets with Eben Spencer while his daughter slept in the next room, then I kicked him out of bed so he could go take my dog for a run?"

Lindsey laughed. "Okay. Stupid hypothesis. I have a feeling if a woman had a man like that in bed, she wouldn't kick him out if the house was on fire, forget about making him walk her dog."

"He's here to buy The Sea Urchin and will only be in town for a few days. Not even long enough for a summer fling, if I were into that kind of thing. Which I most assuredly am not. It happened just as I told you. I was jogging past his house and he was outside and offered to take Conan for his jog. Since you know I'm not excessively fond of that particular activity myself, I decided I would be stupid to refuse."

"Too bad." Lindsey grinned. "I like my version better. For a man like that, I might reconsider my strict hands-off policy toward tourists."

"He's too old for you."

"Mr. Delarosa in his Speedo is too old. Eben Spencer? Not even close."

To her relief, Sage was spared having to continue the conversation by the arrival of the first campers.

She was showing the children how to identify the different tracks of birds in the sand—and doing her level best *not* to pay more than her usual attention to the front door—when it opened suddenly and a little dark-haired sprite rushed through and headed straight for her.

"Hi Sage! My dad says he went running with Conan this morning while I was still sleeping."

Her skin suddenly itchy and tight, she drew in a breath and lifted her gaze to find Eben standing a short distance away watching her out those glittering green eyes.

She couldn't read anything at all in his expression—regret, renewed heat, even mild interest.

Fine. She could pretend nothing happened, too. "True enough," she answered Chloe.

"Why didn't anybody wake me up?" she pouted. "I would have gone jogging, too!"

"Conan has pretty long legs, honey. It's hard for me to keep up with him sometimes."

"I'm a slow runner," Chloe said glumly, then her face lit up. "I could ride a bike, though. I do that sometimes back home. I ride my bike and my dad has to run to catch up with me."

Sage couldn't help giving Eben a quick look, endeared despite herself at the image of Eben jogging while his daughter rode her bike alongside.

It seemed incongruous with everything else she had discerned about the man—but she supposed one brief kiss didn't automatically make her an expert.

"If I can find a bike, can I go with you next time?"

"I don't know if there will *be* a next time," she pointed out. "You're leaving in a few days."

That apparently was the wrong thing to say. Chloe's bottom lip jutted out and her green eyes looked as wounded as if Sage had just kicked her in the shins.

"I don't want to go. I like it here. I like you and I like your dog and I like finding sand dollars."

Sage gave her a little hug. "It's fun going on vacation and meeting new people, isn't it? When you came in, did you notice that Lindsey has some sea glass in a jar? Whoever guesses how many pieces are inside gets a prize."

Distracted for the moment, Chloe's truculence faded. "Really? What kind of prize?"

"A toy stuffed sea otter. It's really cool."

"I bet I can win it! I'm really good at guessing stuff." Chloe rushed away, leaving Eben and Sage alone.

She was intensely aware of him, the smell of expensive cologne that clung to his skin, his tailored blue shirt, the crisp folds in his silk power tie.

His business attire ought to be a major turn-off for her. It should have reminded her just how very far apart they were.

She had always thought she preferred someone like Will, who wasn't afraid to get his hands dirty. But she couldn't seem to control the wild impulse to loosen that tie a little, to spread her hands over the strong muscles beneath the expensive tailoring.

She cleared her throat and forced herself to meet his still-veiled gaze. "Chloe should have a great day today. We have lots of fun things planned for the children."

"Great. I know she's excited—more excited than she's been about anything in a long time."

"That's what we like to hear."

"Okay, then. I guess I'll see you later."

He turned away and headed out the door. Sage watched him for only a moment—but even that was too long and too revealing, apparently. When she turned back to her campers she found her assistant director watching her with a knowing look.

"You know, it's really too bad you're not the kind of

woman who would consider a summer fling," Lindsey murmured as Eben closed the door behind him.

Wasn't it? Sage thought, but she quickly turned her attention to the children.

He was dead meat.

Roast him, fry him, stick him on a spit. Sage Benedetto was going to kill him.

With one eye on the digital clock on the dashboard, Eben accelerated to pass a slow-moving minivan towing a pop-up trailer. He was supposed to have been at the nature center to pick up Chloe twenty minutes ago and he was still an hour away from Cannon Beach.

Sage might have disliked him before—their disturbing, heated morning kiss notwithstanding—but her mild antipathy was going to move into the territory of loathing if he didn't reach her soon to explain.

He was beyond tardy, approaching catastrophically, negligently late.

He steered the Jag off the highway and dialed the center's number again, as he had done a half-dozen times since the moment he had emerged late from meeting with his team of Portland attorneys.

He'd gotten a busy signal for the last half-hour, but this time to his relief the phone rang four times before someone picked up. He recognized Sage's low, sexy voice the moment she said hello.

"Hello. Eben Spencer here," he said, feeling far more awkward and uncomfortable than he was accustomed to.

Somehow she seemed to bring out the worst in him and he didn't like it at all.

"I've, uh, got a slight problem."

"Oh?"

"I'm afraid I'm just leaving Portland. I had a meeting that ran long and, to be perfectly honest, I wasn't paying attention to the time. I'm hurrying as fast as I can, but I won't be there for another hour, even if the traffic cooperates. I'm very sorry."

He heard a slight pause on the line and could almost hear her thinking what a terrible father he was. Right now, he couldn't say he disagreed.

"No problem," she finally said. "I'll just take her to Brambleberry House with me. Conan will be over the moon to see her again."

"I can't ask you to do that."

"You didn't ask. I offered. And anyway, I certainly can't leave her here by herself. I could take her to your beach house but I wouldn't feel right about leaving her alone there either. I don't mind taking her home with me. Like I said, Conan will love the company."

"In that case, thank you." He had to struggle not to grovel with gratitude.

Until this week when he'd been forced by circumstance to bring Chloe along, he wasn't sure he had fully comprehended how much he relied on nannies to take care of details like making sure Chloe was picked up on time. It was all a hell of a lot harder on his own.

He always considered himself a pretty good employer but he was definitely going to make sure he paid the next nanny more.

"You live in the big yellow Victorian down the beach, right?"

"Right. It's got a wrought-iron fence and a sign above the porch that says Brambleberry House."

"I'll be there as soon as I can." He paused. "Thank you again. I owe you."

"No problem. You can pay me back by taking Conan for another run in the morning."

Her words conjured up that kiss again, Sage all sleepy and warm and desirable in his arms, and his stomach muscles tightened.

"That's not much of a punishment. I enjoyed it more than he did," he said, his voice suddenly rough. He had to hope his sudden hunger didn't carry through the phone line. "I'll be glad for the chance to do it again."

"Don't speak too quickly. The weather forecast calls for a big storm the rest of tonight and in the morning. You'll be soaked before you even make it out the front door. I, on the other hand, will be warm and dry and cozy in my bed."

He didn't even want to go there. "I still think I'll be getting the better end of the stick, but you've got a deal."

"We'll see you in a while, then. And Eben, you really don't have to rush. Chloe will be fine."

He severed the connection and sat for a moment in the car, surrounded by lush green foliage in every direction.

He shouldn't be filled with anticipation at seeing her again. He couldn't afford the distraction—and even if he could, he shouldn't want so much to be distracted by *her*.

What was the point, really? He wasn't interested in anything short-term. How could he even think about it, with his eight-year-old daughter around? And he certainly wasn't looking for any kind of longer commitment or if he were, it would never be with a wild, free-spirited woman like Sage.

With a sigh, he put the Jag into gear again and pulled back onto the highway. Best to just work as hard as he could to finalize the deal with the Wus so he could take Chloe back to San Francisco, back to his comfort zone where everything was safe and orderly and predictable.

The storm Sage had mentioned hit just as he reached the outskirts of town. The lights of Brambleberry House gleamed in the pale, watery twilight, a beacon of warm welcome against the vast, dark ocean just beyond it.

The house was a bit more than she described, a rambling Queen Anne Victorian with a wide front porch, elaborate gingerbread trim and a voluptuous tangle of gardens out front. Painted a cheery yellow with multi-colored pastel accents, it looked bright and homey, the kind of place that for some reason always made him picture bread baking and the sweet, embracing scents of home.

He blinked the random image away and hurried through the rain to ring the doorbell, grateful for the wide porch that kept him mostly dry.

Despite the sign above the porch, he thought for a moment he might have come to the wrong house when a stranger answered the door. She had dark hair, solemn eyes, and an air about her of efficient competence.

Her mouth lifted in an impersonal, slightly wary smile. "Yes?"

"Hello. I was certain I was in the right place but now I'm beginning to doubt myself. This is Brambleberry House, isn't it?"

"Yes." She still kept the door only slightly ajar— probably a smart self-defense move so she could slam it quickly shut if he should try anything threatening.

"I'm Eben Spencer. I believe Sage Benedetto is expecting me."

She seemed to relax a little and the door opened wider, letting out a bigger slice of light and warmth to fight back the rainy evening. "You must be Chloe's father."

He held out a hand and she took it. Again, he gathered the vague impression of competence, though he wasn't sure what about her spoke so solidly of it.

"I'm Anna Galvez. I live on this floor and Sage is upstairs, all the way at the top."

"Which means you probably get roped into answering the door for her more often than you'd like."

Her smile warmed. "I don't mind, usually, unless I'm in the middle of something. Sage has a separate doorbell to her apartment but it hasn't been working for awhile. We're working on it. Sage's apartment is all the way to the top of the staircase."

The wide, sweeping staircase was the center core of the magnificent house, he saw, rising straight up from the entry through two other floors. A shame the house had been split into apartments, he thought. It would have made a stunning bed and breakfast, though he supposed it could be converted back if someone had the money, time and energy.

"Thank you," he said to Anna. "Sorry to bother you."

"Not a problem."

He followed the curve of stairs, his hand on the mahogany rail that had been worn smooth over generations.

Outside the door at the top, he heard laughter, then a dog's loud barking. He picked up Chloe's voice, then Sage's. The sound of it, rich and full and sexy, strummed down his spine.

He knocked and the dog's barking increased. He heard Sage order the dog to be stay and be quiet. It seemed to work—when she opened the door, Conan was sitting perfectly still beside the door, though he was practically vibrating with impatience.

Sage had changed yet again—the third outfit he'd

seen her in that day. Instead of her jogging clothes or the conservative navy knit shirt and khaki slacks she wore to work, she wore a flowery tunic-style blouse in some kind of sheer material over a pale pink tank top, dangly earrings and a pair of faded jeans.

She looked heart-stoppingly gorgeous, lush and appealing, and he couldn't seem to focus on anything but their kiss that morning.

He knew he didn't mistake the memory of it flaring in her dark eyes. Her mouth parted slightly and beneath the memory was a faint sheen of trepidation.

Did she think he was going to grab her right here in front of her dog and his daughter for a repeat performance?

"You made good time from Portland." In seconds, she shunted away the brief flicker of remembered heat from her gaze and became as coolly polite as her downstairs neighbor.

"I was afraid you'd be ready to string me up if I didn't hurry."

"I told you not to worry about it. Chloe's a joy."

He raised an eyebrow at that, not used to hearing such praise of his daughter. Before he could respond, Chloe rushed to him.

"Hi Daddy! I had a *super* day today. We learned about the different habitats in the ocean at camp and then when we came here, we went outside on the beach and played catch with Conan and then we made lasagna with zucchini and carrots! It's almost ready. Sage says I can stay and have some. Can I, Daddy?"

He glanced at Sage and saw her mouth tighten slightly. He was quite certain the invitation would never have been extended if she had expected him to be here before the meal was ready.

But how could he disappoint Chloe by telling her they needed to go, that they had already imposed on Sage enough for the day?

Sage must have sensed his indecision. She smiled brightly, though it didn't quite reach her eyes. "You're certainly both welcome to stay. There's plenty for everyone and Chloe did work hard to help me fix it. It's only fair she get to enjoy the fruits of her labor."

"Did we put fruit in there too?" Chloe asked, a baffled expression on her face. "I thought it was just vegetables."

"Well, remember, technically tomatoes are a fruit. So I guess that counts. Seriously, you're both welcome to stay."

Though he knew it was a mistake to spend more time with Sage, he couldn't figure out any way out without hurting Chloe.

"All right. Thank you."

He was quite certain *he* was the one with trepidation in his eyes now as he stepped into her apartment. Only after he crossed the threshold did Conan hurry to him for attention and Eben could swear the dog looked pleased.

Chapter 6

Sage had always considered her apartment to be a perfect size, roomy without being huge. The rooms were all comfortably laid out and she loved having an extra bedroom in case any friends from college came to stay. It had always seemed just right for her.

How was it that Eben Spencer seemed to fill up every available inch?

His presence was overwhelming. He wore the same pale blue dress shirt he'd had on that morning, though his tie was off and his sleeves were rolled up. Afternoon stubble shadowed his jawline, giving him a slightly disreputable look she guessed he would probably find appalling if he were aware of it.

He looked so damn gorgeous, it was infuriating.

She shouldn't even be noticing how he looked, not after she had spent all day sternly reminding herself they had nothing in common, no possible reason for this unwanted attraction that simmered between them.

He represented wealth and privilege and all the things she had turned her back on after a lifetime of struggling—and failing—to find her place there. He was no doubt just like her father, obsessed with making and keeping his money.

Good grief, the cost of his tailored shirt alone could probably feed a family of four for a month.

She didn't like him, she told herself. While her brain might be certain of that, the rest of her was having a tougher time listening to reason when she just wanted to curl against his strength and heat like Conan finding a sunbeam shooting through the window.

She sighed and pulled her lasagna out, attributing her flushed and tight skin to the heat pouring from the oven.

"Can I help with anything?" he asked, standing in the doorway.

Yeah. Go away.

She forced herself to stuff the thought back into the recesses of her mind. She was a strong, independent woman. Surely she was tough enough to endure an hour or so with the man.

"Everything's just about ready. Chloe and I were finishing things up in here when you arrived. Would the two of you mind setting the table?"

She regretted the question as soon as she asked it. Eben Spencer probably had a legion of servants to do that sort of grunt work at his house. To her surprise, he didn't hesitate.

"No problem. Come on, Chloe."

Through the doorway beyond him, Sage saw Chloe

get up from the floor where she had been playing with Conan. She and the dog both tromped into the kitchen, making Sage even more claustrophobic.

"You'll have to point me in the right direction for plates and silverware," Eben said.

"I'll grab them for you."

She pulled out her favorite square chargers—she'd bought them from a ceramics studio in Manzanita, attracted by their wild, abstract designs—and the contrasting plates she always used with them, then held them out for Eben to take.

Their hands connected when he reached for them and a spark jumped between them.

Sage flushed. "Sorry. It's the, uh, hardwood floors. Makes electricity jump in the air, especially when there are a lot of negative ions flying around from the storm."

She was babbling, she realized, and forced herself to clamp her lips shut. She didn't miss the long, considering look Eben gave her.

"Oh, is that what it's from?" he murmured.

Before she could formulate what would no doubt be a sharp retort, he grabbed the plates and carried them out of the kitchen. Only after he left did she release the breath she suddenly realized she was holding.

"Silverware is in the top drawer to the left of the dishwasher," she told Chloe. "Glasses are in the overhead cupboard."

She didn't have the luxury of a dining room in her apartment, but she had commandeered a corner of the good-sized living room for the table Will Garrett had made her.

The chairs were a mismatched jumble picked up here and there at thrift stores and yard sales, but she coordinated them with cushions in vivid colors to match the placemats and chargers.

She always thought the effect was charming but she imagined to someone of Eben Spencer's sophisticated tastes, her house probably reeked of a lousy attempt at garage-sale chic.

She didn't care, she told herself.

It was a waste of time even worrying about what he might think of her and her apartment. In a week, Eben and Chloe Spencer would just be a memory, simply two more in a long line of transitory visitors to her corner of the world.

The thought left her vaguely depressed so she pushed it away and pulled the salad she and Chloe had tossed earlier out of the refrigerator. After a few more moments of them working together, the meal was laid out on the table.

"Everything looks delicious," Eben said, taking the seat across from her.

"Sage is a vegetarian, Daddy," Chloe announced with fascinated eagerness.

"Is that right?"

"Not militant, I promise," she answered. "Steak lovers are usually still welcome at my table."

A corner of his mouth lifted. "Good thing. I do enjoy a good porterhouse, I'm sorry to say."

"You can enjoy it all you want somewhere else, but I'm afraid you won't find any steaks here tonight."

"I can be surprisingly adaptable." Again that half smile lifted his features, made him seem much less formidable. Her insides trembled but she stubbornly ignored them, serving the lasagna instead.

They were all quiet for a few moments as they dished breadsticks and salad.

Sage braced herself for a negative reaction to her favorite lasagna dish. She wasn't the greatest of cooks but after choosing a vegetarian lifestyle in college, she had worked hard to find dishes she found good, nutritious and filling.

But her tastes were likely far different than Eben's. He probably had at least one Cordon Bleu-trained personal chef to go along with the legion of servants she'd imagined for him.

To her relief and gratification, he closed his eyes in appreciation after the first taste. "Delicious. My compliments to the chefs."

Chloe giggled. "There weren't any chefs, Daddy. Just Sage and me."

"You two have outdone yourselves."

"It's super good, Sage," Chloe agreed. "I wasn't sure I'd like it but I can't even taste the carrots and stuff."

Sage smiled, charmed all over again by this little girl with the inquisitive mind and boundless energy.

"Thank you both. I'm glad you're enjoying it."

"Maybe you could give me the recipe and I could make it sometime at home, if the new nanny helps me," Chloe suggested. "I like to cook stuff sometimes, when I have a chance."

"I'll do that. Remind me before you leave and I'll make a copy of the recipe for you."

"Thank you very much," Chloe said, with a solemn formality that made Sage smile again. She shifted her gaze from the girl to her father and immediately wished she hadn't.

Eben watched her, an odd expression in those brilliant green eyes. It left her breathless and off balance. He quickly veiled it in that stiff, controlled way of his she was coming to despise.

"This is a beautiful house," he said into the sudden silence. "Have you lived here long?"

"Five years or so—I moved in a few weeks after I came to Cannon Beach."

"You're not from here? I wondered. You have a slight northeast accent every once in a while, barely noticeable."

Her mouth tightened as if she could clamp down all trace of the past she didn't like remembering. "Boston," she finally said.

"That's what I would have guessed. So what brought you to Oregon?"

"When I graduated from Berkeley, I took an internship at the nature center. I spent the first few weeks in town renting a terrible studio apartment a few blocks from here. It was all I could afford on an intern's salary, which was nothing."

"You worked for free?" Chloe asked and Sage had to smile a little at the shock in her voice.

"I was fresh out of college and ready to see the world, try anything. But I did hate living in that terrible apartment."

"How did you end up here?" Eben asked. He sounded genuinely interested, she realized, feeling ashamed of herself for being so surprised by it.

"One day at the grocery store I helped a local woman with her bags and she invited me home for dinner." Her heart spasmed a little and she suddenly missed Abigail desperately.

She managed a smile, though she suspected it didn't look very genuine. "I've been here ever since."

Eben was silent for a long moment. By the time he spoke, Sage had regained her composure.

"How many apartments are in this place?"

"Three. One on each floor, but the middle floor is empty right now."

"Your neighbor on the first floor let me in."

"Right. Anna."

Conan barked a little from under the table when she said Anna's name and Sage covered her annoyance by taking a sip of the wine she had set out for her and Eben.

Eben and Anna Galvez would be perfect for each other. The hotel tycoon and the sharp, focused businesswoman. They were both type A personalities, both probably had lifetime subscriptions to *The Wall Street Journal*, both probably knew exactly the difference between the Dow Jones and the NASDAQ—and how much of their respective portfolios were tied up in each, down to the penny.

Sage could barely manage to balance her checkbook most months and still carried a balance on her credit card from paying a down-on-his-luck friend's rent a few months earlier.

Yeah, Eben and Anna would make a good pair. So why did the idea of the two of them together leave her feeling vaguely unsettled?

"You said the second floor is empty?"

"Yes. We're still trying to figure out what we want to do, whether we want to fix it up and rent it out or leave things as is. Too many decisions to make all at once."

"I didn't understand that you owned the place. I thought you were renting."

She made a face. "I own it as of a month ago. Well, sort of."

"How do you sort of own something?"

"Anna and I co-inherited the place and everything in it, including Conan."

He looked intrigued and she didn't like feeling her life was one interesting puzzle for him to solve. "So the dog came with the house?" he asked.

"Something like that."

"So are you and Anna related in some way?"

"Nope." She sipped at her wine. "It's a long story."

She didn't want to talk about Abigail so she deliberately changed the subject.

"I understand from Chloe you're in town to buy The Sea Urchin from Stanley and Jade Wu."

Frustration flickered in his green eyes. "That's the plan, anyway."

"When do you expect to close the sale?"

"Good question. There have been a few…complications."

"Oh?"

"Everything was supposed to be done by now but I'm afraid the Wus are having second thoughts. I'm still working hard to convince them."

"My daddy has a lot of other hotels," Chloe piped up, "but he really, really wants The Sea Urchin."

Of course. No doubt it was all about the game to him, the acquisition of more and more. Just like her own father, who had virtually abandoned his child to the care of others, simply to please his narcissistic, self-absorbed socialite of a second wife.

"And I imagine whatever you want, you get, isn't that right?"

She meant to keep her voice cool and uninterested,

but she was fairly sure some of her bitterness dripped into her words.

He studied her for a long moment, long enough that she felt herself flush at her rudeness. He didn't deserve to bear the brunt of an old, tired hurt that had nothing to do with him.

"Not always," he murmured.

"Can I have another breadstick?" Chloe asked into the sudden awkward silence.

Her father turned his attention to her. "How many have you had? Four, isn't it?"

"They're so good, though!"

Sage had enough experience with both eight-year-olds and dogs to know exactly where the extra breadsticks were going—under the table, where Conan lurked, waiting patiently for anything tossed his way.

She handed Chloe another breadstick with a conspiratorial smile. "This is the last one, so you'd better make it last."

"I'm going to have to roll you down the stairs, I'm afraid."

Chloe snickered at her father. "Conan could help you carry me down. He's way strong."

"Stronger than me, probably, especially with all those breadsticks in his system."

Chloe jerked her hand above the table surface with a guilty look, but her father didn't reprimand her, he only smiled.

Sage gazed at his light expression with frustration. Drat the man. Just when she thought she had him pegged, he had to act in a way that didn't match her perception.

It was becoming terribly difficult to hang on to her dislike of him. Though her first impression of him had been

of a self-absorbed businessman with little time for his
child, she was finding it more difficult to reconcile that
with a man who could tease his daughter into the giggles.

She had always made a practice of looking for the
good in people. Even during the worst of her childhood
she had tried to find her stepmother's redeeming quali-
ties. So why was she so determined to only see nega-
tives when she looked at Eben Spencer?

Maybe she was afraid to notice his good points. If she
could still be so attracted to him when she was only focusing on the things she disliked, how much more vulnerable would she be if she allowed herself to see the
good in him?

The thought didn't sit well at all.

What was her story? Eben wondered as Sage dished
out a simple but delicious dessert of vanilla ice cream
and fresh strawberries. She was warm and approachable
one moment, stiff and cool the next. She kissed like a
dream then turned distant and polite.

Her house was like her—eclectic, colorful, with a
bit of an eccentric bent. One whole display case in the
corner was filled with gnarled pieces of driftwood inter-
spersed with various shells and canning jars filled with
polished glass. Nothing in the house looked extravagant
or costly, but it all seemed to work together to make a
charming, cozy nest.

He was intensely curious about how she came to own
the house after five years of renting it, but she obviously
hadn't want to talk about it so he had let her turn the
conversation in other directions. He wondered if that had
something to do with the pain that sometimes flickered
in her gaze.

"I *love* strawberries," Chloe announced. "They're my very favorite thing to have on ice cream."

"You need to try some of the Oregon berries sometime," Sage said with a smile.

She maintained none of her stiff reserve with Chloe. She was genuinely warm all the time and he found it entrancing.

"And before you leave, remind me to give you some of the wild raspberry jam I made last summer," she went on.

"You made jam all by yourself?"

"It's not hard. The toughest thing is not eating the berries the minute you pick them so you've got enough left to use for the jam."

Before Chloe could ask the million questions Eben could see forming in her eyes, Sage's dog slithered out from under the table and began to bark insistently.

"Uh-oh. That's his ignore-me-at-your-peril bark," Sage said quickly, setting her unfinished dessert down on the table. "I had better let him out."

"I'll do it!" Chloe exclaimed. Her features—so much like her mother's—were animated and excited.

She had been remarkably well-behaved through dinner—no tantrums, no power struggles. It was a refreshing change, he thought. Sage Benedetto had a remarkably positive effect on her. He wasn't sure what she did differently, but Chloe responded to her in a way his daughter hadn't to anyone else in a long time.

"Thanks, Chloe," Sage said. "Just make sure the gate is closed around the yard so he can't take off. He's usually pretty good about staying on his own territory, but all bets are off if he catches sight of a cat."

Chloe paused at the door. "Can I ask Miss Galvez if I can look at the dolls while I'm downstairs?"

Sage shifted her gaze to meet Eben's. "You'll have to ask your father that."

"Someone will have to clue me in. What dolls?"

"The woman who left the house to me and to Anna Galvez had a huge doll collection. It takes up an entire room in Anna's apartment now. I promised Chloe we could take a look at them before dinner, but time slipped away from us and then you arrived."

"Can I see it, Daddy?"

"If Miss Galvez doesn't mind showing you, I can't see any reason why not."

"Yay!" Chloe raced out the door, though Conan shot ahead of her and Eben could hear his paws click furiously down the stairs.

The moment they left, Eben realized he was alone with Sage—not a comfortable situation given the tension still simmering between them. She was obviously suddenly cognizant of that fact as well. She jerked to her feet and started clearing away their dinner dishes.

He finished the last of his dessert and rose to help her. "Thank you again for dinner. I can't remember a meal I've enjoyed more."

It was true, he realized with surprise. Chloe was usually in bed when he returned home from work, but on the rare occasions he dined with her, he typically found himself bracing for her frequent emotional outbursts.

It had been wonderful to enjoy his daughter's company under Sage's moderating influence.

Sage didn't look convinced by his words. "It was only vegetarian lasagna. Probably nothing at all like you're used to. You don't have to patronize me."

Her words surprised a laugh from him. "I don't think I could patronize you, even if I tried. I doubt anyone

can. I mean it. I enjoyed the meal—and the company—
immensely."

She studied him for a moment then nodded. "So did I."

"You sound surprised. It's not very flattering, I must
admit."

"I am surprised, I suppose. I don't entertain a great
deal. When I do, it's usually friends in my own circle."

"I appreciate you making an exception in our case."

He was intensely aware of her, of the way her dangly
earrings caught the lamplight, the smell of her, feminine and enticing, her mobile expressions. He wanted
to kiss her again, with a fierce ache, though he knew it
was impossible, not to mention extremely unwise.

He didn't want to destroy this fragile peace—especially when his intentions could never be anything other
than a quick fling, something he guessed wasn't typical
for her, either.

In an effort to cool his growing awareness, he
searched his mind for a change of topic as he followed
her into the small kitchen with his hands full of dishes.

"Tell me the truth, now that Chloe is gone for a
moment. How was she today?"

Surprise widened her eyes at the question. "Fine.
She's a little energetic, but no worse than any of the other
eight-year-olds at the camp. Better than some. She's very
sweet."

She studied him and he was certain some of his relief
must have shown on his features.

"You look like you expected a different answer."

He sighed and put the dishes down on the countertop next to the sink. "I love my daughter, but I have to
admit that *sweet* is not an adjective many people use to
describe her these days."

"That surprises me. She seems to me a typical kid, just like the others in the class."

"I think you have an extraordinary rapport with her.'"

"I'm not sure why that would be."

"I'm not, either. Chloe is…challenging. She's bright and creative and funny most of the time, but she has these mood swings. Her mother's death two years ago affected her strongly. She and Brooke were very close. Her mother doted on her—maybe too much."

"I don't think you can ever love a child too much."

There was that stiffness in her voice again. "I don't, either. Please don't misunderstand. I only meant that losing her mother was a fierce and painful blow to Chloe. As a parent, I'm afraid I'm a poor substitute for my wife."

Her gaze flashed to his and he regretted exposing so much truth about himself.

"I tried to give her some leeway for her grief for several months but I'm afraid I let her get away with too many things and now that's her expectation all the time. In the last year and a half she's been through four schools and a half-dozen nannies. She's moody and unpredictable. Defiant one moment, deceptively docile the next."

Without really thinking about it, he started to load the dishes in the dishwasher. "The other morning was a perfect example," he continued. "She could have been seriously hurt sneaking out so early. I wouldn't do as she demanded the night before and stay out late hunting up seashells with her, so she countermanded me by sneaking out on her own."

She opened her mouth slightly then closed it again.

"What were you going to say?" he pressed.

"Nothing. Never mind." She turned away to run water in the sink for the soiled dishes.

Eben leaned against the counter next to her, enjoy-ing her graceful movements.

"You probably would have been right out there with her in the middle of the night with a flashlight and a bucket looking for sand dollars, wouldn't you?"

She gave him a sidelong look, then smiled. "Prob-ably."

"I let her get away with too much right after Brooke died and I need to set some boundaries now. Children needs rules and structure."

"Is that the kind of childhood you had? Regimented, toe-the-line. Military school, right?"

He laughed, though he heard the harsh note in it and wondered if she did as well. "Not quite. I would have given my entire baseball card collection for a little struc-ture and discipline. My parents were of the if-it-feels-good-just-do-it school of thought. It destroyed them both and they nearly took me and my sister along with them. I can't do that to Chloe."

Her hands paused in the sink and her eyes widened with sympathy. He shifted, uncomfortable. Where the hell had that come from? He didn't share these pieces of his life with anyone. He wasn't sure he'd ever even ar-ticulated that to Brooke. If he had, maybe she wouldn't have expected so many things from him he wasn't at all sure he had been capable of offering.

He certainly had no business sharing them with Sage. She was quiet for a long moment, watching him out of intense brown eyes. The only sound was the rain click-ing against the window and the soft sound of their min-gled breathing.

"I'm sorry," she finally murmured.

He shrugged. "It was a long time ago. I just don't want to make the same mistakes with Chloe."

"But you can go too far in the other direction, can't you?"

"I'm doing my best. That's all I can do."

He didn't want to talk about this anymore. With her so close, he was having a tough time hanging on to any coherent thought anyway. All he could think about was kissing her again.

But he couldn't.

The thought had no sooner entered his head than he could swear he felt a soft hand in the small of his back from out of nowhere pushing him toward her.

She gave him a quick startled look then her gaze seemed to fasten on his mouth.

What other choice did he have but to kiss her?

Chapter 7

She sighed as if she'd been waiting for his kiss and she tasted heady and sweet from the wine and the strawberries.

Having her in his arms felt *right*, in a way he couldn't explain. On an intellectual level, it made absolutely no sense and every voice in his head was clamoring to tell him why kissing her again was a colossal mistake.

He shut them all out and focused only on the silky smoothness of her hair, her soft curves against him.

Her hands were warm, wet from the dishwater. He could feel the palm prints she left against his shirt, a temporary brand.

He had been thinking of their earlier kiss all day. As he drove to Portland and back, as he listened to his attorneys ramble on and on. Like the low murmur of the sea outside, she had been a constant presence in his mind.

Their kiss that morning had been heated and intense, more so because it had been so unexpected.

This, though, was different. Eben closed his eyes at the astonishing gentleness of it, the quiet peace that seemed to swirl around them, wrapping them together with silken threads.

He still wanted her fiercely and the hunger thrumming inside him urged him to deepen the kiss but he kept it slow and easy, reluctant to destroy the fragile beauty of the moment.

"All day long, I've been telling myself a thousand reasons why I shouldn't do that again," he murmured after a long, drugging moment.

He could see a pulse flutter in her throat, feel her chest rise and fall with her accelerated breathing. She dropped her hands from his shirt, but not before he was certain he felt their slight tremble.

"I can probably give you a couple thousand more why I shouldn't have let you."

"Yet here we are."

She sighed and he heard turmoil and regret in the sound. "Right. Here we are."

She stepped away from him and immersed her hands in the dishwater, a slight brush of color on her cheeks as she started scrubbing a pan with fierce concentration.

He sighed, compelled to honesty. "I'm not looking for anything. You need to know that. This just sort of… happened."

The temperature in the room suddenly seemed to dip a dozen degrees and he could swear the rain lashed the windows with much more force than before.

When she spoke, her voice was as cool as the rain. "That makes two of us, then."

"Right."

He was digging himself in deeper but he had to attempt an explanation. "We just have this…thing between us. I have to tell, I don't quite understand it."

"Don't you?" Her voice was positively icy now and he realized how his words could be construed.

He sighed again, hating this awkward discomfort. "You're a beautiful woman, Sage. You have to know that. Any man would be crazy not to find you attractive. But I swear, until this morning I have never in my life kissed a woman I haven't at least taken on two or three dates. I've never known anything like this. You just do something to me. I can't explain it. To be honest, I'm not sure I like it."

The ice in her eyes had thawed a little, he saw, though he wasn't sure he was thrilled with the shadow of amusement that replaced it.

"I'm sure you don't."

"I haven't dated in a decade," he confessed. "My wife and I were married for seven years and Brooke has been gone for two years now. I'm afraid I'm out of practice at this whole man–woman thing."

She sent him a sidelong look he couldn't read. "I wouldn't exactly say that."

Oddly, he could swear he heard a ripple of low laughter coming from the other room. He shifted his gaze to the doorway into her living room and saw Sage do the same, almost as if she could hear it, too.

No one was there, he could tell in an instant, but his attention was suddenly caught by a picture he hadn't noticed before hanging on the wall of the kitchen.

He stared at the image of two women on what looked

like a sea cliff, their cheeks pressed together as they embraced, deep affection in their eyes.

One was Sage, a lighthearted joy in her expression he hadn't seen before. But his shock of recognition was for the other person, the one with the wrinkled features and mischievous eyes…. He moved closer for a better look.

"I know this woman!"

Sage blinked a little at his abrupt change of topic. "Abigail? You know Abigail?"

"Yes! Abigail, that's her name!"

"Abigail Dandridge. She's the one who left me this house. She was my best friend in the world."

"I never knew her last name. She's dead, then." An obvious statement, but he couldn't for the world think of what else to say.

She nodded, her eyes suddenly dark with emotion. "It's been almost five weeks now. Her heart just stopped in her sleep one night. No warning signs at all. I know she would have wanted to go that way, but…I didn't have a chance to say goodbye—you know?—and everything feels so *unfinished*. I still feel her here, in the house. At random moments I think I smell her favorite scent or feel the touch of her hand in my hair. It's a cliché, but I still keep thinking I'll hear her voice any minute now, calling me down the stairs to share some gossip over tea."

He suddenly understood the sorrow he glimpsed every once in a while in Sage's eyes. He wanted to comfort her but couldn't find the words, not through his own shock and sadness.

She looked at him with puzzlement in her eyes. "I'm sorry. How did you say you knew her?"

"I suppose I can't really say I knew her. I met her only briefly but the encounter was…unforgettable."

She smiled, a little tremulously. "Abigail often had that effect on people."

"I should have figured it out. You know, I thought Conan looked familiar but I didn't put the pieces together until right this moment. I can't believe she's gone."

"You met her then? She didn't say anything about it."

"It probably wasn't as significant a meeting for her as it was for me. I came to town scouting locations for a new property. I was jogging early one morning and I saw her and I guess it was Conan. I don't know why I stopped to talk to her—maybe I stopped to tie my shoe or something—but we struck up a conversation. It was the oddest thing. After we talked for awhile, she insisted on taking me to breakfast at The Sea Urchin—and I went, which isn't at all like me."

What also hadn't been like him was the way the woman's warm, kind eyes had led him to telling her far more about himself than he did with most people.

By the time they'd finished their divine breakfast of old-fashioned French toast with mountains of fresh whipped cream and bacon so crisp it melted in his mouth, Abigail knew about Chloe, about Brooke's death, even about those last years of their troubled marriage.

"Abigail was always doing things like that, grabbing a stranger to take out for a meal," Sage said into his sudden silence. "She loved to meet new people. She used to say she knew everything there was to know about the locals and she got damn sick and tired of hearing the same boring old stories a hundred times."

"She was wonderful. Sharp. Funny. Kind. After breakfast at The Sea Urchin, she suggested I talk to

Stanley and Jade Wu about buying it. You know, the whole thing was her idea. She told me they were thinking about retiring, but I have to say, until I approached them with an offer, I don't think it had even occurred to them to sell the place."

"I told you Abigail knew everything about the locals, sometimes things they didn't even know themselves."

Abigail had certainly been able to see deep into Sage's own mind. From the moment Sage arrived in Cannon Beach, Abigail had seemed to know instinctively how much Sage longed for a family and home of her own.

The remarkable thing had been her way of finding the best in everyone she met and helping them see it as well.

Why on earth would Abigail have picked Eben Spencer to be one of her pet projects? Sage couldn't for the life of her figure it out. And she had steered him toward buying The Sea Urchin? It didn't make sense. Abigail would never have suggested he buy the place if she didn't trust him to take care of it.

Maybe Sage needed to reconsider her perceptions of the man. If Abigail had approved of him to that extent, perhaps she saw deeper into him than Sage could.

"That morning at breakfast with Abigail felt like an omen. I have to admit, from the moment we stepped into the place, I set my heart on purchasing The Sea Urchin and I'm afraid I haven't been able to even entertain the idea of any other property for Spencer Hotels' next project. I'm only sorry I didn't have the chance to meet up with her again."

What weird twist of fate had led her to Chloe on the beach that morning, to someone peripherally connected to Abigail? Or *had* it been a coincidence? She shivered a little, remembering how Conan had greeted Chloe like an old friend, as if he had been expecting her.

"Everything okay?" Eben asked.

He would probably mock any woo-woo speculation on her part. She had a feeling Eben was a prosaic man not given to superstition.

"Fine. Just thinking how odd it was that you're here now, in Abigail's house."

"*Your* house, now."

"In my mind, it will always belong to her. She loved every inch of this place."

Before he could answer, they heard footsteps bounding up the stairs. A moment later, Chloe and Conan burst into the apartment, with Anna Galvez in tow.

"Daddy, Daddy, guess what?"

"What, sweetheart?"

"There's a whole room of dolls downstairs. It's huge. I've never *seen* so many dolls. Miss Galvez says if it's okay with you, I can pick one out and keep it. May I, Daddy? Oh please, may I?"

"Chloe—" He shifted, obviously uncomfortable with the idea.

Sage sent a swift look to Anna, surprised she would make such an offer. She wouldn't have expected such a generous gesture from Anna, especially after their conversation the day before about keeping the collection intact.

But somehow it seemed exactly the right thing to do, precisely what Abigail would have wanted, for them to give this sweet daughter of the man Abigail had known one of her beloved dolls.

"Several of the dolls have resin faces and aren't breakable. They're completely safe for her," Anna said somewhat stiffly.

Eben looked at Sage with a question in his eyes. She nodded. "Abigail would have wanted her things to be loved," she said. "She adored showing them off to children."

She got the impression it wasn't an easy thing for Eben to accept anything from anyone. He was a hard, self-contained man, though it appeared he had a soft spot for his daughter, something she wouldn't have expected just a few days before.

"All right," he finally said. "If you're certain you don't mind."

Chloe squealed with excitement. "You have to help me choose one. Both of you."

She grabbed Sage with one hand then Eben with the other and started tugging them both toward the stairs. Conan barked once and Sage could swear he was grinning again.

She didn't know which she found more disturbing, her dog's pleased expression or Anna's speculative one.

For the next ten minutes, she, Anna and Eben helped Chloe peruse Abigail's vast collection, doing their best to point her toward the sturdier, more age-appropriate dolls.

Sage had never been one to play with girlie things, but even she had to admit how much she enjoyed walking into the doll room. She couldn't help feeling close to Abigail here, amid the collection that had been such a part of her friend.

Abigail never married and had no children of her own. She had a great-nephew somewhere, but he hadn't even bothered coming to his great-aunt's funeral. In many ways, the dolls were Abigail's family, the inanimate counterpoints to the living, breathing strays she collected.

Sage loved seeing them, remembering the joy Abigail had found every time she added a new doll to her collection.

She especially loved the dolls Abigail had made herself over the decades, with painted faces and elaborate hand-sewn clothes. Victorian dolls with flounced dresses and parasols, teenyboppers with ponytails and poodle skirts, dolls with bobbed hair and flapper dresses.

There was no real rhyme or reason to the collection—no common theme that Sage had ever been able to discern—but each was charming in its own way.

"I can't decide. There are too many."

A spasm of irritation crossed Eben's features at Chloe's whiny tone. Sage could tell the girl was tired after their big day on the shore then coming back to Brambleberry House afterward. She hoped Eben was perceptive enough to pick up on that as well.

To her relief, after only a moment his frustration slid away, replaced by patience. He pulled his daughter close and kissed her on the top of her dark curls and Sage could swear she felt her heart tumble in her chest.

"Pick out your favorite three and maybe we can help you make your final choice," he suggested, a new gentleness in his voice.

That seemed a less daunting task to his daughter. With renewed enthusiasm she studied the shelves of dolls, pulling one out here and there, returning another, choosing with care until she had three lined up in the middle of the floor.

They were an oddly disparate trio: a little girl with pigtails holding a teddy bear, a curvy woman in a grass Hawaiian skirt and lei, then an elegant woman with blond hair and a white dress.

Chloe studied them for a moment, then reached for

the one in white. "You don't have to help me pick. This is the one I want. She looks just like an angel."

The doll was simple but lovely. "Good choice," Sage said, admiring the doll when Chloe held her out.

"Her name is Brooke."

"Of course it is," Eben murmured.

Sage glanced at him and was surprised to see a pained look in his eyes as he studied the doll. Only then did she remember his wife's name had been Brooke.

For the first time, Sage picked up the resemblance in the doll's features to Chloe's. Only their hair color was different.

Chloe must have picked the doll because it looked like her mother. Oh, poor little pumpkin. Sage wanted to gather her up and hold her tight until she didn't hurt anymore.

So much pain in the world.

"I'm going to put her on my bureau at home," Chloe announced. "That way I can see her every morning."

"Good plan," Anna said. Her eyes met Sage's and Sage could see her own supposition mirrored there.

"Okay, kiddo," Eben interjected, the shadows still in his gaze, "you need to say thanks to Sage and Ms. Galvez for the doll, then we should head home. You've had a big day and need to get some rest so you'll be a good little camper in the morning."

"Thank you very much for the doll. I will love her forever," the girl said solemnly to them, then turned back to her father. "I'm not tired at all, though. I would like to stay longer."

Eben smiled, Sage could see the lines around the corners of his mouth that only served to make him look more ruggedly handsome.

"*You* might not be tired, but I certainly am and I

imagine Sage and Ms. Galvez are as well. Come on, let's take your new friend home."

Chloe paused, then ran to Anna and threw her arms around her waist. "I mean it. Thank you for the doll. I'll take super good care of her, I promise."

Anna looked discomfited by the girl's hug, but there was a softness in her eyes Sage hadn't seen before. "I'm glad to hear that. Bring her back anytime to see the rest of her friends."

Chloe giggled, then turned to Sage and embraced her as well. That tumble in her heart before was nothing compared to the hard, swift fall she felt as she fell head over heels for this sweet, motherless little girl.

"Thank you for letting me help you make vegetable lasagna and play with Conan and see where you live. I think Brambleberry House is the most beautiful house in the world."

Sage hugged her back. "You're very welcome. I'll see you in the morning, okay? Don't forget your raincoat. We're in for some nice Oregon sunshine. That means rain, by the way."

Chloe giggled, then slipped her hand in her father's.

Though Anna and Conan stayed in her apartment, Sage followed them outside. The rain had nearly stopped and only a light drizzle fell.

On the porch, she stopped, feeling as awkward as if they'd been on a date. That stunning, gentle kiss in her apartment seemed to shimmer through her mind and she couldn't seem to think of anything but his warm mouth and his strong, hard arms around her.

Though Chloe ran ahead and climbed into the back seat of the Jag, Eben paused and met her gaze, the re-cessed porch lights reflecting in his eyes. He grabbed her hand, his fingers enfolded around hers. "Thank you again for taking Chloe later than you planned, and for dinner and everything."

"You're very welcome. She was no trouble."

"Only because you're amazing with her."

Sage shook her head, slipping her hand from his, needing the safety of physical distance from him even as her emotions seemed to tug her ever nearer. "I find her a joy. I told you that."

"I'll be ready in the morning to run with Conan."

"I promise, I won't hold you to that. I was joking."

"I'm looking forward to it. This morning was wonderful and I'd love a repeat. The, uh, run I meant."

She was certain if the light had been brighter she would have seen faint color on his features. Somehow his discomfort over their unexpected kiss charmed her beyond measure.

She didn't need to spend more time with him or with Chloe. Both of them were already sneaking their way into her heart. More time would only make their departure that much more difficult. She already dreaded thinking about when they left Cannon Beach.

"Don't count on it," she answered. "If I'm lucky, my furry alarm clock will sleep in tomorrow."

"I'll be waiting if he doesn't."

Without another word, he turned and hurried down the steps into the drizzle.

Chapter 8

Long after the car drove away, headlights reflecting on the wet streets, Sage stood on the porch of Brambleberry House, hugging her arms to her against the evening chill and worrying.

She had to find it in her heart to push them both away. That was the only solution. Her emotions were too battered right now, raw and aching from Abigail's death.

She wasn't strong enough to sustain another devastating loss. That's what it would be, she feared, if she let them inside any farther. She was afraid she would find it entirely too easy to fall for both of them. Already she was halfway to being in love with Chloe, with her sweet eyes and her quirky sense of humor and her desperate eagerness to please.

She sighed as an owl called somewhere in the distance, then Sage opened the door into the house.

She expected Anna to be cloistered in Abigail's apartment by the time she returned. Instead, she found her waiting in the foyer, one hand absently rubbing Conan's head. She looked softer, somehow, more approachable—perhaps because she'd changed out of her work clothes while Sage, Eben and Chloe had been upstairs having dinner.

She should have invited Anna to join them, she thought, ashamed of herself for not thinking of it.

"Thank you for the whole doll thing," she said. "It seemed to be a big hit with Chloe."

"I probably should have talked to you first about giving her one before I suggested it to her. I know what you said the other day about the collection staying together. Technically, they belong to both of us and they're not really mine to give away."

Would she ever escape the complexities of that blasted will? "Despite what you might think, I honestly don't want to hoard all of Abigail's things forever, to freeze everything in the house just as it is and never alter so much as a nail hole."

"I know you don't," Anna said stiffly. "I'm sorry if I gave you the impression I thought otherwise."

Sage sighed. "I'm sorry to be short with you. This is all so awkward, isn't it?"

Anna was quiet for a moment. "I know you loved Abigail deeply and she felt the same way about you. There was an unbreakable bond between the two of you. Everyone could see it. I understand how painful her death is for you. Believe me, I understand. Maybe you loved her longer but…I loved her, too. I miss her."

Guilt lodged in her throat at her weeks of coldness toward Anna, at her ridiculous resentment—as if it were

Anna's fault they found themselves in this tangled arrangement.

She had never felt so small and petty.

Abigail would have been furious with her, would have given her a stern look out of those blue eyes and told her to put on her big girl panties and just deal.

"Would you…like to come in?" Anna asked at Sage's continued silence. "I was about to have some tea and you're welcome to share it. You don't have to, of course."

She was exhausted suddenly, emotionally and physically. Her day had been tumultuous from that first kiss in Eben's beach house and she wanted nothing more than to climb into her bed and yank the quilt over her head and shut out the world.

But how could she rebuff such a clearcut overture of friendship?

"Sure. Okay."

Anna looked surprised, then thrilled, which only added to Sage's guilt level. The other woman led the way into her apartment, toward the little kitchen that still looked as it had the day Abigail died. Her gaze landed on the calendar still turned back to April and Abigail's handwritten little notes in the date squares.

Conan, shots, 10:30.

Lunch with the girls.

Will's birthday.

It was a snapshot of her life, busy and fulfilling. Why hadn't Anna taken it down? Sage would have thought that to be one of the first things an efficient, orderly woman like Anna would make an effort to do when she moved her own things in.

Did she find some kind of comfort from this small

reminder of Abigail and her life? Sage resolved to try harder to forge a connection with Anna.

"What kind of tea would you like? I think there's every kind imaginable here."

Chai was her favorite but she wasn't sure she could drink it here in this kitchen out of Abigail's favorite teacups, not with her emotions so close to the surface.

"It's late. I don't need more caffeine with my head already buzzing. I'd better go for chamomile."

Anna smiled and found teabags in the cupboard, then pulled a burbling kettle off the stove and poured it over the bags.

Sage watched for a moment, awkward at the silence. "Thank you again for the doll thing," she said. "It was a great idea. Chloe was thrilled."

"She picked an angel doll and named her Brooke. Am I crazy or was there some deeper significance to that?"

"It was her mother's name."

Anna pursed her lips in distress. "That's what I thought. Poor little thing."

Anna studied her for a moment as if she wasn't sure whether to ask the questions Sage could see forming in her eyes. "You do know that's Eben Spencer, the CEO of Spencer Hotels, right?" she finally said.

"I hope so. If not, he's doing a fairly credible job of masquerading as the man."

"And do you realize he's brilliant? I read about him in *Fortune* a few months ago. The man has single-handedly rescued a small, floundering hotel company and turned it into a major player in the hospitality industry with small luxury properties around the globe."

"Yippee for him."

And she had fed him vegetarian lasagna and breadsticks at her dining table with the mismatched chairs. She wanted a do-over on the whole evening.

No, she corrected herself. She wouldn't allow him to make her feel ashamed of her life or what she had worked hard to build for herself. After severing the last fragile ties with her father, she had started with nothing and had built a rich, fulfilling life here.

"While we were looking at the dolls, Chloe told me he's looking to buy The Sea Urchin."

"That's what I understand."

"It's a perfect property for Spencer Hotels. It will be interesting to see what he can do with the place."

"I like The Sea Urchin exactly the way it is," she muttered.

"So do I," Anna assured her. "But Spencer Hotels has a reputation for taking great properties and making them even better. It will be interesting to watch."

"If Stanley and Jade ultimately decide to sell. I don't believe Eben has convinced them yet."

"If what I've heard about him is halfway true, he will." She paused and gave Sage a careful look as she handed her the cup of tea. "Was I crazy or did I pick up some kind of vibe between you two?"

Sage could feel herself flush and was grateful again for her Italian heritage. She could taste his mouth again on hers, feel the silky softness of his hair beneath her fingertips. "You have a much more vivid imagination than I ever gave you credit for."

She immediately wished she could call the words back, but to her surprise, Anna only laughed. "Sorry. Not much imagination here, but I do pride myself on my keen powers of observation. Comes from reading too many mysteries, I think."

"What did you see?" Sage asked warily.

"Wet handprints. They were all over his shirt. Unless the man has some kind of weird, acrobatic agility, I don't believe he could put handprints on his own back. And since you were the only one in the apartment with him, I guess that leaves you. Not that it's any of my business."

Sage could feel herself flush and for the life of her, she couldn't think how to respond.

"I hope this doesn't offend you," Anna went on, "but I have to tell you, he doesn't seem like your usual type."

"I wasn't aware I had a *type*."

"Of course you do. Everyone does."

She told herself she was grateful the conversation had turned from handprints—or anything else she might have put on Eben. "Okay, I'll bite. What's my type?"

Anna added at least three teaspoons of sugar to her own cup as she gave Sage a sidelong look. "I don't know. Maybe some shaggy-haired, folk-singer guy who smells like patchouli and drives a hybrid with a Peace-Out bumper sticker on the back bumper."

She was too tired to be offended, she decided. Besides, she had to admit it was a pretty accurate description of the guys she usually dated. She sipped at her tea and grinned a little, astonished to find a sense of humor in Anna Galvez—and more astonished to find herself enjoying their interaction.

"All right, Ms. Know-it-All. What's your type, then?"

She was certain Anna's smile slipped a bit. "Well, probably not shaggy-haired folk singers."

Her evasion only made Sage more curious. She had never given much thought to Anna's social life, though she thought she remembered something about a broken engagement in the last few years.

"Seriously, are you dating anybody? Since we're living in the same house, it would be good to be prepared if I encounter some strange man on the stairway in the middle of the night."

Anna sighed. "No. I'm currently on sabbatical from men."

For some reason—probably because of her exhaustion—Sage found that hilarious. "Is there a stipend that goes with that?"

The other woman laughed and shook her head. "No, it's all purely gratis. But the benefits to my mental health are enormous."

No wonder Abigail had loved Anna. It was a surprising revelation in a day full of them, but by the time Sage finished her tea fifteen minutes later, all her misconceptions about Anna Galvez had flown out the window. The other woman wasn't at all the stuffy, serious businesswoman she presented herself as most of the time, at least the way she had always presented herself to Sage.

Why the facade? Sage wondered. Why had she always acted so cool and polite to her? Was it only a protective response to some latent, unconscious hostility Sage might have been projecting? She didn't want to think so, especially tonight when she was too tired for such deep introspection, but she had a feeling she may have been largely to blame for the awkwardness between them.

At least they had made this shaky beginning to building a friendship. They had a house and a dog and a life in common now. They should at least get a friendship out of the deal, too.

As the thought flickered through her mind, the scent of freesia seemed to drift through the room.

"Can you smell that?"

An odd look sparked in Anna's dark eyes and she set down her teacup. "I smell it all the time. It's like she's right here with me sometimes. But of course that's crazy."

"Is it?"

"I don't believe in ghosts. I'm sorry. I'm sure I'm a little more prosaic than you. I can't buy that Abigail still lingers at Brambleberry House."

"So what explanation do you have for it?"

Anna shrugged and spoke so quickly Sage was certain she must have given the matter some thought. "Abigail loved the smell of freesias. I think over her eighty years of living here and wearing the scent, some of it must have just absorbed into the walls and the carpet. Every once in a while, it's released by a shifting of molecules or something."

Sage wasn't convinced but she wasn't about to risk this tentative friendship by arguing. "Maybe," she answered. "I like it, whatever the explanation."

Anna smiled a little tremulously. "So do I."

"I should go. It's getting late." When Sage set down her teacup and rose, Conan didn't move from his spot curled up on his side by Anna's feet like a huge red footwarmer. Apparently he was settled for the night. She felt a little twinge of jealousy but pushed it away. For some reason, she sensed Anna needed his company more than she did right now.

"I guess he's yours for the night."

"I guess."

"Good night. I, uh, enjoyed the tea."

Anna smiled. "So did I."

"Next time it's my treat."

"I'll count on it."

She said good-night to Conan, who slapped his tail

against the floor a few times before going back to sleep, then she headed up the stairs to her apartment.

No freesia lingered in the air here, only the spicy scent of lasagna—and perhaps a hint of Eben's expensive cologne.

What was she going to do about the man?

Nothing, she answered her own question. What could she do? He would be leaving in a few days when his business here was done and she would go back to her happy, fulfilling life.

What other choice did she have? They were worlds apart in a hundred different ways. He was the CEO of a multinational corporation and she was a vegetarian nature-girl with a spooky, omniscient dog and a rambling old house full of ghosts and problems.

Yeah, the two of them seemed to generate this unlikely heat between them, but even if she were stupid enough to indulge herself by playing with it for awhile, dry tinder could only burn so long. Without the steady fuel of shared interests and emotional compatibility, the heat between them would probably flare and burn out quickly.

That thought depressed her more than it ought to.

She had a great life here in Cannon Beach, she reminded herself. Everything she could ever need. She knew that eventually this ache in her heart over losing Abigail would ease. She hurt a little less again than she had yesterday, a little less then than the day before that.

She would never stop missing her friend, but she knew eventually she would find her way back to homeostasis and begin to find happiness and joy in her life again.

Eben and Chloe Spencer would leave Cannon Beach in a few days and be just another memory. A pleas-

ant one, yes, like all her many birdwatching hikes with
Abigail and their hundreds of shared cups of tea, but a
memory nonetheless.

"It's a good thing you're cute or I could definitely
grow to loathe you for these morning tortures."

The object of her ire simply sat waiting by the door
with an impatient scowl for Sage to lace up her running
shoes. Despite spending the night in Anna's apartment,
Conan must have squeezed out of his doggie door so he
could come up the stairs and bark outside her door at
the usual time to go running.

She yawned and tied her other shoe, dearly wishing
she were back in her bed, that she had the nerve to send
the mongrel down the beach to Eben's rental unit to drag
him out of bed.

Since that conjured up too many enticing images of
wavy dark hair against a pillow, of whisker-roughened
skin and sleepy smiles, she jerked her mind back to
Conan, who was quivering with impatience. He barked
again and she sighed.

"All right, all right. I'm ready. Let's do this."

Conan bounded down the stairs of Brambleberry
House, dancing around in the foyer in his eagerness to
be gone as she followed more slowly, yanking her hair
back into a ponytail as she went.

The morning air was cool and the rain had stopped
sometime in the night, leaving wisps of fog to wrap
through the garden and around the coastal pines
beyond.

She stood on the porch stretching her hamstrings and
listening to the distant sound of the sea and the call of
that screech owl she'd heard the night before.

Maybe she didn't hate these runs with Conan after all, she decided. If not for them, she would miss all this morning splendor, simply for the sake of an extra hour of sleep.

The dog seemed wildly eager to go, whining impatiently and racing back and forth in the yard. Apparently he'd never heard of pulled muscles or torn ligaments, she thought sourly, then gave up stretching and followed him to the backyard, to the latched gate there that led directly to the beach.

The dog rushed out but Sage had to pause for a moment to prop the gate open so they could return that way instead of having to take a more circuitous route to the front of the house.

She straightened from the task and nearly collided with a solid wall of muscle.

"Oh," she exclaimed. She would have fallen if strong arms hadn't reached to keep her upright.

"Sorry," Eben murmured, heat flaring in his green eyes. "I thought you saw me."

"No. I wasn't paying attention."

After a moment's hesitation, he released her arm and she managed to find her footing as she caught sight of Conan a few yards away, racing around a giggling Chloe.

"Chloe! You're up early."

"Don't I know it." Eben looked at his daughter with disgruntled affection. "She woke me an hour ago, begging me to take her jogging with Conan this morning. We couldn't quite figure out the logistics, though. We didn't want to bang on your door at 6:00 a.m. just to pick up your dog, but then we saw your lights go on and headed over, hoping to catch you."

"Conan didn't give me a lot of choice this morning. He seemed particularly insistent on running today. Sometimes I think he's psychic. Maybe he knew you and Chloe were going to be here and wanted to make sure we didn't miss you."

"We came to take him running, so you can go back to bed," Chloe said with her guileless smile.

Tempting offer, Sage thought. That would certainly be the prudent course, to climb back into her bed, yank the covers over her head and pretend this was all a weird dream.

She couldn't do it, though. The morning was too lovely and she discovered she wasn't willing to relinquish the chance to be with them again, even though she knew it couldn't possibly be healthy for her.

"I've got a better idea," she said suddenly. "Come on inside to the garage for a moment."

Eben looked puzzled but he followed her and Chloe and Conan did the same. Sage quickly programmed the code to open the garage door. Inside she found one of Abigail's favorite toys propped against one wall and wheeled it out to where they waited for her.

Chloe's eyes widened when she saw Sage pushing the tandem bike out of the garage.

"Cool!" she exclaimed. "Is that yours?"

"It belonged to a friend of mine. We used to love to take bike rides together."

What a wealth of information that revealed about Abigail, she thought, that an independent woman in her eighties who lived with only an upstairs tenant for family would invest in a tandem bike. With her skill of gathering people around her, she never had a dearth of people to take rides with, from Will Garrett to Mr. Delarosa to the high school kids who delivered the newspaper.

"Can we ride it? You and me?" Chloe asked.

"I think that's a great idea. Your dad and that beastly dog can run if they want and get all sweaty and gross. We girls will enjoy a leisurely morning ride."

Chloe's glee nearly matched Conan's excitement. Sage glanced over at Eben and found him watching her with a murky look in his eyes that made her suddenly as breathless as if she'd just biked up the hill to Indian Beach.

It took Chloe a few moments to get the hang of the tandem bicycle, but by the time they made it a block, she was riding like a pro, giggling for the sheer joy of it.

Sage knew just how she felt. She wanted to laugh, as well. How could she ever have thought staying back in her apartment in bed would be preferable to this?

They stuck to pavement since she knew the soft sand of the beach would prove a challenge for Chloe. On impulse, she guided them south, away from town, with a specific destination in mind.

They encountered little traffic here this early in the morning. Conan and Eben ran ahead of them, Conan resigned to the leash. She had to admit, she enjoyed watching the play of Eben's muscles as he ran. Not a bad way to start the day, she decided.

She lifted her face to the pale streaks of sunlight shining toward the ocean. A strange emotion fluttered through her and it took her a while to recognize it.

She was happy, she realized.

For the first time since Abigail's death, she remembered what it was to savor life.

It was a gift, she decided, one she wasn't about to waste.

Chapter 9

On a purely intellectual level, Eben knew he shouldn't be enjoying himself so much.

It was only a run, after all, just a brief interlude before he jumped right back into his normal routine of business calls and strategy sessions.

But the air was cool and sweet, his muscles had that pleasant burn of a good workout and the scenery was beyond spectacular, with the broad expanse of beach below them and the needles and sea stacks jutting into the sky offshore.

He wasn't sure where he was going, but Sage obviously had a destination in mind. Every once in a while she called out a direction—turn here, over that hill. They continued to head south until they finally turned into a parking area with no cars in sight.

She parked the bike on the pavement, then led them

down a short trail to a gorgeous, isolated beach, complete with an intriguing sea cave and gnarled, funky rocks.

He let Conan off the leash when they were away from the road and the dog and Chloe both jumped around in the sand with delight.

Sage watched them, the seabreeze playing in her hair.

"This is one of my favorite spots along the northern coast."

"I can see why."

"I like it not only for its beauty, but for its interesting history. It gives a rare glimpse into an earlier time."

"How?"

She led him to a rocky outcropping that looked as if it had been blasted through at one point. "See that? That was once a road carved into the headland there."

"A road?" Chloe asked. "For what?"

"Well, the highway we came here on wasn't built until the 1930s. Before then, this was the only way carriages and early cars could move up and down the coast, right on the beach."

For the next fifteen minutes, she gave them a guided tour of the place she called Hug Point. She pointed out many features Eben knew he wouldn't have paid any attention to had he been on his own and many more he wouldn't have understood even if he'd noticed them.

He was particularly fascinated by the stoplight still embedded high on the rocky headland, more evidence of the beach highway.

"You have to be careful here, though," Sage said with a serious look. "The tide comes in faster than you expect. I have a friend who was trapped in the cavern for several hours by the tide and had to be rescued by the Coast Guard."

"I love it here." Chloe twirled her arms around, whirling across the sand with Conan barking alongside her.

Sage smiled at her with a soft affection that did weird things to Eben's insides. "I do, too. I think it's my favorite place on earth."

"Can we come back here tomorrow, Daddy?"

Eben wasn't quite sure how to answer. On the one hand, he hoped he could conclude his business with Stanley and Jade today and be back on his way to San Francisco by morning.

On the other hand, he hated the thought of leaving behind this smart, fascinating woman who made him feel things he never thought he would again.

"We'll have to see," he said, giving the classic parental cop-out. Chloe didn't seem to mind, especially when Sage picked up a piece of driftwood and tossed it far down the beach. An exuberant Conan bounded through the sand after it, then delivered it back, not to Sage but to Chloe. His daughter giggled and threw it again—not quite as far as Sage had, but far enough to make Conan work for it.

He and Sage stood some ways off and he was astonished again at the peace he felt with her.

He wasn't used to these moments of quiet. Usually his life was busy with troubleshooting and meetings and conference calls. Taking a few moments to pause the craziness, to focus only on breathing in sea air and savoring the morning, seemed healing in a way he wouldn't have expected.

He caught a glimmer of something in the sand and reached to pick it up—a baby-pink agate.

"Wow! That's really rare. Finding one is supposed to be lucky. Go ahead, make a wish."

He glanced at Chloe, too far down the beach with

Conan to overhear them, then spoke with heartfelt—though no doubt unwise—honesty. "Okay. I wish I could kiss you again right now."

She froze and sent him a quick, startled look. Heat flashed there for a moment but she quickly veiled it. "Probably not a good idea."

"On several levels," he agreed. "I'll give it to Chloe and let her make the wish."

They were quiet for several moments as they watched the delighted dog and equally delighted child romp across the sand.

"Did you say you expect to be done with The Sea Urchin purchase in a few days?"

It was an obvious play to change the subject but he didn't argue. They were both probably better off pretending to ignore this heat they seemed to generate.

"I have to be," he answered. "I'm due in Tokyo by Tuesday of next week."

She gave him a piercing look as she pushed a strand of wind-tossed hair out of her face, tucking it behind her ear. "Are you planning to take Chloe along?"

He couldn't contain a little shudder at the idea of letting Chloe loose in a foreign country. The havoc she could wreak boggled his mind.

"While we're here enjoying the beaches of Oregon, my assistant has been busy interviewing new nanny applicants. She e-mailed me with the names of a couple of possibilities. I'll try to choose one when we return home this weekend."

He wasn't completely surprised to see storm clouds scud across her dark-eyed gaze. She stopped stock-still on the sand and stared at him.

"Let me get this straight. You're going to dump your

daughter on a stranger picked by your *assistant* while you go out of the country?"

Despite her deceptive calm, she certainly knew just how to raise his hackles and put him on the defensive.

"I said I was choosing the nanny. My assistant is merely offering me a list of possibilities."

"Are you planning on actually meeting any of these worthy applicants before you fly out of the country and leave your daughter with them?"

"Yes. I'm not completely irresponsible, contrary to what you apparently think."

"But you won't stick around to see how she gets along with Chloe?"

"My plans can't be changed at this late date."

"So why don't you just take her and the new nanny with you?"

"Haul Chloe halfway across the world to Tokyo so she can sit in a hotel room with a stranger for a week?"

"Why not? At least then she wouldn't feel completely abandoned. You're the one stable thing in her life right now. You're all she has, Eben. Can't you see that?

"Of course I see that!" He was astonished how quickly his own much-vaunted calm seemed to be slipping away with the tide. "I live with the responsibility of it every moment of my life. I love my daughter, Sage, despite what you might think."

"I know you do. I can see it. But I'm just not sure Chloe is quite as convinced."

"What do you mean? I've never given her any reason to doubt it." At least he didn't think so.

"Children are resilient and bend with the wind like that seagrass over there, but they're not unbreakable, Eben."

"I have to go to Tokyo next week. Taking her along

sounds perfectly reasonable in theory. But have you ever tried to keep an eight-year-old happy on a ten-hour flight?"

"I'm sure it's not easy. But isn't your daughter's sense of emotional security worth a little inconvenience?"

"It's more than inconvenience! It's impossible."

"Nothing is impossible for a man like you. You have the money and the power and the resources at your disposal to make anything happen. You just have to want to make it work."

He started to lash back at her—what the hell did this do-gooder know about his life?—then he took a good look at her. She was angry with him, unquestionably, but there was something else in her eyes, something deeper. An old hurt he couldn't begin to guess at.

He opened his mouth to ask why this seemed so important to her. Before he could formulate the words, Conan raced to them, with the driftwood in his mouth, and dropped it at their feet.

He was followed immediately by Chloe, wind-whipped color on her cheeks and her hand outstretched.

"Look at this cool thing I found. What is it?"

He was fascinated to watch Sage inhale and exhale a long breath and then pick up the item in Chloe's hand. "Cool!" she exclaimed, with no trace of hurt or anger in her voice. "That's a little piece of petrified wood. You and your dad are great at beachcombing. He found a baby-pink agate. Maybe he'll let you make a wish on it."

"Oh, may I, Daddy?"

Grateful he hadn't tossed it back in the sand, he dug it from the pocket of his Windbreaker and handed it to her. She screwed her eyes shut for a moment, her mouth moving with words he couldn't understand, then she opened her mouth and handed it back to him.

"What did you wish?"

"Not telling. Then it won't come true."

"Fair enough. We should probably be heading back."

Chloe shook her head. "I want to keep looking for cool stuff on the beach."

"It's getting late," he insisted after a quick look at his watch. "Nearly a quarter to seven."

"No!" she said hotly. "I'm going to find more shells!"

He should have picked up on the signs. Chloe had been up for several hours already and was overstimulated by the excitement of the bike ride and playing hard with Conan. But she'd been on such good behavior in Sage's presence that her recalcitrance took him completely by surprise.

"Maybe we can make time later to look for shells, but we already have to hurry so you and Sage aren't late at the center."

"Not later! Now!"

"Chloe, get back here, young lady!"

Instead of obeying, she ran farther down the shore, coming dangerously close to the cold Pacific waters.

He headed after her, but the closer he got to her, the faster she ran, sending backward glances over her shoulder.

He saw truculence and defiance in her gaze, all the things he had become accustomed to seeing there the last two years. Though he tried to hang on to his temper, it was fraying already from his argument with Sage and he could feel it slipping through his fingers.

"Chloe Elizabeth Spencer, get your behind back here right now," he ordered. "You're in serious trouble."

"I don't care! I want to find more petrified wood."

And Sage thought he should subject the good citizens of Tokyo to Chloe?

He wouldn't put it past her to cause some kind of international incident and get them both thrown out of Japan.

He was within a few yards of grabbing her and tossing her, shrieking like a banshee, over his shoulder when Sage suddenly rode up on the tandem bike. He had no idea how she'd retrieved it from the parking lot so quickly or how she maneuvered it with such ease across the soft sand. He only knew he'd never been so grateful to see anyone in his life as he was to see Sage placidly pedaling toward them.

"Come on, Chloe. I need help getting back across the sand," she said calmly.

His daughter paused, still poised for flight but with a confused look on her features, as if she didn't quite how to react. "I want to find more petrified wood."

"I'm sure you do. But I'm afraid if we don't leave now, you and I will both be late for nature camp. Today I promised we were going to Ecola and Indian Beach, remember? I'm sure you'll find all kinds of shells there. You wouldn't want to miss it, would you?"

After a moment's reflection, Chloe shook her head and climbed onto the bicycle seat behind Sage.

"We'll have to use all our muscles to get across the sand. It's hard work. Are you ready?"

"Ready!" Chloe exclaimed, all signs of defiance miraculously gone.

Frustration simmered through him as Eben watched them work to pedal back toward the trail to the parking lot.

Even strangers were better at dealing with his daughter than he was. He was far too reactionary, far too quick to let her push his buttons. She knew just how to make him lose his temper and she didn't hesitate to push her advantage.

Perhaps sending her to boarding school to learn control would give him at least a semblance of the upper hand in their relationship.

"Are you coming?" Sage asked at the parking lot. With a sigh of defeat, he nodded and jogged toward them.

The trip back toward town wasn't nearly as pleasant as the trip away from it. Conan seemed to be the only one enjoying himself, even with the leash he obviously despised firmly attached to his collar.

Sage seemed pensive and Chloe sulked while pedaling along on the back half of the bike.

Eben was almost glad they were all working harder to go back uphill. He didn't have the breath left to make conversation, even if he'd been able to find the inclination.

He wouldn't have expected it earlier in the morning, but he was relieved when they finally reached Brambleberry House.

"Why don't you take the bike the rest of the way back to your beach house?" Sage asked. "You'll get home faster on it. Perhaps you can find time to use it tonight or tomorrow to see some sights around town if you're still here. You can just drop it back here on your way out of town."

He didn't like thinking about saying goodbye, despite their earlier conflict and the inevitability of their parting. "Thank you," he answered. "And thank you also for the inside tour of Hug Point. It was nice to have our own private naturalist."

"You're very welcome."

She mustered a smile that didn't quite reach her eyes.

In the widening sunlight, she looked lovely—fresh and untamed, her honey-gold hair slipping from its ponytail and curling riotously around her face, her cheeks flushed from the wind and the exercise.

"Bye Sage," Chloe chirped. "I'll see you in a while."

Sage waved to them as they took off down the road. Eben, busy with figuring out a tandem bike for the first time, could spare only one quick look behind him. She was watching after them, one hand on her dog, the other in her pocket.

Was that sadness he saw in her eyes? he wondered. He didn't have time to look closer, since he had to turn his attention to the road in order to keep both him and Chloe upright.

A curious ache caught in her throat as Sage watched them ride away on Abigail's bike. She told herself it was just because the fragile loveliness of the morning was ending. She had found unexpected pleasure in sharing the morning with Eben and Chloe, even the rough patch at the end.

She shouldn't have been so critical of his parenting. It had been presumptuous and rude and she winced now, remembering it. No wonder he had reacted so strongly.

Eben was not Tommy Benedetto, she reminded herself sharply. She was finding it far too easy to forget that, to project her own childhood and her father's emotional abandonment onto the dynamics between Eben and Chloe.

She had all but accused him of neglect. She supposed she needed to find a way to apologize to the man.

Conan barked what sounded suspiciously like agreement and settled at her feet, for all appearances completely worn out from the morning run.

She sighed. She was becoming entirely too wrapped up in the lives of two strangers she likely would never see after a few more days. Still, she couldn't help wishing she could find a way to help Eben see how very much his daughter needed him.

The strength of her desire took her by surprise. Gathering strays had been Abigail's specialty, not Sage's.

She had many friends in town but she had no misconceptions about herself. Most of her friendships were casual, superficial. She didn't allow people into her life easily. She wasn't standoffish or rude—at least she didn't think she was—but she was uncomfortable letting people see too deeply into her psyche.

Those protective instincts had been learned early at the prestigious boarding school she'd been sent to when she was around Chloe's age, around the time her father's new wife decided she didn't like competition for Thomas's attention.

At school, Sage had been immediately ostracized, marginalized. The stench of new money had clung to her—an insurmountable obstacle, especially since it was new money obtained only through her father marrying it.

She didn't want to think those years had shaped the rest of her life, but she couldn't deny that she was as cautious as a hermit crab about letting people too close to her.

What was different about Eben Spencer and his gamine little daughter? Already she cared about them and she couldn't quite figure out how it had happened so quickly. They were transitory in her life, she knew that, yet in only a few days they had both become dear to her—so dear she wanted to do all she could to smooth their path.

Maybe she had inherited that from Abigail, along with a rambling old house and a mongrel of a dog.

"Everything okay out here?"

She glanced up at the front porch to find Anna just leaving the house, dressed in a black pinstriped suit with a leather briefcase slung over her shoulder.

Neat and orderly, with her dark hair pulled back into a sleek chignon, she made Sage feel frumpy and sweaty. Big surprise there. She *was* frumpy and sweaty.

Anna also looked worlds different from the soft, approachable woman who had shared tea with her the night before.

"It's fine," she finally answered. "Just woolgathering for a moment but I suppose I'd better get moving if I want to have any chance of making it to work on time."

"Since Conan was gone when I woke up, I figured he was with you. Looks like you've been out early this morning."

"He doesn't give me a whole lot of choice some days. It's hard to roll over and go back to sleep with him barking outside my apartment. I'm not sure which is worse, his insistent call outside the door or his big wet nose nudging me out of bed."

Anna grimaced. "I'm sorry. I've been letting you carry most of the burden for taking care of him and it's not fair to you. I'll take my turn tomorrow on the morning run."

"I complain about it but I don't really mind," she said quickly, and realized it was true. Somehow over the last month she had come to enjoy their solitary mornings.

"Well, I'll take a turn sometime, I promise. And don't worry about him this afternoon, either. I've got meetings this morning for my new store in Lincoln City and I should be home early."

She stared. "You never told me you were opening a store in Lincoln City. I had no idea."

Beneath her trim exterior, Anna brimmed with suppressed excitement. "The grand opening is in two weeks. We were trying to have it ready before the summer tourists started showing up, but we didn't quite make it."

"If it's opening by mid-June, you'll hit most of the high season, anyway."

"That's the plan."

Anna was quiet for a moment then she sighed. "I'm scared to death," she admitted.

Sage had a feeling that kind of raw truth was something the brisk, in-control Anna didn't share with many people and it warmed her to know Anna trusted her with it.

"Are you crazy? By-The-Wind rocks here in Cannon Beach. You're always busy. The new store will be great."

"I know, but we're entering a whole new demographic in Lincoln City. I've done the market studies and it looks like it will be feasible, but you never know what's going to click with people. Entering a new market is always a risk."

"If anyone can handle it, you can."

Anna look surprised, then pleased. "Thanks. That means a lot." She paused. "Everything has been so overwhelming the past month, with Abigail's death and the house and everything. If I could postpone the opening of the new store for a few weeks until I find my feet again, I would, but this has been planned for months. I don't have any choice."

No wonder Anna seemed so stressed and stiff all the

time. Sage regretted again her rudeness, the deliberate distance she had imposed between them.

Eben and Chloe weren't the only ones she was letting deeper into her life, she realized. She was coming to consider Anna a friend as well.

Somehow she suspected that was exactly what Abigail had intended.

Chapter 10

"Did everybody have fun at Ecola?" Sage asked the thirteen tired, sweaty children gathered around her at the end of the day.

"Yeeeessss!" came the resounding cheer from the campers.

"I did, too. Remember, if the weather cooperates, tomorrow is our beach day. We're going to spend the whole day on Cannon Beach, so make sure you have your hats and your sunscreen and a warm jacket. We'll be tide-pooling near Haystack Rock, flying kites and having a sand-castle competition."

She smiled as the campers cheered with excitement. "Now your parents will be here in a few moments. It's time to gather up your backpacks and the projects we did today so you're all ready to hit the road."

The campers jumped up and dispersed to the class-room where they stowed their gear. As she helped find missing jackets and refereed arguments over whose watercolor of aggregating anemone was better, she was aware of the anticipation curling through her.

Your parents will be here in a few moments, she had told the children, but it was the thought of only one parent's arrival that churned her pulse and sent wild-edged nerves zinging through her.

Ridiculous, she reminded herself.

Eben Spencer was just another parent and that's exactly the way she had to treat him. She certainly should not have spent what seemed like the entire day remembering their morning together—his powerful muscles as he ran beside her toward Hug Point, his slow smile as he enjoyed the sunshine, his low words when he said he wished he could kiss her again.

Even though they had argued, she couldn't seem to stop thinking about him.

She needed a good dousing in the Pacific.

Perhaps if she had seen him when he dropped off Chloe in the morning she wouldn't feel this glittery anticipation, but she had been busy on the phone arranging a field trip for the next session of camp. By the time she emerged from her office, Chloe had been working with Lindsey and several of the other children in a gathering activity to identify different sea creatures and their typical habitat and Eben had been nowhere in sight.

"Sage! There you are! I've been trying to catch you all week."

She groaned at the perky voice ringing through the center. Damn Eben Spencer anyway! If she hadn't been so distracted by thoughts of him, she might have been able to employ her usual tactics to avoid Tracy Harder. Now she had nowhere safe to go.

"Hi, Tracy. How are you?"

The other woman beamed at her. "Just great. I got the listings for two new properties today, right next to each other in Manzanita. They're half a block from the ocean and ought to move fast. So how were my two little terrors?"

She forced a smile. Tracy had been bringing her twins to camp for three years, ever since they turned old enough to attend, and right around the time their parents divorced.

The boys *were* terrors but she liked to chalk it up to high energy, not maliciousness.

"We had a great day today. I tried to keep them too busy to get into trouble."

"You are amazing with them, Sage. Thanks for putting up with them every year. I just wish you had camp year-round. I'd pull them out of school in a heartbeat and sign them up to every session."

Sage managed to contain a slight shudder. Fortunately, Tracy didn't require an answer before she went on. "So, let's talk," she said abruptly. "Brambleberry House."

Though she mentally groaned, she managed to keep a polite expression. "We've had this discussion already, Tracy. Several times. And nothing has changed at all since the last time we discussed it. I'm sorry, but Anna and I aren't selling."

"You two are crazy! Do you realize how much I can ask for a fifteen-room mansion on the beach? The place is a gold mine! With a little creative investment, you and Anna could be set for life."

"We can't do that, Tracy. I'm sorry, but Abigail would have hated to see us sell it."

"Abigail is not the one who will have to deal with all the repairs and the property taxes and the gigantic utility bills. Do you want to be tied to that house for the rest of your life?"

She had a brief, stark image of living forever in her turret apartment, growing old like Abigail, alone except for a big furry red dog who had been rescued from the pound.

A week ago, she would have found that image comforting. She wanted nothing more than to emulate Abigail, to be as feisty and independent as her friend for the rest of her days.

She wasn't sure what she wanted anymore. Her old childhood dreams of having a family of her own, born out of empty loneliness, had somehow re-emerged.

"You need to think long and hard about this," Tracy pressed. "I know you're still grieving for Abigail—we all are—but you're a young, beautiful woman. Trust me, someday you're going to want options."

She opened her mouth to answer but Tracy cut her off. "I've got a couple of Portland clients looking for a property for a bed and breakfast in town. Brambleberry House would be perfect. They have money to spare and I'm sure we could push the asking price well into seven figures. Talk to Anna about it. You have to!"

Sage shook her head. "No, Tracy. We're not selling."

The other woman's attention suddenly caught at something in the doorway, at the same time a tiny shiver skittered down Sage's spine.

Tracy's eyes widened and she let out a long breath. "Oh. My. Word. Who's the yummy guy? No, don't turn around."

She didn't need to turn around to know who it must be.

Since this session of camp contained mostly local children, Tracy had to know all their parents—except one.

"How can I know who it is if you won't let me turn around to look?" she asked.

Tracy's eyes widened. "He's coming this way! Unless my eyes deceive me—and I don't think they do, trust me, I've got radar for these things—I can't see a ring. How's my hair?"

Sage studied her polished friend. Her makeup was perfect and not a strand of her highlighted blonde hair dared escape its trendy style.

In contrast, Sage didn't need a mirror to tell her what she must look like. Her dratted hair was probably falling out of the ponytail again, her skin felt tight and itchy, probably from a slight sunburn, and she didn't doubt she smelled as if she'd been chasing thirteen active elementary school students all day.

She sighed. "You look beautiful, as always."

"Liar!" Tracy purred, then her white teeth widened and she thrust out a hand, complete with the French manicure Sage knew she drove to Astoria to get and no trace of a callus or wrinkle.

"Hi there. I don't believe we've met. I'm Tracy Harder with Harder Realty. Welcome to Cannon Beach! Are you a summer visitor or are you moving in? Before you answer, let me just say how much I sincerely hope it's the latter. We just love new faces around here, don't we, Sage?"

"Uh, sure."

Eben blinked a few times at her gushing warmth, but finally held out his hand. "Hello. Eben Spencer. I'm afraid my daughter and I are only here until the weekend."

Tracy's face fell and she didn't look like she wanted to

let go of his hand, as if she could change his mind just with her force of will. Eben finally managed to slip it away.

"Too bad for us. But if you ever think about moving back permanently, give me a call. Let me give you my card. Now you hang on to that, promise? I have listings up and down the northern/central coast, from Astoria to Newport. From luxury beachside houses to small two-room cottages, I can hook you up with anything you want. Anything."

Sage certainly didn't mistake the intent in that single, flirtatious word and Eben obviously didn't either.

"Uh, thank you."

"Oh, you're welcome. For instance, I just picked up two new listings today in Manzanita. The master suite in one of them is huge with one full wall of windows overlooking the ocean. Truly stunning and it's listed at several thousand dollars below appraisal. At that price, it's not going to last long. And the other one has four bedrooms, including one that would be perfect for an in-law suite."

Before Tracy could get revved up into a full-scale sales pitch, Sage took pity on Eben's glazed expression and stepped in. "Mr. Spencer, I imagine you're probably looking for the hiking trail guides we talked about this morning, aren't you?"

He looked baffled for only half a second, then seized on the excuse. "Yes. Exactly. I'm very anxious to see the area."

"I'm sorry, I meant to have them ready for you when you arrived to pick up Chloe, but it's been a rather busy day. It won't take me a second to dig them out of my files, though. They're back in my office, if you want to come with me. Tracy, will you excuse us?"

Tracy opened her mouth to object, but Sage didn't

give her a chance, she just led Eben through the center to her office.

"Trail guides?" he murmured when they were safely out of earshot.

"I couldn't think of anything else. Sorry. Tracy's a sweetheart but she can be a bit of a piranha if she smells fresh meat."

He raised an eyebrow and Sage could feel herself flush. "Completely in the real estate sense of the word, I mean. Potential customers."

"Right."

He looked tired, she thought. His shirtsleeves were rolled up, his tie loose and that hint of disreputable stubble was back on his jawline. No wonder Tracy went into hungry mode.

"Uh, long day?"

He shrugged. "We're having some labor issues with a couple of our European properties. It took some serious negotiations, but I think we've finally got a handle on it."

He studied her for a long moment, a light in his eyes that left her suddenly breathless. "How about you?"

"It's been a good day. The kids seemed to enjoy Ecola. What's not to love? The place looks prehistoric, like dinosaurs will come stalking through the plants any minute now."

"How was Chloe today?"

"Tired, I think."

"I suppose that's what happens when she wakes us both up before five o'clock."

"Probably. She was a little bit cranky, but we didn't have any real problems. She fell asleep for a few moments in the van on the way back."

"She'll probably zonk out right after dinner, which will be good since I'm suddenly slammed with paperwork my assistant sent by courier."

She had a sudden fierce longing to run a finger down the tired lines at the corner of his mouth, as if she could soothe them. The impulse appalled her. "And are you the proud owner of a certain Cannon Beach landmark yet?"

"Not yet. They're stalling with every possible tactic they can come up with."

"Yet you're not giving up?"

He sighed. "I don't know. At this point, I'm not sure what else I can do. I can't force Stanley and Jade to sell, nor would I want to."

"Someone unscrupulous probably could figure out a way to do just that."

To her surprise, hurt flickered in his gaze. "Is that what you think of me?"

She considered the idea then rejected it. "Not at all. I think you're very determined but I don't believe you're ruthless."

"We need The Sea Urchin. I'm afraid nothing else will do."

"You need it or you want it? Big difference, Eben."

"Both. The more time I spend in Cannon Beach, the more I know this is the ideal location for another Spencer Hotel. It's perfect."

Before she could answer, Chloe skipped in and threw her arms around Eben's waist. "Hi Daddy. What are you doing in here?"

"Just talking to Sage."

She seemed to accept that with equanimity. "I'm

hungry. Can we have dinner at Brambleberry House again tonight?"

Eben looked taken aback at Chloe's question and sent a swift look toward Sage. Her first inclination was to go ahead and extend the invitation Chloe was angling for in her not-so-subtle manner, but she quickly checked the impulse. Eben said he had paperwork to finish.

Beyond that, she needed a little space and distance from the two of them to see if she could rebuild the protective barriers around her heart.

She forced a smile to Chloe. "I'm sorry, honey, but I've got other plans tonight."

It wasn't a lie. She was supposed to have her monthly book club meeting at By-The-Wind tonight, though all day she had been planning to do her best to wiggle out of it.

"What about tomorrow?" Chloe asked.

"We'll have to see," Eben stepped in. "Come on, Chloe. We'd better get out of Sage's hair and it looks like you need to get cleaned up before dinner. What do you say to pizza tonight?"

"I say *yum*," Chloe chirped.

Sage walked them to the door of the center. "Bye, Chloe. Don't forget your hat tomorrow. Remember, it's beach day."

"I can't wait! Can we ride bikes again tomorrow morning while Daddy and Conan run and go to Hug Point?"

She'd had a tough enough time getting the image of Eben's muscles out of her head all day today. She didn't need a repeat performance in the morning. "Guess what? I get to sleep in tomorrow since Anna wants to take a turn running with Conan in the morning."

To her surprise, disappointment sparked in Eben's gaze but he said nothing about it. "Come on, kid."

"Bye Sage," Chloe said reluctantly. She hugged Sage then grabbed her father's hand and walked outside.

This was becoming a habit Eben had a feeling would be tough to break when they returned to San Francisco.

Early the next morning, Eben stood at the deck railing watching the ocean change color with the sunrise, from black to murky blue to a deep, rich green. He was coming to depend entirely too much on these moments of solitude, when he had the vast beach to himself, sharing it only with the occasional shore bird.

He had intended to sleep in at least until six, but he woke an hour before his travel alarm had been set to go off. Restless and edgy, he had opted to come out here and enjoy the morning.

The beauty of the Oregon coast had somehow seeped into him. Despite the frustration over The Sea Urchin, he felt calmer here than he had in a long time. Maybe since those rough last few months of his marriage.

He shifted. He didn't like dwelling on Brooke and all the ways he had failed her. The worst of it was that now he wasn't even sure when he had stopped loving his wife.

She had been a friend of his sister Cami's and he had known her since she was a girl. He had been her escort at her debutante ball, had dated her through college. Theirs had never been a grand passion, but in the early days at least it had been comfortable.

And then after Chloe was born, she had wanted so much more from him. She had become clingy, demanding. She had hated his work schedule, had resented the hours he spent rebuilding the company, then had started accusing him of a long string of affairs.

Her emotional outbursts had all seemed so much like his parents' marriage—with the exception that his father *had* been having affairs, buckets of them, and no one could ever have called Hastings Spencer a workaholic. Alcoholic? Yes. Workaholic? Not a chance.

The last few years of their marriage had been miserably unhappy and he had worked even more to avoid the tumult he hated so much at home. He imagined if Brooke hadn't died, they would have been well on their way to divorce by now.

And most of it had been his fault. He acknowledged that now. He had been consumed with proving he was *not* his father, that he had inherited nothing from his unstable mother. As a result, he had refused to fight with Brooke, had refused to show much emotion at all.

He had lived with that guilt for two years now. The past couldn't be changed. Perhaps it was time to let it go.

He watched a black oystercatcher hop down the shore and his muscles hummed with a fierce desire to be out there on the hard-packed sand running for all he was worth.

He couldn't leave Chloe sleeping alone inside their beach house, so he had to be content with watching the daybreak from the sidelines.

He sipped his coffee, remembering the morning only a few days ago when Sage had taken it out of his hand and sent him off running with her dog. Had it only been a few days ago? It seemed like forever since he had returned to find her asleep on the couch, warm and tousled and sexy, and had stolen a kiss.

He jerked his mind away from the memory and focused instead on the day ahead. He was meeting with

Stanley and Jade that afternoon, for possibly the last time. If they still balked at the sale, he knew he would have to return to San Francisco and all the work waiting for him there. He couldn't linger here indefinitely, hoping he could change their minds.

He sighed, depressed at the realization that this would likely be his last Oregon sunrise for some time.

It was a glorious one, he had to admit. The sun coming over the Coast Range to the east tinted the sky above the ocean a pearly pink, with shades of lavender and pale orange.

Sage would love this.

He sighed. Couldn't he go five seconds without thinking about her? He was obsessed. He definitely needed to return to San Francisco soon so he could start shaking her from his mind.

As if in response to the direction of thoughts, he suddenly spied two shapes running down the beach, one of which was unmistakably a familiar shaggy red dog.

Anticipation curled through him and he knew with grim realization this was the reason he stood here at the railing—not to watch the sunrise, but on the off chance she might run past with Conan.

As they drew closer, he saw immediately his subconscious hope of seeing her would be dashed. Conan's companion didn't have unruly honey-gold curls. Instead, she had dark hair scraped back into a sleek ponytail.

Anna Galvez was taking her turn with the dog's morning run, just as Sage had told them the day before she planned to do.

The depth of his disappointment shocked the hell out of him.

How had a wild-haired nature girl become so important to him in a few short days? His fingers curled around the coffee mug. He should have done a much better job of keeping her out. What was the point of coming to care about her? He was leaving soon, tomorrow at the latest.

With sudden, hard dread lodged in his gut, he hated the idea of saying goodbye to her.

Conan barked an exuberant greeting and rushed over to his deck. Eben unlatched the gate and headed down the wooden stairs.

"Hey bud. No Chloe this morning. She's still sleeping." He scratched the dog's chin and was rewarded by furious tail-wagging.

Anna arrived several moments after the dog, panting hard. "My gosh, he's fast. I had no idea. Morning."

He smiled. "Good morning."

"How does Sage do this every morning? It's torture!" She straightened and he thought again that she was a remarkably lovely woman, with her glossy dark hair and delicate features.

He could appreciate her loveliness on a purely detached basis but he realized she did nothing for him. The realization was unsettling. He wasn't at all attracted to Anna Galvez—because all he could think about was Sage and her winsome smile and her untamed beauty.

"I guess you're the reason he insisted on dragging me in this direction," Anna said.

"Sorry."

She smiled. "I'm not. At least he's giving me a breather for a minute. Anyway, the ocean view is spectacular in any direction. I never tire of it."

"You're lucky to see it every day."

"I think so, too." She paused. "I never intended to stay

here forever but I came a few years ago for a... vacation and I never left. I think seawater seeped into my blood or something. Now here I am a homeowner, a business owner. Settled. Life takes some strange twists sometimes."

He sensed there was more to her story, but didn't feel he knew her well enough to pry.

"I understand you may be joining the ranks of Cannon Beach property owners."

"Your mouth to God's ear."

She smiled again. "Will you be sticking around if you buy The Sea Urchin?"

Three days ago he would have given an unequivocal no to that question. The fact that he couldn't honestly offer her the answer he knew he should stunned him.

"Sorry. Not my business," she said, her voice somewhat stiff and he abruptly realized he must have been staring at her without speaking for several seconds.

"No, it's not that. I just don't quite know how to answer. Our hotel corporate office is in San Francisco, so I would have to say probably not. But I have a couple of great people in mind to run the place after we finish a few upgrades."

Conan barked and for some reason, Eben was quite certain that look in his eyes was disapproval. Did he need to consult a dog now on his business decisions?

"Well, Cannon Beach is a great place to raise a family if you should decide differently."

"I'll keep that in mind," he answered.

"Good luck with the Wus," she said. "I've read a little about Spencer Hotels and I think your company would treat The Sea Urchin exactly as it deserves."

"Thank you. Now if you wouldn't mind stopping at the hotel on your run and telling Stanley and Jade just what you told me," he joked, "maybe I could wrap things up here before Independence Day."

She laughed. "I'm not sure they'd listen to me. I've only been here three years so I'm still very much a newcomer."

Conan suddenly wriggled away from Eben and started heading up the beach. Anna gave a rueful smile. "I guess that's the boss's way of telling me it's time to head off. Thanks for giving me a chance to catch my breath."

"No problem."

She waved and headed off after the dog.

Six hours later, Eben wished for a little of Anna Galvez's encouragement as he sat in the elegantly appointed conference room of The Sea Urchin, frustration burning his insides.

He had been running his family's hotel company since he graduated from The Wharton School in his early 20s. The company's assets and reputation had increased exponentially under his command.

With a far-ranging strategic plan, he had worked as hard as he knew how, had sacrificed and planned and maneuvered Spencer Hotels to emerge from near-bankruptcy to its current healthy market share.

Through all the years of toil and negotiations, he had never felt as completely inept as he did right this moment, gazing at Stanley Wu's smooth, inscrutable features.

The man was harder to read than the framed Chinese calligraphy hanging on the wall above his head.

"Mr. Wu, I'm sorry, but I don't know what else you and Mrs. Wu want from me. I have tried to convince you Spencer Hotels doesn't plan any radical changes to The Sea Urchin. You've seen our business plan and the blueprints for the minor renovations we would like to see.

You have physically toured each of our two other hotels in Oregon as well as two in Washington and I've showed you multimedia tours of several others. I've given you my personal promise that I will treat this establishment with the same care and attention you and Mrs. Wu have showered on it for thirty-five years. I want this hotel, I've made no secret of that fact, but my time here is running out. What else can I do to convince you?"

Stanley studied him for a full minute without saying anything—an eternity, Eben thought. Finally Stanley's mouth lifted slightly in what Eben supposed passed for a smile.

"Come to dinner tonight. Seven o'clock. Bring your daughter."

Eben gave a mental groan. Of all the things he might have expected, that was way down at the bottom of his list. It was also the one thing he did *not* want to do. The way things were going, Chloe would pitch a fit and destroy any chance he had of making this deal.

This was one more hoop the Wus were making him jump through. Perhaps one too many.

"I don't know if that's a good idea. Chloe's only eight. Her manners are not exactly what you might call impeccable."

"Bring her," Stanley said sternly. "My father used to say, if you want to know the health of the tree, study the fruit."

Eben had to fight to keep from banging his head on the conference table a few times as he felt his chances for buying The Sea Urchin slipping through his fingers like sand.

This was a certifiable nightmare. His entire plans—

all the months of study and work—hinged on the table manners of a moody, unpredictable eight-year-old girl.

He should just tell the man to go to hell. Eben had worked harder on this deal than anything in the dozen years since he took over at the helm of Spencer Hotels. If it wasn't enough for Stanley Wu, so be it.

Even as he opened his mouth to tell the man to forget the whole thing, something stopped him.

"Of course," he found himself murmuring instead, at the same moment a germ of an idea sprouted.

He thought of Chloe a few nights before at dinner, how polite and patient she had been while they ate vegetarian lasagna at Brambleberry House. If he could somehow replicate that behavior, there was a tiny—miniscule—chance he might pull this off.

Sage's presence had made all the difference. She had some uncanny moderating effect on Chloe's misbehavior. If she could distract his daughter long enough, convince her to behave for one simple evening, perhaps all hope was not completely lost.

"Do you mind if I bring along a guest?" he asked before he gave himself time to think it through.

Stanley studied him across the conference table. "What guest is this?"

How exactly did he explain? "My daughter and I have befriended a Cannon Beach resident, Sage Benedetto. I would like to bring her along, if it would be acceptable to you and Mrs. Wu."

This time the cool look in the other man's eyes was replaced with the first genuine smile Eben had seen there. "Ah. Sage. Yes. A beautiful woman always improves the digestion."

"More wisdom from your father?"

Stanley laughed. "I don't need my father to tell me this truth. I have eyes, don't I?"

"Uh, right."

"So you will come for dinner and bring your daughter and our friend Abigail's beautiful wild rose, yes?"

"Yes," he answered.

Now he just had to convince Sage.

Chapter 11

"Now remember, what's the most important tide-pool rule?"

"Look but don't touch!" the six campers in her group recited as one and Sage beamed.

"Exactly right. The rocky shore ecosystem is very fragile and you never know what harm you could do even by picking up a piece of kelp. It's much better just to take pictures and look. All right, everybody grab your disposable cameras and let's start recording our observations."

The kids broke off into their pre-assigned teams of two and, chattering with excitement, headed on their field assignments to record as many tide-pool creatures as they could find.

Sage watched their eager faces and had to smile. This was close to her idea of a perfect day. The sun, making a brief appearance between storms, was bright and warm on her face, the water a spectacularly beautiful shade of deep olive. She had a bright group of children soaking in knowledge like little sea sponges.

For the next half hour, she wandered through the three teams, answering questions, making observations, pointing them toward species they may have missed: tiny porcelain crabs and Hopkin's roses.

She loved it out here. She didn't need anything else, certainly not any sharp-eyed executives who smelled like heaven and kissed like a dream.

She pushed thoughts of Eben away—again—and focused on the tide-poolers until her stopwatch beeped, then she gathered them around to compare notes.

"Excellent job, all of you. You're now official junior naturalists for Cannon Beach."

"Ms. B., when can we have the crab race? You promised you'd let me whip your butt this year."

She laughed at Ben Harder, one of Tracy's twins. "Excuse me, but I believe I promised I would let you *try* to whip my butt. Big difference there, kiddo."

"When? Can we do it now?"

She checked her watch. They had split the campers into two groups so they didn't stress the tide-pool residents with too much attention at once. Lindsey had the other group down the beach flying kites and they weren't due to switch places for another twenty minutes.

"Okay. Crab races it is. We need start and finish lines."

Two of the boys found a piece of driftwood and charted a race course of about thirty feet—far too long in Sage's book, but the children insisted they could go that far.

Her idea was for one-on-one races, but eventually

everybody wanted to compete against her and it turned into a free-for-all.

It was a fight to the finish but she came in a respectable third—behind Ben Harder and Leilani Stein. At the finish line, panting and aching, she collapsed into the sand. How did she seem to forget every year until the first camp of the summer how blasted hard it was to walk backward on her hands and feet? It took her abs all summer long to relearn how to crab race.

"Good race," she said, gasping. "But I think you got a head start."

"No way," Ben exclaimed. "It was totally fair!"

"Need a hand up?"

At the low, masculine voice, Sage opened her eyes and found Eben standing over her, his hand outstretched.

Her heart gave a sharp kick in her chest at his features silhouetted in the sunshine. He looked gorgeous in a pair of khaki slacks and a casual cotton shirt.

Of course he would. She was hot and sweaty and probably smelled like a tide-pool again. She wanted to burrow into the sand like a geoduck clam. Instead, she released a tiny sigh, reached for his hand and let him help her to her feet.

"I have to say, the kid's right. It looked fair to me. If anybody jumped the gun, I think it was you."

She brushed sand off her butt. "Whose side are you on?"

He grinned and she forgot to breathe. She had no idea he could look so lighthearted. It was a disturbing revelation.

"Did you need Chloe?" she asked to cover her reaction. "Her group is down the beach. See the kites down there?"

"No. I saw them first and already stopped to talk to her," he answered. "Your assistant—Lindsey, I think is her name—told me I could find you out here."

Note to self, she thought, *remind Lindsey not to send gorgeous men out searching for me when I'm crab-walking in the sand.*

She pushed wind-tossed hair out of her face. "Is there some problem with Chloe?"

"In a way."

His temporary lightheartedness seemed to slide away again and he shifted a little, looking suddenly uncomfortable.

She had no idea what he wanted and he didn't seem in any big hurry to enlighten her. "Do you need me to keep her after camp ends again?" she said, hazarding a guess. "It's really no problem."

"It's not that." He let out a long breath. "The truth is, I need to ask a huge favor and I'm not sure quite how to go about it."

The kids in her group seemed happy enough with continuing their crab races so she led him down the sand a little. "Just ask, Eben."

"You make it sound easy." He paused. "All right. Will you come to dinner at The Sea Urchin tonight?"

She gave a surprised laugh. "This is your huge favor? Inviting me to dine at the finest restaurant on the northern coast? By the tone of your voice, I was expecting you to ask me to donate a kidney or something."

"That might be less painful in the long run. The truth is, I need help with Chloe. Stanley has invited me to dinner tonight." He paused. "No, that's not right. There was no invitation involved. He *ordered* me to come to dinner tonight and to bring Chloe along. Apparently, before the man will make a final decision to trust me with his hotel, he wants to see how I interact with my daughter."

Sage flushed, embarrassed that she had initially allowed herself to feel flattered, to imagine he might have been asking her on a date. "And how do I fit into the picture?"

"You're so good with Chloe. With you, she's a different girl. She's polite and well-mannered. Happy. I need her to be on her best behavior and you seem to bring the best out in her where I seem to usually have the opposite effect."

It was ridiculous to feel this hurt that spread out from her stomach like the paralyzing venom of a jellyfish sting.

"So you're inviting me as your daughter's handler in order to help you clinch the deal?"

He winced. "Put like that, it sounds pretty damn nervy, doesn't it?"

"Yes," she clipped off the word.

"I'm asking you to help me for one night. This is important to me. You have the magic touch with Chloe. Everything seems to go more smoothly when you're around. Please, Sage. It's one night."

All her instincts cried out for her to tell him to go to hell. She thought of that kick in her heart when she first saw him. How ridiculous. She was allowing herself to have feelings for a man who only viewed her as a convenient caregiver for his daughter.

With every ounce of her, she wanted to tell him no. She even started to form the word, but her mouth seemed to freeze.

She couldn't do it.

He wanted The Sea Urchin desperately—he had made no secret of that—and she cared about him and about Chloe enough that some part of her wanted to help him reach his goal.

Four days ago she might have scoffed and told him to go back to his business meetings and his conference calls. But that was before she had come to know him.

The truth was, she had become convinced Spencer Hotels would be good for Cannon Beach and The Sea Urchin. Abigail must have thought so or she never would have suggested the idea. It seemed a betrayal of her friend to refuse to help Eben simply because some foolish part of her hoped he wanted more from her than etiquette lessons for his daughter.

"Please," he repeated.

She was going to bleed from a thousand gashes in her heart when he and Chloe left. Helping him tonight would only accelerate that inevitable heartbreak. She knew it perfectly well, could already feel the ache, but from somewhere deep she still managed to dredge up a smile.

"What time?"

The pure delight on his face almost broke her heart right there. "Seven. Will that work for you?"

Her mind raced with the million things she would have to do between the time she finished work and seven o'clock. Foremost was the purely feminine lament that she had nothing to wear and no time to run to her favorite vintage boutique in Portland to find something.

"If Anna's home to stay with Conan, it should be fine."

He reached for her hands and she was certain if they weren't standing on a public beach in broad daylight with a hundred other people, he would have kissed her right then.

"My debt to you seems to grow larger by the minute. Somehow I'll find a way to pay you back, I swear it."

"Don't worry about it. I'll see you at seven."

* * *

"No, no, *no*!" Sage wailed, her breath coming in short gasps as she pedaled hard up the hill toward Brambleberry House. With one hand on the handlebars, she used the other to hold her umbrella over the dress that had just cost her an entire week's paycheck.

It was wrapped in plastic but she bemoaned every single raindrop that made it around the umbrella to splatter against her precious cargo. The whole dress was going to be ruined, she just knew it. Worse, her hair was drenched and would take hours to dry.

She had exactly forty-five minutes to ride the half-mile home and to shower and primp for her dinner with Eben and Chloe and the damn pouring rain wasn't making this any easier.

She could barely see and didn't have a spare hand to wipe the rain out of her eyes and she lived in mortal dread her tires were going to slip in the mud at the shoulder of the road and dump her *and* the dress.

A vehicle drove slowly past and she shifted the umbrella over the dress until it was almost vertical like a warrior's shield, just in case the driver hit a puddle and splattered it everywhere.

Instead, the vehicle slowed even further, then she saw brakelights through the rain. She could barely make out that the truck belonged to Will Garrett until the driver's door opened and he climbed out.

"Get in," he called. "I'll throw your bike in the back of the truck and drive you the rest of the way home."

"I'm almost there."

"Get in, Sage. It's not safe for you to be riding your bike in these conditions. It's slick and visibility is terrible, though I have to say, the bright pink umbrella does tend to draw the eye."

She winced at the ridiculous picture she must make. "I bought a fancy new dress. I didn't want it to get wet."

Will's eyes widened, but to her relief, he said nothing as he took the bicycle from her and effortlessly lifted it into the back while she rushed to open the passenger door. Inside the cab, she laid her dress carefully on the bench seat then climbed in behind it, closing her vivid umbrella.

Will's heater blared full force and she relished the warmth seeping into her chilled muscles for the few moments before he joined her and pulled back onto the road toward Brambleberry House.

"Do I dare ask what's up with the dress? It's not your usual kind of thing, is it?"

She could feel her face flame. "I'm having dinner at the Sea Urchin tonight and it occurred to me I don't have a lot of grown-up clothes to wear. I splurged a bit."

She glanced at it, a sleek midnight blue dream of a dress shot through with the barest trace of iridescent rainbow thread. *Splurge* was a bit of an understatement. She had spent more on this one dress than she usually spent on clothes all year long. Her Visa balance would probably never recover.

It had been purely an impulse buy, too. She hadn't really intended a whole new dress. Since she couldn't make it to her favorite shop in Portland, she thought she would only take a quick look at some of the local stores on the off chance she might find a blouse on clearance she could wear with her usual black dress skirt.

She had just about given up on finding anything when she wandered into a new shop and saw this dress hanging in a corner.

The moment she saw it, she had fallen in love, despite the hefty price tag.

"So what do you think?" she asked Will.

He smiled ruefully. "I'm the wrong guy to ask. Afraid I'm not the best judge of that kind of thing. Robin used to throw a fit because I usually didn't even notice when she bought something new."

He didn't often refer to his late wife or their life together and she could tell it still bothered him to do so because he quickly changed the subject.

"The Sea Urchin, huh? Hot date?"

If only. She burned with embarrassment again, remember her first conclusion when Eben asked her. "Not quite. I'm taking an eight-year-old. One of my day campers. Her dad is negotiating with Stanley and Jade to buy the hotel and he and his daughter have been invited to dinner. Eben, in turn, invited me. They're coming in exactly—" she glanced at her watch as they pulled into the Brambleberry House driveway "—forty minutes now."

"You'd better hurry then. Run in and put on your fancy dress. I'll put your bike away in the garage for you."

On impulse, she leaned across her dress and kissed his cheek, smelling sawdust and sweat, a surprisingly pleasant combination.

"Thanks, Will. I owe you. Come for dinner next week, okay?"

"As long as there's no tofu on the menu."

"I'll see what I can do."

She opened her umbrella, clutched her dress to her as if it were spun gold—a fair description, really, penny for penny—and dashed out into the rain.

She reached the porch just as Anna opened the door to let Conan out. The dog barked a greeting, but to her vast relief he didn't jump all over her in his usual away, almost as of the uncanny beast knew she didn't have time to play.

"That looks like something fabulous," Anna exclaimed, gazing at the dress. "Let's see."

Sage held it up, gratified by Anna's moan of appreciation.

"Gorgeous!" she exclaimed. "What's the occasion?"

"I'm having dinner at The Sea Urchin tonight with Eben and Chloe."

Anna gave her a careful look, then smiled. "Do you have any jewelry to match?"

Ha. After buying the dress, her budget barely stretched to a new pair of pantyhose. "I'll find something."

"Don't forget we have Abigail's whole glittery collection to choose from. Go get dressed and I'll bring her jewelry box up and see what we can dig out."

Sage raced up the stairs two at a time. This excitement pumping through her was only adrenaline, she told herself, just a normal reaction to her urgency and the ever-ticking clock.

She hadn't been on a date in a long time. Did this qualify, since Chloe would be along? Probably not. But she still couldn't shake the bubbling anticipation and she took the fastest shower on record.

She raced through her makeup—something she rarely bothered with—then took a page out of Anna's fashion book and pulled her still-damp hair into as smooth an updo as she could manage with her unruly frizz.

She had just slipped into the dress and was working the zipper when Anna knocked on the door.

"It's open. Come in," she called.

Anna's arms overflowed with Abigail's huge jewelry

box, but all Sage focused on was the astonished admiration in her eyes.

"Wow. That's all I can say. Wow. That dress is perfect for you. The coloring, the style, everything."

"That's why I spent far more than I could afford on it. Stupid, isn't it, for a dress I'll probably only wear once."

"Every girl needs something completely, outrageously impractical hanging in her closet."

"I guess I'm covered, then."

"Not yet. Let's see what Abigail has in her magic box." She held out the jewelry box that contained what had been another of Abigail's passions—vintage costume jewelry, which she wore loads of at every opportunity.

Even when she worked in the garden, Abigail would wear some kind of gorgeous jeweled earbobs and a matching necklace.

"I need to glitter," she used to say with that mischievous gleam in her blue eyes. "It takes the attention away from my wrinkles."

To Sage's shock, Anna turned the box with its jumbled contents and upended the whole thing onto her bed.

The two of them stared at the huge sparkly pile for a long moment. Sage hadn't given much thought to the collection, but now she couldn't seem to look away.

"Do you suppose any of it's real?" Sage whispered.

"I don't know." Anna spoke in the same hushed tone. "I'm not sure I *want* to know."

She started pawing through the collection, pulling out a gleaming strand of pearls here, a chunky citrine and topaz necklace there.

Finally she stopped and pulled out an Art Deco

choker in stones the exact midnight shade of the dress. "This is it. It's perfect."

The stones felt as smooth and cool as polished sea glass. After another moment of treasure hunting, Anna pulled out a pair of matching dangly earrings that seemed to capture the light and reflect it back in a hundred different shades of blue.

"I guess we really should have this collection appraised," Anna said while Sage put them in.

"You don't sound any more enthusiastic than I am."

"They're Abigail's. I hate the idea of parting with *any* of her things. But let's face it, the upkeep on the house is going to be more than either of us can afford. The heating bill alone is almost as much as I was paying for rent on my condo."

"We'll figure it out."

"You're right. No depressing talk," Anna said firmly. "Let's just get you ready. We can worry about heating bills and extravagant jewelry collections another day."

Already Sage could feel her hair slipping out of the style. Before the whole thing could fall apart, Anna fiddled with a few strands, smoothed a few more, then stepped back to admire her handiwork.

"All done. What do you think?"

Sage stared at her full-length mirror at the stranger gazing back at her. Not a stranger, she corrected. She only had a single picture of the slim, lovely mother she barely remembered, a picture rescued and hidden away when her father started to purge that part of his life after his second marriage.

She hadn't looked at it in a long time, but somehow she knew if someone snapped a picture of her right now and compared it with that precious photograph, the two women would be nearly a match.

Tears burned behind her eyelids, but she choked them back. "Oh, Anna. Thank you. The necklace and earrings are exactly right."

Anna stepped back and studied her. "It's almost spooky the way they match, as if Abigail bought them just to go with that dress."

Maybe because she had been thinking of her mother, but Sage could swear she felt invisible fingers gently brush her cheek.

She shivered a little and was grateful when the door-bell rang.

"There's Eben," she said, then felt ridiculous for the inanity. Who else would it be?

"Have a wonderful time," Anna said. "Give my love to Stanley and Jade."

"I will."

Anna looked bright and animated, Sage thought, so very different from the stiff businessman she had always considered her. She really was becoming a dear friend, something Sage never would have expected.

She reached out and gave Anna a quick, impulsive hug. "Thank you again."

Anna looked stunned but pleased. "You're very wel-come. I'll go let him in. Wait up here a moment so you can make a grand entrance down the stairs."

"Oh, for heaven's sake. I'm not in high school."

"Trust me. Stay here."

Anna flew down the stairs and a moment later, Sage heard Eben's deep voice greeting her. She tried to count to twenty but only made it to fifteen before she started down the stairs, certain she was going to trip in the un-accustomed high heels and break her neck.

Eben stood at the bottom of the stairs waiting for her in a dark suit and tie. He looked sinfully gorgeous and she had to admit his thunderstruck expression more than made up for the sheer extravagance of the dress.

By the time she reached the bottom step, Anna was ushering Conan into her apartment and closing the door behind them both with one last delighted smile at Sage and Eben in the entryway.

Eben grabbed her hand and brought it to his mouth in a gesture that should have felt foolish but seemed exactly right.

"You look stunning," he murmured.

"I feel like I'm on the way to the prom."

He gave a surprised laugh. "I sincerely hope I've moved beyond the arrogant jackass I was at seventeen."

"Well, I have to admit my prom date didn't bring along his eight-year-old daughter."

"Left her home with a sitter, did he?"

She laughed at the sheer unexpectedness of his teasing. "Something like that."

"I should probably tell you, Chloe's over the moon about spending the evening with grown-ups. We had to rush out and buy her a new dress and everything."

Thank heavens they hadn't bumped into each other in the few Cannon Beach clothing stores. "The Wus have a dozen grandchildren. Trust me, they're going to adore her."

He drew in a deep breath, his eyes filled with doubt. "I guess we'll find out in a few moments, right?" He held out his arm. "Shall we?"

She slipped her arm through his. The rain forced them

to stand close together and share his umbrella and she could smell the deliciously spicy scent of his aftershave.

This was a make-believe night, she reminded herself as he helped her into his luxurious rental car. She needed to remember that by morning this would all be a memory.

A wonderful, glorious, heartbreaking memory.

Chapter 12

"Mrs. Wu, this fortune cookie is delicious. I like it very much. Would you mind if I had a second one?"

Eben observed his daughter's careful politeness with amazement. What kind of well-mannered gremlin had snuck in when he wasn't paying attention and replaced his headstrong daughter with this sweet, polite little person?

He glanced over at Sage and caught her suppressing a smile.

Jade Wu only beamed at Chloe, her lovely, ageless features glowing with delight. "You have as much as you want, child. Fortune cookies are not really from China, did you know that?"

"I didn't know that. Really?" Chloe looked enthralled.

"They were invented right in your town of San Francisco by a smart baker at a Japanese restaurant. But our guests expect them, so we have perfected our own recipe."

"You make them here?"

Jade smiled at her. "They are not hard. I can show you how, if you would like."

Chloe's eyes widened with delight. "Oh, could you? That would be so cool! Can you show me now?"

Sage made tiny sound in her throat, enough that Chloe gave her a careful look, then moderated her glee to a respectful smile toward Jade Wu. "Only if it wouldn't put you to too much trouble, of course."

Jade looked as amused as Eben had ever seen her in their brief acquaintance. "Not at all. Not at all. I am certain we could find a good apron to put over your lovely dress."

"Thank you very much," Chloe said calmly but Eben could see her nearly vibrating with excitement.

He couldn't help breathing a huge sigh of relief. Chloe had been perfectly behaved all evening. She had been respectful of both of the Wus, had waited her turn to interject a comment or question and had used impeccable table manners.

He knew exactly who deserved the credit for the remarkable transformation—the stunning woman sitting beside him. Sage caught his gaze again and smiled in a conspiratorial way and his heart seemed to stutter in his chest.

Emotions tangled in his throat as he looked at her— tenderness and admiration and something else, something deeper he wasn't sure he could afford to examine closely.

"You should ask your father first, of course."

Chloe grabbed his hand and pressed it between both of hers in her dramatic way, as if she were pleading to save a life instead of only asking permission to bake a cookie. "Oh, please, may I, Daddy?"

"Of course, as long as Mrs. Wu doesn't mind showing you and you do exactly what she says."

She kissed his cheek and Sage smiled at him again. For some silly reason, Eben felt as if he had just hand-delivered the moon to both of them.

"Sage, would you care to come with us?" Jade asked her. "I will find an apron for you as well."

"I'd love to see how it's done," she answered. "But I believe I'll just watch, apron or not."

Eben rose when the three lovely females did and watched them head for the kitchen, Jade in the lead, leaving him alone with Stanley.

The other man didn't seem in any hurry to resume his seat even after the door closed behind the women, so Eben stayed on his feet as well. "Thank you for dinner. It was exceptional, as usual. Tonight, I especially enjoyed the duckling."

Stanley continued to study him out of impassive eyes. Just before the pause between them would have turned awkward, Stanley turned and headed away from the table. "Come with me, Eben Spencer."

Baffled and more than a little edgy, he followed Stanley to the suite of rooms that contained the hotel's administrative offices.

Stanley sat behind his elegantly simple desk and with a solemn look in his eyes he gestured for Eben to take a seat.

"My wife and I have loved this hotel," he said after a long moment. "It has been our home and our lives for many, many years. We have raised two strong sons here and had hoped one of them would choose to carry on for us, but our sons have chosen other paths to follow."

Eben wasn't quite sure where Stanley was steering

the conversation so he opted to remain silent and let the man lead.

"My wife and I are old and we are tired. We spend so much time caring for those who stay here that we have no time to enjoy our older years. The moment has come for us to make a decision about the future of this place we love."

Eben held his breath, doing his best to contain the nerves shooting through him.

"I know you have been impatient with us for the delays. But I hope you understand how difficult it is for us to let go and surrender our dream to another. We needed to be certain. Completely certain. Tonight, seeing you with your beautiful daughter, we are sure of our decision. A man who could raise such a delightful child will take good care of this hotel, the child of our hearts."

The other man pulled out the file Eben knew contained the paperwork for the sale of The Sea Urchin to Spencer Hotels. He signed it in his small, neat script, then handed the papers over to Eben.

He had negotiated hundreds of deals in his dozen years at Spencer Hotels, but Eben couldn't remember any victory tasting as sweet as this one. He wanted to laugh out loud, to throw his fists in the air.

To find Sage and kiss her senseless.

She deserved every bit of credit for this. If not for her and her miraculous effect on Chloe, he wouldn't be sitting here watching Stanley Wu hand him exactly what he wanted, ownership of this graceful old hotel.

Instead of leaping up to go in search of Sage, he settled for holding his hand out across the desk to shake the other man's hand.

"Thank you, Mr. Wu. I give you my solemn vow that you will not regret this."

They would have to go through this again in the morning with attorneys present, but Eben knew Stanley would not change his mind now, not after he had given his word.

They spent several moments discussing a few of the myriad details involved in the sale. He tried his best to focus, but inside he couldn't wait to find Sage and tell her.

Stanley must have finally sensed his impatience.

"All this can wait until tomorrow with the lawyers. Tonight is for being with those we love," Stanley said, then paused. "Our Sage, I have never seen her looking so lovely."

An odd segue, he thought, rather discomfited. "Uh, right."

"And she is just as lovely on the inside. A man would be a fool to let such a rare and precious flower slip through his fingers."

Eben couldn't have said why this particular conversational detour left him slightly panicked. Would Stanley rip up the papers if Eben told him things weren't serious between him and Sage?

He searched the other man's features but could see nothing behind Stanley's serenity.

"Shall we join our women in the kitchen? I am always looking for good fortune."

Still feeling a bit off center, Eben followed Stanley into the kitchen. They stood in the doorway, admiring the lovely picture of women across three generations working together.

The delicious-smelling kitchen was busy and crowded

as the head chef and his workers served the other dinner guests. Jade had taken over a workspace in the corner and was overseeing as Chloe and Sage—aprons tucked carefully over their dresses—folded thin circles of soft-cooked cookies into half-moons around little slips of paper, then curved and tucked them into the traditional fortune-cookie shape.

Chloe was laughing with delight as she worked, he saw, and so was Sage, her lovely features bright and animated.

He could barely look away.

Something shivered in his chest, a sense of rightness, of belonging, that had been missing for a long time.

She glanced up and for a tiny sliver of time, their gazes locked together. Her smile slid away, her eyes suddenly as deep and fathomless as the Pacific.

He would be leaving her tomorrow. The grim knowledge churned through him and he suddenly hated the very thought of it. But what other choice did he have?

Chloe caught sight of him. "Daddy, come and see my fortune cookies! I made one just for you. I even wrote the fortune and put it inside and everything."

He jerked his gaze away from Sage, from that stunning, tensile connection between them, and smiled at the cookie in her outstretched hand. "Thanks, kiddo. It's too pretty to eat, though."

"But if you don't eat it, you won't get to see the message."

Four sets of eyes watched him as he broke open the cookie and pulled out the folded slip of paper inside. He unfolded it, only to find Chloe's girlish handwriting, much tinier than usual, was almost indecipherable.

With effort, he was finally able to read the message

aloud. To the best Daddy ever. I love you better than all the fortune cookies in the world.

To his complete astonishment—and no small amount of dismay—tears welled up in his eyes. Eben blinked them back rapidly, shoving them down as far as he could into his psyche.

"It's great," he said brusquely when he trusted his voice again. "Thank you very much."

Chloe was obviously looking for more from him. Her features fell. "You don't like it."

"I do." He tried a little more enthusiasm. "I love it. The cookie tastes great and the fortune is…well, it's not true."

Now she looked close to tears. "It is *too*. I do love you more than all the fortune cookies in the world."

He would have preferred this conversation anywhere else than in the busy, noisy kitchen of the hotel he had just agreed to buy—and anywhere else but in front of Stanley and Jade Wu and Sage Benedetto. "I know you do, sweetheart. I just meant the first part isn't true. I'm far from the best daddy in the world, but I'm trying."

She smiled her relief and threw her flour-covered hands around his waist. "Well, I think you're the best."

He hugged her back. "That's the important thing, then, isn't it?"

He had won. The Sea Urchin was his.

Neither Eben nor Stanley mentioned the matter for the rest of the evening. Even after the three of them took their leave of the Wus, Eben didn't say anything, but Sage somehow knew.

She didn't need to possess any kind of psychic ability to correctly read the suppressed excitement in his features.

So this was it. They would be leaving soon. His mind was probably already spinning as he made plans. For all she knew, he may even have made arrangements for a flight out tonight.

She sat beside him battling down a deep ache as he drove down the long driveway of The Sea Urchin, then turned in the direction toward Brambleberry House.

She wasn't ready for another loss so soon. She was still reeling from Abigail's death and now she would lose Eben and Chloe as well. How could she ever be happy in her quiet life without them?

She should never have let them so far into her world. It had been a huge mistake and she was very much afraid she would be paying the price for that particular error in judgment for a long time.

He would probably return to Cannon Beach at some point. She could at least console herself with that. His company had dozens of other hotels around the world, but The Sea Urchin was important to him, he had made no secret of it.

Now that she knew how much he cared about the hotel, she couldn't imagine him just buying the place for acquisition's sake alone. While Sage doubted he would have direct involvement in the future management of the hotel, she expected he would at least have some participation in decision-making.

Even if he left tonight, she knew it was unlikely she would never see him again.

In many ways, she almost thought she would prefer that alternative—that he leave Cannon Beach now that the papers were signed and never look back. How much harder would those occasional visits be, knowing she would have to steel herself to say goodbye to him again?

The rain had eased to a light, filmy drizzle. They were almost to Brambleberry House when she knew she had to say something.

"It's done, then?" she asked.

His brilliant, boyish smile cut through the darkness inside the Jaguar and, absurdly, made her want to weep. "It's done. The papers are signed. We'll need to have our attorneys go over everything in the morning but as far as I'm concerned, it's official."

"Congratulations."

She thought she had done a fairly credible job of cloaking her ambivalence behind enthusiasm, but some of it must have filtered through.

Eben sent her a swift look across the vehicle. "I know The Sea Urchin is a local landmark and has great meaning for the people of Cannon Beach. I've told you this before, but I think it bears repeating. I promise, I don't plan any major changes. A few coats of paint, maybe, a few modernizations here and there, but that's it."

"I believe you." She smiled, a little less feigned this time. "I'm thrilled for you, Eben. Really, I am. You got exactly what you wanted."

He opened his mouth to say something, then closed it again and she couldn't read his expression in the dim light. "Yes. Exactly what I wanted," he murmured.

"You said you had papers to sign tomorrow. I guess that means you're not leaving tonight, then?"

She saw his gaze shift to the rearview mirror, where Chloe was admiring her substantial pile of fortune cookies and not paying them any attention.

"No. We'll wait until the morning. The Wus and I will have to go through everything with the attorneys at The Sea Urchin first thing and then I'll have my pilot meet Chloe and me at the airport in Seaside when we're done."

She thought of the field trip they had planned all week for their last day of camp, to visit the Cape Meares Lighthouse and Wildlife Refuge. Chloe would be so disappointed to miss it but she knew Eben no doubt had many things to do back in the Bay Area and wouldn't delay for a little thing like a camp field trip.

As they reached Brambleberry House, some of Eben's excitement seemed to have dimmed—or perhaps he was merely containing it better.

Sage, on the other hand, felt ridiculously close to tears. She wasn't sure why, she only knew she couldn't bear the thought of saying goodbye to them in the car.

Besides that, Conan would never forgive her if she let them leave without giving him one last chance to see his beloved Chloe.

She injected an enthusiasm she was far from feeling into her voice. "Do you both want to come in for a few minutes? I've got a frozen cheesecake Abigail made me a…a few weeks before she died. I've been looking for a good occasion to enjoy it with some friends."

"I *love* cheesecake," Chloe offered from the backseat.

"You love anything with sugar in it, monkey."

She giggled at her father. "It's true. I do."

"It's settled, then." Sage smiled.

"Are you sure?" Eben asked.

"Absolutely. We need to celebrate. I'll have to take it out of the freezer but it should only take a few moments to thaw."

He seemed as reluctant as she for the evening to end. "Thank you, then," he said.

He reached behind the seat for the umbrella and came around to her door to open it for her. As he reached to help her from the vehicle, her nerves tingled at the touch of his hand.

"You and Chloe take the umbrella," he said. "You're the ones with the fancy dresses."

Sage found it particular bittersweet to hold Chloe's little hand tightly in hers as the two of them raced through the drizzle to the porch.

Oh, she would miss this darling child. Again she had to swallow down the ache in her throat.

Water droplets glistened in Eben's hair as he joined them on the porch while she unlocked the door.

"Is Conan upstairs or with Ms. Galvez?" Chloe asked when they were inside the entryway.

"He would have been lonely upstairs in my apartment by himself. I think he and Anna were watching a movie when I left."

"Can I take him upstairs with us for cheesecake?"

"Well, we can get him but I should warn you that Conan doesn't like cheesecake. His favorite dessert is definitely apple pie."

Chloe giggled, as Sage had intended. She kept her hand firmly in Sage's as they knocked on Anna's door. For just an instant, Sage caught Eben watching her and she shivered at the glittery expression there.

Conan rushed through the door the moment Anna opened it. "Hey," Anna exclaimed. "How was dinner?"

"You know The Sea Urchin. It couldn't be anything other than exquisite," Sage answered. "Sorry to bother you but we're having an impromptu little party. I'm going to take out the frozen cheesecake Abigail made."

"What's the occasion?"

"We're celebrating," she said, forcing a smile. "Stanley and Jade agreed to sell to Spencer Hotels."

"Oh, that's wonderful! Congratulations."

Eben smiled, though in the better lighting of the entryway, Sage was certain he didn't look quite as thrilled as he had earlier.

"You and Conan have to join us while we celebrate," she said.

"May I look at the dolls first?" Chloe asked.

Anna sent a quick look at Sage and Eben. Her dark eyes danced with mischief for a moment in an expression that suddenly looked remarkably like one of Abigail's.

"Sure," she finally answered. "You two go ahead. Conan, Chloe and I will be up in a moment. Well, probably closer to ten or fifteen."

She ushered the girl into her apartment and closed the door firmly before Conan could bound up the stairs, leaving Eben and Sage alone in the entryway.

Feeling awkward—and more than a little mortified by Anna's not-so-subtle maneuvering to give her and Eben some private time—Sage led the way up the stairs and into her apartment.

Eben closed the door behind him. She wasn't quite sure how he moved so quickly, but an instant later she was in his arms.

His kiss was firm, demanding, stealing the breath from her lungs. She wrapped her arms around him, exulting in his strength beneath her fingers, in the taste and scent of him.

For long, drugging moments, nothing else mattered but his mouth and his hands and the wild feelings inside her, fluttering to take flight.

"I've been dying to do that all night." His low voice sent shivers rippling down her spine.

She shivered and pulled his mouth back to hers, wondering if he could taste the edge of desperation in the kiss. She forgot about Chloe and Anna and Conan downstairs, she forgot about The Sea Urchin, she forgot everything but the wonder of being in his arms one more time.

One *last* time.

"I don't want to leave tomorrow."

At the ragged intensity of his voice, she blinked her eyes open. The reminder of her inevitable heartbreak seemed to jar her back into her senses.

What was the point in putting herself through this? The more she touched him, experienced the wild joy of being in his arms, the harder she knew it would be to wrench her heart away from him and return to her quiet, safe life before he and Chloe had stumbled into it.

She swallowed. "But you have to."

"I have to," he agreed, reluctance sliding through his voice. "I can't miss these Tokyo meetings."

He pressed his forehead to hers. "But I could try to rearrange my schedule to come back in a few weeks. A month on the outside."

She allowed herself a brief moment to imagine how it might be. Despite the heat they generated and these fragile emotions taking root in her heart, she knew she would merely be a convenience for him, never anything more than that.

She drew in a shuddering breath and slid out of his arms, desperate for space to regain her equilibrium. "I should, uh, get the cheesecake out of the freezer."

He raised an eyebrow at her deliberate evasion but said nothing, only followed her into the kitchen. She opened the small freezer and quickly found Abigail's foil-wrapped package.

Her hands shook a little as she pulled it out—from the embrace with Eben, but also from emotion. This was one more tie to Abigail that would be severed after tonight.

She looked at Abigail's handwriting on the foil with the date a few weeks before her death and one simple word: Celebrate.

Eben looked at the cheesecake from over her shoulder. He seemed to instinctively know how difficult it was for her to lose one more connection to Abigail. "Are you certain you don't want to save this a little longer, for some other occasion?"

She shook her head with determination. "I have the oddest feeling Abigail would approve. She was the one who introduced you to the Wus, after all. She never would have done that if she didn't want you to buy The Sea Urchin. I think she would be happy her cheesecake is being put to good use. In fact, if I know Abigail, she's probably somewhere lifting a glass of champagne to you right now."

He tilted his head and studied her for a long moment, then smiled softly. "I have you to thank as much as Abigail."

"I didn't do anything."

"Not true. You know it's not. I honestly think Stanley and Jade were ready to pull out until dinner tonight, until you and Chloe both charmed them."

He grabbed her fingers. "You reach Chloe in ways I don't think anyone has since her mother died."

She shifted and slid her hand away, uncomfortable with his praise. How could she tell him she understood

Chloe's pain so intimately and connected with her only because her life had so closely mirrored the little girl's?

"What can I do to reach her that way?" Eben asked. By all appearances, he looked completely sincere. "You need to give me lessons."

"Just trust your instincts. That's the only lesson I can give."

"Following my instincts hasn't turned out well so far. Maybe if I had better success at this father business, I wouldn't have to send her to boarding school in the fall."

At first, she thought—hoped—she misheard him. He couldn't possibly be serious.

"Boarding school? You're sending her to *boarding school?*"

He shrugged, looking as if he wished he hadn't said anything. "Thinking about it. I haven't made a final decision."

"You have. Admit it."

She was suddenly trembling with fury. She was again eight years old, lost and alone, with no friends and a father who wanted little to do with her. "You've probably already signed her up and paid the first year's tuition, haven't you?"

Guilt flitted across his features. "A deposit, only to hold her spot. It's a very good school outside Newport, Rhode Island. My sister went there."

"Half a world away from you!"

"What do you want me to do, Sage? I've been at my wit's end. You've seen a different child this week than the one I've lived with for two years. Here, Chloe has been sweet and easygoing. Things are different at home. She's moody and angry and deceitful and nothing I do gets through to her. I told you she's been through half a dozen nannies and four different schools since her mother died. Every one of them says she has severe behavior problems and needs more structure and order. How am I supposed to give her that with my travel schedule?"

"You're the brilliant businessman. You don't need me to help you figure it out. Stop traveling so much or, if you have to go, take her with you. That's your answer, not dumping her off at some boarding school and then forgetting about her. She's a child, Eben. She needs her father."

"Don't you get it? I'm not the solution, I'm the damn problem."

As quickly as it swelled inside her, her anger trickled away at the despair in his voice. She longed, more than anything, to touch him again.

"Oh, Eben. You're not. She's a little girl who's lost her mother and she's desperate for her father's attention. Of course she's going to misbehave if that's the only time she can get a reaction from you. But she doesn't need a boarding school, she needs you."

"How do you know it won't help her?"

"Because I lived it! You want to know how I'm able to reach Chloe so well? Because I'm her with a few more years under my belt. I was exactly like Chloe, shunted away by my father to boarding school when I was eight simply because I no longer fit his lifestyle."

Chapter 13

Eben stared at her. Of all the arguments he might have expected her to make, that particular one wouldn't have even made his list.

"Sage—"

She let out a long breath. Still in her party clothes, she looked fragile and heartbreakingly beautiful.

"My mother died when I was five," she went on. "I was seven when my father married his second wife, a lovely, extremely wealthy socialite who didn't appreciate being reminded of his previous wife and the life they had together. I was an inconvenience to both of them."

An inconvenience? How could anyone consider a child an inconvenience? For all his frustration with Chloe, none of it hinged on a word as cold as that one.

"I was dumped into boarding school when I was eight. The same age as Chloe. For the next decade, I saw my father about three weeks out of every year—

one week during the Christmas holidays and two weeks in the summer."

He remembered her disdain for him early in their acquaintance, the contempt he saw in her eyes that first morning on the beach, the old pain he had seen in her eyes when they argued about whether he should take Chloe with him on his trip to Tokyo.

No wonder.

She thought of him as someone like her father, someone too busy for his own child. He ached to touch her but couldn't ignore the *hands-off* signals she was broadcasting around herself like a radio frequency.

"I'm so sorry, Sage."

Her chin lifted. "I survived. Listen to me complain like it was the worst thing that could ever happen to a child. It wasn't. I was always fed, clean, warm. I know many children endure much worse than an exclusive private boarding school in Europe. But I have to tell you, part of me has never recovered from that early sense of abandonment."

He pictured a younger version of Sage, lost and lonely, desperate for attention. He ached to imagine it.

But she was right, wasn't she? If he sent Chloe to boarding school, she would probably suffer some of those same emotions—perhaps for the rest of her life.

What the hell was he supposed to do?

"Boarding school doesn't have to be as you experienced it," he said. "My sister and I both went away for school when we were about Chloe's age. We did very well."

For him and, he suspected, for his sister, school had offered security and peace from the tumult and chaos of their home life. He had relished the structure and order he found there, the safety net of rules. He had thrived there in a way he never could have at home with his parents. In his heart, he supposed he was hoping Chloe would do the same.

"You don't have any scars at all?"

"A few." The inevitable hazings and peer cruelty had certainly left their mark until he'd found his feet. "But I don't know anyone who survives childhood without a scar or two."

"She's already lost her mother, Eben. No matter how lofty you tell yourselves your motives might be, I can promise that if you send Chloe away, she'll feel as if she's losing you, too."

"She won't be losing me. I'm not your father, Sage. I don't plan to send her away and ignore her for months at a time."

All his excitement at closing The Sea Urchin deal was gone now, washed away under this overwhelming tide of guilt and uncertainty.

"Besides, I told you I haven't made a final decision yet. This week has been different. *Chloe* has been different and I probably have been, too. If I can recapture that when we're back in our regular lives, there's no reason I have to follow through and send her to boarding school."

A small gasp sounded from the doorway. In the heat of the discussion with Sage—wrapped up in his dismay over inadvertently putting those shadows in her eyes—he had missed the sound of the door opening. Now, with a sinking heart, he turned to find Chloe standing there, her little features pale and her eyes huge and wounded.

"Chloe—"

"You're sending me to *boarding school?*" she practically shrieked. "You can't, Daddy. You *can't!*"

She was hitching her breath in and out rapidly, on the brink of what he feared would be a full-blown tantrum.

Helpless and frustrated, he went to her and tried to hug her, tangentially aware as he did so of Anna Galvez and Conan standing behind her in the hallway outside Sage's apartment.

"I didn't say I was sending you to boarding school."

She was prickly and resistant and immediately slid away from him. "You said you might not have to but that means you're thinking about it, doesn't it?"

He couldn't lie to her. Not about something as important as her future. "We don't have to talk about this right now. We're all tired and overexcited. Come on, let's have some of Sage's cheesecake."

"I don't want cheesecake! I don't want *anything*."

"Chloe—"

"I won't go! Do you hear me? I'll run away. I'll come here and live with Sage."

She burst into hard, heaving sobs and buried her face in Conan's fur. The dog licked her cheek then turned and glared at Eben.

Join the club, he thought. Everybody else in the room was furious with him.

He didn't know what to do, certain that if he tried to comfort his daughter he would only make this worse. To his vast relief, Sage stepped in and sat on the floor right there in the doorway in her elegant dress and pulled Chloe onto her lap.

She murmured soft, soothing words and after a few tense moments, Chloe's tears began to ease.

"I don't want to go to boarding school," she mumbled again.

"I know, baby."

Sage ran a hand over her hair but he noted she didn't give Chloe any false reassurances. "Do you think you're going to be up for cheesecake tonight? If you're not, you could always take some home with you."

"I'm not hungry now," Chloe whispered. "If it's okay with you, I'll take it home. Thank you."

By the time Sage cut into her friend's ironically labeled cheesecake—he had never felt *less* like celebrating—and packaged up two slices for them, Chloe had reverted to an icy, controlled calm that seemed oddly familiar. It took him a moment to realize she was emulating the way he tried to stuff down his emotions and keep control in tense situations.

Somebody ought to just stick a knife through his heart, Eben thought. It would be far less painful in the long run than this whole parenting thing.

Anna had disappeared back to her apartment earlier during the worst of Chloe's outburst and Sage and Conan walked them down the stairs and to his car.

The rain had stopped, he saw. The night was cool and sweet with the scent of Abigail's flowers.

Chloe gave Sage an extra-long hug. If he wasn't mistaken, he saw Sage wipe her eyes after Chloe slid into the back seat, but when she lifted her gaze to his, it was filled with a Zen-like calm.

"This isn't the way I wanted the evening to end," he murmured. *Or the week, really.*

Their time with her had been magical and he hated to see it end.

He gazed at her features in the moonlight, lovely and exotic, and his chest ached again at the idea of leaving her.

"Will you come running with Chloe and me in the morning? Just one more time?"

She drew in a sharp breath. "I don't know if that's a good idea. It's late and Chloe probably will need sleep after tonight. Perhaps we should just say our goodbyes here."

"Please, Sage."

She closed her eyes. When she opened them, they brimmed with tears again and his heart shattered into a million pieces.

"I can't," she whispered. "Goodbye, Eben. Be well."

She turned and hurried up the sidewalk and slipped inside the house before he could even react.

After a long moment of staring after her, he climbed into the car, fighting the urge to press a hand to his chest to squeeze away the tight ache there.

Despite his halfhearted efforts to engage her in conversation, Chloe maintained an icy silence to him through the short distance to their rented beach house.

He couldn't blame her, he supposed. It had been a fairly brutal way to find out that he was considering sending her to boarding school. He had planned to broach the idea when he returned from Tokyo and slowly build to it over the summer, give her time to become adjusted to it.

"You know you're going to have to talk to me again sometime," he finally said when they walked to the door of their rented beach house. In answer, she pointedly turned her back, crossed her arms across her chest and clamped her lips shut.

He sighed as he unlocked the door and disengaged the security system. The moment they were inside, Chloe raced to her bedroom and slammed the door.

Eben stood for a moment in the foyer, his emotions a thick, heavy burden. He didn't know what the hell to do with them.

He needed a drink, he decided, and crossed to the small, well-stocked bar. A few moments later, snifter in hand, he sat in the small office calling his assistant to set up the meeting with his attorneys at The Sea Urchin in the morning and to arrange for the company Learjet to meet them at the airport in Seaside.

After he hung up, he sat for a moment wondering how a night that had started out holding such promise could have so quickly turned into an ugly disaster.

Now Sage was angry and disappointed in him, his daughter wasn't speaking to him, he was even getting the cold shoulder from a blasted dog, for heaven's sake.

The way his evening was going, he would probably be getting a phone call from the Wus telling him they had changed their minds *again*.

By the time he finished the tiny splash of brandy, he knew he had to face Chloe, if only to address her fears.

He knocked on her bedroom door. "Chloe? Let's talk about this. Come on."

Only silence met his knock. Surely she couldn't have fallen asleep already, could she? He knocked harder and tried the door, only to find it locked.

He didn't need this tonight. Frustration whipped through him and he banged even harder. "Chloe, open this door, young lady. Right now."

Still no answer. For the first time, unease began to filter through his frustration. He should never have let her come here and stew. It had been only a cowardly attempt to delay the inevitable. He should have just confronted the problem head-on the minute they walked into the house.

The lock on the bedroom door was flimsy. He quickly grabbed a butter knife from the kitchen, twisted the mechanism, then swung the door open.

A quick sweep of the darkened room showed the bed was still made, with no sign of his daughter.

"Chloe? Where are you hiding? This isn't funny."

He flipped on the light. The dress she had adored so much was discarded in a pile of taffeta on the floor and the shelves of the bureau were open, their contents spilling out, as if she had rummaged through looking for something in a hurry.

He barely saw any of that. His attention was suddenly focused on the curtains fluttering in the breeze and instantly Eben's unease turned to cold-edged fear.

The window was open to the sea-soaked night air and there was no sign of his daughter.

"Yeah, I know. I don't need a second piece of cheesecake. Or the first one, for that matter. You're one to talk. You pig out on *dog food*, for crying out loud."

Conan snickered and dipped his head back to his forepaws as he watched her lame attempts to drown her misery in a decadent swirl of sugar and cream cheese.

"It's not working, anyway," she muttered, setting the plate down on the coffee table in front of her.

She should be in bed, she knew. The day had been long, the evening painfully full and her muscles ached with exhaustion, but she knew she wouldn't be able to sleep.

Her emotions were too raw, too heavy. She had a sinking suspicion that when the sun rose, she would probably still be sitting right here on her couch in her bathrobe, red-eyed and wrung-out and three pounds heavier from the cheesecake.

Damn Eben Spencer anyway.

He had no business sweeping into her life, shaking up her status quo so dramatically, then riding off into the blasted sunset—especially not when her grief for Abigail still had such a stranglehold around her life.

Conan made a sad sound suddenly, as if he sensed she was thinking about his human companion.

He had seemed much less depressed these last few days with Eben and Chloe. How would their leaving affect him, poor dog? She had a feeling her quad muscles were in for some good workouts the next few mornings.

He had been acting strangely ever since Eben and Chloe had left for the evening. Now he stood again. Instead of going to the door to signal he needed to go out, he went to the windows overlooking the ocean and stared out into the night for a long moment then whined plaintively.

That was the third time he had repeated the same odd behavior in the last half-hour. It was starting to freak her out.

"What's the matter, bud?" she asked him.

Before the words were even out of her mouth, she heard a sharp knocking at the door downstairs.

Who on earth would be coming to call at—she checked her clock—eleven o'clock at night?

She went to the opposite windows but couldn't see a car in the driveway. The caller knocked again and Sage moved warily down the stairs, one hand on Conan's collar.

The best Conan would do was probably sniff an intruder to death but he was big and could look menacing if the light wasn't great and the intruder had bad eyes.

She left the chain in the door and peered through, but her self-protective instincts flew out into the night when she saw Eben standing on the porch, a frantic expression in his eyes.

"Eben! What is it? What's happened?"

He studied her for a moment, then raked a hand through his hair. "She's not here, is she?"

She blinked, trying to make sense of his appearance on her doorstep so late. "Chloe? No. I haven't seen her since the two of you left. She's not at home?"

"I thought she was just sulking in her bedroom. I gave her maybe twenty minutes to get it out of her system while I made a few calls. But when I went into her room to talk to her, she was gone and her window was open. I was certain she must have come here to find you. That's what she said, right? That she would run away and find you."

Conan whined and ran past them sniffing around the perimeter of the wrought-iron fence.

"You checked the beach?" Sage asked.

"That's the way I came. I ran the whole way, sure I would bump into her any minute, but I couldn't see any sign of her. I called and called but she didn't answer."

His eyes looked haunted. "I have to find her. Anything could happen to her alone in the middle of the night!"

His desperation terrified her as nothing else could. "Let me throw on some clothes and get a jacket and shoes. Perhaps we can split up, cover more ground."

Anna's door suddenly opened and she poked her head out, her hair as messy as Sage had ever seen it and her dark eyes bleary with sleep. "What's wrong?"

"Sorry we woke you," Sage spoke quickly. "Chloe's missing. She was angry with her father about what happened earlier and it looks as if she snuck out her window."

She couldn't help but be impressed at the rapid way Anna pushed aside the cobwebs and became her normal brisk, businesslike self. "What can I do? Do you want me to call the police?"

Eben drew in a sharp breath. "I don't know. I just keep thinking she didn't have enough time to go far. Where could she have gone? There aren't that many places she's familiar with around here."

"I don't know. We've explored the area around here quite a bit this week in camp." Her voice trailed off and she gazed at Eben and saw the exact same realization hit him.

"Hug Point," Sage said. The beach they had visited when they took the tandem bicycle.

"Would she have time to get there?"

"She's fast. She could make it."

"That's a hell of a long way for an eight-year-old in the dark," Eben said, and she ached at the fledgling hope in his eyes.

"She has a flashlight. It's part of the survival kit we did the first day of camp."

"That must have been what she was rummaging through her room to find. That's something, isn't it?"

"Maybe." She paused, loathe to tell him more bad news but she knew she had no choice. "Eben, the tide is coming in fast. High tide will be in about ninety minutes."

She saw stark fear in his eyes and knew it mirrored her own.

"We should split up," he said. "One of us search down the beach in case she hasn't made it that far yet and is still on her way and the other one start at Hug Point and head back this direction."

"Good idea. I'll drive to Hug Point and start backtracking this way. You take Conan with you."

She thought of the way the dog had immediately gone

to Chloe that first day, as if he'd been looking just for her. "If she's out there, he'll help us find her."

"Okay."

She grabbed his hand, heartsore for him. "Eben, we'll find her."

He looked slightly buoyed by her faith and squeezed her fingers, then took off through the backyard to the beach access gate.

"Maybe I ought to call the police chief and give him a heads-up, just in case your hunch is wrong," Anna said.

"Do it," Sage said on her way up the stairs two at a time.

For all her reassurances to Eben, she knew exactly what dangers awaited a little girl on the beach in the dark at high tide and she couldn't bear to think of any of them.

Though it only took a few moments to reach Hug Point by car, it felt like a lifetime. The whole way, Sage gripped the steering wheel of her aging Toyota and tried to battle back her terror and her guilt.

She was as much to blame for this as Eben. If she hadn't overreacted so strongly at his mention of boarding school for Chloe, they wouldn't have been arguing about it and Chloe wouldn't have overheard.

It was none of her business what school Eben sent his daughter to. She had been presumptuous to think otherwise. In her usual misguided attempt to save the world, she had ended up hurting the situation far more than she helped.

She pulled into the parking lot as a light drizzle started again. Heedless of the rain or the wind that whipped the hood of her Gore-Tex jacket, she cupped her hands and called Chloe's name.

She strained hard to hear anything over the wind and the murmur of the sea. In the distance, somewhere beyond the headland, she thought she heard a small cry.

Though she knew well how deceiving sounds could be out here—for all she knew, it could have been a nocturnal shorebird—she decided she had to head in the direction of the sound.

In the dark, the shore was far different than it was in the daylight, though it had a harsh beauty here as well, like some wild moonscape, twisted and shaped by the elements.

She rounded the cluster of rocks, straining to see anything in the darkness.

She heard the same cry again and aimed her flashlight along the beach but it was a pitiful weapon to fight back the vast, unrelenting dark.

Suddenly on the wind, she could swear she heard Chloe's voice. "Help. Please!"

She turned the flashlight toward the water and her heart stopped when she saw several yards away a small figure in a pink jacket on one of the rocks they had played on the other day. She was surrounded by water now and the tide was rising quickly.

Far down the beach from the direction of Brambleberry House, she saw a tiny spark of light on the beach and knew it was Eben. There wasn't time to wait for him but she whistled hard, hoping Conan would hear and come running. Perhaps Eben would pick up on the dog's urgency.

"I'm coming, baby," she called as she hurried down the sand. "Stay there. Just hang on."

When she was parallel on the shore with Chloe on her watery perch, she headed through the surf. She was prepared for the cold but it still clutched at her with icy fingers and she couldn't contain a gasp. No matter how cold she knew the ocean could be along the Pacific Northwest coast, even in June, it still took her by surprise.

She knew hypothermia could hit out here in a matter of minutes.

Chloe's rock was probably only twenty yards from shore but that seemed far enough as she waded through the icy water, now up to her knees. She was laboring for breath by the time she reached her. "Hi, sweetie,"

The sobbing girl threw her arms around Sage. She was wet and shivering and Sage knew she had to get her out of the water immediately.

"You came for me!" she sobbed. "I was so scared. I want my daddy."

Sage held her close and buried her face in the girl's hair, her heart full. She could barely breathe around the emotions racing through her.

"I know you want your daddy, honey. I know. He and Conan are coming down the beach from my house looking for you, but they'll be here in a minute. He'll be so happy to see you."

"Am I in big trouble?"

"What do you think?" she asked, trying to sound stern through her vast relief.

"I snuck out again, even though I promised I wouldn't. I went on the beach at night, even though you told me I shouldn't. I broke a lot of rules. I bet my dad's really mad."

Sage kept one eye on the rising tide. A wave hit her, soaking her to her waist and she knew they had to move. "Let's worry about that when we get out of here, okay? How about a piggyback ride?"

"Okay. My hands are really cold, though. I don't know if I can hang on."

"You can. Just pretend you're a crab and I'm your dinner and you don't want to let me go."

Chloe giggled and gripped her arms around Sage's neck. Sage could feel her shiver even through her jacket.

It was tough going on the way back. She couldn't see where she was going and she felt as if she were walking through quicksand. For the first time, she was grateful for the last month of morning runs that had built up her muscles. If not for those runs, she wasn't sure she would have had the endurance to get to shore.

A journey that had only been twenty yards on the way out now seemed like miles. They were almost to the sand when a sneaker wave came out of nowhere and slammed into the backs of her legs.

Tired and off balance with Chloe on her back, Sage swayed from the force of it and stumbled to her knees. She managed to keep her hold on Chloe but then another one washed over them and drove her face into the surf.

Spluttering and coughing, she wrenched her face free of the icy water. She had to get to her feet now, she knew, but she felt as if she were fighting the whole ocean.

At last, with a great surge of adrenaline, she staggered to her feet. Chloe was crying in earnest now.

"We're okay. We're okay. Only a little farther," she managed, then she heard the most welcome sounds she had ever heard—a dearly familiar bark and Eben's strong voice.

"Chloe! Sage!" he called. "Hang on. I'm coming."

She sobbed out a breath of relief and made it only another few feet before he reached them and guided them all back to safety.

Chapter 14

By the time he reached them, both Sage and Chloe were soaked and shivering violently. He grabbed Chloe in one arm while he drew Sage against his body with the other. Together, the three of them made their way to the shore. Only when they were above the high tide line did Eben pause to take a breath.

His heart still pounded with rapid force from that terrible moment when he saw them both go down in the water and struggle so hard against the waves to come up.

"Are you both okay?" he asked.

In his arms, Chloe nodded and sniffled. "I'm sorry, Daddy. I'm sorry. I'm sorry. I shouldn't have run away. No wonder you want to send me away to boarding school."

He closed his eyes, pained that they had come back to this. "We need to get you both warmed up. Come on. Let's get you home."

"There's a trail back to the road from here. That's probably the easiest way to get to the parking lot and my car."

After the longest fifteen minutes of his life, they made it to Sage's car.

"There's a b-blanket in the b-back for Chloe," she mumbled. "It's probably covered in dog hair but it's the b-best I can do."

He found it quickly and also a fleece jacket of Sage's, which he handed to her.

"I'll drive," he insisted. "You work on getting warm."

After Chloe was settled in the back wrapped in the blanket and cuddled next to Conan's heat, Eben climbed into the driver's seat and turned her heater on high.

His emotions were thick, jumbled, and his heart still pounded with remembered fear as he drove toward Brambleberry House.

"I should call Anna, tell her to call off the police," Sage said after a moment. Her trembling had mostly stopped, he saw with vast relief.

"The police were looking for me?" Chloe asked in a small voice from the back seat. "I'm in big trouble, aren't I?"

"Everybody was worried about you," Eben said.

Sage called Anna on her cell phone and for the next few moments their one-sided conversation was the only sound in the small vehicle.

"She's fine. We're all fine. Cold and wet but everybody's okay. Yeah, I'll be home in a minute. I'll tell her. Thanks, Anna."

She closed her phone and turned to the back seat. "Anna says to tell you she's so glad you're okay."

"Me, too," Chloe said sleepily. "I was so scared. The

water wasn't high when I went out to the rock but then it started coming in fast and I didn't know what to do."

"You did the right thing to stay where you were," Sage said.

"I remembered what we talked about in camp. I tried to do just what you said."

He couldn't bear to think about what might have happened if Chloe hadn't had a little survival training through Sage's camp or if they hadn't found her in time.

With the resilience of the young, Chloe was nearly asleep by the time they reached Brambleberry House, her arms wrapped around Conan and her cheek resting against the top of his furry head.

He feared it would be as tough to wean her from the dog as it would be to leave this place.

"Just drop me off," Sage said. "I can pick up my car at your place tomorrow on my way to the center."

In the driveway, he put the car in park and finally reached for her hand. "Sage, I don't know how I can ever thank you."

She shook her head. "Don't. You know you don't need to thank me. I'm just so grateful everything turned out okay."

He was quiet for a moment, hot emotion choking his throat. He wanted to shunt it all away as he usually did, to lock it down deep inside him, but this wild tangle was too huge, to overwhelming.

He knew he couldn't leave things between them like this, tainted by this stilted awkwardness, not after everything that had happened.

"I know it's late but…I need to talk to you. After I get Chloe settled into bed, I would like to call Stanley and Jade, see if they could send someone over to stay with her for a little while."

She drew in a breath that ended in a little shiver, though he wasn't sure if it resulted from the cold or something else. "We don't really have anything left to say, do we?"

He squeezed her fingers. "I think we do. Please, Sage."

After an agonizingly long moment, she shrugged. "I'll try to watch for you so you don't have to ring the doorbell and wake Anna again."

He nodded. He had no idea what he wanted to say to her, he only knew he couldn't return home in the morning without seeing her again.

She opened the rear door for Conan and gave Chloe another hug, then hurried into her house.

Chloe said little as they drove back to their cottage. She was nearly asleep by the time he pulled into the driveway behind his rental, her head lolling back against the upholstery.

"Just a few more minutes, baby," he said as he helped her inside. "A hot shower will help warm you up the rest of the way and wash away the saltwater."

She sighed. "I'd rather just go to bed. I'm so tired."

"I know, but you'll feel better, I promise. You're not going to fall asleep in there, are you?"

"No," she said, her voice subdued. "I'll be okay."

While he listened to the sounds of the shower, he changed out of wet khakis and shoes. He'd had it easy compared to Chloe and Sage and had only gotten wet up to mid-calf, but just that slight dousing left him cold.

He called The Sea Urchin front desk and, to his surprise, Jade answered. He left out a few details but explained he needed someone to come and sit with Chloe. Despite his best efforts to dissuade her, she insisted on coming herself and said she would be there in a few moments.

He was waiting in the living room when Chloe came out of the shower in her warmest flannel nightgown.

She hurried to him at once and wrapped her arms around his waist. She smelled sweet, like lavender soap and baby shampoo, and he held on tightly as more emotions caught in his throat.

"I really am super sorry I ran away, Daddy. I was just so mad at you but I wasn't thinking right."

He kissed the top of her head. "Trying to escape our problems doesn't work and usually only creates more trouble. Either they come right along with us or they're waiting where we left them when we get back."

She nodded, her damp hair leaving a mark against his shirt.

"I love you, baby," he said after a moment. "Please don't forget that. No matter what, I love you."

"I want to stay with you, Daddy. Please don't send me away. I'll try harder, I promise."

Sage had been right. He couldn't do it. Imperfect though he was—inadequate as he felt as a father—his daughter needed him.

"Same here, okay? I'll try harder, too. We both have to figure out how to make this work. I'll try to cut down my travel schedule so I'm home to spend more time with you."

"Oh, would you?"

More guilt sliced him at the stunned disbelief in her voice. "Yes. But you have to promise me that you'll settle down and work harder in school and that you'll take it easy on the new nanny when we get one."

Though she was about to fall over with exhaustion,

she still managed to get a crafty look in her eyes. "Can I help pick her?"

"Well, I can't promise I'll let you make the final decision but you can have input. Deal?"

"Deal." She beamed at him. "I know just what I want. Somebody like Sage. She's pretty and she smells good and she's super nice."

That just about summed it up, Eben thought. "We'll have to see what we can do. I think Sage is one of a kind."

"You like her, too, don't you, Daddy?"

"Sure, baby." He wasn't quite ready to examine his emotions too closely—nor did he want to explain them to his eight-year-old daughter. Instead, he scooped her into his arms, earning a sleepy giggle.

"Come on, let's get you into bed, okay? Jade Wu is coming over to stay with you so I can take Sage's car back to Brambleberry House after you're asleep."

"Okay. Give Sage and Conan a big kiss for me, okay?"

He grimaced. He wasn't sure either of those creatures in question were very happy with him right now. "I'll see what I can do," he murmured as he tucked her into her bed, then kissed her forehead and slipped from the room to wait for Jade.

What the hell was he doing here?

Twenty minutes later, Eben drove Sage's car into the driveway of Brambleberry House, turned off the engine and sat for a moment in the dark silence.

He should just leave her car here, tuck the keys under the doormat and walk back down the beach. The smartest thing to do would be to leave things as they were and continue with his plans to leave in the morning.

But just the thought of it made him ache inside. He sighed, still not certain what he wanted to say to her.

He was still trying to puzzle it out when the porch light flipped on. A moment later, she opened the door and stood in the doorway, a slim, graceful silhouette, and his heart bumped in his chest.

Her hair was damp and she had a blanket wrapped around her shoulders and one hand on the dog. He let out a long breath and slid from the car. The night air was cool and moist from the rains earlier, sweet with Abigail's flowers and the salty undertone of the ocean.

Neither of them spoke until he reached the porch.

"I wasn't sure you were coming." Her voice was low and strummed down his spine as if she'd caressed his skin.

"I probably shouldn't have."

"Why are you here, then? You're not a man who does things he shouldn't."

He gave a rough laugh. "Aren't I?" Unable to resist, he stepped forward and framed her face in his hands. She was so achingly beautiful and the air eddying around them was sweetly magical and he had no choice but to kiss her.

She was perfect in his arms and as her mouth moved softly under his, he felt something tight and hard around his heart shudder and give way.

This was why he came. He knew it with sudden certainty. Because somehow when he was here, with this woman in his arms, all the tumult inside him seemed to go still.

He found a peace with Sage Benedetto he had never even realized had been missing in his life.

She wanted to cherish every second of this.

Sage twisted her arms around his neck, trying to burn

each memory into her mind. She couldn't quite believe she had the chance to touch him and to taste him again when only a few short hours ago she thought he would be leaving her world forever.

"You're shivering," he murmured.

She knew it was in reaction to the wild chaos of emotions storming through her, but she couldn't tell him that. "I'm fine. My hair's just a little damp. That's all."

"You shouldn't be out here in the cool night air."

She was silent for a moment, gazing at the masculine features that had become so dear to her. "You're probably right," she finally murmured. "Come inside."

She knew exactly what she was offering—just as she knew she was signing herself up for even more heartache.

But she loved him. The truth of it had hit her the moment she saw him coming walking up the path. She was in love with Eben Spencer, billionaire hotelier and the last man on the planet a wild, flyaway nature girl from Oregon would ever have a forever-chance with.

This was all she would have with him and she couldn't make herself turn away now.

She walked up to her apartment without looking back. Over the pounding of her heart, she heard his footsteps behind her but he didn't say anything as they climbed the two flights of stairs.

Once inside, she frowned. She could swear she had left several lights on when she walked downstairs to let him in, but now only a single lamp was burning.

She had been reading while she waited and watched for him, listening to a Nanci Griffith CD but she must have bumped her stereo on her way out the door because now soft jazz played.

The whole room looked as if she had set the scene

for romance, which she absolutely had *not*. Despite her conviction that she wanted this, wanted him, she felt her face flame and hit the overhead light switch.

Nothing happened. The bulb must have burned out, she thought, mortified all over again.

Eben came into the room alone and she looked behind him. "Where's Conan?"

"I think he went through his door into Anna's apartment."

"Ah."

They stood looking at each other for a long moment and Sage could swear she could hear the churn of her blood pulsing through her body. She didn't think she had ever wanted anything in her life as much as she wanted him right now.

She opened her mouth to ask if he would like a drink or something—not that she had much, just some wine left over from the other night—but before any words could escape, he stepped forward and kissed her again.

Who needed alcohol when Eben Spencer was around? It was the last thought she had for a long time as she lost herself in the wonder of his strength, his touch.

After several long, glorious moments, he lifted his mouth away and pressed his forehead to hers. "I don't want to lose you, Sage."

She raised an eyebrow. "You can't lose what you don't have. An astute businessman like you should already know that."

He laughed, a low, amused sound that rippled over her nerve endings. "You're very good at putting me in my place, aren't you?"

She smiled, liking the place he was in very, very much.

"I mean it," he said. "I have to leave in the morning but I don't want this to be the end for us."

She didn't want to think about his leaving or about the emptiness he would leave behind. "Eben—"

He stepped away from her, raw emotion on his face. He was usually a master at concealing his thoughts. To see him in such an unveiled moment shocked her.

He gripped her hands in his and brought them to his chest, where she could feel the wild pulse of his heartbeat. Had she done that to him? She wondered with surprise.

"I was terrified tonight," he said, his voice low. "I've never known anything like that."

"You were worried for your daughter," she said. "That was completely normal."

"My fear wasn't only for Chloe." His gaze locked with hers and she couldn't look away from the stunning tenderness in the glittery green depths of his eyes. "My world stopped when I saw that wave hit. All I could think was that I couldn't bear the thought of anything happening to either of you."

Sharp joy exploded inside her and she couldn't breathe around it.

"I care about you, Sage. You've become desperately important to me and to my daughter this week."

Close on the heels of the joy was an even bigger terror. This couldn't be real. Hadn't she just spent a week convincing herself of all the reasons there could never be anything between them?

"You'll go back to California and forget all about me."

"I don't think so." He brought their clasped hands to his mouth, his gaze still locked with hers. "I'm in love with you, Sage."

She swallowed, feeling lightheaded with shock. "You're not," she exclaimed.

"I've been fighting it with everything I have. Falling in love is not what I planned in my life right now—or ever."

He let go of her hands and stepped away from her. "My marriage was a mess, Sage. It taught me that love is complicated and confusing and…messy. I didn't want that again. I've done everything I can to talk myself out of it this week, but I can't deny it anymore. I'm in love with you, Sage. I don't want to be, but there it is. I think I have been since you showed up on my doorstep with Chloe that first morning."

I don't want to be in love with you.

She heard his words as if from a long distance, but they still managed to pierce the haze of disbelief around her.

He didn't want to love her. He had done all he could to talk himself out of it, had been fighting it with everything he had. He didn't want to be in love, didn't want the complications or the mess.

Panic fluttered through her and she was suddenly desperate for space to breathe, to think.

She couldn't do this. She *couldn't*. She had spent her childhood trying desperately to gain the attention of a man who didn't want to love her, who had shut his emotions off abruptly when he married her stepmother, leaving Sage with nothing.

She couldn't put herself through this again.

It was a simple matter of self-preservation. She loved him. The surety of it washed over her like the most powerful of sneaker waves.

She loved him and she knew all about how messy and painful love could be. She was terrified that she would give everything to Eben and he would destroy her.

She drew in a shaky breath and pressed a hand to her stomach, to the fear that roiled and churned there. He was watching her out of those vivid green eyes and she knew she had to say something.

Something cold and hard.

Final.

She was weak, desperate, and very much feared she had no willpower at all when it came to Eben Spencer.

"You're not in love with me, Eben. You're attracted to me, just as I am to you, but it's not love. How could it be? We barely know each other. We're far too different. We…we want different things out of life. You want to conquer the world and I want to clean it up and leave it a better place."

"A little simplistic, don't you think?"

She grabbed the blanket that had fallen during the heat of their embrace and wrapped it around her shoulders again, hoping he wouldn't notice her trembling.

"Maybe it is simplistic. But look at us! You're the CEO of a billion-dollar hotel dynasty and I'm perfectly happy here in my little world, showing kids how to tell the difference between a clingfish and a sculpin. When you think about it, you have to see we have nothing in common."

"We can get past the few differences between us."

"I don't *want* to get past them."

For once in her life, she desperately wished she were a better liar. She could only pray he wouldn't look closely enough to see right through her. "I'm physically attracted to you, Eben, I can't deny that. I'm attracted to you and I adore Chloe. But I'm…I'm not in love with you. You're not the kind of man I want."

She was trembling in earnest now, sick with the lie

and had to pull the blanket tighter around her shoulders to hide it from him.

He gazed at her for a long moment and she forced herself to lift her chin and return his gaze, praying she could keep all trace of emotion from her features.

"Fair enough," he finally said, his voice quiet. "I guess that's all that really matters, isn't it?"

A few more moments, she told herself. *Keep it together just a few more moments and he'll be gone.*

"I'm sorry," she murmured.

His laugh was rough, humorless. "You don't have to apologize for not sharing my feelings, Sage. I told you love was messy. There's nothing messier than one person feeling things that aren't returned."

She could say nothing, could only clutch the blanket around her with nerveless fingers.

"I guess this is goodbye, then," he said, reaching for the doorknob. "I have to come back to Cannon Beach. There's no avoiding that—I just bought a hotel here. But on the rare occasions I come back to oversee the transition of The Sea Urchin to Spencer Hotels ownership, I'll do my best to stay out of your way."

She thought her heart would crack apart again. How many times was she going to have to say goodbye to him? She couldn't bear this. "You don't have to do that."

One corner of his mouth lifted in a grim ghost of a smile. "Yeah. Yeah, I do."

He opened the door but turned back before he passed through it for the last time. "Goodbye, Sage. Thank you again for tonight, for Chloe. You gave me back my daughter and I don't just mean by rescuing her from the tide. I'm not sending her to school, if that makes you feel any better. The two of us will tough it out and try to figure things out together."

"That's good. I'm happy for you both."

Oh, please go! She couldn't bear this.

He gave that ghost of a smile again then walked out, closing the door behind him.

She managed to keep it together, her hands gripping the blanket tightly while she listened to his footsteps down the stairs and then the creak of the outside door opening and closing.

She waited a few more moments, until she could be certain he was on his way back to his beach house, then a wild sob escaped her, then another and another.

By the time Conan climbed the stairs a few moments later, she had collapsed on the couch and was sobbing in earnest.

Her dog raced into the room, sniffed around the entire apartment, then barked. She opened her gritty eyes to find him giving her what she could only describe as an accusing stare.

She was *not* in the mood to deal with another contrary male.

"Don't look at me like that," she tried to snap, though it came out more like a wail. "You're supposed to be on my side, aren't you?"

Conan barked and she could swear he shook his head.

"It's better this way. You're smart enough to know that," she muttered. "It never would have worked out. We're just too different. Eventually he would figure out I'm not what he needs or wants. I can't go through that. You understand, don't you? I *can't*."

She knew the tears she was wiping away probably

negated some of the resoluteness of her voice but she couldn't seem to make them stop.

After another moment of glaring at her, Conan made a snorting, disgusted kind of sound. She thought he would amble back down to Anna's apartment. Instead, he came to her and licked at the tears on her cheeks, then settled beside her.

Sage wrapped her arms around his solid mass and wept.

Chapter 15

She finally fell into a fitful sleep sometime in the early hours of the morning, only to be awakened a short time later by a cold nose snuffling the side of her neck.

"Oh, for the love of Pete," she grunted. "Why don't you go harass Anna for once?"

Now the cold nose was joined by a paw on her shoulder. Conan threw in a whine for good measure.

She glanced at her alarm clock. Six o'clock. He'd at least given her an extra half-hour of sleep. She supposed she ought to be grateful for that much. She scrubbed at her face with one hand and sat up. Every single muscle in her body ached.

Her penance, she supposed, for a night of only a few moments' sleep. Conan whined impatiently at the emerging signs of life from her.

She frowned at him. "I guess a broken heart doesn't win me any amnesty when it comes to your daily run, does it?"

He moved his head from side to side in that uncanny way he had. Obstinate male. He barked and cocked his head toward the door. *Come on. Let's go, lazybones.*

For a nonverbal creature, he was remarkably communicative. She sighed, surrendering to the inevitable. She had to be up soon for work anyway. Perhaps a few moments of fresh sea air would help clear this wool from her head.

Ten minutes later, still aching and exhausted but now in her workout clothes, her hair yanked back into a ponytail, she followed Conan down the stairs at a much slower pace than his eager gallop.

Outside, the sun was just beginning its rise above the Coast Range. The sweetness of Abigail's flowers mingled with the sharp, citrusy scent of the Sitka spruce and pines. It was a beautiful morning. She only wished she had room in her heart past this pain to enjoy it.

Still, the cool air did help her wake up and by the time she propped open the beach access gate and took off across the sand, she was moving a little less gingerly.

As usual, the moment they hit the beach, he tugged the leash for her to head downtown—exactly the direction she did not want to go. She couldn't take the chance that Eben might be outside his beach house again. She just couldn't face him this morning.

Or ever.

"No, bud. This way."

Conan barked and kept going to the very limit of his retractable leash. She managed to find the strength to give him the resistance to keep him from dragging her up the beach with him.

Sage pointed stubbornly in the other direction, as far

away from Eben's beach house as she could get. "This way," she repeated.

Conan whined but had no choice but to comply. When she started a halfhearted jog down the beach, he came along with a huffy reluctance that might have made her smile under other circumstances.

"It's no fun when somebody makes you go somewhere you don't want to, is it?" she muttered, wondering if his keen communication skills stretched to understanding irony.

After a few moments of running, she had to admit she felt slightly better. The slanted light of day breaking across the wild, rugged shoreline didn't calm her soul, but at least the endorphins helped take the edge off the worst of her despair.

She had the grim feeling it would take many more of these morning runs before she could find the peace her heart needed.

Why did Eben and Chloe have to come into her life now—and leave it again—when she was still reeling from losing Abigail? It hardly seemed fair.

If she had met them both before Abigail died, would she have even let them into her life? She didn't know. Perhaps she wouldn't have been as vulnerable to falling for both of them if her emotions hadn't been so raw and unprotected.

No, that was a cop-out. She had a feeling she would have fallen hard for them no matter what the circumstances. Chloe was completely irresistible and Eben… well, Eben reached her heart in ways no man ever had.

Or ever would again, she was very much afraid.

She sobbed out a little breath. Just from exertion, she

told herself. It was good for her. Maybe if she ran hard enough, she could outpace the pain.

The tide rose and fell on Oregon's coast approximately every twelve hours. It was almost low tide now, the perfect time for beachcombing. She passed a few early-morning adventurers as she ran, most of them tourists who waved at her and smiled at Conan's friendly bark.

After a mile and a half, she stopped, her breath heaving in her lungs. That first rush of endorphins could only take her so far. She wasn't up for their full five-mile round trip, she decided. Three would have to do for today. She started to turn around, when suddenly Conan barked sharply and tugged his leash so hard he nearly toppled her into the sand.

"What's the matter with you?" She pulled after him to follow her but he gave another powerful lunge away from her and the leash slipped out of her perspiration-slicked hands.

In seconds, he was gone, tearing down the beach in the direction of Hug Point.

"Conan, get back here!" she yelled, but he completely ignored her, racing toward a couple of beachcombers several hundred yards away.

He was going to scare the life out of them if he raced up to them at full-speed, a big hairy red beast rocketing out of nowhere. She had to hope it wasn't a couple of senior citizens with an aversion to dogs and a team of attorneys on retainer.

She groaned and hurried after him.

"Conan! Get back here."

From here, she saw him jump all over one of them and she groaned.

And then she saw a small figure hugging Conan, heard a high, girlish giggle drift toward her on the breeze, and her heart seemed to stop. She shifted her gaze to see the other person on the beach who stood watching her approach, his dark hair gleaming in the dawn.

Eben and Chloe.

She wanted to turn and run hard in the other direction. She couldn't handle this. Not now. She needed time to restore the emotional reserves that had been depleted by her crying jag the night before.

Were her eyes as puffy and red as they felt? Oh, she hoped not.

It was far too late to turn and run back to the safety of Brambleberry House. Conan was already wriggling around them both with enthusiasm and Chloe was waving for all she was worth.

"Sage! Hi Sage!"

Somehow from deep inside her, she dug around until she found the courage to meet Eben's gaze. His features were impassive and revealed nothing as he watched her approach.

I'm in love with you.

For an instant, she could hear nothing but those words, not even the low murmur of the ocean.

He had offered her a priceless gift and she had rejected it with cruel finality.

I don't love you. You're not the kind of man I want.

She wanted to sob all over again at the lie. How could she face him in the cold light of day?

She looked away quickly and turned her attention back to Chloe. "Hey. Good morning. I didn't expect to see you today."

Or you can bet I would have been back at my house with the covers over my head right now.

"My dad woke me up. He said we had to try to find

a few more sand dollars to take home today so we can always remember our trip together. Look at how many we have. He's the best at finding them."

"You're lucky to get them before the gulls do. That's terrific."

"I'm going to make something cool with them. I don't know what yet but I'll figure something out."

"Great."

Oh, she did not want to be here. She wanted to grab her dog and run as far and as fast as they could until both of them collapsed in the sand.

"Look! My dad doesn't have his shoes on, either. Don't you think that's funny? He said he wanted to wriggle his toes in the sand one more time before we leave."

Against her will, Sage shifted her attention to Eben and saw that, indeed, his bare feet were covered in sand. She couldn't seem to look away from the sight.

"This isn't going to last long." His voice sounded tight, slightly strangled, and her gaze flew to his. A glimmer of emotion slipped through his steely reserve and she could swear he looked as if this was as awkward for him as it was for her. "To be honest, it's not what I expected. The sand is much colder than I thought it would be and I'm a little nervous about being pinched by a hermit crab."

"But you tried it, just like you said you wanted to, didn't you, Daddy?" Chloe chirped, oblivious to the currents zinging between them.

He smiled, more than a little self-consciousness in his expression, his eyes shimmering with love for his daughter.

As she gazed at him, something inside her seemed to shatter apart.

The stiff, controlled businessman she had mistaken

him for early in their relationship was nowhere in sight. She was stunned by the transformation. His jeans were rolled up, his toes were bare and he had his hands full of sand dollars.

She thought of him that first day when she had taken Chloe home to their beach house. He had been angry and humorless and she never would have imagined in a million years that one day she would find him digging his toes in the sand, laughing with his daughter, hunting for the treasures delivered by the sea.

Or that she would come to love him so dearly.

"Did *you* get pinched by a crab?" Chloe asked her. "You look funny."

Everything inside her began a slow, achy tremble and she suddenly felt as if her heart was like one of the gulls overhead, wheeling and diving across the sky.

"I'm…I'm fine."

Her voice sounded scratchy, and drew Eben's gaze. She saw echoes of longing in his eyes and a pain that matched her own.

She let out a breath, trying so hard to hang on to some shred of sanity. Nothing had changed. Not really. She was still terrified she would be left bruised and bloody.

No. She gazed at his bare feet and at the sight of them, it seemed as if her fear ebbed out to sea with the tide.

She loved him. More than that, she trusted him. He might not be comfortable digging his feet into the sand, but he had done it for his daughter's sake. And for his own. Because he wanted to know what it was like, even if it wasn't the most comfortable feeling in the world.

He was a good man. A wonderful man. If she didn't reach for the priceless gift he had offered her, she suddenly knew she would spend every moment of the rest of her life regretting it.

She wanted desperately to tell him but knew she could say nothing in front of Chloe. As if reading her mind, Conan, bless him, suddenly barked and took off after a gull down the beach.

"Hey! Get back here," Chloe giggled, running after him.

"I'm sorry," Eben finally said when the two of them were alone. He sat on a rock and started slipping his shoes back on. "I assumed with the late night and… everything…that you and Conan probably wouldn't be running this morning. I didn't mean to make you uncomfortable by forcing you to have to see us again."

She shook her head. "I'm not uncomfortable."

"No?" He rose from the rock. "Well, that makes one of us."

How difficult must it be for him to meet up with the woman who had coldly rejected him the night before?

"Don't be uncomfortable. Please."

"Sorry. I haven't had a lot of experience with this. I'm not exactly sure the correct protocol here. How does a man act smooth and urbane around the woman in front of whom he's made a complete ass of himself?"

She closed her eyes, hating the echo of hurt in his voice. She couldn't do this. She had to tell him the truth, no matter how painful.

"I lied, okay?" she finally blurted out. "I lied."

A dead silence met her pronouncement, with no sound at all but the waves and the gulls overhead.

"You…lied about what?"

She went to him and reached for his hand, wishing

she wasn't disheveled and sweaty for this. He seemed to always see her at her worst.

Yet he loved her anyway.

"I lied when I told you you weren't the kind of man I want, that I didn't love you. I've never told such a shocking untruth."

He suddenly looked as astonished as if she had just knocked him into the cold waves.

"You don't have to do this."

"Yes, I do." She squeezed his fingers. "I love you, Eben. I have from the beginning."

"Sage—"

She didn't give him time to say anything, just blurted out the rest. "I'm such a coward. I never realized that about myself until last night. I always thought I had everything figured out, that I was so in control of my world. I thought I had worked through all the stuff of my past and become a capable, well-adjusted adult."

"You are."

She shook her head, fighting tears. "No. Inside I'm eight years old again, watching my father walk away without a backward look. I was so afraid to admit my feelings, a-afraid to give you that same kind of power to hurt me. Instead, I decided I would be the one doing the walking."

He said nothing, just continued to watch her, as if he didn't quite know what to believe.

She drew in a breath and reached for his other hand. "I love you, Eben. I'm sorry if I…hurt you by lying and saying I didn't."

He gazed at her for one stunned moment and then he gave a little, disbelieving laugh and tugged her into his arms. As his hard mouth covered hers, Sage wrapped her arms around his waist and held on for dear life. The tight ache inside her eased and she could finally breathe again, for the first time in hours.

This was right. This was exactly where she belonged, right here in his arms.

"It was ripping my heart out to leave you," he murmured against her mouth. "I came down to the beach with Chloe one more time because I wanted one last connection to you. I felt closer to you here by the ocean than anywhere."

She kissed him again and the tenderness in his touch brought tears to her eyes.

"Don't cry," Eben murmured, kissing her cheeks where a few tears trickled down.

She laughed, wondering if her heart could burst from happiness. "These are happy tears. Not like the ones I cried all night. Conan had to drag me out of bed to run. All I wanted to do was pull the covers over my head and hibernate there for a few weeks."

"What if I'd missed you this morning?" he asked. "If I hadn't decided to bring Chloe here one last time? If you and Conan had decided to go in the other direction?"

She hugged him. "We're both here. That's the important thing."

"I think you're the reason I came back for The Sea Urchin, why it seemed so vital to me that I buy it. The hotel was only part of it. Call it fate or destiny or dharma or whatever, but I think everything that's happened was leading me right here, to this moment and to you."

It was the perfect thing to say and she could swear she tumbled even deeper in love with him. This was her prosaic, austere businessman, talking of fate and destiny?

Dharma? Had she ever been so wrong about a person in her life?

"I think it was Abigail."

He blinked. "Abigail?"

"I think she met you and fell for those gorgeous green eyes of yours."

She could swear a touch of color dusted his cheek-bones. "She did not."

"You didn't know her as well as I did. She always was a sucker for a gorgeous man. Since she couldn't have you for herself, I think she handpicked you for me and she's been doing everything she can since she met you to throw the two of us together."

Eben didn't look convinced, but since he reached for her and kissed her again, she decided the point wasn't worth arguing.

She received confirmation of it a moment later, though, when a sudden bark managed to pierce the lovely fog of desire swirling around her. She wrenched her mouth from Eben's to gaze at her dog.

Conan watched them from a few feet away with that uncanny intelligence in his eyes. He barked again, a de-lighted sound. It seemed ridiculous, but she could swear he looked pleased.

Chloe was close on the dog's heels and she studied them with startled concern in her green eyes. "Daddy, why are you holding on to Sage? Did she fall?"

His expression filled with sudden panic, as if he hadn't quite thought far enough ahead about explaining this to his daughter. Sage took pity on him and stepped in.

"You're exactly right. I fell, really hard. Harder than I ever thought I could. But you know what? Your dad was right there to pick me back up and help me find my feet. Isn't that lucky?"

Chloe's brow furrowed as she tried to sift through the layers of the explanation. Sage could tell she wasn't quite buying it. "So why is he still holding on to you?"

She laughed and slanted Eben a look out of the corner of her eyes. "I'll let you answer that one," she murmured.

He gave her a mock glare then turned to his daughter, "Well, after I helped her up, I discovered I didn't want to let her go."

Chloe seemed to accept that with surprising equanimity. She studied them for a moment longer, then shrugged. "You guys are weird," she finally said, then chased Conan across the sand again.

"I meant it. I *don't* want to let you go," Eben repeated fiercely after they were gone.

She wrapped her arms around his neck and held on tight. "I'm not going anywhere."

As he kissed her again, she could swear she heard Abigail's wicked laughter on the wind.

* * * * *

HIS SECOND-CHANCE FAMILY

Chapter 1

As signs from heaven went, this one seemed fairly prosaic.

No choir of angels, no booming voice from above or anything like that. It was simply a hand-lettered placard shoved into the seagrass in front of the massive, ornate Victorian that had drifted through her memory for most of her life.

Apartment For Rent.

Julia stared at the sign with growing excitement. It seemed impossible, a miracle. That *this* house, of all places, would be available for rent just as she was looking for a temporary home seemed just the encouragement her doubting heart needed to reaffirm her decision to pack up her twins and take a new teaching job in Cannon Beach.

Not even to herself had she truly admitted how worried she was that she'd made a terrible mistake moving here, leaving everything familiar and heading into the unknown.

Seeing that sign in front of Brambleberry House seemed an answer to prayer, a confirmation that this was where she and her little family were supposed to be.

"Cool house!" Maddie exclaimed softly, gazing up in awe at the three stories of Queen Anne Victorian, with its elaborate trim, cupolas and weathered shake roof. "It looks like a gingerbread house!"

Julia squeezed her daughter's hand, certain Maddie looked a little healthier today in the bracing sea air of the Oregon Coast.

"Cool dog!" Her twin, Simon, yelled. The words were barely out of his mouth when a giant red blur leaped over the low wrought-iron fence surrounding the house and wriggled around them with glee, as if he'd been waiting years just for them to walk down the beach.

The dog licked Simon's face and headbutted his stomach like an old friend. Julia braced herself to push him away if he got too rough with Maddie, but she needn't have worried. As if guided by some sixth sense, the dog stopped his wild gyrations and waited docilely for Maddie to reach out a tentative hand and pet him. Maddie giggled, a sound that was priceless as all the sea glass in the world to Julia.

"I think he likes me," she whispered.

"I think so, too, sweetheart." Julia smiled and tucked a strand of Maddie's fine short hair behind her ear.

"Do you really know the lady who lives here?" Maddie asked, while Simon was busy wrestling the dog in the sand.

"I used to, a long, long time ago," Julia answered. "She was my very best friend."

Her heart warmed as she remembered Abigail Dandridge and her unfailing kindness to a lonely little girl. Her mind filled with memories of admiring her vast doll collection, of pruning the rose hedge along the fence with her, of shared confidences and tea parties and sand dollar hunts along the beach.

"Like Jenna back home is my best friend?" Maddie asked.

"That's right."

Every summer of her childhood, Brambleberry House became a haven of serenity and peace for her. Her family rented the same cottage just down the beach each July. It should have been a time of rest and enjoyment, but her parents couldn't stop fighting even on vacation.

Whenever she managed to escape to Abigail and Brambleberry House, though, Julia didn't have to listen to their arguments, didn't have to see her mother's tears or her father's obvious impatience at the enforced holiday, his wandering eye.

Her fifteenth summer was the last time she'd been here. Her parents finally divorced, much to her and her older brother Charlie's relief, and they never returned to Cannon Beach. But over the years, she had used the image of this house, with its soaring gables and turrets, and the peace she had known here to help center her during difficult times.

Through her parents' bitter divorce, through her own separation from Kevin and worse. Much worse.

"Is she still your best friend?" Maddie asked.

"I haven't seen Miss Abigail for many, many years,"

she said. "But you know, I don't think I realized until just this moment how very much I've missed her."

She should never have let so much time pass before coming back to Cannon Beach. She had let their friendship slip away, too busy being a confused and rebellious teenager caught in the middle of the endless drama between her parents. And then had come college and marriage and family.

Perhaps now that she was back, they could find that friendship once more. She couldn't wait to find out.

She opened the wrought-iron gate and headed up the walkway feeling as if she were on the verge of something oddly portentous.

She rang the doorbell and heard it echo through the house. Anticipation zinged through her as she waited, wondering what she would possibly say to Abigail after all these years. Would her lovely, wrinkled features match Julia's memory?

No one answered after several moments, even after she rang the doorbell a second time. She stood on the porch, wondering if she ought to leave a note with their hotel and her cell phone number, but it seemed impersonal, somehow, after all these years.

They would just have to check back, she decided. She headed back down the stairs and started for the gate again just as she heard the whine of a power tool from behind the house.

The dog, who looked like a mix between an Irish setter and a golden retriever, barked and headed toward the sound, pausing at the corner of the house, head cocked, as if waiting for them to come along with him.

After a wary moment, she followed, Maddie and Simon close on her heels.

The dog led them to the backyard, where Julia found a couple of sawhorses set up and a man with brown hair and broad shoulders running a circular saw through a board.

She watched for a moment, waiting for their presence to attract his attention, but he didn't look up from his work.

"Hello," she called out. When he still didn't respond, she moved closer so she would be in his field of vision and waved.

"Excuse me!"

Finally, he shut off the saw and pulled his safety goggles off, setting them atop his head.

"Yeah?" he said.

She squinted and looked closer at him. He looked familiar. A hint of a memory danced across her subconscious and she was so busy trying to place him that it took her a moment to respond.

"I'm sorry to disturb you. I rang the doorbell but I guess you couldn't hear me back here with the power tools."

"Guess not."

He spoke tersely, as if impatient to return to work, and Julia could feel herself growing flustered. She had braced herself to see Abigail, not some solemn-eyed construction worker in a sexy tool belt.

"I...right. Um, I'm looking for Abigail Dandridge."

There was an awkward pause and she thought she saw something flicker in his blue eyes.

"Are you a friend of hers?" he asked, his voice not quite as abrupt as it had been before.

"I used to be, a long time ago. Can you tell me when she'll be back? I don't mind waiting."

The dog barked, only with none of the exuberance he had shown a few moments ago, almost more of a whine than a bark. He plopped onto the grass and dipped his chin to his front paws, his eyes suddenly morose.

The man gazed at the dog's curious behavior for a moment. A muscle tightened in his jaw then he looked back at Julia. "Abigail died in April. Heart attack in her sleep. I'm sorry to be the one to tell you."

Julia couldn't help her instinctive cry of distress. Even through her sudden surge of grief, she sensed when Maddie stepped closer and slipped a small, frail hand in hers.

Julia drew a breath, then another. "I…see," she mumbled.

Just one more loss in a long, unrelenting string, she thought. But this one seemed to pierce her heart like jagged driftwood.

It was silly, really, when she thought about it. Abigail hadn't been a presence in her life for sixteen years, but suddenly the loss of her seemed overwhelming.

She swallowed hard, struggling for composure. Her friend was gone, but her house was still here, solid and reassuring, weathering this storm as it had others for generations.

Somehow it seemed more important than ever that she bring her children here.

"I see," she repeated, more briskly now, though she thought she saw a surprising understanding in the deep blue of the man's eyes, so disconcertingly familiar. She knew him. She knew she did.

"I suppose I should talk to you, then. The sign out front says there's an apartment for rent. How many bedrooms does it have?"

He gave her a long look before turning away to pick up another board and carry it to the saw. "Three bedrooms, two of them on the small side. Kitchen's been redone in the last few months and the electricity's been upgraded but the bathroom plumbing's still in pretty rough shape."

"I don't care about that, as long as everything works okay. Three bedrooms is exactly the size my children and I need. Is it still available?"

"Can't say."

She pursed her lips. "Why not?"

He shrugged. "I don't own the place. I live a few houses down the beach. I'm just doing some repairs for the owners."

Something about what he said jarred loose a flood of memories and she stared at him more closely. Suddenly everything clicked in and she gasped, stunned she hadn't realized his identity the instant she had clapped eyes on him.

"Will? Will Garrett?"

He peered at her. "Do I know you?"

She managed a smile. "Probably not. It's been years."

She held out a hand, her pulse suddenly wild and erratic, as it had always been around him.

"Julia Blair. You knew me when I was Julia Hudson. My parents rented a cottage between your house and Brambleberry House every summer of my childhood until I was fifteen. I used to follow you and my older brother Charlie around everywhere."

Will Garrett. She'd forgotten so much about those summers, but never him. She had wondered whether she would see him, had wondered about his life and where he might end up. She never expected to find him standing in front of her on her first full day in town.

"It's been years!" she repeated. "I can't believe you're still here."

At her words, it took Will all of about two seconds to remember her. When he did, he couldn't understand why he hadn't seen it before. He had yearned for Julia Hudson that summer as only a relatively innocent sixteen-year-old boy can ache. He had dreamed of her green eyes and her dimples and her soft, burgeoning curves.

She had been his first real love and had haunted his dreams.

She had promised to keep in touch but she hadn't called or answered any of his letters and he remembered how his teenage heart had been shattered. But by the time school started a month later, he'd been so busy with football practice and school and working for his dad's carpentry business on Saturdays that he hadn't really had much time to wallow in his heartbreak.

Julia looked the same—the same smile, the same auburn hair, the same appealing dimples—while he felt as if he had aged a hundred years.

He could barely remember those innocent, carefree days when he had been certain the world was his for the taking, that he could achieve anything if only he worked hard enough for it.

She was waiting for a response, he realized, still holding her hand outstretched in pleased welcome. He held up his hands in their leather work gloves as an excuse not to touch her. After an awkward moment, she dropped her arms to her side, though the smile remained fixed on her lovely features.

"I can't believe you're still here in Cannon Beach," she repeated. "How wonderful that you've stayed all these years! I remember how you loved it here."

He wouldn't call it wonderful. There were days he felt like some kind of prehistoric iceman, frozen forever in place. He had wondered for some time if he ought to pick up and leave, go *anywhere*, just as long as it wasn't here.

Someone with his carpentry skills and experience could find work just about any place. He had thought about it long and hard, especially at night when the memories overwhelmed him and the emptiness seemed to ring through his house but he couldn't seem to work past the inertia to make himself leave.

"So how have you been?" Julia asked. "What about family? Are you married? Any kids?"

Okay, he wasn't a prehistoric iceman. He was pretty certain they couldn't bleed and bleed and bleed.

He set his jaw and picked up the oak board he was shaping for a new window frame in one of the third-floor bedrooms of Brambleberry House.

"You'll have to talk to Sage Benedetto or Anna Galvez about the apartment," he said tersely. "They're the new owners. They should be back this evening."

He didn't quite go so far as to fire up the circular saw but it was a clear dismissal, rude as hell. He had to hope she got the message that he wasn't interested in any merry little trips down memory lane.

She gave him a long, measuring look while the girl beside her edged closer.

After a moment, she offered a smile that was cool and polite but still managed to scorch his conscience. "I'll do that. Thank you. It's good to see you again, Will."

He nodded tersely. This time, he did turn on the circular saw, though he was aware of every move she and her children made in the next few moments. He knew just when they walked around the house with Abigail's clever Irish Setter mix Conan following on their heels.

He gave up any pretense of working when he saw them head across the lane out front, then head down the beach. She still walked with grace and poise, her chin up as if ready to take on the world, just as she had when she was fifteen years old.

And her kids. That curious boy and the fragile-looking girl with the huge, luminescent blue eyes. Remembering those eyes, he had to set down the board and press a hand to the dull ache in his chest, though he knew from two years' experience nothing would ease it.

Booze could dull it for a moment but not nearly long enough. When the alcohol wore off, everything rushed back, worse than before.

He was still watching their slow, playful progress down the beach when Conan returned to the backyard. The dog barked once and gave him a look Will could only describe as peeved. He planted his haunches in front of the worktable and glared at him.

Abigail would have given him exactly the same look for treating an old friend with such rudeness.

"Yeah, I was a jerk," he muttered. "She caught me off guard, that's all. I wasn't exactly prepared for a ghost from the past to show up out of the blue this afternoon."

The dog barked again and Will wondered, not for the first time, what went on inside his furry head. Conan had a weird way of looking at everybody as if he knew exactly what they might be thinking and he managed to communicate whole diatribes with only a bark and a certain expression in his doleful eyes.

Abigail had loved the dog. For that reason alone, Will would have tolerated him since his neighbor had been one of his favorite people on earth. But Conan had also showed an uncanny knack over the last two years for knowing just when Will was at low ebb.

More than once, there had been times when he had been out on the beach wondering if it would be easier just to walk out into the icy embrace of the tide than to survive another second of this unrelenting grief.

No matter the time of day or night, Conan would somehow always show up, lean against Will's legs until the despair eased, and then would follow him home before returning to Brambleberry House and Abigail.

He sighed now as the dog continued to wordlessly reprimand him. "What do you want me to do? Go after her?"

Conan barked and Will shook his head. "No way. Forget it."

He *should* go after her, at least to apologize. He had been unforgivably rude. The hell of it was, he didn't really know why. He wasn't cold by nature. Through the last two years, he had tried to hold to the hard-fought philosophy that just because his insides had been ripped apart and because sometimes the grief and pain seemed to crush the life out of him, he hadn't automatically been handed a free pass to hurt others.

Lashing out at others around him did nothing to ease his own pain so he made it a point to be polite to just about everybody.

Sure, there were random moments when his bleakness slipped through. At times, Sage and Anna and other friends had been upset at him when he pushed away their efforts to comfort him. More than a few times, truth be told. But he figured it was better to be by himself during those dark moments than to do as he'd just done, lash out simply because he didn't know how else to cope.

He had no excuse for treating her poorly. He had just seen her there looking so lovely and bright with her energetic son and her pretty little daughter and every muscle inside him had cramped in pain.

The children set it off. He could see that now. The girl had even looked a little like Cara—same coloring, anyway, though Cara had been chubby and round where Julia's daughter looked as if she might blow away in anything more than a two-knot wind.

It hadn't only been the children, though. He had seen Julia standing there in a shaft of sunlight and for a moment, long-dormant feelings had stirred inside him that he wanted to stay dead and buried like the rest of his life.

No matter how screwed up he was, he had no business being rude to her and her children. Like it or not, he would have to apologize to her, especially if Anna and Sage rented her the apartment.

He lived three houses away and spent a considerable amount of time at Brambleberry House, both because he was busy with various remodeling projects and because he considered the new owners—Abigail's heirs—his friends.

He didn't want Julia Hudson Blair or her children here at Brambleberry House. If he were honest with himself, he could admit that he would have preferred if she had stayed a long-buried memory.

But she hadn't. She was back in Cannon Beach with

her children, looking to rent an apartment at Bramble-berry House, so apparently she planned to stay at least awhile.

Chances were good he would bump into her again, so he was going to have to figure out a way to apologize.

He watched their shapes grow smaller and smaller as they walked down the beach toward town and he rubbed the ache in his chest, wondering what it would take to convince Sage and Anna to find a different tenant.

Chapter 2

"Will we get to see inside the pretty house this time, Mommy?"

Julia lifted her gaze from the road for only an instant to glance in the rearview mirror of her little Toyota SUV. Even from here, she could see the excitement in Maddie's eyes and she couldn't help but smile in return at her daughter.

"That's the plan," she answered, turning her attention back to the road as she drove past a spectacular hotel set away from the road. Someday when she was independently wealthy with unlimited leisure time, she wanted to stay at The Sea Urchin, one of the most exclusive boutique hotels on the coast.

"I talked to one of the owners of the house an hour ago," Julia continued, "and she invited us to walk through and see if the apartment will work for us,"

"I hope it does," Simon said. "I really liked that cool dog."

"I'm not sure the dog lives there," she answered. "He might belong to the man we talked to this morning. Will Garrett. He doesn't live there, he was just doing some work on the house."

"I'm glad he doesn't live there," Maddie said in her whisper-soft voice. "He was kind of cranky."

Julia agreed, though she didn't say as much to her children. Will had been terse, bordering on rude, and for the life of her she couldn't figure out why. What had she done? She hadn't seen him in sixteen years. It seemed ridiculous to assume he might be angry, after all these years, simply because she hadn't written to him as she had promised.

They had been friends of a sort—and more than friends for a few glorious weeks one summer. She remembered moonlight bonfires and holding hands in the movies and stealing kisses on the beach.

She would have assumed their shared past warranted at least a little politeness but apparently he didn't agree. The Will Garrett she remembered had been far different from the surly stranger they met that afternoon. She couldn't help wondering if he treated everyone that way or if she received special treatment.

"He was simply busy," she said now to her children. "We interrupted his work and I think he was eager to get back to it. We grown-ups can sometimes be impatient."

"I remember," Simon said. "Dad was like that sometimes."

The mention of Kevin took her by surprise. Neither twin referred to their father very often anymore. He had died more than two years ago and had been a distant presence for some time before that, and they had all walked what felt like a million miles since then.

Brambleberry House suddenly came into view, rising above the fringy pines and spruce trees. She slowed, savoring the sight of the spectacular Victorian mansion silhouetted against the salmon-colored sky, with the murky blue sea below.

That familiar sense of homecoming washed over her again as she pulled into the pebbled driveway. She wanted to live here with her children. To wake up in the morning with that view of the sea out her window and the smell of roses drifting up from the gardens and the solid comfort of those walls around her.

As she pulled into the driveway and turned off the engine, she gave a silent prayer that she and the twins would click with the new owners. The one she'd spoken with earlier—Sage Benedetto—had seemed cordial when she invited Julia and her children to take a look at the apartment, but Julia was almost afraid to hope.

"Mom, look!" Simon exclaimed. "There's the dog! Does that mean he lives here?"

As she opened her door to climb out, she saw the big shaggy red dog waiting by the wrought-iron gates, almost as if he somehow knew they were on their way.

"I don't know. We'll have to see."

"Oh, I hope so." Maddie pushed a wisp of hair out of her eyes. She looked fragile and pale. Though Julia would have liked to walk from their hotel downtown to enjoy the spectacular views of Cannon Beach at sunset, she had been afraid Maddie wouldn't have the strength for another long hike down the beach and back.

Now she was grateful she had heeded her motherly

instincts that seemed to have become superacute since Maddie's illness.

More than anything—more than she wanted to live in this house, more than she wanted this move to work out, more than she wanted to *breathe*—she wanted her daughter to be healthy and strong.

"I hope we can live here," Maddie said. "I really like that dog."

Julia hugged her daughter and helped her out of her seatbelt. Maddie slipped a hand in hers while Simon took his sister's other hand. Together, the three of them walked through the gate, where the one-dog welcoming committee awaited them.

The dog greeted Simon with the same enthusiasm he had shown that morning, wagging his tail fiercely and nudging Simon's hand with his head. After a moment of attention from her son, the dog turned to Maddie. Julia went on full mother-bear alert, again ready to step in if necessary, but the dog showed the same uncanny gentleness to Maddie.

He simply planted his haunches on the sidewalk in front of her, waiting as still as one of those cheap plaster dog statues for Maddie to reach out with a giggle and pet his head.

Weird, she thought, but she didn't have time to figure it out before the front door opened. A woman wearing shorts and a brightly colored tank top stepped out onto the porch. She looked to be in her late twenties and was extraordinarily lovely in an exotic kind of way, with blonde wavy hair pulled back in a ponytail and an olive complexion that spoke of a Mediterranean heritage.

She walked toward them with a loose-hipped gait and a warm smile.

"Hi!" Her voice held an open friendliness and Julia instinctively responded to it. She could feel the tension in her shoulders relax a little as the other woman held out a hand.

"I'm Sage Benedetto. You must be the Blairs."

She shook it. "Yes. I'm Julia and these are my children, Simon and Maddie."

Sage dropped her hand and turned to the twins. "Hey kids. Great to meet you! How old are you? Let me guess. Sixteen?"

They both giggled. "No!" Simon exclaimed. "We're seven."

"Seven? Both of you?"

"We're twins." Maddie said in her soft voice.

"Twins? No kidding? Cool! I've always wanted to have a twin. You ever dress up in each others' clothes and try to trick your mom?"

"No!" Maddie said with another giggle.

"We're not *identical* twins," Simon said with a roll of his eyes. "We're *fraternal.*"

"Of course you are. Silly me. 'Cause one of you is a boy and one is a girl, right?"

Sage obviously knew her way around children, Julia thought as she listened to their exchange. That was definitely a good sign. She had observed during her career as an elementary school teacher that many adults didn't really know how to talk to kids. They either tried too hard to be buddies or treated them with obvious condescension. Sage managed to find the perfect middle ground.

"I see you've met Conan," Sage said, scratching the big dog under the chin.

"Is he your dog?" Simon asked.

She smiled at the animal with obvious affection. "I

guess you could say that. Or I'm his human. Either way, we kind of look out for each other, don't we, bud?"

Oddly, Julia could swear the dog grinned.

"Thank you again for agreeing to show the apartment to us tonight," she said.

Sage turned her smile to Julia. "No problem. I'm sorry we weren't here when you came by the first time. You said on the telephone that you knew Abigail."

That pang of loss pinched at her again as she imagined Abigail out here in the garden, her big floppy straw hat and her gardening gloves and the tray of lemonade always waiting on the porch.

"Years ago," she answered, then was compelled to elaborate.

"Every summer my family rented a house near here. The year I was ten, my brother and I were running around on the beach and I cut my foot on a broken shell. Abigail heard me crying and came down to help. She brought me back up to the house, fixed me a cookie and doctored me up. We were fast friends after that. Every year, I would run up here the minute we pulled into the driveway of our cottage. Abigail always seemed so happy to see me and we would get along as if I had never left."

The other woman smiled, though there was an edge of sorrow to it. Julia wondered again how Sage had ended up as one of the two new owners of Brambleberry House after Abigail's death.

"Sounds just like Abigail," Sage said. "She made friends with everyone she met."

"I've been terrible about keeping in contact with her," Julia admitted with chagrin as they walked into the entryway of the house, with its sweeping staircase and polished honey oak trim. "I was so sorry to hear about her death—more sorry than I can say that I let so much time go by without calling her. I suppose some foolish part of me just assumed she would always be here. Like the ocean and the seastacks."

The dog—Conan—whined a little, almost as if he understood their conversation, though Julia knew that was impossible.

"I think we all felt that way," Sage said. "It's been four months and it still doesn't seem real."

"Will said she died of a heart attack in her sleep."

"That's right. I find some comfort in knowing that if she could have chosen her exit scene, that's exactly how she would have wanted to go. The doctors said she probably slept right through it."

Sage paused and gave her a considering kind of look. "Do you know Will, then?"

Julia could feel color climb her cheekbones. How foolish could she be to blush over a teenage crush on Will Garrett, when the man he had become obviously wanted nothing to do with her?

"Knew him," she corrected. "It all seems so long ago. The cottage we rented every year was next door to his. We socialized a little with his family and he and my older brother Charlie were friends. I usually tried to find a way to tag along, to their great annoyance."

She had a sudden memory of mountain biking through the mists and primordial green of Ecola National Park, then cooling off in the frigid surf of Indian Beach, the gulls wheeling overhead and the ocean song a sweet accompaniment.

Will had kissed her for the first time there, while her brother was busy body surfing through the baby breakers and not paying them any attention. It had just been a quick, furtive brush of his lips, but she could suddenly remember with vivid clarity how it had warmed her until she forgot all about the icy swells.

"He was my first love," she confessed.

Oh no. Had she really said that out loud? She wanted to snatch the words back but they hung between them. Sage turned around, sudden speculation sparking in her exotic, tilted eyes, and Julia could feel herself blushing harder.

"Is that right?"

"A long time ago," she answered, though she was certain she had said those words about a million times already. So much for making a good impression. She was stuttering and blushing and acting like an idiot over a man who barely remembered her.

To her relief, Sage didn't pursue it as they reached the second floor of the big house.

"This is the apartment we're renting. It's been vacant most of the time in the five years I've lived here. Once in a while Abigail opened it up on a short-term basis to various people in need of a comfortable place to crash for a while. Since Anna and I inherited Brambleberry House, we've kept Will busy fixing it up so we could rent out the space."

Will again. Couldn't she escape him for three seconds? "Convenient that he lives close," she said.

"It's more convenient because he's the best carpenter around. With all the work that needs to be done to Brambleberry House, we could hire him as our resident carpenter. Good thing for us he likes to stay busy."

She remembered again the pain in his eyes. She

wanted to ask Sage the reason for it, but she knew that would be far too presumptuous.

Anyway, she wasn't here to talk about Will Garrett. She was trying to find a clean, comfortable place for her children.

When Sage opened the door to the apartment, Julia felt a little thrill of anticipation.

"Ready to take a look?" Sage asked.

"Absolutely." She walked through the door with the oddest sense of homecoming.

The apartment met all her expectations and more. Much, much more. She walked from room to room with a growing excitement. The kitchen was small but had new appliances and what looked like new cabinets stained a lovely cherry color. Each of the three bedrooms had fresh coats of paint. Though two of them were quite small, nearly every room had a breathtaking view of the ocean.

"It's beautiful," she exclaimed as she stood in the large living room, with its wide windows on two sides that overlooked the sea.

"Will did a good job, didn't he?" Sage said.

Before Julia could answer, the children came into the room, followed by the dog.

"Wow. This place is so cool!" Simon exclaimed.

"I like it, too," Maddie said. "It feels friendly."

"How can a house feel friendly?" her brother scoffed. "It's just walls and a roof and stuff."

Sage didn't seem to mind Maddie's whimsy. Her features softened and she laid a hand on Maddie's hair with a gentleness that warmed Julia's heart.

"I think you're absolutely right, Miss Maddie," she answered. "I've always thought Brambleberry House was just about the friendliest house I've ever been lucky enough to live in."

Maddie smiled back and Julia could see a bond forming between the two of them, just as the children already seemed to have a connection with Conan.

"When can we move in?" Simon asked.

Julia winced at her son's bluntness. "We've still got some details to work out," she said quickly, stepping in to avoid Sage feeling any sense of obligation to answer before she was completely comfortable with the idea of them as tenants. "Nothing's settled yet. Why don't the two of you play with Conan for a few moments while I talk with Ms. Benedetto?"

He seemed satisfied with that and headed to the window seat, followed closely by his sister and Sage's friendly dog.

Her children were remarkably adept at entertaining themselves. Little wonder, she thought with that echo of sadness. They had spent three years developing patience during Maddie's endless string of appointments and procedures.

When they seemed happily settled petting the dog, she turned back to Sage. "I'm sorry about that. I understand that you need to check references and everything and talk to the co-owner before you make a decision. I'm definitely interested, at least through the school year."

Sage opened her mouth to answer but before she could speak, the dog gave a sudden sharp bark, his ears on alert. He rushed for the open door to the landing and she could hear his claws scrabbling on the steps just an instant before the front door opened downstairs.

Sage didn't even blink at the dog's eager behavior. "Oh, good. That's Anna Galvez. I was hoping she'd be home before you left so she could have a chance to meet you. Anna took over By-the-Wind, Abigail's old book and giftshop in town."

"I remember the place. I spent many wonderful rainy afternoons curled up in one of the easy chairs with a book."

"Haven't we all?" Sage said with a smile, then walked out to the stairs to call down to the other woman.

A moment later, a woman with dark hair and petite, lovely features walked up the stairs, her hand on Conan's fur.

She greeted Julia with a smile slightly more reserved than Sage's warm friendliness. "Hello."

Her smile warmed when she greeted the curious twins. "Hey, there," she said.

Sage performed a quick introduction. "Julia and her twins are moving to Cannon Beach from Boise. Julia's going to be teaching fifth grade at the elementary school and she's looking for an apartment."

"Lovely to meet you. Welcome to Oregon!"

"Thank you," Julia said. "I used to spend summers near here when I was a child."

"She's one of Abigail's lost sheep finally come home," Sage said with a smile that quickly turned mischievous. "Oh, you'll be interested to know that Will was her first love."

To Julia's immense relief, Sage added the latter in an undertone too low for the children to hear, even if they'd been paying attention. Still, she could feel herself blush again. She really *had* to stop doing that every time Will Garrett's name was mentioned.

"I was fifteen. Another lifetime ago. We barely recognized each other when I bumped into him earlier today outside. He seems…very different than he was at six-teen."

Sage's teasing smile turned sober. "He has his rea-sons," she said softly.

She and Anna gave each other a quick look loaded with layers of subtext that completely escaped Julia.

"Thank you for showing me the apartment. I have to tell you, from what I see, it would be perfect for us. It's exactly what I'm looking for, with room for the children to play, incredible views and within walking distance to the school. But I certainly understand that you need to check references and credit history before renting it to me. Feel free to talk to the principal of the elementary school who hired me, and any of the other references I gave you in our phone conversation. If you need any-thing else, you have my cell number and the number of the hotel where we're staying."

"Or we could always talk to Will and see what he re-members from when you were fifteen."

Julia flashed a quick look to Sage and was relieved to find the other woman smiling again. She had no idea what Will Garrett remembered about her. Nothing pleas-ant, obviously, or he probably would have shown a little more warmth when she encountered him earlier.

"Will may not be the best character reference. If I remember correctly, I still owe him an ice-cream cone. He bet me I couldn't split a geoduck without using my hands. I tried for days but the summer ended before I could pay him back."

"Good thing you're sticking around," Anna said. "You can pay back your debt now. We've still got ice cream."

"And geoducks," Sage said. "Maybe you're more agile than you used to be."

She laughed, liking both women immensely. As she gathered the children and headed down the stairs to her car, Julia could only wish for a little more agility. Then she would cross her toes and her fingers that Sage Benedetto and Anna Galvez would let her and her twins rent their vacant apartment.

She couldn't remember when she had wanted anything so much.

"So what do you think?" Sage asked as she and Anna stood at the window watching the schoolteacher strap her children into the backseat of her little SUV.

She looked like she had the process down to a science, Sage thought, something she still struggled with when she drove Chloe anywhere. She could never figure out how to tighten the darn seat belt over the booster chair with her stepdaughter-to-be. She ought to have Julia give her lessons.

"No idea," Anna replied. "I barely talked to her for five minutes. But she seems nice enough."

"She belongs here."

Anna snorted. "And you figured that out in one quick fifteen-minute meeting?"

"Not at all." Sage grinned. She couldn't help herself. "I figured it out in the first thirty seconds."

"We still have to check her references. I'm sorry if this offends you, but I can't go on karma alone on this one."

"I know. But I'm sure they'll check out." Sage couldn't have said how she knew, she just did. Somehow she was certain Abigail would have wanted Julia and her twins to live at Brambleberry House.

"Did you see her blush when Will's name came up?"

Anna shook her head. "Leave it alone, Sage. You engaged women think you have to match up the entire universe."

"Not the entire universe. Just the people I love, like Will."

And you, she added silently. She thought of the loneliness in Anna's eyes, the tiny shadow of sadness she was certain Anna never guessed showed on her expression.

Their neighbor wasn't the only one who deserved to be happy, but she decided she—and Abigail—could only focus on one thing at a time. "Will has had so much pain in his life. Wouldn't you love to see him smile again?"

"Of course. But Julia herself said she hadn't seen him in years and they barely recognized each other. And we don't even know the woman. She could be married."

"Widowed. She told me that on the phone. Two years, the same as Will."

Compassion flickered in Anna's brown eyes. "Those poor children, to lose their father at such a young age." She paused. "That doesn't mean whatever scheme you're hatching has any chance of working."

"I know. But it's worth a shot. Anyway, Conan likes them and that's the important thing, isn't it, bud?"

The dog barked, giving his uncanny grin. As far as Sage was concerned, references or not, that settled the matter.

Chapter 3

Sage and Anna apparently had a new tenant.

Will slowed his pickup down as he passed Bramble-berry House coming from the south. He couldn't miss the U-Haul trailer hulking in the driveway and he could see Sage heading into the house, her arms stacked high with boxes. Anna was loading her arms with a few more while Julia's children played on the grass not far away with Conan. Even from here he could see the dog's glee at having new playmates.

Damn. This is the price he paid for his inaction. He should have stopped by a day or two earlier and at least tried to dissuade Anna and Sage from taking her on as a tenant.

It probably wouldn't have done any good, he acknowledged. Both of Abigail's heirs could be as stubborn as crooked nails when they had their minds made up about something. Still, he should have at least made the attempt.

But what could he have said, really, that wouldn't have made him sound like a raving lunatic?

Yeah, she seems nice enough and I sure was crazy about her when I was sixteen. But I don't want her around anymore because I don't like being reminded I'm still alive.

He sighed and turned off his truck. He wanted nothing more than to drive past the house and hide out at his place down the beach until she moved on but there was no way on earth his blasted conscience would let him leave three women and two kids to do all that heavy lifting on their own.

He climbed out of his pickup and headed to the trailer. He reached it just as the top box on Anna's stack started to slide.

He lunged for it and plucked the wobbly top box just before it would have hit the ground, earning a surprised look from Anna over the next-highest box.

"Wow! Good catch," she said, a smile lifting her studious features. "Lucky you were here."

"Rule of thumb—your stack of boxes probably shouldn't exceed your own height."

She smiled. "Good advice. I'm afraid I can get a little impatient sometimes."

"Is that it? I thought you just like to bite off more than you can chew."

She made a wry face at him. "That, too. How did you know we needed help?"

He shrugged. "I was driving past and saw your leaning tower and thought you might be able to use another set of arms."

"We've got plenty of arms. We just need some arms with muscle. Thanks for stopping."

"Glad to help." It was a blatant lie but he decided she didn't need to know that.

She turned and headed up the stairs and he grabbed several boxes from inside the truck and followed her, trying to ignore the curious mingle of dread and anticipation in his gut.

He didn't want to see Julia again. He had already dreamed about her the last two nights in a row. More contact would only wedge her more firmly into his head.

At the same time, part of him—maybe the part that was still sixteen years old somewhere deep inside—couldn't help wondering how the years might have changed her.

Anna was breathing hard by the time they reached the middle floor of the house, where the door to the apartment had been propped open with a small stack of books.

"I could have taken another one of your boxes," he said to Anna.

She made a face. "Show-off. Are you even working up a sweat?"

"I'm sweating on the inside," he answered, which was nothing less than the truth.

The source of his trepidation spoke to Anna an instant later.

"Thanks so much," Julia Blair said in her low, sexy voice. "Those go in Simon's bedroom."

Will lowered his boxes so he could see over them and found her standing in the middle of the living room directing traffic. She wore capris and a stretchy yellow T-shirt. With her hair pulled back into a ponytail, she looked fresh and beautiful and not much older than she'd been that last summer together.

He didn't miss the shock in her eyes when she spied him behind the boxes. "Will! What are you doing here?"

He shrugged, uncomfortable at her obvious shock. Why *shouldn't* he be here helping? It was the neighborly thing to do. Had he really been such a complete jerk the other day that she find his small gesture of assistance now so stunning?

"Do these go into the same room?"

She looked flustered, her cheeks slightly pink. "Um, no. Those are my things. They go in my bedroom, the big one overlooking the ocean."

He headed in the direction she pointed, noting again no sign of a Mr. Blair. On some instinctive level, he had subconsciously picked up the fact that she wore no wedding ring when he had seen her the other day and she had spoken only of herself and her children needing an apartment. Was she widowed, divorced, or never married?

He only wondered out of mild curiosity about the road she might have traveled in the years since he had seen her. Or at least that's what he told himself.

In her bedroom, he found stacks of boxes, some of them open and overflowing with books. The queen-size bed was already made up with a cozy-looking comforter in soft blue tones, with piles of pillows against the headboard.

An image flashed in his head of her tousled and welcoming, her auburn hair spread out on those pillows and a soft, aroused smile teasing the edges of those lovely features.

He dropped the boxes so abruptly he barely missed his toe.

Whoa. Where the hell did that come from?

He had no business thinking about her at all, forget about in some kind of sultry, welcoming pose.

When he returned to the living room, her cheeks were still flushed and she didn't meet his gaze, as if she were embarrassed about something. It was a damn good thing she couldn't know the inappropriate direction of his thoughts.

"I'm sorry." She fidgeted with a stack of books in her hand. "I probably sounded terribly ungracious when you first came in. I just didn't expect you to show up and start hauling my boxes inside."

"No problem."

He started to head toward the door, but she apparently wasn't content with his short response. "Why, again, are you helping me move in?"

He shrugged. What did it matter? He was here, wasn't he? Did they really have to analyze the reasons why? "I was heading home after a job south of here and saw your U-Haul out front. I figured you could use a hand."

"How...neighborly of you."

"Around here we look out for each other." It was nothing less than the truth.

"I remember." She smiled a little. "That's one of the reasons I wanted to come back to Cannon Beach. I remembered that sense of community with great affection."

She set the stack of books down on the coffee table, then turned a searching gaze toward him. "Forgive me, Will, but...for some reason I had the impression you weren't exactly overjoyed to see me the other day."

And he thought he'd been so careful at hiding his

reaction. He shifted his weight, not sure how to answer. Any apology would only lead to explanations he was eager to avoid at all costs.

"You took me by surprise, that's all," he finally said.

"A mysterious stranger emerging from your distant past?"

"Something like that. Sixteen seems like a long, long time ago."

She nodded solemnly but said nothing. After an awkward moment, he headed for the door again.

"Anyway, I'm sorry if I seemed less than welcoming." It needed to be said, he decided. Apparently, she was going to be his neighbor and he disliked the idea of this uneasiness around her continuing. That didn't make the words any easier to get out. "You caught me at a bad moment, that's all. But I'm sorry if I gave you the impression I didn't want you here. It was nothing personal."

"I must say, that's a relief to hear."

She smiled, warm and sincere, and for just an instant he was blinded by it, remembering the surge of his blood every time he had been anywhere close to her that last summer.

Before he could make his brain work again, Sage walked up carrying one bulky box.

"What do you have in these, for Pete's sake? Did you pack along every brick from your old place?"

Julia laughed, a light, happy sound that stirred the hair on the back of his neck.

"Not bricks, but close, I'm afraid. Books. I left a lot in storage back in Boise but I couldn't bear to leave them all behind."

So that hadn't changed about her. When she was a kid, she always seemed to have her nose in a book. He and her brother used to tease her unmercifully about being a bookworm.

That last summer, he had been relentless in his efforts to drag her attention away from whatever book she was reading so she would finally notice him....

He dragged his mind away from the past and the dumb, self-absorbed jerk he'd been. He didn't want to remember those times. What was the damn point? That stupid, eager, infatuated kid was gone, buried under the weight of the years and pain that had piled up since then.

Instead, he left Sage and Julia to talk about books and headed back down the sweeping Brambleberry House stairs. On the way, he passed Anna heading back up, carrying a suitcase in each hand. He tried to take them from her but she shook him off.

"I've got these. There are some bulkier things in the U-Haul you could bring up, though."

"Sure," he answered.

In the entryway on the ground floor, he heard music coming from inside Anna's apartment. Through the open doorway, he caught a glimpse of her television set where a Disney DVD was just starting up.

Julia's twins must have finished playing and come inside. He spotted Julia's boy on the floor in front of the TV, his arm slung across Conan's back. Both of them sensed Will's presence and looked up. He started to greet them but the boy put a finger to his mouth and pointed to Abigail's favorite armchair.

Will followed his gaze and found the girl—Maddie—curled up there, fast asleep.

She looked small and fragile, with her too-pale skin and thin wrists. There was something going on with her, but he was pretty sure he was better off not knowing.

He waved to the boy, then headed down the porch steps to the waiting U-Haul.

It was nearly empty now except for perhaps a half-dozen more boxes, a finely crafted Mission-style rocking chair and something way in the back, a bulky-looking item wrapped in an old blanket that had been secured with twine.

He went for the rocking chair first. Might as well get the tough stuff out of the way. It was harder to carry than he expected—wide and solid, made of solid oak—but more awkward than really heavy.

He made it without any trouble up the porch steps and was trying to squeeze it through the narrow front door without bunging up the doorframe moldings when Sage came down the stairs.

"Okay, Superman. Let me help you with that."

"I can handle it."

"Only because of your freakish strength, maybe."

He felt his mouth quirk. Sage always managed to remind him he still had the ability to smile.

"I had my can of spinach just an hour ago so I think I've got this covered. There are a few more boxes in the U-Haul. Those ought to keep you busy and out of trouble."

She stuck her tongue out at him and he smiled at the childish gesture, with a sudden, profound gratitude for the friendship of those few people around him who had sustained him through the wrenching pain of the last two years.

"Which is it? Are you Popeye or Superman?"

"Take your pick."

"Or just a stubborn male, like the rest of your gender?" She lifted the front end of the chair. "Even

Popeye and Superman need help once in awhile. Besides, we wouldn't want you to throw your back out. Then how would all our work get done around here?"

He knew when he was defeated. With a sigh, he picked up the other end. They had another minor tussle about who should walk backward up the stairs but he won that one simply by turning around and starting up.

She didn't let him gloat for long. "I understand you know our new tenant."

His gaze flashed to hers. *Uh-oh. Here comes the inquisition*, he thought. "Knew. Past tense. A long time ago."

The words were becoming like a mantra since she showed up again in Cannon Beach. *A long time ago.* But not nearly long enough. Like a riptide, the memories just seemed to keep grabbing him out of nowhere and sucking him under.

"She's lovely, isn't she?" Sage pressed as they hit the halfway mark on the stairs. "And those kids of hers are adorable. I can't wait until Eben and Chloe finish up their trip to Europe in a few weeks. Chloe's going to be over the moon at having two new friends."

"How are the wedding plans?" he asked at her mention of her fiancé and his eight-year-old daughter. The question was aimed more at diverting her attention than out of much genuine interest to hear about her upcoming nuptials, but it seemed to work.

Sage made a face. "You know I'm not good at that kind of thing. If I had my way, I would happy with something simple on the beach, just Eben and me and Chloe and the preacher."

"I guess when you marry a gazillionaire hotel magnate, sometimes you have to make sacrifices."

"It's still going to be small, just a few friends at the ceremony then a reception later at the Sea Urchin. I'm leaving all the details to Jade and Stanley Wu."

"Smart woman."

She went on about wedding plans and he listened with half an ear.

In a million years, he never would have expected a hippie-chick like Sage to fall for a California business-man like Eben Spencer but somehow they seemed to fit together.

Sage was more at peace than he'd ever known her, settled in a way he couldn't explain.

She was one of his closest friends and had been since she moved to town five years ago and found herself im-mediately drawn into Abigail's orbit. He loved her as a little sister and he knew she deserved whatever joy she could find.

He wanted to be happy for her—and most of the time he was—but every once in awhile, seeing the love and happiness that seemed to surround her and Eben when they were together was like a slow, relentless trickle of acid on an open wound.

Despite knowing Julia was inside, he was relieved as hell when they reached the top of the stairs and turned into the apartment.

"Oh, my Stickley! We bought that when I was preg-nant with the twins. I know the apartment is furnished but I couldn't bear to leave it behind. Thank you so much for carrying that heavy thing all that way! That goes right here by the window so I can sit in it at night and watch the moonlight shining on the ocean."

He set it down, his mind on the rocking chair he had made Robin when she was pregnant with Cara. It was still sitting in the nursery along with the toddler bed he had made, gathering dust.

He really ought to do something with the furniture. Sage would probably know somebody who could use it....

Not today, he thought abruptly. He wasn't ready for that yet.

He turned on his heel and headed back down the stairs to retrieve that mysterious blanket-wrapped item. When he reached the U-Haul, he stood for a moment studying it, trying to figure out what it might be—and how best to carry it up the Brambleberry House stairs—when the enticing scent of cherry blossoms swirled around him.

"It's a dollhouse." Julia spoke beside him in a low voice and he automatically squared his shoulders, though what he was bracing for, he wasn't quite sure.

"My father made it for me years ago. My...late husband tried to fix it up a little for Maddie but I'm afraid it's still falling apart. I really hope it survived the trip."

So she was a widow. They had that in common, then. He cleared his throat. "Should we take the blanket off?"

She shrugged, which he took for assent. He unwrapped the cord and heard a crunching kind of thud inside. Uh-oh. Not a good sign. With a careful look at her and a growing sense of trepidation, he pulled the blanket away and winced as Julia gasped.

Despite her obvious efforts to protect the dollhouse, the piece hadn't traveled well. The construction looked flimsy to begin with and the roof had collapsed.

One entire support wall had come loose as well and the whole thing looked like it was ready to implode.

"I'm sorry," he said, though the words seemed grossly inadequate.

"It's not your fault. I was afraid it wouldn't survive the trip. Oh, this is going to break Maddie's heart. She loved that little house."

"So did you," he guessed.

She nodded. "For a lot of reasons." She tilted her head, studying the wreckage. "You're the carpentry expert. I don't suppose there's any way I can fix this, is there?"

He gazed down at her, at the fading rays of the sun that caught gold strands in her hair, at the sorrow marring those lovely features for a lost treasure.

He gave an inward groan. Dammit, he didn't want to do this. But he was such a sucker for a woman in distress. How could he just walk away?

He cleared his throat. "If you want, I could take a look at it. See what I can do."

"Oh, I couldn't ask that of you."

"You didn't ask," he said gruffly.

She sent him a swift look. "No. I didn't."

"I'm kind of slammed with projects right now. It might take me awhile to get to it. And even then, I can't make any guarantees. That's some major damage there. You might be better just starting over."

She forced a smile, though he could see the sadness lingering in her eyes. Her father had made it for her, she had said. He didn't remember much about her father from their summers in Cannon Beach, mostly that the man always seemed impatient and abrupt.

"I can't make any promises," he repeated. "But I'll see what I can do."

"Oh, that would be wonderful. Thank you so much, Will."

Together, they gathered up the shattered pieces of the dollhouse and carried them to his truck, where he set them carefully in the back between his toolbox and ladder.

"I'm happy to pay you for your time and trouble."

As if he would ever accept her money. "Don't worry about it. Let's see if I can fix it first."

She nodded and looked as if she wanted to say something more. To his vast relief, after a moment, she closed her mouth, then returned to the U-Haul for the last few boxes.

Chapter 4

Between the two of them, they were able to carry all but a few of the remaining boxes from the U-Haul up the stairs, where they found Sage and Julia pulling books out of boxes and placing them on shelves.

"You're all so wonderful to help me," Julia said, gratitude coursing through her as she smiled at all three of them. "I have to tell you, I never expected such a warm welcome. I thought it would be weeks before I would even know a soul in Cannon Beach besides Abigail. I haven't even started teaching yet but I feel as if I have instant friends."

Sage smiled. "We're thrilled to have you and the twins here. And I think Abigail would be, too. Don't you think, Will?"

He set down the boxes. "Sure. She always loved kids."

"She was nothing but a big kid herself. Remember

how she used to sit out on the porch swing for hours with Cara, swinging and telling stories and singing."

"I remember," he said, his voice rough.

Color flooded Sage's features suddenly. "Oh, Will. I'm sorry."

He shook his head. "Don't, Sage. It's okay. I'd better get the last load of boxes."

He turned and headed down the stairs, leaving behind only the echo of his workboots hitting the wooden steps. Julia turned her confused gaze to Anna and Sage and found them both watching after Will with identical expressions of sadness in their eyes.

"I missed something, obviously," she said softly.

Sage gave Anna a helpless look and the other woman shrugged.

"She'll find out sooner or later," Anna said. "She might as well hear it from us."

"You're right," Sage said. "It just still hurts so much to talk about the whole thing."

"You don't have to tell me anything," Julia said quickly. "I'm sorry if I've wandered into things that are none of my business."

Sage glanced down the stairs as if checking to see if Will was returning. When she was certain he was still outside, she turned back, her voice pitched low. "Will had a daughter. She would have been a couple years younger than your twins. Cara. That's who I was talking about. Abigail adored her. We all did. She was the cutest little thing you've ever seen, just full of energy, with big blue eyes, brown curls and dimples. She was full of sugar, our Cara."

Had a daughter. Not has. An ache blossomed in her chest and she knew she didn't want to hear any more.

But she had learned many lessons over the last few years—one of the earliest was that information was empowering, even if the gaining of it was a process often drenched in pain.

"What happened?" she forced herself to ask.

Sage shook her head, her face inexpressibly sad. Anna squeezed her arm and picked up the rest of the story.

"Cara was killed along with Will's wife, Robin, two years ago." Though Anna spoke in her usual no-nonsense tone, Julia could hear the pain threading through her words.

"They were crossing the street downtown in the middle of the afternoon when they were hit by a drunk tourist in a motorhome," she went on. "Robin died instantly but Cara hung on for two weeks. We all thought—hoped—she was going to pull through but she caught an infection in the hospital in Portland and her little body was too weak and battered to fight it."

She wanted to cry, just sit right there in the middle of the floor and weep for him. More than that, she wanted to race down the stairs and hug her own precious darlings to her.

"Oh, poor Will. He must have been shattered."

"We all were," Sage said. "It was like a light went out of all of us. Will used to be so lighthearted. Like a big tease of an older brother. It's been more than two years since Robin and Cara died and I can count on one hand the number of times I've seen him genuinely smile at something since then."

The ache inside her stretched and tugged and her eyes burned with tears for the teenage boy with the mischievous eyes.

Sage touched her arm. "I'm so glad you're here now."

"Me? Why?"

"Well, you've lost someone, too. You understand, in a way the rest of us can't. I'm sure it would help Will to talk to someone who's experienced some of those same emotions."

Julia barely contained her wince, feeling like the world's biggest fraud.

"Grief is such a solitary, individual thing," she said after an awkward moment. "No one walks the same journey."

Sage smiled and pressed a cheek to Julia's. "I know. But I'm still glad you're here, and I'm sure Will is, too."

Julia was saved from having to come up with an answer to that when she again heard his footsteps on the stairs. A moment later, he came in, muscles bulging beneath the cotton of his shirt as he carried in a trio of boxes.

He had erased any trace of emotion from his features, any sign at all that he contained any emotions at all. Finding out about his wife and daughter explained so much about him. The hardness, the cynicism. The pain in his eyes when he looked at Maddie.

She had a wild urge to take the boxes from him, slip her arms around his waist and hold him until everything was all right again.

"This is the last of it. Where do these go?"

Her words tangled in her throat and she had to clear her throat before she could speak. "The top one belongs in my bedroom. The others are Simon's."

With an abrupt nod, he headed first to her room and then to the one down the hall where Simon slept.

He returned to the living room just as the doorbell downstairs rang through the house.

"Hey, Mom!" Simon yelled up the stairs an instant later. "The pizza guy's here!"

Conan started barking in accompaniment and Julia rolled her eyes at the sudden cacophony of sound. "Are you sure about this? The house was so quiet before we showed up. If you want that quiet again, you'd better speak now while I've still got the U-Haul."

Sage shook her head with a laugh. "No way. I'm not lugging those books back down the stairs. You're stuck here for awhile."

Right now, she couldn't think of anywhere she would rather be. Julia flashed a quick smile to the other two women and Will, grabbed her purse, and headed down the stairs to pay for the pizza.

Simon stood at the door holding on to Conan's collar as the dog wriggled with excitement, his tail wagging a mile a minute.

Her son giggled. "I think he really likes pizza, Mom."

"I guess. Maybe you had better take him into Anna's apartment so he doesn't attack the pizza driver."

With effort, he wrangled the dog through the door and closed the door behind him. Finally, Julia opened the door and found a skinny young man with his cap on backward and his arms full of pizza boxes.

She quickly paid him for the pizza—adding in a hefty tip. She closed the door behind him and backed into the entry, her arms full, and nearly collided with a solid male.

Strong arms came around her to keep her upright.

"Oh," she exclaimed to Will. "I didn't hear you come down the stairs."

"You were talking to the driver," he answered. He quickly released her—much to her regret. She knew she shouldn't have enjoyed that brief moment of contact, but it had been so very long…

She couldn't help noticing the boy she had known now had hard strength in his very grown-up muscles.

"I thought you said the trailer was empty," she said with some confusion as he headed for the door.

"It is. You're done here so I'm heading home."

"You can't leave!" she exclaimed.

He raised an eyebrow. "I can't?"

She held out the boxes in her arms. "You've got to stay for pizza. I ordered way too much for three women and two children."

"Don't forget Conan," he pointed out. "He's crazy about pizza, even though all that cheese is lousy for him."

"Knowing my kids, I'm sure he'll be able to sneak far more than is good for him."

The scent of him reached her, spicy and male and far more enticing than any pizza smells. "I still have too much. Please stay."

He gazed at the door with a look almost of desperation in his eyes. But when he turned back, she thought he might be weakening.

"Please, Will," she pressed.

He opened his mouth to answer but before he could, the door to Abigail's apartment opened and Maddie peeked her head out, looking tousled and sleepy.

"Can we come out now?" she asked.

"As long as the dog's not going to knock me down to get to the Canadian bacon."

At Maddie's giggle, Julia saw a spasm of pain flicker across Will's features and knew the battle was lost.

"I really can't stay." He reached for the doorknob.

"Thanks anyway for the invitation, but I've got a lot of work to do at home."

She couldn't push him more, not with that shadow of pain clouding his blue eyes. Surrendering to the inevitable, she simply nodded. "You still need to eat. Take some home with you."

She could see the objections forming on his expression and decided not to take no for an answer. Will Garrett didn't know stubborn until he came up against her.

"What's your pleasure? Pepperoni or Hawaiian? I'd offer you the vegetarian but I think Sage has dibs on that one."

"It's not necessary, really."

"It is to me," she said firmly. "You just spent forty-five minutes helping me haul boxes up. You have to let me repay you somehow. Here, I hope you still like pepperoni and olive."

His eyes widened that she would remember such a detail. She couldn't have explained why—it was just one of those arcane details that stuck in her head. Several times that last summer, they'd gone to Mountain Mike's Pizza in town with her brother and Will always had picked the same thing.

"Maddie, can you hold this for a second?"

She gave the box marked pepperoni to her daughter, then with one hand she opened it and pulled out half the pizza, which she stuck on top of the Hawaiian.

He looked as if he wanted to object, but he said nothing when she handed him the box with the remaining half a pizza in it.

"Here you go. You should have enough for dinner tonight and breakfast in the morning as well. Consider it a tiny way to say thank you for all your hard work."

He shook his head but to her vast relief, he didn't hand the pizza back to her.

"Mom, I can't hold him anymore!" Simon said from behind the door. "He's starving and so am I!"

"You'd better get everyone upstairs for pizza," Will said.

"Right. Good night, then."

She wanted to say more—much more—but with a rambunctious dog and two hungry children clamoring for her attention, she had to be content with that.

Blasted stubborn woman.

Will sat on his deck watching the lights of Cannon Beach flicker on the water as he ate his third piece of pizza.

He had to admit, even lukewarm, it tasted delicious—probably a fair sight better than the peanut butter sandwich he would have scrounged for his meal.

He didn't order pizza very often since half of it usually went to waste before he could get to the leftovers so this was a nice change from TV dinners and fast-food hamburgers.

He really needed to shoot for a healthier diet. Sage was always after him to get more vegetables and fewer preservatives into his diet. He tried but he'd never been a big one for cooking in the first place. He could grill steaks and burgers and the occasional chicken breast but he usually fell short at coming up with something to go alongside the entree.

He fell short in a lot of areas. He sighed, listening to the low rumble of the sea. He spent a lot of his free time puttering around in his dad's shop or sitting out here watching the waves, no matter what the weather. He just hated the emptiness inside the house.

He ought to move, he thought, as he did just about every night at this same time when the silence settled over him with like a scratchy, smothering wool blanket.

He ought to just pick up and make a new start somewhere. Especially now that Julia Hudson Blair had climbed out of the depths of his memories and taken up residence just a few hundred yards away.

She knew.

Sometime during the course of the evening, Sage or Anna must have told her about the accident. He wasn't quite sure how he was so certain, but he had seen a deep compassion in the green of her eyes, a sorrow that hadn't been there earlier.

He washed the pizza down with a swallow of Sam Adams—the one bottle he allowed himself each night.

He knew it shouldn't bother him so much that she knew. Wasn't like it was some big secret. She would find out sooner or later, he supposed.

He just hated that first shock of pity when people first found out—though he supposed when it came down to it, the familiar sadness from friends like Sage and Anna wasn't much easier.

Somehow seeing that first spurt of pity in Julia's eyes made it all seem more real, more raw.

Her life hadn't been so easy. She was a widow, so she must know a thing or two about loss and loneliness. That didn't make him any more eager to have her around— or her kids.

He shouldn't have made a big deal out of the whole thing. He should have just sucked it up and stayed for pizza with her and Sage and Anna. Instead, his kneejerk reaction had been to flee and he had given into it, something very unlike him.

He sighed and took another swallow of beer. From here, he could see her bedroom light. A dark shape moved across the window and he eased back into the shadows of his empty house.

Why was he making such a big deal about this? Julia meant nothing to him. Less than nothing. He hadn't thought about her in years. Yeah, years ago he had been crazy about her when he was just a stupid, starry-eyed kid. He had dreamed about her all that last summer, when she came back to Cannon Beach without her braces and with curves in all the right places.

First love could be an intensely powerful thing for a sixteen-year-old boy. When she left Cannon Beach, his dreams of a long-distance relationship were quickly dashed when she didn't write to him as she had promised. He had tried to call the phone number she'd given him and left several messages that were never returned.

He was heartbroken for a while but he'd gotten over it. By spring, when he'd taken Robin Cramer to the prom, he had completely forgotten about Julia Hudson and her big green eyes.

Life had taught him that a tiny little nick in his heart left by a heedless fifteen-year-old girl was nothing at all to the pain of having huge, jagged chunks of his soul ripped away.

Now, sixteen years later, Julia was nothing to him. He just needed to shake this weird feeling that the careful order of the life he had painstakingly managed to piece together in the last two years had just been tossed out to sea.

He could think of no earthly reason he shouldn't be able to treat her and her children with politeness, at least.

He couldn't avoid interacting with Julia, for a dozen reasons. Beyond the minor little fact that she lived three houses down, he was still working on renovating several of the Brambleberry House rooms. He couldn't avoid her and he sure as hell couldn't run away like a coward every time he saw her kids.

He looked up at Brambleberry House again and his gaze automatically went to the second-floor window. A shape moved across again and a moment later the light went out and somehow Will felt more alone than ever.

"Thank you both again for your help today." Julia smiled at Sage and Anna across the table in her new apartment as they finished off the pizza. "I don't know what I would have done without you."

Anna shook her head. "We only helped you with the easy part. Now you have to figure out where to put everything."

"We have dishes in the kitchen and sheets on the beds. Beyond that, everything else can wait until the morning."

"Looks like some of us need to find that path there sooner than others," Sage murmured, gesturing toward Maddie.

"Not me," Maddie instantly protested, but Julia could clearly see she was drooping tonight, with her elbow propped on the table and her head resting on her fist.

Even with her short nap, Maddie still looked tired. Julia sighed. Some days dragged harder than others on Maddie's stamina. They had spent a busy day making all the arrangements to move into Brambleberry House. Maddie had helped carry some of her own things to her bedroom and had delighted in putting her toys and clothes away herself.

With all the craziness of moving in, Julia hadn't been as diligent as usual about making sure Maddie didn't overextend herself and now it looked as if she had reached the limit of her endurance.

"Time for bed, sweetie. Let's get your meds."

"I'm not ready for bed," she protested, sending a pleading look to Anna and Sage, as if they could offer a reprieve. "I want to stay up and help move in."

"I'm tuckered myself," Julia said. "I'll leave all the fun stuff for tomorrow when we're all rested, okay?"

Maddie sighed with a quiet resignation that never failed to break her heart. She caught herself giving into the sorrow and quickly shunted it away. Her daughter was still here. She was a miracle and Julia could never allow herself to forget that.

Before she brought in any other boxes, she had made sure to put Maddie's pill regimen away in a cabinet by the kitchen sink. She poured a glass of water and handed them to her. With the ease of long, grim practice, Maddie downed the half-dozen pills in two swallows, then finished the water to flush down the pills.

Because her daughter seemed particularly tired, Julia helped her into her pajamas then did a quick set of vitals. Everything was within normal ranges for Maddie so Julia pushed away her lingering worry.

"Good night, sweetie," she said after a quick story and kiss. "Your first sleep in the new house!"

"I like this place," Maddie said sleepily as Julia pulled the nightgown over her thin shoulders.

"I like it, too. It feels like home, doesn't it?"

Maddie nodded. "And the lady is nice."

Julia smiled. "Which one? Sage or Anna? I think they're both pretty nice."

Maddie shook her head but her eyes drooped closed before she could answer.

Julia watched her sleep for a moment, marveling again at the lessons in courage and strength and grace her daughter had taught her these last few years.

A miracle, she thought again. As she stood watching over her, she felt the oddest sensation, almost like feather-light fingers touching her cheek.

Weird, she thought. Sage and Anna had warned her Brambleberry House was a typical drafty old house. She would have to do her best to seal up any cracks in Maddie's room.

When she returned to the other room, she found only Simon, curled up in the one corner of the couch not covered in boxes. He had a book in one hand and was petting Conan absently with the other.

What a blessing her son loved to read. Books and his Game Boy had sustained him through many long, boring doctor appointments.

"Did Sage and Anna go downstairs?" she asked.

"I think they're still in the kitchen," Simon answered without looking up from his book.

She heard low, musical laughter before she reached the kitchen. For a moment, she stood in the doorway watching them as they unloaded her grandmother's china into the built-in cabinet.

Here was another blessing. She was overflowing with them. She had come back to Cannon Beach with only a teaching position and her hope that everything would work out. Now she had this great apartment overlooking the sea and, more importantly, two unexpected new friends who were already becoming dear to her.

She didn't think she made a sound but Sage suddenly sensed her presence. She glanced toward her, her exotic tilted eyes lighting in welcome.

"Our girl is all settled for the night?"

Julia nodded. "It was a hectic day. She wore herself out."

"Is she all right?" Anna asked, her features tight with concern.

"Yes. She's fine. She just doesn't have the stamina she used to have." She paused, deciding it was time to reveal everything. "It's one of the long-term side effects of her bone marrow transplant."

"Bone marrow transplant?" Anna exclaimed, her eyes wide with a shock mirrored on Sage's features.

Julia sighed. "Yes. And a round of radiation and two rounds of chemotherapy. I probably should have told you this earlier but Maddie is in remission from acute lymphocytic leukemia."

Chapter 5

Saying the words aloud always left her feeling vaguely queasy, as if she were the one who had endured months of painful treatments, shots, blood draws, the works.

She found it quite a lowering realization that Maddie had faced her cancer ordeal with far more courage than Julia had been able to muster as her mother.

"Oh, Julia." Sage stepped forward and wrapped her into a spontaneous hug. "I'm so sorry you've all had to go through this."

"It's been a pretty bumpy road," she admitted. "But as I said, she's in remission and she's doing well. Much better since the bone marrow transplant. Simon was the donor. We were blessed that they were a perfect match."

"You've had to go through this all on your own?" Anna's dark eyes looked huge and sad.

She knew Anna was referring to Kevin's death and the timing of it. She decided she wasn't quite ready to delve into those explanations just yet so she chose to evade the question.

"I had a strong support network in Boise," she said instead. "Good friends, my brother and his wife, my co-workers at the elementary school there. They all think I'm crazy to move away."

"Why did you?" Anna asked.

"We were all ready for a change. A new start. Three months ago, Maddie's oncologist took a new job at the children's hospital in Portland. Dr. Lee had been such a support and comfort to us and when she moved, it seemed like the perfect time for us to venture back out in the world."

She sometimes felt as if their lives had been on hold for three years. Between Maddie's diagnosis, then Kevin's death, she and her children had endured far too much.

They needed laughter and joy and the peace she had always found by the ocean.

She smiled at the two other women. "I have to tell you both, I was still wondering if I had made a terrible mistake leaving behind our friends and the safe cushion of support we had in Boise, until we saw the for-rent sign out front of Brambleberry House. It seemed like a miracle that we might have the chance to live in the very house I had always loved so much when I was a little girl, the house where I had always found peace. I took that sign as an omen that everything would be okay."

"We're so glad you found us," Anna said.

"You belong here," Sage added. She squeezed Julia's fingers with one hand and reached for Anna's hand with the other, linking them all together and Julia had to fight back tears, overwhelmed by their easy acceptance of her.

She realized she felt happier standing in this warm kitchen with these women than she could remember being in a long, long time.

"Thank you," she said softly. "Thank you both."

"You smell that?" Sage demanded after a moment.

Anna rolled her eyes. "Cut it out, Sage."

"Smell what?" Julia asked.

"Freesia," Sage answered. "You smelled it, too, didn't you?"

"I thought it was coming from the open window."

Sage shook her head. "Nope. As much as she loved it, Abigail could never get any freesia bulbs to survive in her garden. Our microclimate is just not conducive to them."

"I hope you're not squeamish about ghosts," Anna said after a long sigh. "Sage insists Abigail is still here at Brambleberry House, that she flits through the house leaving behind the freesia perfume she always wore."

Julia blinked, astonished. It seemed preposterous—until she remembered Maddie's words that the lady was nice, and that soft brush against her skin when she had been standing in Maddie's room looking over her daughter almost as if someone had touched her tenderly.

She fought back a shiver.

"You don't buy it?" she said to Anna.

Anna laughed. "I don't know. I usually tend to fall on the side of logic and reason. My intellect tells me it's a complete impossibility. But then, I can't put anything past Abigail. It wouldn't surprise me at all if she decided to defy the rules of metaphysics and stick around in this house she loved. If it's at all within the realm of possibility, Abigail would find a way."

"And Conan is her familiar," Sage added. "You

probably ought to know that up front, too. I think the two of them are a team. If Abigail is the brains of the outfit, he's the muscle."

"Okay, now you're obviously putting me on."

Sage shook her head.

"Conan. The dog."

Sage grinned. "Don't look at me like I'm crazy. Just watch and see. The dog is spooky."

"On that, at least, we can agree," Anna said, setting the last majolica teacup in the cupboard. "He's far smarter than your average dog."

"I've seen that much already," Julia admitted. "I'm sorry, but it's a bit of a stretch for me to go from thinking he's an uncommonly smart dog to buying the theory that he's some kind of conduit from the netherworld."

Sage laughed. "Put like that, it does sound rather ridiculous, doesn't it? Just keep your eyes open. You can judge for yourself after you've been here awhile. I wanted to put a disclosure in the rental agreement about Abigail but Anna wouldn't let me."

Anna made a face. "It's a little tough to find an attorney who will add a clause that we might have a ghost in the house."

"There's no *might* about it. You wait and see, Julia."

A ghost and a dog/medium. She supposed there were worst things she could be dealing with in an apartment. "I hope she is still here. I can't imagine Abigail would be anything but a benevolent spirit."

Sage grinned at her. Anna shook her head, but she was smiling as well. "I see I'm outnumbered in the sanity department."

"You're just better at being a grown-up," Sage answered. Her teasing slid away quickly, though, replaced with concern. "And on that note, is there anything special we need to worry about with Maddie? Environmental things she shouldn't be exposed to or anything?"

Julia sighed. She would much rather ponder light-hearted theories of the supernatural than bump up against the harsh reality of her daughter's illness and recovery.

"It's a tough line I walk between wrapping her up in cotton wool to protect her and encouraging as normal a life as possible. Most of the time she's fine, if a little more subdued than she once was. You probably wouldn't know it but she used to be the spitfire of the twins. When they were toddlers, she was always the one leading Simon into trouble."

She gave a wobbly smile and was warmed when Anna reached out and squeezed her hand.

A moment passed before she could trust her voice to continue. "Right now we need to work on trying to regain the strength she lost through the month she spent in the hospital with the bone marrow transplant. I hope by Christmas things will be better."

Sage smiled. "Well, now you've got two more of us— four, counting Abigail and Conan—on your side."

"Thank you," she whispered, immeasurably touched at their effortless acceptance of her and her children.

After Simon was finally settled in bed, Julia stood in her darkened bedroom gazing out at the ripples of the sea gleaming in the moonlight. Though she had a million things to do—finding bowls they could use for cereal in the morning hovered near the top of her list— she decided she needed this moment to herself to think, without rushing to take care of detail after detail.

Offshore some distance, she could see the moving

lights of a sea vessel cutting through the night. She watched it for a moment, then her gaze inexorably shifted to the houses along the shore.

There was the cottage where her family had always stayed, sitting silent and dark. Beyond that was Will Garrett's house. A light burned inside a square cedar building set away from the house. His father's workshop, she remembered. Now it would be Will's.

She glanced at her watch and saw it was nearly midnight. What was he working on so late? And did he spend his time out in his workshop to avoid the emptiness inside his house?

She pressed a hand to her chest at the ache there. How did he bear the pain of losing his wife and his child? She remembered the vast sorrow in his gaze when he had looked at Maddie and she wanted so much to be able to offer some kind of comfort to him.

She sensed he wouldn't want her to try. Despite his friendship with Sage and Anna, Will seemed to hold himself apart, as if he had used his carpentry skills to carefully hammer out a wall between himself and the rest of the world.

She ached for him, but she knew there was likely very little she could do to breach those walls.

She could try.

The thought whispered through her head with soft subtlety. She shook her head at her own subconscious. No. She had enough on her plate right now, moving to a new place, taking on a new job, dealing with twins on her own, one of whom still struggled with illness.

She didn't have the emotional reserves to take on anyone else's pain. She knew it, but as the peace of the house settled around her, she had the quiet conviction that she could at least offer him her friendship.

As if in confirmation, the sweet, summery scent of freesia drifted through the room. She smiled.

"Abigail, if you are still here," she whispered, "thank you. For this place, for Anna and Sage. For everything."

For just an instant, she thought she felt again the gentle brush of fingers against her cheek.

Will managed to avoid his new neighbors for several days, mostly because he was swamped with work. He was contracted to do the carpentry work on a rehab project in Manzanita. The job was behind schedule because of other subcontractors' delays and the developer wanted the carpentry work done yesterday.

Will was pouring every waking moment into it, leaving his house before the sun was up and returning close to midnight every night.

He didn't mind working hard. Having too much work to do was a damn sight better than having too little. Building something with his hands helped fill the yawning chasm of his life.

But his luck where his neighbors were concerned ran out a week after he had helped carry boxes up to the second-floor apartment of Brambleberry House.

By Friday, most of the basic work on the construction job was done and the only thing left was for him to install the custom floor and ceiling moldings the developer had ordered from a mill in Washington State. They hadn't been delivered yet and until they arrived, he had nothing to do.

Finally he returned to Cannon Beach, to his empty house and his empty life.

After showering off the sawdust and sweat from a hard day's work, he was grilling a steak on the deck—his nightly beer in hand—watching tourists fly kites and play in the sand in the pleasant early evening breeze when he suddenly heard excited barking.

A moment later, a big red mutt bounded into view, trailing the handle of his retractable leash.

As soon as he spied Will, he switched directions and bounded up the deck steps, his tongue lolling as he panted heavily.

"You look like a dog on the lam."

Conan did that weird grin thing of his and Will glanced down the beach to see who might have been on the other end of the leash. He couldn't see anyone—not really surprising. Though he seemed pondeorus most of the time, Conan could pour on the juice when he wanted to escape his dreaded leash and be several hundred yards down the beach before you could blink.

When he turned back to the dog, he found him sniffing with enthusiasm around the barbecue.

"No way," Will muttered. "Get your own steak. I'm not sharing."

Conan whined and plopped down at his feet with such an obviously feigned morose expression that Will had to smile. "You're quite the actor, aren't you? No steak for you tonight but I will get you a drink. You look like you could use it."

He found the bowl he usually used for Conan and filled it from the sink. When he walked back through the sliding doors, he heard a chorus of voices calling the dog's name.

Somehow, he supposed he wasn't really surprised a

moment later when Julia Blair and her twins came into view from the direction of Brambleberry House.

Conan barked a greeting, his head hanging over the deck railing. Three heads swiveled in their direction and even from here, he could see the relief in Julia's green eyes when she spotted the dog.

"There you are, you rascal," she exclaimed.

With her hair held back from her face in a ponytail, she looked young and lovely in the slanted early evening light. Though he knew it was unwise, part of him wanted to just sit and savor the sight of her, a little guilty reward for putting in a hard day's work.

Shocked at the impulse, he set down Conan's bowl so hard some water slopped over the side.

"I'm so sorry," Julia called up. Though he wanted to keep them off the steps like he was some kind of medieval knight defending his castle from assault, he stood mutely by as she and her twins walked up the stairs to the deck.

"We were taking him for a walk on the beach," Julia went on, "but we apparently weren't moving quickly enough for him."

"It's my fault," the boy—Simon—said, his voice morose. "Mom said I had to hold his leash tight and I tried, I really did, but I guess I wasn't strong enough."

"I'm sure it's not your fault," Will said through a throat that suddenly felt tight. "Conan can be pretty determined when he sets his mind to something."

Simon grinned at him with a new warmth. "I guess he had his mind set on running away."

"We were going to get an ice cream," the girl said in her whispery voice. He had no choice but to look at her, with her dark curls and blue eyes. A sense of frailty clung to her, as if the slightest breeze would pick her up and carry her out to sea.

He didn't know how to talk to her—didn't know if he could. But he had made a pledge not to hurt others simply because he was in pain. He supposed that included little dark-haired sea sprites.

"That sounds like fun. A great thing to do on a pretty summer night like tonight."

"My favorite ice cream is strawberry cheesecake," she announced. "I really hope they have some."

"Not me," Simon announced. "I like bubblegum. Especially when it's blue bubblegum."

To his dismay, Julia's daughter crossed the deck until she was only a few feet away. She looked up at him out of serious eyes. "What about you, Mr. Garrett?" Maddie asked. "Do you like ice cream?"

Surface similarities aside, she was not at all like his roly-poly little Cara, he reminded himself. "Sure. Who doesn't?"

"What kind is your favorite?"

"Hmmm. Good question. I hate to be boring but I really like plain old vanilla."

Simon hooted. "That's what my mom's favorite flavor is, too. With all the good flavors out there—licorice or coconut or chocolate chunk—why would you ever want plain vanilla? That's just weird."

"Simon!" Julia's cheeks flushed and he thought again how extraordinarily lovely she was—not much different from the girl he'd been so crazy about nearly two decades ago.

"Well, it is," Simon insisted.

"You don't tell someone they're weird," Julia said.

"I didn't say *he* was weird. Just that eating only vanilla ice cream is weird."

Will found himself fighting a smile, which startled him all over again. "Okay, I'll admit I also like praline ice cream and sometimes even chocolate chip on occasion. Is that better?"

Simon snickered. "I guess so."

He felt the slightest brush of air and realized it was Maddie touching his arm with her small, pale hand. Suddenly he couldn't seem to catch his breath, aching inside.

"Would you like to come with us to get an ice-cream cone, Mr. Garrett?" she asked in her breathy voice. "I bet if you were holding Conan's leash, he couldn't get away."

He glanced at her sweet little features then at Julia. The color had climbed even higher on her cheekbones and she gave him an apologetic look before turning back to her daughter.

"Honey, I'm sure Mr. Garrett is busy. It smells like he's cooking a steak for his dinner."

"Which I'd better check on. Hang on."

He lifted the grill and found his porterhouse a little on the well-done side, but still edible. He shut off the flame, using the time to consider how to answer the girl.

He shouldn't be so tempted to go with them. It was an impulse that shocked the hell out of him.

He had spent two years avoiding social situations except with his close friends. But suddenly the idea of sitting here alone eating his dinner and watching others enjoy life seemed unbearable.

How could he possibly go with them, though? He wasn't sure he trusted himself to be decent for an hour or so, the time it would take to walk to the ice-cream place, enjoy their cones, then walk home.

What if something set him off and brought back that bleak darkness that always seemed to hover around the edges of his psyche? The last thing he wanted to do was hurt these innocent kids.

"Thanks for the invitation," he said, "but I'd better stay here and finish my dinner."

Conan whined and butted his head against Will's leg, almost as if urging Will to reconsider.

"We can wait for you to eat," Simon said promptly. "We don't mind, do we, Mom?"

"Simon, Mr. Garrett is busy. We don't want to badger him." She met his gaze, her green eyes soft with an expression he couldn't identify. "Though we would love to have you come along. All of us."

"I don't want you to have to wait for me to eat when you've got strawberry cheesecake and bubblegum ice-cream cones calling your name."

Julia nodded rather sadly, as if she had expected his answer. "Come on, kids. We'd better be on our way."

Conan whined again. Will gazed from the dog to Julia and her family, then he shook his head. "Then again, I guess there's no reason I can't warm my steak up again when we get back from the ice-cream parlor. I'm not that hungry right now anyway."

His statement was met with a variety of reactions. Conan barked sharply, Julia's eyes opened wide with surprise, Simon gave a happy shout and Maddie clapped her hands with delight.

It had been a long time since anyone had seemed so thrilled about his company, he thought as he carried his steak inside to cover it with foil and slide it in the refrigerator.

He didn't know what impulse had prompted him to agree to go along with them. He only knew it had been a long while since he had allowed himself to enjoy the quiet peace of an August evening on the shore.

Maybe it was time.

Chapter 6

This was a mistake of epic proportions.

Will walked alongside Julia while her twins moved ahead with Conan. Simon raced along with the dog, holding tightly to his leash as the two of them scared up a shorebird here and there and danced just out of reach of the waves. Maddie seemed content to walk sedately toward the ice-cream stand in town, stopping only now and again to pick something up from the sand, study it with a serious look, then plop it in her pocket.

Will was painfully conscious of the woman beside him. Her hair shimmered in the dying sunlight, her cheeks were pinkened from the wind, and the soft, alluring scent of cherry blossoms clung to her, feminine and sweet.

He couldn't come up with a damn thing to say and he felt like he was an awkward sixteen-year-old again.

Accompanying her little family to town was just about

the craziest idea he had come up with in a long, long time.

She didn't seem to mind the silence but he finally decided good manners compelled him to at least make a stab at conversation.

"How are you settling in?" he asked.

She smiled softly. "It's been lovely. Perfect. You know, I wasn't sure I was making the right choice to move here but everything has turned out far better than I ever dreamed."

"The apartment working out for you, then?"

"It's wonderful. We love it at Brambleberry House. Anna and Sage have become good friends and the children love being so close to the ocean. It's been a wonderful adventure for us all so far."

He envied her that, he realized. The sense of adventure, the willingness to charge headlong into the unknown. He had always been content to stay in the house where he had been raised. He loved living on the coast—waking up to the sound of scoters and grebes, sleeping to the murmuring song of the sea—but lately he sometimes felt as if he were suffocating here. It was impossible to miss the way everyone in town guarded their words around him and worse, watched him out of sad, careful eyes.

Maybe it was time to move on. It wasn't a new thought but as he walked beside Julia toward the lights of town, he thought perhaps he ought to do just as she had—start over somewhere new.

She was looking at him in expectation, as if she had said something and was waiting for him to respond. He couldn't think what he might have missed and he hesitated to ask her to repeat herself. Instead, he decided to pick a relatively safe topic.

"School starts in a few weeks, right?" he asked.

"A week from Tuesday," she said after a small pause. "I plan to go in and start setting up my classroom tomorrow."

"Does it take you a whole week to set up?"

"Oh, at least a week!" Animation brightened her features even more. "I'm way behind. I've got bulletin boards to decorate, class curriculum to plan, students' pictures and names to memorize. Everything."

Her voice vibrated with excitement and despite his discomfort, he almost smiled. "You can't wait, can you?"

She flashed him a quick look. "Is it that obvious?"

"I'm glad you've found something you enjoy. I'll admit, back in the day, I wouldn't have pegged you for a schoolteacher."

She laughed. "I guess my plans to be a rich and famous diva some day kind of fell by the wayside. Teaching thirty active fifth-graders isn't quite as exciting as going on tour and recording a platinum-selling record."

"I bet you're good at it, though."

She blinked in surprise, then gave him a smile of such pure, genuine pleasure that he felt his chest tighten.

"Thank you, Will. That means a lot to me."

Their gazes met and though it had been a long, long time, he knew he didn't mistake the currents zinging between them.

A gargantuan mistake.

He was almost relieved when they caught up with Maddie, who had slowed her steps considerably.

"You doing okay, cupcake?" Julia asked.

"I'm fine, Mommy," she assured her, though her

features were pale and her mouth hung down a little at the edges.

He wondered again what the story was here—why Julia watched her so carefully, why Maddie seemed so frail—but now didn't seem the appropriate time to ask.

"Do you need a piggyback ride the rest of the way to the ice-cream stand?" Julia asked.

Maddie shook her head with more firmness than before, as if that brief rest had been enough for her. "I can make it, I promise. We're almost there, aren't we?"

"Yep. See, there's the sign with the ice-cream cone on it."

Somehow Maddie slipped between them and folded her hand in her mother's. She smiled up at Will and his chest ached all over again.

"I love this place," Maddie announced when they drew closer to Murphy's Ice Cream.

"I do, too," Will told her. "I've been coming here for ice cream my whole life."

She looked intrigued. "Really? My mom said she used to come here, too, when she was little." She paused to take a breath before continuing. "Did you ever see her here?"

He glanced at Julia and saw her cheeks had turned pink and he wondered if she was remembering holding hands under one of the picnic tables that overlooked the beach and stealing kisses whenever her brother wasn't looking.

"I did," he said gruffly, wishing those particular memories had stayed buried.

Maddie looked as if she wanted to pursue the matter but by now they had reached Murphy's.

He hadn't thought this whole thing through, he

realized as they approached the walk-up window. Rats. Inside, he could see Lacy Murphy Walker, who went to high school with him and whose family had owned and operated the ice-cream parlor forever.

She had been one of Robin's best friends—and as much as he loved her, he was grimly aware that Lacy also happened to be one of the biggest gossips in town.

"Hi, Will." She beamed with some surprise. "Haven't seen you in here in an age."

He had no idea how to answer that so he opted to stick with a polite smile.

"We're sure loving the new cabinets in the back," she went on. "You did a heck of a job on them. I was saying the other day how much more storage space we have now."

"Thanks, Lace."

Inside, he could see the usual assortment of tourists but more than a few local faces he recognized. The scene was much the same on the picnic tables outside.

His neck suddenly itched from the speculative glances he was getting from those within sight—and especially from Lacy.

She hadn't stopped staring at him and at Julia and her twins since he walked up to the counter.

"You folks ready to order?"

He hadn't been lumped into a *folks* in a long time and it took him a moment to adjust.

Sometimes he thought that was one of the things he had missed the most the last two years, being part of a unit, something bigger and better than himself.

"Hang on," he said, turning back to Julia and her twins. "Have you decided?" he asked, in a voice more terse than he intended.

"Bubblegum!" Simon exclaimed. "In a sugar cone."

Lacy wrote it down with a smile. "And for the young lady?"

Maddie gifted Lacy with a particularly sweet smile. "Strawberry cheesecake, please," she whispered. "I would like a sugar cone, too."

"Got it." Again Lacy turned her speculative gaze at him and Julia, standing together at the counter. "And for the two of you?"

The two of you. He wanted to tell her there was no *two of you*. They absolutely were *not* a couple, just two completely separate individuals who happened to walk down the beach together for ice cream.

"Two scoops of vanilla in a sugar cone," he said.

"Make that two of those." Julia smiled at Lacy and he felt a little light-headed. It was only because he hadn't eaten, he told himself. Surely his reaction had nothing to do with the cherry blossom scent of her that smelled sweeter than anything coming out of the ice cream shop.

Lacy gave them the total and Will pulled out his wallet.

"My treat," he said, sliding a bill to Lacy.

She reached for it at the same time Julia did.

"It is not!" Julia exclaimed. "You weren't even planning to come along until we hounded you into it. Forget it, I'm paying."

Even more speculative glances were shooting their way. He could see a couple of his mother's friends inside and was afraid they would be on the phone to her at her retirement village in San Diego before Lacy even scooped their cones.

Above all, he wanted to avoid attention and just win

this battle so they could find a place to sit, preferably one out of view of everyone inside.

"Nobody hounded anybody. I wanted to come." *For one brief second of insanity,* he thought, but didn't add. "I'm paying this time. You can pick it up next time."

The minute the words escaped his mouth, he saw Lacy's eyes widen. *Next time,* he had said. Rats. He could just picture the conversation that would be buzzing around town within minutes.

You hear about Will Garrett? He's finally dating again, the new teacher living in Abigail's house. The pretty widow with those twins. Remember, her family used to rent the old Turner place every summer.

He grimaced to himself, knowing there wasn't a darn thing he could do about it. When a person lived in the same town his whole life, everybody seemed to think they had a stake in his business.

"Are you sure?" Julia still looked obstinate.

He nodded. "Take it, Lace," he said.

To his vast relief, she ended the matter by stuffing the bill into the cash register and handing him his change.

"It should just be a minute," she said in a chirpy kind of voice. She disappeared from the counter, probably to go looking for her cell phone so she could start spreading the word.

"Thank you," Julia said, though she still looked uncomfortable about letting him treat.

"No problem."

"It really doesn't seem fair. You didn't even want to come with us."

"I'm here, aren't I? It's fine."

She looked as if she had something more to say but

after a moment she closed her mouth and let the matter rest when Lacy returned with the twins' cones.

"Here you go. The other two are coming right up."

"Great service as always, Lacy," he said when she handed him and Julia their cones. "Thanks."

"Oh, no problem, Will." She smiled brightly. "And let me just say for the record that it's so great to see you out enjoying…ice cream again."

Heat soaked his face and he could only hope he wasn't blushing. He hadn't blushed in about two decades and he sure as hell didn't want to start now.

"Right," he mumbled, and was relieved when Simon spoke up.

"Hey, Mom, our favorite table is empty. Can we sit out there and watch for whales?"

Julia smiled and shook her head ruefully. "We've been here twice and sat at the same picnic table both times. I guess that makes it our favorite."

She studied Will. "Are you in a hurry to get back or do you mind eating our cones here?"

He would rather just take a dip in the cold waters of the Pacific right about now, if only to avoid the watching eyes of everyone in town. Instead, he forced a smile.

"No big rush. Let's sit down."

He made the mistake of glancing inside the ice-cream parlor one time as he was sliding into the picnic table across from her—just long enough to see several heads swivel quickly away from him.

With a sigh, he resigned himself to the rumors. Nothing he could do about them now anyway.

She was quite certain Conan was a canine but just now he was looking remarkably like the proverbial cat with its mouth stuffed full of canary feathers.

Julia frowned at the dog, who settled beside the picnic table with what looked suspiciously like a grin. Sage and Anna said he had an uncanny intelligence and some hidden agenda but she still wasn't sure she completely bought it.

More likely, he was simply anticipating a furtive taste of one of the twins' cones.

If Conan practically hummed with satisfaction, Will resembled the plucked canary. He ate his cone with a stoicism that made it obvious he wasn't enjoying the treat—or the company—in the slightest.

She might have been hurt if she didn't find it so terribly sad.

She grieved for him, for the boy she had known with the teasing smile and the big, generous heart. His loss was staggering, as huge as the Pacific, and she wanted so desperately to ease it for him.

What power did she have, though? Precious little, especially when he would only talk in surface generalities about mundane topics like the tide schedule and the weather.

She tried to probe about the project he was working on, an intriguing rehabilitation effort down the coast, but he seemed to turn every question back to her and she was tired of talking about herself.

She was also tired of the curious eyes inside. Good heavens, couldn't the poor man go out for ice cream without inciting a tsunami of attention? If he wasn't being so unapproachable, she would have loved to give their tongues something to wag about.

How would Will react if she just grabbed the cone out of his hand, tossed it over her shoulder into the sand, and planted a big smacking kiss on his mouth, just for the sheer wicked thrill of watching how aghast their audience might turn?

It was an impulse from her youth, when she had been full of silly dreams and impetuous behavior. She wouldn't do it now, of course. Not only would a kiss horrify Will but her children were sitting at the table and they wouldn't understand the subtleties of social tit-for-tat.

The idea was tempting, though. And not just to give the gossips something to talk about.

She sighed. It would be best all the way around if she just put those kind of thoughts right out of her head. She had been alone for two years and though she might have longed for a man's touch, she wasn't about to jump into anything with someone still deep in the grieving process.

"What project are you working on next at Brambleberry House?" she asked him.

"New ceiling and floor moldings in Abigail's old apartment, where Anna lives now," he answered. "On the project I'm working on in Manzanita, the developer ordered some custom patterns. I liked them and showed them to Anna and she thought they would be perfect for Brambleberry House so we ordered extra."

"What was wrong with the old ones?"

"They were cracking and warped in places from water damage a long time ago. We tried to repair them but it was becoming an endless process. And then when she decided to take down a few walls, the moldings in the different rooms didn't match so we decided to replace them all with something historically accurate."

He started to add more, but Maddie slid over to him and held out her cone.

"Mr. Garrett, would you like to try some of my strawberry cheesecake ice cream? It's really good."

A slight edge of panic appeared around the edges of his gaze. "Uh, no thanks. Think I'll stick with my vanilla."

She accepted his answer with equanimity. "You might change your mind, though," she said, with her innate generosity. "How about if I eat it super slow? That way if decide you want some after all, I'll still have some left for you to try later, okay?"

He blinked and she saw the nerves give way to astonishment. "Uh, thanks," he said, looking so touched at the small gesture that her heart broke for him all over again.

Maddie smiled her most endearing smile, the particularly charming one she had perfected on doctors over the years. "You're welcome. Just let me know if you want a taste. I don't mind sharing, I promise."

He looked like a man who had just been stabbed in the heart and Julia suddenly couldn't bear his pain. In desperation, she sought a way to distract him.

"What will you do on Brambleberry House after you finish the moldings?" she finally asked.

He looked grateful for the diversion. "Uh, your apartment is mostly done but the third-floor rooms still need some work. Little stuff, mostly, but inconvenient to try to live around. I figured I would wait to start until after Sage is married and living part-time in the Bay Area with Eben and Chloe."

"I understand they're coming back soon from an extended trip overseas. We've heard a great deal about them from Sage and Anna. The twins can't wait to meet Chloe."

"She's a good kid. And Eben is good for Sage. That's the important thing."

He was a man who loved his friends, she realized. That, at least, hadn't changed over the years.

He seemed embarrassed by his statement and quickly returned to talking about the repairs planned for Brambleberry House. She listened to his deep voice as she savored the last of her cone, thinking it was a perfect summer evening.

The children finished their treats—Maddie's promise to Will notwithstanding—and were romping with Conan in the sand. Their laugher drifted on the breeze above the sound of the ocean.

For just an instant, she was transported back in time, sitting with Will atop a splintery picnic table, eating ice-cream cones and laughing at nothing and talking about their dreams.

By unspoken agreement, they stood, cones finished, and started walking back down the beach while Conan herded the twins along ahead of them.

"I'm boring you to tears," Will said after some time. "I'm sorry. I, uh, don't usually go on and on like that about my work."

She shook her head. "You're not boring me. On the contrary. I enjoy hearing about what you do. You love it, don't you?"

"It's just a job. Not something vitally important to the future of the world like educating young minds."

She made a face. "My, you have a rosy view of educators, don't you?"

"I always had good teachers when I was going to school."

"Good teachers wouldn't have anywhere to teach

those young minds if not for great carpenters like you," she pointed out. "The work you've done on Bramble-berry House is lovely. The kitchen cupboards are as smooth as a satin dress. Anna told me you made them all by hand."

"It's a great old house. I'm trying my best to do it justice."

They walked in silence for a time and Julia couldn't escape the grim realization that she was every bit as attracted to him now as she had been all those years ago.

Not true, she admitted ruefully. Technically, anyway. She was far *more* aware of him now, as a full-grown woman—with a woman's knowledge and a woman's needs—than she ever would have been as a naive, idealistic fifteen-year-old girl.

He was bigger than he had been then, several inches taller and much more muscled. His hair was cut slightly shorter than it had been when he was a teenager and he had a few laugh lines around his mouth and his eyes, though she had a feeling those had been etched some time ago.

She was particularly aware of his hands, square-tipped and strong, with the inevitable battle scars of a man who used them in creative and constructive ways.

She didn't want to notice anything about him and she certainly wasn't at all thrilled to find herself attracted to him again. She couldn't afford it. Not when she and her children were just finding their way again.

Hadn't she suffered enough from emotionally unavailable men?

"Look what I found, Mom!" Maddie uncurled her fingers to reveal a small gnarled object. "What is it?"

As she studied the object, Julia held her daughter's

hand, trying not to notice how thin her fingers seemed. It appeared to be an agate but was an odd color, greenish gray with red streaks in it.

"We forgot to bring our rocky coast field book, didn't we? We'll have to look it up when we get back to the house."

"Do you know, Mr. Garrett?" Maddie presented the object for Will's inspection.

"I'm afraid I'm not much of a naturalist," he said, rather curtly. "Sage is your expert in that department. She can tell you in a second."

"Oh. Okay." Maddie's shoulders slumped, more from fatigue than disappointment, Julia thought, but Will didn't pick up on it. Guilt flickered in his expression.

"I can look at it," he said after a moment. "Let's see."

Will reached for her hand and he examined the contents carefully. "Wow. This is quite a find. It's a bloodstone agate."

"I want to see," Simon said.

"It's pretty rare," Will said. He talked to them about some of the other treasures they could find beachcombing on the coast until they reached his house.

"I guess this is your stop," Julia said as they stood at the steps of his deck.

He glanced up the steps, as if eager to escape, then looked back at them. "I'll walk you the rest of the way to Brambleberry House. It's nearly dark. I wouldn't want you walking on your own."

It was only three houses, she almost said, but he looked so determined to stick it out that she couldn't bring herself to argue.

"Thank you," she said, then gave Maddie a careful

look. Her daughter hadn't said much for some time, since finding the bloodstone.

"Is it piggyback time?" Julia asked quietly.

Maddie shrugged, her features dispirited. "I guess so. I really wanted to make it the whole way on my own this time."

"You made it farther this time than last time. And farther still than the time before. Come on, pumpkin. Your chariot awaits." Julia crouched down and her daughter climbed aboard.

"I can carry her," Will said, though he looked as if he would rather stick a nail gun to his hand and pull the switch.

"I've got her," she answered, aching for him all over again. "But you can make sure Simon and Conan stay away from the surf."

They crossed the last hundred yards to Brambleberry House in silence. When they reached the back gate, Will held it open for them and they walked inside where the smells of Abigail's lush late-summer flowers surrounded them in warm welcome.

She eased Maddie off her back. "You two take Conan inside to get a drink from Anna while I talk to Mr. Garrett, okay?"

"Okay," Simon said, and headed up the steps. Maddie followed more slowly but a moment later Julia and Will were alone with only the sound of the wind sighing in the tops of the pine trees.

"What's wrong with Maddie?"

His quiet voice cut through the peace of the night and she instinctively bristled, wanting to protest that nothing was wrong with her child. Absolutely nothing. Maddie was perfect in every way.

The words tangled in her throat. "She's recovering from a bone marrow transplant," she answered in a low voice to match his. It wasn't any grand secret and he certainly deserved to know, though she didn't want to go through more explanations.

"It's been four months but she hasn't quite regained her strength. She's been a fighter through everything life has thrown at her the last two and a half years, though—two rounds of chemo and a round of radiation—so I know it's only a matter of time before she'll be back to her old self."

Chapter 7

He heard her words as if she whispered them on the wind from a long distance away.

Bone marrow transplant. Chemotherapy. Radiation. Cancer.

He had suspected Maddie was ill, but *cancer*. Damn it. The thought of that sweet-faced little girl enduring that kind of nightmare plowed into him like a semitruck and completely knocked him off his pins.

"I'm sorry, Julia."

The words seemed horrifyingly inadequate but he didn't have the first idea what else to say in this kind of situation. Besides, hadn't he learned after the dark abyss of the last two years that sometimes the simplest of sentiments meant the most?

The sun had finally slipped beyond the horizon and in the dusky twilight, she looked young and lovely and as fragile as her daughter.

"It's been a long, tough journey," she answered. "But I have great hope that we're finally starting to climb through to the other side."

He envied her that hope, he realized. That's what had been missing in his world for two years—for too long there had seemed no escape to the unrelenting pain. He missed Robin, he missed Cara, he missed the man he used to be.

But this wasn't about him, he reminded himself. One other lesson he had learned since the accident that stole his family was that very few people made it through life unscathed, without suffering or pain, and Julia had obviously seen more than her share.

"A year and a half, you said. So you must have had to cope with losing your husband in the midst of dealing with Maddie's cancer?"

In the twilight, he saw her mouth open then close, as if she wanted to say something but changed her mind.

"Yes," she finally answered, though he had a feeling that wasn't what she intended to tell him. "I guess you can see why I felt like we needed a fresh start."

"She's okay now, you said?"

"She's been in remission for a year. The bone marrow transplant was more a precaution because the second round of chemo destroyed her immune system. We were blessed that Simon could be the donor. But as you can imagine, we're all pretty sick of hospitals and doctors by now."

He released a breath, his mind tangled in the vicious thorns of remembering those last terrible two weeks when Cara had clung to life, when he had cried and prayed and begged for another chance for his broken and battered little girl.

For nothing.

His prayers hadn't done a damn bit of good.

"It's kind of surreal, isn't it?" Julia said after a moment. "Who would have thought all those summers ago when we were young that one day we'd be standing here in Abigail's garden together talking about my daughter's cancer treatment?"

He had a sudden, savage need to pummel something—to yank the autumn roses up by the roots, to shatter the porch swing into a million pieces, to hack the limbs off Abigail's dogwood bushes.

"Life is the cruelest bitch around," he said, and the bitter words seemed to scrape his throat bloody and raw. "Makes you wonder what the hell the point is."

She lifted shocked eyes to his. "Oh, Will. I'm so sorry," she whispered, and before he realized her intentions, she reached out and touched his arm in sympathy.

For just a moment the hair on his arm lifted and he forgot his bitterness, held captive by the gentle brush of skin against skin. He ached for the tenderness of a woman's touch—no, of *Julia's* touch— at the same time it terrified him.

He forced himself to take a step back. Cool night air swirled between them and he wondered how it was possible for the temperature to dip twenty degrees in a millisecond.

"I'd better go." His voice still sounded hoarse. "Your kids probably need you inside."

Her color seemed higher than it had been earlier and he thought she looked slightly disconcerted. "I'm sure you're right. Good night, then. And…thank you for the ice cream and the company. I enjoyed both."

She paused for the barest of moments, as if waiting for him to respond. When the silence dragged on, an instant's disappointment flickered in her eyes and she began to climb the porch steps.

"You're welcome," he said when she reached the top step. She turned with surprise.

"And for the record," he went on, "I haven't enjoyed much of anything for a long time but tonight was...nice."

Her brilliant smile followed him as he let himself out the front gate and headed down the dark street toward his home, a journey he had made a thousand times.

He didn't need to think about where he was going, which left his mind free to wander through dark alleys.

Cancer. That cute little girl. Hell.

Poor thing. Julia said it was in remission, that things were better except lingering fatigue. Still, he knew this was just one more reason he needed to maintain his careful distance.

His heart was a solid block of ice but if it ever started to melt, he knew he couldn't let himself care about Julia Blair and her children. He couldn't afford it.

He had been through enough pain and loss for a hundred lifetimes. He would have to be crazy to sign up for a situation with the potential to promise plenty more.

When he was ready to let people into his life again—if he was ever ready—it couldn't be a medically fragile little girl, a boy with curious eyes and energy to burn, and a lovely auburn-haired widow who made him long to taste life again.

She didn't see Will again for several days. With the lead-up to the start of school and then the actual chaos of adjusting to a new classroom and coming to know thirty new students, she barely had time to give him more than a passing thought.

But twice in the early hours of the morning as she graded math refresher assignments and the obligatory essays about how her students had spent the summer, she had glimpsed the telltale glimmer of lights in his workshop through the pines.

Only the walls of Abigail's old house knew that both times she had stopped what she was doing to stand at the window for a few moments watching that light and wondering what he was working on, what he was thinking about, if he'd had a good day.

It wasn't obsession, she told herself firmly. Only curiosity about an old friend.

Other than those few silent moments, she hadn't allowed herself to think about him much. What would be the point?

She had seen his reaction to the news of Maddie's cancer, a completely normal response under the circumstances. He had been shocked and saddened and she certainly couldn't blame him for the quick way he distanced himself from her.

She understood, but it still saddened her.

Now, the Friday after school started, she pulled into the Brambleberry House driveway to find his pickup truck parked just ahead of her SUV. Before she could contain the instinctive reaction, her stomach skittered with anticipation.

"Hey, I think that's Mr. Garrett's truck," Simon exclaimed. "See, it says Garrett Construction on the side."

"I think you must be right." She was quite proud of herself for the calm reply.

"I wonder what's he doing here." Simon's voice

quivered with excitement and she sighed. Her son was so desperately eager for a man in his life. She couldn't really blame him—except for Conan, who didn't really count, Simon was surrounded by women in every direction.

"Do you think he's working on something for Sage and Anna? Can I help him, do you think? I could hand him tools or something. I'm really good at that. Do you think he'll let me?"

"I don't know the answer to any of your questions, kiddo. You'll have to ask him. Why don't we go check it out?"

Both children jumped out of the vehicle the moment she put it in park. She called to them to wait for her but either they didn't hear her or they chose to ignore her as they rushed to the backyard, where the sound of some kind of power tool hummed through the afternoon.

She caught up with them before they made it all the way.

"I don't want you bothering Will—Mr. Garrett—if he's too busy to answer all your many questions. He has a job to do here and we need to let him."

The rest of what she might have said died in her throat when they turned the corner and she spotted him.

Oh mercy. He wore a pair of disreputable-looking jeans, a forest green T-shirt that bulged with muscle in all the right places, and a leather carpenter's belt slung low like a gunfighter's holster. The afternoon sun picked up golden streaks in his brown hair and he had just a hint of afternoon stubble that made him look dangerous and delectable at the same time.

Oh mercy.

Conan was curled under the shade nearby and his bark of greeting alerted Will's to their presence.

The dog lunged for Simon and Maddie as if he hadn't seen them in months instead of only a few hours and Will even gifted them with a rare smile, there only for an instant before it flickered away.

He drew off his leather gloves and shoved them in the back pocket of his jeans. "School over already? Is it that late?"

"We have early dismissal on Fridays. It's only three o'clock," Julia answered.

"We've been out for a few hours already," Maddie informed him. "Usually we get to stay at the after-school club until Mama finishes her work in her classroom."

"Is that right?"

"It's really fun," Simon answered. "Sometimes we have to stay in Mom's room with her and do our homework if we have a lot, but most of the time we go to extracurriculars. Today we played tetherball and made up a skit and played on the playground for a long time."

"Sounds tiring."

"Not for me," Simon boasted. "Maybe for Maddie."

"I'm not tired," Maddie protested.

His gaze met Julia's in shared acknowledgment that Maddie's claim was obviously a lie.

"What's the project today?" she asked.

"Last time I was here I noticed the back steps were splintering in a few places. I had a couple of hours this afternoon so I decided to get started on replacing them before somebody gets hurt."

Simon looked enthralled. "Can we help you fix them? I could hand you tools and stuff."

That subtle panic sparked in his eyes, the same

uneasiness she saw the day they went for ice cream, whenever she or the children had pushed him for more than he was willing to offer.

She could see him trying to figure a way out of the situation without hurting Simon and she quickly stepped in.

"We promised Sage we would pick a bushel of apples and make our famous caramel apple pie, remember? You finally get to meet Chloe in a few hours when she and her father arrive."

Simon scowled. "But you said in the car that if Mr. Garrett said it was okay, we could help him."

She sent a quick look of apology to Will before turning back to her son. "I know, but I could really use your help with the pies."

"Making pies is for girls. I'd rather work with tools and stuff," Simon muttered.

Will raised an eyebrow at this blatantly chauvinistic attitude. "Not true, kid. I know lots of girls who are great at using tools and one of my good friends is a pastry chef at a restaurant down the coast. He makes the best brambleberry pie you'll ever eat in your life."

"Brambleberry, like our house?" Maddie asked.

"Just like."

"Cool!" Simon said. "I want some."

"No brambleberries today," Julia answered. "We're making apple, remember? Let's go change our clothes and get started."

Simon's features drooped with disappointment. "So I don't get to help Mr. Garrett?"

"Simon—"

"I don't mind if he stays and helps," Will said.

"Are you sure?"

He nodded, though she could still see a shadow of reluctance in his eyes. "Positive. I'll enjoy the company. Conan's a good listener but not much of a conversationalist."

She smiled at the unexpected whimsy. "Conversing is one thing Simon does exceptionally well, don't you, kiddo?"

Simon giggled. "Yep. My dad used to say I could talk for a day and a half without needing anybody to answer back."

"I guess that means you probably talk in your sleep, right?"

Simon giggled. "I don't, but Maddie does sometimes. It's really funny. One time she sang the whole alphabet song in her sleep."

"I was only five," Maddie exclaimed to defend herself.

"And you're going to be fifteen before we finish this pie if we don't hurry. We all need to change out of school clothes and into apple-picking and porch-fixing clothes."

Simon looked resigned, then his features brightened. "Race you!" he called to Maddie and took off for the house. She followed several paces behind with Conan barking at their heels, leaving Julia alone with Will.

"I hope he doesn't get in your way or talk your ear off."

"Don't worry. We'll be fine."

"Feel free to send him out to play if you need to."

They lapsed into silence. She should go upstairs, she knew, but she had suddenly discovered she had missed him this last week, silly as that seemed after years when she hadn't given the man a thought.

She couldn't seem to force herself to leave. Finally she sighed, giving into the inevitable.

She took a step closer to him. "Hold still," she murmured.

Wariness leapt into the depths of his blue eyes but he froze as if she had just cast his boots in concrete.

He smelled of leather and wood shavings, and hot, sun-warmed male, a delicious combination, and she wanted to stand there for three or four years and just enjoy it. She brushed her fingers against the blade of his cheekbone, feeling warm male skin.

At her touch, their gazes clashed and the wariness in his eyes shifted instantly to something else, something raw and wild. An answering tremble stirred inside her and for a moment she forgot what she was doing, her fingers frozen on his skin.

His quick intake of breath dragged her back to reality and she quickly dropped her hand, feeling her own face flame.

"You, um, had a little bit of sawdust on your cheek. I didn't want it to find its way into your eye."

"Thanks." She wasn't sure if it was her imagination or not but his voice sounded decidedly hoarse.

She forced a smile and stepped back, though what she really wanted to do was wrap her arms fiercely around his warm, strong neck and hold on for dear life.

"You're welcome," she managed.

With nothing left to be said, she turned and hurried into the house.

She tried hard to put Will out of her mind as she and Maddie plucked Granny Smith apples off Abigail's tree. She might have found it a bit easier to forget about him if the ladder didn't offer a perfect view of the porch steps he was fixing.

Now she paused, her arm outstretched but the apple she was reaching to grab forgotten as she watched him smile at something Simon said. She couldn't hear them from here but so far it looked as if Simon wasn't making too big a pest of himself.

"Is this enough, Mama?" Maddie asked from below, where she stood waiting by the bushel basket.

Julia jerked her attention back to her daughter and the task at hand. "Just a moment." She plucked three more and added them to the glistening green pile in the basket.

"That ought to do it."

"Do we really need that many apples?"

"Not for one pie but I thought we could make a couple of extras. What do you think?"

She thought for a moment. "Can we give one to Mr. Garrett?"

Maddie looked over at the steps where Simon was trying his hand with Will's big hammer and Julia saw both longing and a sad kind of resignation in her daughter's blue eyes.

Maddie could be remarkably perceptive about others. Julia thought perhaps her long months of treatment—enough to make any child grow up far too early—had sensitized her to the subtle behaviors of others toward her. The way adults tried not to stare after she lost her hair, the stilted efforts of nurses and doctors to befriend her, even Julia's attempts to pretend their world was normal. Maddie seemed to see through them all.

Could Maddie sense the careful distance Will seemed determined to maintain between them?

Julia hoped not. Her daughter had endured enough. She didn't need more rejection in her life right now when she was just beginning to find her way again.

"That's a good idea," she finally answered Maddie, hoping her smile looked more genuine than it felt. "And perhaps we can think of someone else who might need a pie."

She lifted the bushel and started to carry it around the front of the house. She hadn't made it far before Will stepped forward and took the bushel out of her hands.

"Here, I'll carry that up the stairs for you."

She almost protested that it wasn't necessary but she could tell by the implacable set of his jaw that he wouldn't accept any arguments from her on the matter.

"Thank you," she said instead.

She and Maddie followed him up the stairs.

"Where do you want this?" he asked.

"The kitchen counter by the sink."

"We have to wash every single apple and see if it has a worm," Maddie informed him. "I hope we don't find one. That would be gross."

"That's a lot of work," he said stiffly.

"It is. But my mama's pies are the best. Even better than brambleberry. Just wait until you try one."

Will's gaze flashed to Julia's then away so quickly she wondered if she'd imagined the quick flare of heat there.

"Good luck with your pies."

"Good luck with your stairs," she responded. "Send Simon up if you need to."

He nodded and headed out the door, probably completely oblivious that he was leaving two females to watch wistfully after him.

Chapter 8

About halfway through helping Julia peel the apples, Maddie asked if she could stop for a few minutes and take a little rest.

"Of course, baby," Julia assured her.

Already Maddie had made it an hour past the time when Julia thought she would give out. School alone was exhausting for her, especially starting at a new school and the effort it took to make new friends. Throw in an hour of after-school activities then picking the apples and it was no wonder Maddie was drooping.

A few moments later, Julia peered through the kitchen doorway to the living room couch and found her curled up, fast asleep.

Julia set down the half-peeled apple, dried her hands off on her apron, and went to double-check on her. Yes, it might be a bit obsessive, but she figured she had earned the right the last few years to a little cautious overreaction.

Maddie's color looked good, though, and she was breathing evenly so Julia simply covered her with her favorite crocheted throw and returned to the kitchen.

Her job was a bit lonely now, without Maddie's quiet observations or Simon's bubbly chatter. With nothing to distract her, she found her gaze slipping with increasing frequency out the window.

She couldn't see much from this angle but every once in awhile Will and Simon would pass into the edge of her view as they moved from Will's power saw to the porch.

She had nearly finished peeling the apples when she suddenly heard a light scratch on the door of her apartment over the steady hammering and the occasional whine of power tools.

Somehow she wasn't surprised to find Conan standing on the other side, his tail wagging and his eyes expectant.

"Let me guess," she murmured. "All that hammering is interfering with your sleep."

She could swear the dog dipped his head up and down as if nodding. He padded through the doorway and into the living room, where he made three circles of his body before easing down to his stomach on the floor beside Maddie's couch.

"Watch over her for me, won't you?"

The dog rested his head on his front paws, his attention trained on Maddie as if the couch where she slept was covered in peanut butter.

"Good boy," Julia murmured, and returned to the kitchen.

She finished her work quickly, slicing enough apples for a half-dozen pies.

She assembled the pies quickly—cheating a little and using store-bought pie shells. She had a good pie crust recipe but she didn't have the time for it today since Eben and Chloe would be returning soon.

Only two pies could cook at a time in her oven and they took nearly forty minutes. After she slid the first pair in, she untied her apron and hung it back on the hook in the kitchen.

Without giving herself time to consider, she grabbed the egg timer off the stovetop, set it for the time the pies needed and stuck it in her pocket, then headed down the stairs to check on Simon.

It was nearly five-thirty but she couldn't see any sign of Anna or Sage yet. Sage, she knew, would be meeting Eben and Chloe at the small airstrip in Seaside, north of Cannon Beach. As for Anna, she sometimes worked late at her store in town or the new one in Lincoln City she had opened earlier in the summer.

She followed the sound of male voices—Will's lower-pitched voice a counterpoint to Simon's mile-a-minute higher tones.

She stepped closer, still out of sight around the corner of the house, until she could hear their words.

"My mom says next year I can play Little League baseball," Simon was saying.

"Hold the board still or we'll have wobbly steps, which won't do anyone any good."

"Sorry."

"Baseball, huh?" Will said a moment later.

"Yep. I couldn't play this year because of Maddie's bone transplant and because we were moving here. But next year, for sure. I can't wait. I played last year, even though I had to miss a lot of games and stuff when Mad was in the hospital."

She closed her eyes, grieving for her son who had suffered right along with his sister. Sometimes it was so easy to focus on Maddie's more immediate needs that she forgot Simon walked each step of the journey right along with her.

"Yeah, I hit six home runs last year. I bet I could do a lot more this year. Did you ever play baseball?"

"Sure did," Will answered. "All through high school and college. Until a few years ago, I was even on a team around here that played in the summertime."

"Probably old guys, huh?"

Julia cringed but Will didn't seem offended, judging by his quick snort of laughter—the most lighthearted sound she had heard from him since she'd been back.

"Yeah. We have a tough time running the bases for all the canes and walkers in the way."

Julia couldn't help herself, she laughed out loud, drawing the attention of both Will and Simon.

"Hi, Mom," Simon chirped, looking pleased to see her. "Guess what? Mr. Garrett played baseball, too."

"I remember," she said. "Your Uncle Charlie dragged me to one of his summer league games the last time I was here and I got to watch him play. He hit a three-run homer."

"Trying to impress you," Will said in a laconic tone.

She laughed again. "It worked very well, as I recall."

That baseball game had been when she first starting thinking of Will as more than just her brother's summer-vacation friend. She hadn't been able to stop thinking about him.

What, exactly, had changed since she came back? she wondered. She still couldn't seem to stop thinking about him.

"My mom likes baseball, too," Simon said. "She said maybe next month sometime we can go to a Mariners game, if they're in the playoffs. It's not very far to Seattle."

His eyes lit up with sudden excitement. "Hey, Mr. Garrett, you could come with us! That would be cool."

Will's gaze met hers and for an instant she imagined sharing hot dogs and listening to the cheers and sitting beside him for three hours, his heat and strength just inches away from her.

"I do enjoy watching the Mariners," Will said, an unreadable look in his eyes. "I'm pretty busy next month but if you let me know when you're going, I can see how it fits my schedule."

"We haven't made any definite plans," Julia said, hoping none of the longing showed in her expression.

She hadn't realized until this moment that Simon wasn't the only one in their family who hungered for a man in their lives.

And not just any man, either. Only a strong, quiet carpenter with callused hands and a rare, beautiful smile.

She decided to quickly change the subject. "The stairs look wonderful. Are you nearly finished?"

Before he could answer, they heard sudden excited barking from the front of the house.

Julia laughed. "I guess Conan needed to go out. It's a good thing he has his own doggy door."

"Hang on a minute," Will said. "That's his *somebody's home* bark."

A moment later they heard a vehicle pull into the driveway.

"Conan!" a high, excited voice shrieked and the dog woofed a greeting.

"That would be Chloe," Will said.

By tacit agreement, the three of them walked together toward the front of the house. When they rounded the corner, Julia saw a dark-haired girl around the twins' age with her arms around the dog's neck.

Beside her, Sage—glowing with joy—stood beside a man with commanding features and brilliant green eyes.

"Hey, guys!" Sage beamed at them. "Julia, this is Chloe Spencer and her dad Eben."

Julia smiled, though she would have known their identities just from the glow on Sage's features—the same one that flickered there whenever she talked about her fiancé and his daughter.

"Eben, this is Julia Blair."

The man offered a smile and his hand to shake. "The new tenant with the twins. Hello. It's a pleasure to meet you finally. Sage has told me a great deal about you and your children the last few weeks."

Sage had told her plenty about Eben and Chloe as well. Meeting them in person, she could well understand how Sage could find the man compelling.

It seemed an odd mix to her—the buttoned-down hotel executive who wore an elegant silk power tie and the free-thinking naturalist who believed her dog communicated with her dead friend. But Julia could tell in an instant they were both crazy about each other.

Eben Spencer turned to Will next and the two of them exchanged greetings. As they spoke, she couldn't help contrasting the two men. Though Eben was probably more classically handsome in a *GQ* kind of way, with his loosened tie and his rolled up shirt sleeves, she had to admit that Will's toolbelt and worn jeans affected her more.

Being near Eben Spencer didn't make her insides flutter and her bones turn liquid.

"And who's this?" Eben was asking, she realized when she jerked her attention back to the conversation.

Color soaked her cheeks and she hoped no one else noticed. "This is one of my kiddos. Simon, this is Mr. Spencer and his daughter Chloe."

"I'm eight," Chloe announced. "How old are you?"

Simon immediately went into defensive mode. "Well," he said slowly, "I won't be eight until March. But I'm taller than you are."

Chloe made a face. "*Everyone* is taller than me. I'm a shrimp. Sage says you have a twin sister. How cool! Where is she?"

He looked to Julia for an answer.

"Upstairs," she answered. "I'll go wake her, though. She's been anxious to meet you."

As if on cue, her timer beeped. "Got to run. That would be my pies ready to come out of the oven."

"You're making pie?" Chloe exclaimed. "That's super cool. I just *love* pie."

She smiled, charmed by Sage's stepdaughter-to-be. "I do, too. But not burnt pie so I'd better hurry."

She tried to be quiet as she slid the pies from the oven and carefully set them on a rack to dry, but she must have clattered something because Maddie began to stir in the other room.

She stood in the doorway and watched her daughter

rise to a sitting position on the couch. "Hey, baby. How are you feeling?"

Maddie gave an ear-popping yawn and stretched her arms above her head. "Pretty good. I'm sorry, Mama. I said I would help you make pies and then I fell asleep."

"You helped me with the hard part, which was picking the apples and washing them all."

"I guess."

She still looked dejected at her own limitations and Julia walked to her and pulled her into a hug. "You helped me a ton. I never would have been able to finish without you. And while you were sleeping soundly, guess who arrived?"

Her features immediately brightened. "Chloe?"

"Yep. She's outside with Simon right now."

"Can I go meet her?"

She smiled at her enthusiasm. One thing about Maddie, even in the midst of her worst fatigue, she could go from full sleep to complete alertness in a matter of seconds.

"Of course. Go ahead. I'll be down in a minute—I just have to put in these other pies."

A few moments later, she closed her apartment door and headed down the stairs. The elusive scent of freesia seemed to linger in the air and she wondered if that was Abigail's way of greeting the newcomers. The whimsical thought had barely registered when Anna's door—Abigail's old apartment—slowly opened.

She instinctively gasped, then flushed crimson when Will walked out, a measuring tape in hand.

What had she expected? The ghostly specter of Abigail, complete with flashy costume jewelry and a wicked smile?

"Hi," she managed.

He gave her an odd look. "Everything okay?"

"Yes. Just my imagination running away with me."

"I was double-checking the measurements for the new moldings in Anna's apartment. I'm hoping to get to them in a week or so."

"All done with the stairs, then?"

"Not quite. I'm still going to have to stain them but the bulk of the hard work is done."

"You do good work, Will. I'm very impressed."

"My dad taught me well."

The scent of freesia seemed stronger now and finally she had to say something. "Okay, tell me something. Can you smell that?"

Confusion flickered across his rugged features. "I smell sawdust and your apple pie baking. That's it."

"You don't smell freesia?"

"I'm not sure I know what that is."

"It's a flower. Kind of light, delicate. Abigail used to wear freesia perfume, apparently. I don't remember that about her but Anna and Sage say she did and I believe them."

He still looked confused. "And you're smelling it now?"

She sighed, knowing she must sound ridiculous. "Sage thinks Abigail is sticking around Brambleberry House."

To her surprise, he laughed out loud and she stared, arrested by the sound. "I wouldn't put it past her," he said. "She loved this old place."

"I can't say I blame her for that. I'm coming to love it, too. There's a kind of peace here—I can't explain it. Maddie says the house is friendly and I have to tell you, I'm beginning to believe her."

He shook his head, but he was smiling. "Watch out or you'll turn as wacky as Sage. Next thing I know, you'll be balancing your chakras every five minutes and eating only tofu and bean sprouts."

She gazed at his smile for a long moment, arrested by his light-hearted expression. He looked young and much more relaxed than she had seen him in a long time, almost happy, and her heart rejoiced that she had been able to make him smile and, yes, even laugh.

His smile slid away after a moment and she realized she was staring at his mouth. She couldn't seem to look away, suddenly wildly curious to know what it would be like to kiss him again.

Something hot kindled in the blue of his eyes and she caught her breath, wanting his touch, his kiss, more than she had wanted anything in a long time.

He wasn't ready, she reminded herself, and eased back, sliding her gaze from his. No sooner had she made up her mind to step away and let the intense moment pass when she could swear she felt a determined hand between her shoulderblades, pushing her forward.

She whirled around in astonishment, then thought she must be going crazy. Only the empty stairs were behind her.

"What's wrong?" Will asked. Though his words were concerned, that stony, unapproachable look had returned to his expression and she sighed, already missing that brief instant of laughter.

"Um, nothing. Absolutely nothing. My imagination seems to be in overdrive, that's all."

"That's what you get for talking about ghosts."

She forced a smile and headed for the door. Just

before she walked through it, she turned and aimed a glare at the empty room.

Stay out of my love life, Abigail, she thought. *Or any lack thereof.*

She could almost swear wicked laughter followed behind her.

Damn it. He wasn't at all ready for this.

Will followed Julia out the door, still aware of the heat and hunger simmering through him.

He had almost kissed her. The urge had been so strong, he had been only seconds away from reaching for her.

She wouldn't have stopped him. He sensed that much—he had seen the warm welcome in her eyes and had known she would have returned the kiss with enthusiasm.

He still didn't know why he had stopped or why she had leaned away then looked behind her as if fearing her children were skulking on the second-floor landing watching them.

He didn't know why they hadn't kissed but he was enormously grateful they had both come to their senses.

He didn't want to be attracted to another woman. Sure, he was a man and he had normal needs just like any other male. But he had been crazy about his wife. Kissing another woman—even *wanting* to kiss another woman—still seemed like some kind of betrayal, though intellectually he knew that was absurd.

Robin had been gone for more than two years. As much as he had loved her, he sometimes had to work hard to summon the particular arrangement of her features and the sound of her voice.

He was forgetting her and he hated it. Sometimes his grief seemed like a vast lake that had been frozen solid forever. Suddenly, as if overnight, the ice was beginning to crack around the edges. He wouldn't have expected it to hurt like hell but everything suddenly seemed more raw than it had since the accident.

He pressed his fist to the ache in chest for just a moment then headed for the backyard, where he had set up his power tools. His gaze seemed to immediately drift to Julia and he found her on the brick patio, laughing at something Sage had said, the afternoon sunlight finding gold strands in her hair. He could swear he felt more chunks of ice break free.

She must have sensed the weight of his stare—she turned her head slightly and their gazes collided for a brief moment before he broke the connection and picked up his power saw and headed for his truck.

On his next trip to get the sawhorses, he deliberately forced himself not to look at her. He was so busy *not* looking at her that he nearly mowed down Eben.

"Sorry," he muttered, feeling like an ass.

Eben laughed. "No problem. You look like your mind's a million miles away."

He judged her to be only about twenty-five feet, but he wasn't going to quibble. "Something like that," he murmured.

He hadn't expected to like Eben Spencer. When Sage had first fallen for the man, Will had been quite certain he would break her heart. As he had come to know him these last few months, he had changed his mind. Eben was deeply in love with Sage.

The two of them belonged together in a way Will couldn't have explained to save his life.

"You look like you could use a hand clearing this up."

He raised an eyebrow. "No offense, but you're not really dressed for moving my grimy tools."

"I don't mind getting a little dirty once in a while." The other man hefted two sawhorses over one shoulder, leaving Will only his toolbox to carry.

"Thanks," he said when everything had been slid into the bed of his pickup truck.

"No problem," Eben said again. "You're staying for dinner, aren't you? Sage has decided to throw an impromptu party since Chloe and I are back in town for a few days. I really don't want to be the only thing around here with a Y chromosome. Beautiful as all these Brambleberry women are, they're a little overwhelming for one solitary man."

"Don't forget you've got Simon Blair around now."

Eben laughed. "Well, that does help even the scales a little, but I have a feeling Sage and the others will be lost in wedding plans. I wouldn't mind company while I'm manning the grill."

He was tempted. He knew he shouldn't be but his empty house had become so oppressive sometimes he hated walking inside it.

"Got anything besides veggie burgers?"

"Sage talked to Jade and Stanley and they're sending over some choice prime-cut steaks from The Sea Urchin—the kind you can't buy at your average neighborhood grocery store."

"Sage *must* be in love if she's chasing down steaks for you," Will said, earning a chuckle from Eben.

"She might be a vegetarian but she's very forgiving of those of us who aren't quite as enlightened yet."

"Maybe she's just biding her time until you're

married, then she'll start substituting your bacon for veggie strips and your hamburgers for mushroom, bean-curd concoctions."

Eben smiled, his expression rueful. "I'm so crazy about her, I probably wouldn't mind." He paused. "Stay, why don't you? Anna and Sage would love to have you."

What about Julia? He wondered. His attention shifted to her and that longing came out of nowhere again, knocking him out at the knees.

"Sure," he said, before he could give himself a chance to reconsider. "I just need to run home and wash off some of this sweat and sawdust."

"Great. We'll see you in a few minutes then."

He drove away, already regretting the momentary impulse to accept the invitation.

Chapter 9

An hour later, after taking a quick shower and changing his clothes, Will stood beside Eben at the grill, beer in hand, asking himself again why he had possibly thought this might be a good idea.

It was a lovely evening, he had to admit that. A breeze blew off the ocean, cool enough to be refreshing but not cold enough to have anybody reaching for a sweater.

The sweet sound of children's laughter rang through the Brambleberry House yard as Chloe and the twins threw a ball for Conan. Sage, Julia and Anna were sitting at a table on the weathered brick patio looking over wedding magazines.

Abigail would have adored seeing those she loved most enjoying themselves together. This casual, informal kind of gathering was exactly the kind of thing she loved best.

He only wished he could enjoy himself as he used to

do, that he didn't view the whole scene with his chest aching and this deep sense of loss in his gut.

"My people at The Sea Urchin tell me the work you've done on the new cabinetry in the lobby is spectacular," Eben said as he turned the steaks one last time.

Will forced a smile. "I had great bones to work with. That helps on any project."

"She's a beautiful old place, isn't she?" Eben's smile was much more genuine. "I'm sorry I haven't had the opportunity yet to see what you've accomplished there. I'm looking forward to tomorrow when I have a chance to check out the progress of the last three weeks while Chloe and I have been overseas. I've been getting daily reports but it's not the same as seeing it firsthand."

"I think you'll be happy with it. You've got some real craftsmen working on The Sea Urchin."

"Including you." He took a sip of his beer, then gave Will an intent look. "In fact, I've got a proposition for you."

Will raised an eyebrow, curiosity replacing the ache, if only temporarily. Another job? he wondered. As far as he knew, The Sea Urchin was the only Spencer Hotels property along the coast.

"Spencer Hotels could always use a master carpenter. We've got rehab projects going in eight different properties right now alone. There's always something popping. What would you say to signing on with us, traveling a little? You could take your pick of the jobs, anywhere from Tokyo to Tuscany. We've got more than enough work to keep you busy, with much more in the pipeline."

He blinked, stunned at the offer. He was just a journeyman carpenter in piddly little Cannon Beach. What the hell did he know about either Tokyo or Tuscany?

"Whoa," he finally managed through his shock. "That's certainly…unexpected."

"I've been thinking about it for awhile. When I received the glowing report from my people here, it just seemed a confirmation of what had already been running around my head. I think you'd be perfect for the job. I usually try to hire workers from the various communities where my hotels are located—good business practice, you know—but I also like to have my own man overseeing the work."

"I don't know what good I would be in that capacity. I don't speak any language except good old English and a little bit of Spanish."

"The Spanish might help. But we always have translators on site, so that's not really a concern. I'm looking for a craftsman. An artisan. From what I've seen of your work, you definitely qualify. I also want someone I can trust to do the job right. And again, you qualify."

He had to admit, he was flattered. How could he not be? He loved his work and took great pride in it. When others saw and acknowledged a job well done, he found enormous satisfaction.

For just a moment, he allowed himself to imagine the possibilities. He had lived his entire life in Cannon Beach—in the very same house, even. Though he loved the town and loved living on the coast, maybe it was time to pick up and try something new, see the world a little.

On the other hand. he wasn't sure the ghosts that haunted him were ready for him to move on.

"You don't have to give me any kind of answer tonight," Eben said at his continued silence. "Just think about it. If you decide you're interested, we can sit down while I'm here and talk details."

"I'll think about it," he agreed. "I…it's a little over-whelming. It would be a huge change for me."

"But maybe not an unwelcome one," Eben said, show-ing more insight than Will was completely comfortable with.

"Maybe not." He paused. "I've got a buddy up in Ketchikan who's been after me to come up and go into business with him. I've been tossing the idea around."

"That might be good for you, too. Look at all your options. Take all the time you need. As far as I'm con-cerned, you can consider the Spencer Hotels offer an indefinite one with no time limit."

"What offer?"

He hadn't even noticed Sage had joined them until she spoke. Now she slipped her arm through the crook of Will's elbow and gave his arm an affectionate squeeze. Of all his friends, Sage was the most physical, and he always appreciated her hugs and kisses on the cheek and the times, like now, when she squeezed his arm.

He didn't like to admit it, but he sometimes ached for the soft comfort of a woman's touch, even the touch of a woman he considered more in the nature of a little sister than anything else.

"You won't like it," Eben predicted.

She made a face. "Try me. Believe it or not, I can be remarkably open-minded sometimes."

"Good. It might be a good idea for you to keep that in mind," Eben said with a wary expression.

"What are you up to?"

"I'm trying to steal Will away from Cannon Beach to come work for Spencer Hotels."

She dropped her arm and glared with shock at both of them. "You can't leave! We need you here."

"Says the woman who's going to be moving to San Francisco herself in a few months," Will murmured.

She tucked a loose strand of wavy blonde hair behind her ear, flushing a little at the reminder. "Not full-time. We'll be here every summer so I can still run the nature center camps. And we're planning to spend as much time up here as we can—weekends and school holidays."

"But you'll still be in the Bay Area most of the time, right?"

"Yes." She made a face. "I'm selfish, I know. I just don't want things to change."

"Things change, Sage. Most of the time we have no choice but to change, too, whether we want to or not."

She squeezed his arm again, her eyes suddenly moist. He saw memories of Robin and Cara swimming there and he didn't want to ruin her night by bringing up the past.

"I'm not going anywhere right now," he said. "Let's just enjoy the evening while we can."

Eben kissed his fiancée on the tip of her nose, an intimate gesture that for some reason made Will's chest ache. "These steaks are just about ready and I think your bean burger is perfect, though I believe that statement is a blatant oxymoron."

She laughed and headed off to tell the others dinner was ready.

"Give my offer some thought," Eben said when Sage was out of earshot. "Like I said, you don't have to answer right away. Maybe you could try it for six months or so to see how the traveling lifestyle fits you."

"I'll think about it," he agreed, which was an understatement of major proportions.

They ate on the brick patio, protected from the wind blowing off the sea by the long wall of Sitka spruce on the seaward edge of the yard.

While he and Eben had been grilling, the women had set out candles of varying heights around the patio and turned on the little twinkling fairy lights he had hung in the trees for Abigail a few summers earlier.

It seemed an odd collection of people but somehow the mix worked. Sage, with her highly developed social conscience. Anna with her quiet ambition and hard work ethic. Eben, dynamic businessman, and Julia, warm and nurturing, making sure plates were full, that the potato salad was seasoned just so, that drinks were replenished.

A group of very different people brought together because of Abigail, really.

Conversation flowed around him like an incoming tide finding small hidden channels in the sand and he was mostly content to sit at the table and listen to it.

"You're not eating your steak."

He looked up to find Julia watching him, her green eyes concerned. Though she sat beside him, he hadn't been ignoring her for the last hour but he hadn't exactly made any effort to seek her out, still disconcerted by that moment in the hallway when he had wanted to kiss her more than he wanted oxygen.

Sorry," he mumbled and immediately applied himself to the delicious cut in front of him.

"You don't have to eat it just because I said something." She pitched her voice low so others didn't overhear. "I was just wondering if everything is okay. You seem distracted."

He was distracted by *her*. By the cherry blossom scent of her, and her softness so close to him and the inappropriate thoughts he couldn't seem to shake.

"You don't know me anymore, Julia. For all you know, maybe I'm always this way."

As soon as the sharp words left his mouth, a cold wind suddenly forced its way past the line of trees to flutter the edges of the tablecloth and send the lights shivering in the treetops.

He didn't miss the hurt that leapt into her eyes or the way her mouth tightened.

He was immediately contrite. "I'm sorry. I'm not really fit company tonight."

"No, you're not. But it happens to all of us." She turned away to talk to Eben, on her other side, and the prime-cut steak suddenly had all the appeal of overdried beef jerky.

He would have to do a better job of apologizing for his sharp words, he realized. She didn't deserve to bear the brunt of his temper.

His chance didn't come until sometime later when everyone seemed to have finished dinner. Julia stood and started clearing dishes and Will immediately rose to help her, earning a surprised look and even a tentative smile from her.

"Where are we taking all this stuff?" he asked when he had an armload of dishes.

"My apartment. My dishwasher is the newest and the biggest. Most of the dishes came out of my kitchen anyway and I can make sure those that belong to Sage or Anna are returned to their rightful homes."

He followed her up the stairs, then headed down for another load. When he returned, she was rinsing and loading dishes in the dishwasher and he immediately started helping.

She flashed him one quick, questioning look, then smiled and made room for him at the sink.

The sheer domesticity of it stirred that same weird ache in his throat and he could feel himself wanting to shut down, to flee to the safety and empty solitude of his house down the beach.

But he had come this far. He could tough it out a little longer.

"I owe you an apology for my sharpness," he said after a moment. "A better one than the sorry excuse I gave you outside."

Her gaze collided with his for just a moment before she returned her attention to the sink. "You don't owe me anything, Will. I overstepped and I'm sorry. I've been overstepping since I came back to Cannon Beach."

She sighed and turned around, her hip leaning against the sink. "You were absolutely right, we don't have any kind of…anything. We were friends a long time ago, when we were both vastly different people. That was in the past. Somehow I keep forgetting that today we're simply two people who happen to live a few houses apart and have the same circle of friends."

"That's not quite true."

She frowned. "Which part isn't true?"

"That we were friends so long ago."

Hurt flickered in her eyes but she quickly concealed it and turned back to the sink. "My mistake, then. I guess you're right. We didn't know each other well. Just a few weeks every summer."

He should just stop now before he made things worse. What was the point in dragging all this up again?

"That's not what I meant. I only meant that the way we left things was definitely more than just friends."

She stared at him, sudden awareness blossoming in the green of her eyes.

"It took me a long time to get over you," he said, and the admission looked as if it surprised her as much as it did him. "When you didn't answer my letters, I figured everything I thought we had was all in my head. But it still hurt."

"Oh, Will." She dried her hands on a dish towel. "I would have written you but…things were so messed up. I was messed up. The day we returned home from our last summer in Cannon Beach, my parents told us they were divorcing. This was only two weeks before school started. My dad ended up with Charlie and the house in Los Angeles, and my mom took me to Sacramento with her. I had to start a new school my junior year, which was terrible. I didn't even get your letters until almost the end of the school year when my dad finally bothered to forward them from L.A."

She touched his arm, much the way Sage had earlier, but Sage's touch hadn't given him instant goosebumps or make him want to yank her into his arms.

"I should have written to explain to you what was going on," she went on. "I'm sorry I didn't, but I never forgot you, Will. This probably sounds really stupid, but the time I spent with you that summer was the best thing that happened to me in a long time, either before it or after, and I didn't want to spoil the memory of it."

She smiled, her hand still on his arm. He was dying here and he doubted she even realized what effect she was having on him. "You have no idea how long it took me to stop comparing every other boy to you."

"What can I say? I'm a hell of a kisser."

He meant the words as a flippant joke and she gave him a startled laugh, then followed up with a sidelong glance. "I do believe I remember that about you," she murmured.

The intimacy of the room seemed to wrap around them. For one wild moment, he felt sixteen again, lost in the throes of first love, entranced by Julia Hudson.

He could kiss her.

The impulse to taste her, touch her, poured through him and he was powerless to fight it. He took a step forward, expecting her to back away. Instead, her gaze locked with his and he saw in her eyes an awareness— even a longing—to match his own.

Still he hesitated, the only sound in the kitchen their mingled breathing. He might have stayed in an eternity of indecision if she hadn't leaned toward him slightly, just enough to tumble the last of his defenses.

In an instant, his mouth found hers and captured her quick gasp of surprise.

So long. So damn long.

He had forgotten how soft a woman's mouth could be, how instantly addictive it could be to taste desire.

Part of him wanted to yank back and retreat to his frozen lake where he was safe. But he was helpless to fight the tide of yearning crashing over him, the heat and sensation and pure, delicious pleasure of her softness against him.

It seemed impossible, but he tasted better than she remembered, of cinnamon and mint and coffee.

She should be shocked that he would kiss her, after being quite blunt that he wasn't interested in starting anything. But it seemed so right to be here in his arms that she couldn't manage to summon anything but grateful amazement.

She slid her arms around his neck, letting him set the pace and tone of the kiss. It was gentle at first, sweet and comfortable. Two old friends renewing something they had once shared.

Just as it had so many years earlier, being in his arms felt right. Completely perfect.

Their bodies had changed over the years—he was much broader and more muscled and she knew giving birth to twins had softened her edges and given her more curves.

But they still seemed to fit together like two halves of the same planed board.

She was aware of odd, random sensations as the kiss lingered—the hard countertop digging into her hip where he pressed her against it, the silk of his hair against her fingers, the smell of him, leathery and masculine.

And freesia.

The smell of flowers drifted through her kitchen so strongly that she opened one eye to make sure Abigail wasn't standing in the doorway watching them.

An instant later, she forgot all about Abigail—or any other ghosts—when Will pulled her closer and deepened the kiss, his tongue playing and teasing in a way that demonstrated quite unequivocally that he had learned more than a few things in the intervening years since their last kiss on the beach.

Heat flared, bright and urgent, and she dived right into the flames, holding him closer and returning the kiss.

She had no idea how long they kissed—or just how long they might have continued. Both of them froze when they heard the squeak of the entry door downstairs.

Will wrenched his mouth away, breathing hard, and stared at her and her heart broke at the expression on his face—shock and dismay and something close to anguish.

He raked a hand through his hair, leaving little tufts looking as if he'd just walked into a wind tunnel.

"That was… I shouldn't have…"

He seemed so genuinely upset, she locked away her hurt and focused on trying to ease his turmoil. "Will, it's okay."

"No. No, it's not. I shouldn't have done that. I've… I've got to go."

Without another word, he hurried out of the kitchen and her apartment and she heard the thud of his boots as he rushed down the wooden stairway and out the door.

She leaned against the counter, her breathing still ragged. She felt emotionally ravaged, wrung out and hung to dry.

She was still trying to figure out what just happened when she heard a knock on her door.

She wasn't sure she was at all ready to face anyone but when the knock sounded again, she knew she wouldn't be able to hide away there in her kitchen forever.

"It's open," she called.

The door swung open and a moment later Anna Galvez walked into the apartment.

"What's up with Will? He passed me on the stairs and didn't even say a word before he headed out the door like the hounds of hell were nipping at his heels."

She gave Julia a careful look. "Are you okay?

You look flushed. Did you and Will have a fight or something?"

"That blasted *or something* will get you every time," Julia muttered under her breath.

"You're going to have to give me a break here. I've been working all day on inventory and my brain is mush. Do you want to explain what that means?"

"Not really." She sighed, not at all comfortable talking about this. But right now she desperately needed a friend and Anna definitely qualified. "He kissed me," she blurted out.

Surprise then delight flickered across Anna's features. "Really? That's wonderful!"

"Is it? Will obviously didn't think so."

"Will doesn't do anything he doesn't want to do. If he hadn't wanted to kiss you, he wouldn't have."

"He was horrified afterward."

"A little overdramatic, don't you think?"

"You should have seen his face! I don't think he's ready. He's lost so much."

"So have you. I don't hear you saying you're not ready."

But their situations were vastly different, a point she wasn't prepared to point out to Anna. Will had been happily married when his wife died. She, on the other hand, had let Kevin go long before his fatal car accident.

"He will figure things out in his own time. Don't worry," Anna went on. "He's a wonderful man who's been through a terrible tragedy. But he'll get through it. Have a little faith."

Right now faith was something Julia had in very short supply. She could tumble hard and fast for Will Garrett. It wouldn't take a hard push—she had been in love with him when she was fifteen years old and she could easily see herself falling again.

But what would be the point, if he had his heart so tightly wrapped in protective layers that he wouldn't let anyone in?

Chapter 10

It was just a damn kiss.

Three weeks later, Will backed his truck into the Brambleberry House driveway, fighting a mix of dread and unwilling anticipation.

He knew both reactions were completely ridiculous. What the hell was he worrying about? She wouldn't even be here—he had finally managed to work the molding job into his schedule only after squeezing in a time when he could be certain Julia and her children were safely tucked away at the elementary school.

The very fact that he had to resort to such ridiculous manipulations of his own schedule simply to avoid seeing a certain woman bugged the heck out of him.

He ought to be tougher than this. He should have been completely unfazed by their brief encounter, instead of brooding about it for the better part of three weeks.

So he had kissed her. Big deal. The world hadn't

stopped spinning, the ocean hadn't suddenly been sucked dry, the Coast Range hadn't suddenly tumbled to dust.

Robin hadn't come back to haunt him.

He knew his reaction to the kiss had been excessive. He had run out of her apartment at Brambleberry House like a kid who had been caught smoking in the boy's room of the schoolhouse.

Yeah, he had overreacted to the shock of discovering not all of him was encased in ice—that he could desire another woman, could long to have her wrapped around him.

He still wanted it. That was what had bothered him for three weeks. Even though he hadn't seen her in all that time, she hadn't been far from his thoughts.

He remembered the taste of her, sweet and welcoming, the softness of her skin under his fingers, the subtle peace he had so briefly savored.

He couldn't seem to shake this achy sense that with that single kiss, everything in his world had changed, in a way he couldn't explain but knew he didn't like.

He didn't want change. Yeah, he hated his life and missed Robin and Cara so much he sometimes couldn't breathe around the pain. But it was *his* pain.

He was used to it now, and somewhere deep inside, he worried that letting go of that grief would mean letting go of his wife and baby girl, something he wasn't ready to face yet.

He knew his reaction was absurd. Plenty of people had lost loved ones and had moved ahead with their lives. His own mother had married again, just a few years after his father died, when Will was in his early twenties. She had moved to San Diego with her new husband, where the two of them seemed to be extremely happy together. They played golf, they went sailing on the bay, they enjoyed an active social life.

Will didn't begrudge his mother her happiness. He liked his stepfather and was grateful his mother had found someone else.

Intellectually, he knew it was possible, even expected, for him to date again sometime. He just wasn't sure he was ready yet—indeed, that he would ever be ready.

It had just been a kiss, he reminded himself. Not a damn marriage proposal.

As he sat in the driveway, gearing himself to go inside, the moist sea breeze drifted through his cracked window and he could suddenly swear he smelled cherry blossoms.

It was nearing the end of September, for heaven's sake, and was a cool, damp morning. He had absolutely no business smelling the spring scent of cherry blossoms on the breeze.

No doubt it was only the power of suggestion at work—he was thinking about Julia and his subconscious somehow managed to conjure the scent that always seemed to cling to her.

He closed his eyes and for just a moment allowed his mind to wander over that kiss again—the way she had responded to him with such warm enthusiasm, the silky softness of her mouth, the comfort of her hands against his skin.

Just a damn kiss!

His sigh filled the cab of the pickup and he stiffened his resolve and reached for the door handle.

Enough. Anna and Sage weren't paying him to sit on his butt and moon over their tenant. He had work to do. He'd been promising Anna for weeks he would get to her moldings and he couldn't keep putting it off.

A Garrett man kept his promises.

He climbed out and strapped on his tool belt with a dogged determination he would have found amusing under other circumstances, then grabbed as many of the moldings out of the back as he could lift.

He carried them to the porch and set them as close to the house as he could, then went back to his pickup for the rest. Judging by the steely clouds overhead, they were in for rain soon and he needed to keep the custom-cut oak dry.

He nearly dropped his second load when the front door suddenly swung open. A second later, Conan bounded through and barked with excitement.

He set the wood down with the other pile and gave the dog the obligatory scratch. "You're opening the door by yourself now? Pretty soon you're going to be driving yourself to the store to pick up dog food. You won't need any of us anymore."

"Until that amazing day arrives, he'll continue to keep us all as willing slaves. Hi, Will."

His entire insides had clenched at the sound of that first word spoken in a low, musical voice, and he slowly lifted his gaze to find Julia standing in the doorway.

She looked beautiful, fresh and lovely, and he could almost feel the churn of his heart.

"What are you doing here?" he said abruptly. "I figured you'd be at school."

Too late, he realized all that his words revealed—that he had given her more than a minute's thought in the last three weeks. She wasn't a stupid woman. No doubt she would quickly read between the lines and figure out he had purposely planned the project for a time when he was unlikely to encounter her.

To his vast relief, she didn't seem to notice. "I should be. At school, I mean. But Maddie's caught some kind of a bug. She was running a fever this morning and I decided I had better stay home and keep an eye on her."

"Is it a problem, missing your class?"

She shook her head. "I hate having to bring in a substitute this early in the school year but it can't be helped. The school district knew when they hired me that my daughter's health was fragile. So far they've been amazingly cooperative."

"She's okay, isn't she?"

All he could think about even as he asked the question was the irony of the whole thing. Above all else, he had tried his best to avoid bumping into her. So how, in heaven's name, had he managed to pick the one day she was home to finish the job?

"I think she's only caught a little cold," Julia answered. "At least that's what I hope it is. She's sniffly and coughing a bit but her fever broke about an hour ago. I hope it's just one of those twenty-four hour bugs."

"That's good."

"Her night was a little unsettled but she's sleeping soundly now. I figured rest was the best thing for her so I'm letting her sleep as long as she needs to beat this thing."

"Sounds like a smart plan."

"I guess you're here to do the moldings in Anna's apartment."

He nodded curtly, not knowing what else to say.

"Do you have more supplies in your truck that need to come in? I can help you carry things."

"This is it." His voice was more brusque than he intended and Conan made a snarly kind of growl at him.

Will just barely managed not to snarl back. He didn't need a dog making him feel guilty. He could do that all on his own.

It wasn't Julia's fault she stirred all kinds of unwelcome feelings in him and it wasn't at all fair of him to take out his bad mood on her.

He forced himself to temper his tone. "Would you mind holding the door open for me, though? It's going to rain soon and I'd hate for all this oak to get wet."

"Oh! Of course." She hurried to open the door. The only tricky part now was that he would have to move past her to get inside, he realized. He should have considered that little detail.

Too late now.

He let out a sigh of defeat and picked up several of the moldings and squeezed past her, doing his best not to bang the wood on the doorway on his way inside.

Going in wasn't so tough. Walking back out for a second load with his arms unencumbered was an entirely different story. He was painfully aware of her—that scent of spring, the heat of her body, the flicker of awareness in her green eyes as he passed.

Oh, he was in trouble.

His only consolation was that she seemed just as disconcerted by his presence.

"I guess you probably have a key to Anna's apartment, don't you?" she asked.

He nodded. "I have keys to the whole house so I can come and go when I'm working on something. All but your apartment. I gave it back to Anna and Sage when I finished up on the second floor."

"Good to know," she murmured.

He cleared his throat, set down the moldings in the

entry and fished in his pocket, then pulled out the Brambleberry keyring. Of course, his hands seemed to fumble
as he tried to find the right one to fit the lock for Anna's
apartment, but he finally located it and opened her door.

"Would you mind holding the apartment door open
as well? I need to be careful not to hit the wood on the
frame. If you could guide it through, that would be
great."

"Sure!" She hurried to prop open the door with an
eagerness that made him blink. Even though it was akin
to torture, he had to walk past her all over again and he
forced himself to put away this sizzle of awareness and
focus on the job.

She followed him inside as he carried the eight-foot-
long moldings in and set them behind Anna's couch.

"Can I give you a hand with anything else?" Julia
asked. "To be honest, I'm a bit at loose ends this morning
and was looking for a distraction. I've already finished
my lesson plans for the next month and I'm completely
caught up with my homework grading. I was just con-
templating rearranging my kitchen cabinets in alphabeti-
cal order, just to kill the boredom. I'd love the chance to
do something constructive."

That was just about the last thing on earth he needed
right now, to have to work with Julia looking on. She
was the very definition of distraction. With his luck,
he'd probably be so busy trying not to smell her that he
would glue his sleeve to the wood.

His hesitation dragged on just a moment too long, he
realized as he watched heat soak her cheeks.

"You're used to working alone and I would probably
only get in the way, wouldn't I? Forget I said anything."

He hated her distress, hated making her think he

didn't want her around. Was he a coward or was he a man who could contain his own unwanted desires?

"I *am* used to working alone," he said slowly, already regretting the words. "But I guess I wouldn't mind the company."

It was almost worth his impending discomfort to see her face light up with such delight. She must really be bored if she could get so excited about handing him tools and watching him nail up moldings.

"I'll just run up and grab the walkie-talkie I let the kids use when they're sick to call out to me when they need drinks and things. That way Maddie will be able to find me when she wakes up."

He nodded, though she didn't seem to expect much of an answer as she hurried out the door and up the stairs.

What the hell had he just done? he wondered. The whole point of scheduling this project during this time had been to avoid bumping into her. He certainly didn't expect to find himself inviting her to spend the next hour or so right next to him, crowding his space, posing far too much of a temptation for his peace of mind.

"What are you grinning at?" he growled to Conan.

The dog just woofed at him and settled onto the rug in front of the empty fireplace. When Abigail was alive, that had always been his favorite place, Will remembered.

He supposed it was nice to see a few things didn't change, even though he felt as if the rest of his life was a deck of cards that had suddenly been thrown into the teeth of the wind.

She was a fool when it came to Will Garrett.

Up in her apartment, Julia quickly ran a brush through her hair. She thought about touching up the quick makeup job she'd done that morning but she figured Will would probably notice—and wonder—if she put on fresh lipstick.

Would he really notice? The snide voice in her head asked. He had made it plain he wasn't interested in her. Or at least that he didn't want to be interested in her, which amounted to the same thing.

More reason she was a fool for Will Garrett. Some part of her held out some foolish hope that this time might be different, that this time he might be able to see beyond the past.

Her conversation with Anna seemed to play through her head again. *He's a wonderful man who's been through a terrible tragedy. But he'll get through it. Have a little faith.*

She understood grief. Understood and accepted it. Despite their marital problems toward the end, she had mourned Kevin's death for the children's sake and for the sake of all those dreams they had once shared, the dreams that had been lost along the way somewhere.

She understood Will's sorrow. But she also accepted that she had missed him these last few weeks.

He hadn't been far from her thoughts, even as she went about the business of living—settling into the school year, getting to know her new students and co-workers at the elementary school, helping Simon and Maddie with their schoolwork.

She glanced out the window at his workshop, tucked away behind his house beneath the trees. How many nights had she stood at the window, watching the lights flicker there, wondering how he was, what he was thinking, what he might be working on?

She was obsessed with the man. Pure and simple. Perhaps they would both be better off if she just stayed up here with her daughter and pushed thoughts of him out of her head.

She sighed. She wasn't going to, because of that whole being-a-fool thing again. She couldn't resist this chance to talk to him again, to indulge herself with his company and perhaps come to know a little more about the man he had become.

She opened Maddie's door and found her daughter still sleeping, her skin a healthy color and her breathing even. Julia scribbled a quick note to tell her where she was.

"I have the other walkie-talkie so just let me know when you wake up," she wrote and slipped the note under the other wireless handset on Maddie's bedside table where she couldn't miss it.

She spent one more moment watching the miracle of her daughter sleeping.

It was exactly the reminder she needed to wake her to the harsh reality of just how cautious she needed to be around Will Garrett.

Girlhood crushes were one thing, but she had two children to worry about now. She couldn't risk their feelings, couldn't let them come to care any more about a man who quite plainly wasn't ready to let anyone else into his life.

She would walk downstairs and be friendly in a polite, completely casual way, she told herself as she headed for the door. She wouldn't push him, she wouldn't dig too deeply.

She would simply help him with his project and try to bridge the tension between them so they could remain on friendly terms.

Anything else would be beyond foolish, when she had her children's emotional well-being to consider.

Chapter 11

When she returned to Anna's apartment, she found Conan sleeping on his favorite rug but no sign of Will. His tools and the boards he had brought in were still in evidence but Will wasn't anywhere to be found so Julia settled down to wait.

A moment later, she heard the front door open. Conan opened one eye and slapped his tail on the floor but didn't bother rising when Will came in carrying a small tool box and a container of nails.

He faltered a little when he saw her, as if he had forgotten her presence, or, worse, had maybe hoped it was all a bad dream. She was tempted again to abandon the whole idea and return upstairs to Maddie. But some part of her was still intensely curious to know why he seemed so uncomfortable in her presence.

He obviously wasn't completely impervious to her or he wouldn't care whether she hung around or not, any more than it bothered him to have Conan watching him work.

Was that a good sign, or just more evidence that she ought to just leave the poor man alone?

"Are you sure there's not anything else I can bring inside for you?" she asked. "I'm not good for much but I can carry tools or something."

"No. This should be everything I need."

He said nothing more, just started laying out tools, and she might have thought he had completely forgotten her presence if not for the barest clenching of muscle along his jawline and a hint of red at the tips of his ears.

She knew she shouldn't find that tiny reaction so fascinating but she couldn't seem to stop staring.

She found *everything* about Will Garrett fascinating, she acknowledged somewhat grimly.

From the tool belt riding low on his hips to the broad shoulders he had gained from hard work over the years to the tiny network of lines around his eyes that had probably once been laugh lines.

She wanted to hear him laugh again. The strength of her desire burned through her chest and she would have given anything just then to be able to come up with some kind of hilarious story that would be guaranteed to have him in stitches.

"Since you're here, can you do me a favor?" he spoke suddenly as she was wracking her brain trying to come up with something.

"Of course." She jumped up, pathetically grateful for any task, no matter how humble.

"I need to double-check my measurements. I've checked them several times but I want to be sure before I make the final cuts."

"I guess you can't be too careful in your line of work."

"Not when you're dealing with oak trim that costs an arm and a leg," he answered.

"It's gorgeous, though."

"Worth every penny," he agreed, and for one breathless moment, he looked as if he wanted to smile. Just before the lighthearted expression would have broken free, his features sobered and he held out the end of the tape measure to her.

He was a man who devoted scrupulous attention to detail, she thought as they measured and re-measured the circumference of the room. He had kissed her the same way, thoroughly and completely, as if he couldn't bear the idea of missing a single second.

Her stomach quivered at the memory of his arms around her and the intensity of his mouth searching hers.

Maybe this hadn't been such a grand idea, the two of them alone here in the quiet hush of a rainy day morning with only Conan for company.

"What do you do when you don't have a fumbling and inept—but well-meaning—assistant to help you out with things like this?" she asked, to break the sudden hushed intimacy.

He shrugged. "I usually make do. I have a couple of high school kids who help me sometimes. Most jobs I can handle on my own but sometimes an extra set of hands can definitely make the work a lot easier."

She was grateful again that she had offered help, even if he still seemed uneasy about accepting.

"Well, I can't promise that my hands are good for much, but I'm happy to use them for anything you need."

As soon as the words left her mouth, she realized how they could be misconstrued. She flushed, but to her vast relief he didn't seem to notice either her blush or her unintentionally provocative statement.

"Thanks. I appreciate that."

He paused after writing down one more measurement then retracting the tape measure. "Robin was always after me to hire a full-time assistant," he said after a moment.

This was the first time he had mentioned his wife to her on his own. It seemed an important step, somehow, as if he had allowed himself to lower yet another barrier between them.

Julia held her breath, not wanting to say anything that might make him regret bringing up the subject.

"You didn't do it, though?"

He shrugged. "I like working on my own. I can pick the music I want, can work at my own pace, can talk to myself when I need to. Yeah, I guess that probably makes me a little on the crazy side."

She laughed. "Not crazy. I talk to myself all the time. It helps to have Conan around, then I can at least pretend I'm talking to him."

He smiled. One moment he was wearing that remote, polite expression, then next, a genuine smile stole over his handsome features. She stared at it, her pulse shivering.

She wanted to leap up and down and shriek with glee that she had been able to lighten his features, even if only for a moment, but then he would definitely think *she* was the crazy one.

"Maybe I need a dog to take on jobs with me, just so I don't get a reputation as the wild-eyed carpenter who carries on long conversations with himself."

"I'm sure Sage and Anna would consider renting Conan out by the hour," she offered.

He smiled again—twice in as many minutes!—and turned to the dog. "What do you say, bud? Want to be my permanent assistant?"

Conan snuffled and gave a huge yawn that stretched his jaws, then he flopped over on his other side, turning his back toward both of them.

Julia couldn't help laughing. "Sorry, Will, but I think that's a definite no. You wouldn't want to interfere with his strenuous nap schedule. I guess you'll have to make do with me for now. I just hope I haven't messed up your rhythm too much."

"No. You're actually helping."

"You don't have to sound so surprised!" she exclaimed. "I do occasionally have my uses."

"Sorry. I didn't mean it that way."

She managed a smile. "No problem. Believe it or not, I've got a pretty thick skin."

They worked in silence and Will seemed deep in thought. When he spoke some time later, she realized his mind was still on what he'd said about hiring an assistant.

"Sometimes Robin would come with me on bigger jobs to lend a hand, until Cara came along, anyway," he said. "She started to crawl early—six months or so—and was into everything. She barely gave Robin a second to breathe for chasing her."

Again, she sensed by the stiff set of his shoulders that he wasn't completely comfortable talking about his family. She wasn't sure why he had decided to share these few details but she was beyond touched that he was willing to show her this snapshot of their life together.

"I can imagine it was hard to get any work done while you were chasing a busy toddler," she said.

He nodded. "She wasn't afraid of anything, our Cara. If Robin or I didn't watch her, she'd be out the back door and halfway to the ocean before we figured out where she had gone. We had to put double child-locks on every door."

He smiled a little at the memory but she could still sense the pain around the edges of his smile. She couldn't help herself, she reached out and touched his forearm, driven only by the need to comfort him.

His skin was warm, covered in a layer of crisp dark hair. He looked down at her fingers on his darker skin and she thought she saw his Adam's apple move as he swallowed.

"Maddie was like that, too," she said after a moment, lifting her hand away.

"Maddie?"

"I know. Hard to believe. She was a much busier toddler than Simon. She was always the ringleader of the two of them."

She smiled at the memory. "When they still could barely walk, they used to climb out of their cribs in the night to play with their toys. I couldn't figure out how they were doing it so I set up the video camera with a motion sensor and caught Maddie moving like a little monkey to climb out of hers. She didn't need any help but Simon apparently wasn't as skilled so Maddie would climb out and then push a half-dozen stuffed animals over the top railing of his crib so he could use them to climb out. It was quite a system the little rascals came up with."

He paused in the middle of searching through his toolbox, his features far more interested than she might have expected. "So what did you do? Take out all the stuffed animals from the room?"

She made a face. "No. Gave into the inevitable. We bought them both toddler beds so they wouldn't break their necks climbing out"

"Did they still get up in the night?"

"Not as much. I think it was the lure of the forbidden that kept them trying to escape."

He laughed—a real, full-fledged laugh. She watched the shadows lift from his eyes for just a moment, saw in that light expression some glimmer of the Will she had known, and she could swear she felt the tumble and thud of her heart.

She was an idiot for Will Garrett, only now she didn't have the excuse of being fifteen, flush with the heady excitement of first love.

After entirely too short a time, his laughter slid away and he turned his attention back to the project. "How do you feel about heights?"

"Moderately okay, within reason."

"It would help if you could hold the trim up while I nail it, as long as you don't mind climbing the ladder."

"Not at all."

For the next twenty minutes, they spoke little as they worked together to hang the trim. They finished two walls quickly but the other two weren't as straightforward. One had a fireplace and chimney flue that Will needed to work the trim around and the other had a jog that she thought must contain ductwork.

As she waited for Will to figure out the angles for the cuts, Julia sat on the couch, enjoying the animation on his features as he calculated. She wondered if he knew how his eyes lit up while he was working, how he seemed to vibrate with an energy she didn't see there at other times.

At last he figured out the math involved to make sure the moldings matched up correctly. He left for a moment and she heard his power saw out on the porch.

"You love this, don't you?" she asked when he returned carrying the cut pieces of trim.

He shrugged. "It's a living."

"It's more than that to you. I can tell. I keep remembering how much you complained about your dad making you go out on jobs with him that summer."

His laugh was rueful, tinged with embarrassment. "I was a stupid sixteen-year-old punk without a brain in my head. All I wanted to do was hang out with my friends and try to impress pretty girls."

She shook her head. "You were *not* a punk. You were by far the most decent boy I knew."

The tips of his ears turned that dusky red again. "Funny, you always seemed like such a sensible kind of girl."

"I was sensible enough to know when a boy is different from the others I'd met. All they wanted to do was flirt and see how many bases they could steal. They weren't interested in talking about serious things like the political science class they had taken the year before or the ecological condition of the shoreline."

"Did I do that?"

"You don't remember?"

He slanted her a sidelong look. "All I remember is trying to figure out whether I dared try sliding into second base."

She blushed, though she couldn't help smiling, too.

"I guess you were just more subtle about that particular goal than the other boys, then."

"Either that or more chicken."

She laughed. She couldn't help herself. To her delight, he laughed along with her and the unexpected sound of it even had Conan lifting his head to watch the two of them with what looked suspiciously like satisfaction.

She remembered Sage's assertion that the dog was working in cahoots with Abigail.

Just now—with the rain pattering softly against the window and this peculiar intimacy swirling around them—the idea didn't seem completely ludicrous.

"Okay, I think I've finally got this figured out," he said after a moment. "I think I'm ready for my assistant."

She pushed her ladder closer to his since they were working with a much smaller length of trim.

As he was only a few feet away from her, she was intensely aware of him—his scent, leathery and masculine, and the heat that seemed to pulse from him.

He wasn't smiling or laughing now, she noted. In fact, he seemed tense suddenly and in a hurry to finish this section of the job.

"I can probably handle the rest on my own," he said, his voice suddenly sounding strained. "None of the remaining lengths of trim are very long so I shouldn't need your help holding them in place."

"I can stick around, just in case you need me."

His gaze met hers and she thought he would tell her not to bother but he simply nodded. "Sure. Okay."

She was so relieved he wasn't going to send her away that she wasn't paying as close attention to what she was doing as she should have been while she descended the ladder at the same time Will descended his own ladder next to her.

In her distracted state, she misjudged the last rung and stumbled a little at the bottom.

"Whoa! Careful there," he exclaimed, reaching out instinctively to catch her.

For one moment, they froze in that suspended state, with his strong arms around her and her arms trapped between their bodies. Her startled gaze flew to his and she thought she saw awareness and desire and the barest shadow of resignation there.

Will stared at her, his heart pumping in his chest like an out-of-control nail gun. A desperate kind of hunger prowled through him, wild and urgent. Though he knew she was far from it, she felt small and fragile in his arms.

He could feel the heat of her burning his skin, could smell that soft, mouthwatering scent of cherry blossoms.

He closed his eyes, fighting the inevitable with every ounce of strength he had left. But when he opened his eyes, he found her color high, her lips parted slightly, her eyes a deep and mossy green, shadowed with what he was almost positive was a heady awareness to match his own.

He should stop this right now, should just release her, push her from Anna's apartment and lock the door snugly behind her. The tiny corner of his brain that could still manage to string together a coherent thought told him that was exactly the course of action he ought to follow.

But how could he? She was so soft, so sweetly, irresistibly warm, and he had been cold for so damn long.

He heard a groan and realized it came from his own

throat just an instant before he lowered his mouth and kissed her.

She sighed his name, just a whispered breath between their mouths, but the sound seemed to sink through all the layers of careful protection around his heart.

She wrapped her arms around his neck, responding eagerly to his kiss. Tenderness surged through him, raw and terrifying. He wanted to hang on tight and never let go, wanted to stand in Abigail's old living room for the rest of his life with a soft rain clicking against the windows and Julia Hudson Blair in his arms.

They kissed for a long time, until he was breathing hard and light-headed, until her mouth was swollen, until his body cried out for more and more.

He didn't know how long they would have continued—forever if he'd had his way—when suddenly he heard the one thing guaranteed to shatter the moment and the mood like a hard, cold downpour.

"Mama? Are you there? I woke up."

The sweet, high voice cut through the room like a buzz saw. He stiffened, his insides cold suddenly, and frantically looked to the doorway, aghast at what he had done and that her daughter had caught them at it.

He only knew a small measure of relief when he realized the voice was coming from the walkie-talkie she had brought downstairs.

Julia was breathing just as hard as he was, her eyes wide and dazed and her cheeks flushed.

Even through his dismay, he had to clench his fists at his side to keep from reaching for her again.

She drew in a deep, shuddering breath, then walked to the walkie-talkie and picked it up.

"I'm here, baby," she said, her voice slightly ragged. "How are you feeling?"

"My throat still hurts a little but I'm okay," Maddie answered. "Where are you, Mama?"

Julia flashed a quick glance at him, then looked away. "Downstairs with W— Mr. Garrett. Didn't you see my note?"

"Yes, when I woke up. But I was just wondering if you were still down there."

"I am."

"Is Conan there with you?"

Will saw her sweep the room with her gaze until she found the dog still curled up by the couch. "He's right here. I'll bring him up with me if you want some company."

"Thanks, Mama."

She clipped the walkie-talkie to her belt, angled slightly away from him so he couldn't see her expression, then she seemed to draw another deep breath before she turned to face him.

"I…have to go up. Maddie needs me."

"Right." He ached to touch her again, just one more time, but he fiercely clamped down on the desire, wanting her gone almost as much as he wanted to sweep her into his arms again.

Without warning, he was suddenly furious. Damn her, *damn her*, for making him want again—for this churn of his blood pouring into the frozen edges inside him. Pain prickled through him, like he had just shoved frostbitten fingers into boiling water.

He didn't want this, didn't want to feel again. Hadn't he made that clear? So why the hell did she have to come in here, with her sweet smile and her warm eyes and her soft curves.

"Will—"

"Don't say anything," he bit out. "This was a mistake. It's been a mistake for me to spend even a minute with you since you came back to town."

At his sudden attack, shock and hurt flared in her green eyes and he hated himself all over again but that didn't change what he knew he had to do.

"You didn't think it was a mistake a moment ago," she murmured.

He couldn't deny the truth of that. "I'm attracted to you. That's obvious, isn't it? I have been since I was sixteen years old. But I don't want to be. You're in my way every single time I turn around."

He lashed out, needing only to make her understand even as he was appalled at his words, at the way her spine seemed to stiffen with each syllable.

Still, he couldn't seem to hold them back once he started. They gushed between them, ugly and harsh.

"You're always coming around to help me work, showing up at my house dragging your kids along, crowding me every second. Don't you get it? I don't want you around! Why can't you just leave me alone?"

Conan rose and growled and for the first time in Will's memory the dog looked menacing. At the same time, a branch outside Anna's apartment clawed and scratched against the window, whipped by a sudden microburst of wind.

Julia seemed to ignore all the external distractions. She drew in a deep breath, her face paler than he had ever seen it.

"That's not fair," she said, her voice low and tight.

He raked a hand through his hair, hating himself, hating her, hating Robin and Cara for leaving him this empty, harsh, cruel husk of a man. "I know. I know it's not fair. You don't deserve to bear the weight of all that, Julia. I know that, but I can't help it. I'm sorry, but it's the truth. I need you to leave me alone. Please. I can't do this anymore. I can't. Not with you. Not with anyone."

The branch scraped the glass harder and he made a mental note to prune it for Sage and Anna, even as he fought down the urge to pound something, to smash his fists hard into the new drywall he had put in a few months earlier.

She studied him for a long moment, her features taut.

"Okay," she finally murmured and headed for the door to Anna's apartment.

Before she left, she turned around to face him one last time. "I appreciate your frankness. Since I know you're a fair man, I'm sure you'll allow me the same privilege."

What the hell was he supposed to say to that? He waited, though he wanted nothing more than to shove the door closed behind her and lock it tight.

"I have something I want to say, though I know it's not my place and none of my business. Still, I think you need to hear it from someone."

She paused, and seemed to be gathering her thoughts. When she spoke, her words sliced at him like a band saw.

"Will, do you really think Robin and Cara would want this for you?"

"Don't."

He couldn't bear a lecture or a commentary or whatever she planned. Not now, not about this.

She shook her head. "No. I'm going to say this. And then you can push me away all you want, as you've been doing since I came back to Cannon Beach. I want you to ask yourself if your wife and little girl would want you to spend the rest of your life wallowing in your pain, smothering yourself in it. From all I've heard about Robin, it sounds as if she was generous and loving to everyone. Sage has told me what a good friend she was to everyone, how people were always drawn to her because of her kindness and her cheerful nature. I'm sorry I never had the chance to meet her. But from what I've heard of her, I can't imagine Robin would find it any tribute to her kind and giving nature that you want you to close yourself away from life as some kind of…of penance because she's gone."

She looked as if she had more she wanted to say, but to his relief she only gave him one more long look then turned to gesture to Conan. The dog added his glare to hers, giving Will what could only be described as the snake-eye, then followed her out the door.

Will stood for a long moment, an ache in his chest and her scent still swirling around him. He closed his eyes, remembering again the sweetness of her touch, how fiercely he had wanted to hold on tight, to surrender completely and let her work her healing magic.

He had to leave.

That was all there was to it. He couldn't stay in Cannon Beach with Julia and her kids just a few houses away. There was no way in the small community of year-round residents that he could avoid her, and seeing her, spending any time with her, was obviously a mistake.

He had meant what he said. She crowded him and he couldn't deal with it anymore.

He knew after his outburst just now that she wouldn't make any effort to spend time with him, but they were still bound to bump into each other once in a while and he had just proved to himself that he had no powers of resistance where she was concerned.

He had no other option but to escape.

He pulled out his cell phone. He knew the number was there—he had dialed it only the night before but in the end he had lost his nerve and hung up.

With the wind still whipping the tree branches outside like angry fists, he found it quickly, hit the button to redial and waited for it to ring.

As he might have expected, he was sent immediately to voice-messaging. For a moment he considered hanging up again but the sweet scent of spring flowers drifted to him and he knew this was what he had to do.

He drew in a breath. "Eben, this is Will Garrett," he began. "I'd like to talk about your offer, if it's still open."

Chapter 12

"Simon, hands to yourself."

Her son snatched his fingers back an instant before they would have dipped into the frosting on the frill-bedecked sheet cake for Sage's wedding shower.

"I only wanted a little smackeral," he complained.

Julia sighed, even as she fought a smile. This was why she was destined to be a lousy mother, she decided. How on earth was she supposed to have the gumption to properly discipline her son when he knew he could charm her every time by quoting Winnie the Pooh?

"No smackerals, little or otherwise," she said as sternly as she could manage. "After the bridal shower you can have all the leftovers you want but Sage wouldn't want grimy little finger trails dipping through her pretty cake, would she?"

"Sage wouldn't mind," he grumbled.

All right, he was probably correct on that observation.

Sage was remarkably even-tempered for a bride and she adored Julia's twins and spoiled them both relentlessly.

But as their mother, it was Julia's responsibility to teach them little things like manners, and she couldn't let him get away with it, smackerals or not.

"I mind," she said firmly. "Tell you what, if you promise to help Anna and me put all the chairs and tables away after the shower, you can appease your sugar buzz with one of the cookies you and Maddie and I made last night."

He grinned and reached for one. "Can I take one to Mad? She's in her room."

"As long as you don't forget where you were taking it and eat that one too along the way."

"I would *never* do that!" he protested, with just a shade too much offended innocence.

Julia shook her head, smiling as she put the finishing touches on the cake.

Simon paused at the doorway. "Can we eat our cookies outside and play with Conan for awhile since the rain *finally* stopped?"

"Of course," she answered. After an entire week straight of rain, she knew both of her children were suffering from acute cases of cabin fever.

A moment later, she heard the door slam then the pounding of two little sets of feet hurtling down the stairs, joined shortly after by enthusiastic barking.

Unable to resist, she moved to the window overlooking the backyard just in time to see Maddie pick up an armful of fallen leaves and toss them into the air, her face beaming with joy at being outside to savor the October sunshine. Not far away, Conan and Simon were already wrestling in the grass together.

The two of them loved this place—the old house, with its quirks and its personality, the yard and Abigail's beautiful gardens, the wild and gorgeous ocean just a few footsteps away.

They were thriving here, just as she had hoped. They already had good friends at school, they were doing well in their classes. Maddie's health seemed to have taken a giant leap forward and improved immeasurably in the nearly two months they had been in Cannon Beach.

She should be so happy. Her children were happy, her job was working out well, they had all settled into a routine.

So why couldn't she shake this lingering depression that seemed to have settled on her shoulders as summer slid into autumn? She shifted her gaze from the Brambleberry House yard to another house just a few hundred yards up the beach.

There was the answer to the question of why she couldn't seem to shake her gray mood. Will Garrett. She hadn't seen him since their disastrous encounter nearly two weeks earlier but her insides still churned with dismay when she remembered his blunt words telling her to leave him alone, and then her own presumptuous reply.

She had been way out of line to bring Robin and Cara into the whole thing, to basically accuse him of dishonoring his wife and daughter's memory simply because he continued to push Julia away.

She had had no right to tell him how he ought to grieve or to pretend she knew what his wife might have wanted for him. She had never even met the woman.

Because of her lingering shame at her own temerity, she was almost grateful she hadn't seen him since, even to catch a glimpse of him through the pines as he moved around his house.

That's what she told herself, anyway. If she stood at her window at night watching the lights in his house, hoping for some shadow to move across a window, well, that was her own pathetic little secret.

With one last sigh, she forced herself to move away from the window and return to the kitchen and the cake. A few moments later, with a final flourish, she judged it ready and carefully picked it up to carry it downstairs to Anna's apartment.

Since her arms were full, she managed to ring the doorbell with her elbow. Anna opened almost immediately. Though she smiled, Julia didn't miss the troubled expression in her eyes.

She was probably just busy setting up for the shower, Julia told herself. She knew Anna had been distracted with problems at her two giftshops as well, though she seemed reluctant to talk about them.

Julia smiled and held out the cake. "Watch out. Masterpiece coming through."

Anna's expression lifted slightly as she looked at the autumn-themed cake, with its richly colored oak and maple leaves and pine boughs, all crafted of frosting.

Sage wasn't one for frilly lace and other traditional wedding decorations. Given her job as a naturalist and her love of the outdoors, Julia and Anna had picked a nature theme for the shower they were throwing and the cake was to be the centerpiece of their decorations.

"Oh! Oh, It's beautiful!"

"Told you it would be," Julia said with undeniable satisfaction as she carried the cake inside Anna's apartment to a table set in a corner.

"You were absolutely right," Sage said from the couch. "I can't believe you did all that in one afternoon!"

Julia shrugged. "I don't have a lot of domestic skills but I can decorate a cake like nobody's business. I told you I put myself through college working in a bakery, so if the teaching thing ever falls through, I've at least got something to fall back on."

She grinned at them both and was surprised when they didn't smile back. Instead, they exchanged grim looks.

"What is it? What's wrong? Is it the cake? I tried to decorate it just as we discussed."

"It's not the cake," Anna assured her. "The cake is gorgeous."

"Did somebody cancel, then?"

"No. Everybody's still coming, as far as I know." Sage sighed. "I just hung up the phone with Eben."

She frowned. "Is everything okay with Chloe?"

"No. Nothing like that. Julia, it's not Eben or Chloe or anything to do with the shower. It's Will."

Her stomach cramped suddenly and for a moment she couldn't seem to breathe. "What…what's wrong with Will?"

"He's leaving," Anna said, her usual matter-of-fact tone sounding strained.

"Leaving?"

Sage nodded, her eyes distressed. "Apparently he's taken a traveling job with Spencer Hotels. A sort of carpentry trouble-shooter, traveling around to their renovation sites and overseeing the work of the local builders. He's starting right after the wedding. He accepted the job a few weeks ago but apparently Eben didn't seem to think it was anything worth mentioning to me until just now on the phone, purely in passing."

She scowled, apparently at her absent fiancé. Julia barely noticed, too lost in her own shock. Two weeks ago. She didn't miss the significance of that, not for a minute.

They had kissed right here in this very living room and she could think of nothing else but how he had all but begged her to leave him alone and then in her hurt, she had said such nervy, terrible things to him.

Ask yourself if your wife and little girl would want you to spend the rest of your life wallowing in your pain, smothering yourself in it.

Oh, what had she done? Now he had taken a traveling job with Eben's company and she could hardly seem to work her brain around it. He was leaving Cannon Beach—the home he loved, his friends, the business he had work so hard to build.

Because of her.

She knew it had to be so. What other reason could he have?

She had made him too uncomfortable, had pushed too hard.

I can't imagine Robin would find it any tribute that you want you to close yourself away from life as some kind of penance because she's gone.

Her face burned and her stomach seemed to twist into a snarled tangle. What had she *done?*

"What do you think, Julia?"

She jerked her mind back to the conversation to realize Sage was speaking to her and as her silence dragged on, both women were giving her curious looks.

It was obvious they expected some response from her but as she hadn't heard the question, she didn't know at all what to say.

"I'm sorry. What?"

"I said that you've known him longer than any of us. What could he be thinking?"

"Oh no. I don't know him," she murmured. "Not really."

Perhaps that was the trouble, she admitted to herself. She had this idealized image of Will from years ago when she had loved him as a girl. Had she truly allowed herself to accept the reality of all the years and the pain between them?

She had pushed him, harder than he was ready to be pushed. She had backed him into a corner and he was looking for some way out.

This was all her fault and she was going to have to figure out a way to make things right. She couldn't let Will leave everything he cared about behind because of her.

The doorbell rang suddenly and Conan jumped up from his spot on the floor where he had been watching them. Now he hurried to Anna's open apartment door, his tail wagging furiously and for one wild moment her heart jumped at the thought that it might be Will.

Foolish, she realized almost instantly. Why would he be here?

More likely it was Becca Wilder, the teenager she had hired to corral the twins for the evening while she was busy with Sage's shower.

Her supposition was confirmed a moment later when Anna went to answer the door and Julia heard the voice of Jewel Wilder, Becca's mother and one of Sage's friends, who had offered to drop Becca off when she came to the shower herself.

She couldn't do anything about Will right now, she

realized. Sage's bridal shower was supposed to start any moment now and she couldn't let the celebration be ruined by her guilt.

Three hours later, as Sage said goodbye to the last of her guests, Julia began gathering discarded plates and cups, doing her best to ignore her head that throbbed and pulsed with pain.

She knew exactly why her head was pounding—the same reason her heart ached. Because of Will and his stubborn determination to shut himself off from life and because of her own stubborn, misguided determination to prevent him.

For Sage's sake, she had done her best to put away her anxiety and guilt for the evening. She had laughed and played silly wedding shower games and tried to enjoy watching Sage open the gifts from her eclectic collection of friends.

Beneath it all, the ache simmered and seethed, like a vat of bitter bile waiting to boil over.

Will was leaving his home, his friends, his wife and daughter's resting places. She couldn't let him do it, not if he was leaving because of her.

She carried the plates and dishes into the kitchen, where she found Anna wrapping up the leftover food.

"It was a wonderful party," Julia said.

"I think everyone had a good time," Anna agreed. "But listen, you don't have to help clean up. I can handle it. Why don't you go on upstairs with the twins?"

"I just checked with Becca and they're both down for the night. She's heading home with her mom and is leaving the door open so we can hear them down here."

Anna stuck a plate of little sandwiches into her refrigerator, then gave Julia a placid smile.

"That's great. Since the twins are asleep, this would be the perfect chance for you to go and talk some sense into Will."

Julia stared at her, completely astounded at the suggestion. "Where did that come from?"

Anna smiled. "My brilliantly insightful mind."

"Which I never realized until this moment is a little on the cracked side. Why would he listen to me?"

"Well, somebody needs to knock some sense into him and Sage and I both decided you're the best one for the job."

"Why on earth would you possibly think *that?* You've both been friends with him for a long time. I just moved back. He'll listen to what you have to say long before he'll listen to me."

Not to mention the tiny little detail that she suspected *she* was the reason he was leaving in the first place—and the fact that he had basically ordered her to stay away from him.

She wasn't about to admit that to Anna, though.

"We're like sisters to him," Anna answered. "Naggy, annoying little sisters. You, on the other hand, are the woman he has feelings for."

She bobbled the plate she was loading into the dishwasher but managed to catch it before it shattered on the floor.

"Wrong!" she exclaimed. "Oh, you couldn't be more wrong. Will doesn't have feelings for me. He…he might, if he would let himself, but he's wrapped himself up so tightly in his pain he won't let anyone through. Or not me, at least. No, he absolutely doesn't have feelings for me."

Anna studied her for a long moment, then smiled unexpectedly. "Our mistake, then, I guess. Sage and I were quite convinced there was something between the two of you. Will's been different ever since you came back to Cannon Beach."

"Different, how?" she asked warily.

"I can't quite put my finger on how, exactly. I wouldn't say he's been happier, but he's done things he hasn't in two years. Going for ice cream with you and your kids. Coming to the barbecue with Eben and Chloe without putting up a fight. Sage and I both thought you were slowly dragging him back to life, whether he wanted you to or not, and we were both thrilled about it. He kissed you, didn't he?"

Julia flushed. "Yes, but he wasn't happy about either time."

Anna's eyebrow rose. "There was more than one time?"

She sighed. "A few weeks ago, when I helped him hang the new moldings in your living room. We had a fight afterward and I said horrible things to him, things I had no right to say. And now I find out he took a job with Eben's company, and accepted it two weeks ago. I just can't believe it's a coincidence."

"All the more reason you should be the one to convince him to stay," Anna said.

"He told me to stay away from him," Julia whispered, hurting all over again at the harshness of his words.

"Are you going to listen to him? Go on," Anna urged. "I'll keep an eye on Simon and Maddie for you. There's nothing stopping you."

Except maybe her guilt and her nerves and the horrible, sinking sensation in her gut that she was pushing a man away from everything that he cared about, just so he could escape from her.

Before she could formulate further arguments, a huge shaggy beast suddenly hurried into the room, a leash in his mouth and Sage right on his heels.

"Conan, what has gotten into you, you crazy dog?" she exclaimed. "I can put you out."

But the dog didn't listen to her. He headed straight to Julia, plopped down at her feet and held the leash out in his mouth with that familiar expectant look.

She groaned. "Not you, too?"

Sage and Anna exchanged glances and Julia was quite certain she heard Sage snigger.

"Looks like you're the chosen one," Anna said with a smile.

"You can't fight your destiny, Jules," Sage piped in. "Believe me, I've tried. The King of Brambleberry House has declared you're tonight's sacrificial lamb. You can't escape your fate."

She closed her eyes, aware as she did that the pain in her head seemed to have lifted while she was talking to Anna. "I suppose you're telling me Conan wants me to talk to Will, too."

"That's what it looks like to me," Sage said.

"Same here."

Julia stared at Anna—prosaic, no-nonsense Anna, who looked just as convinced as Sage.

"You're both crazy. He's a dog, for heaven's sake!"

Sage grinned. "Watch it. If you offend him, you'll be stuck for life giving him his evening walk."

"Rain or shine," Anna added. "And around here, it's usually rain."

She studied them all looking so expectantly at her and gave a sigh of resignation. "This isn't fair, you know. The three of you ganging up on me like this."

In answer, Sage clipped the leash on Conan's collar and held the end out for Julia. Anna left the room, returning a moment later with Julia's jacket from the closet in the entryway.

"What if Will doesn't want to talk to me?"

It was a purely rhetorical question. She knew perfectly well he wouldn't want to talk to her, just as she was grimly aware she was only trying to delay the inevitable moment when she had to gather her nerve and walk down the beach to his house.

"You're an elementary school teacher," Anna said with a confident grin. "You're good at making your students do things they don't want to do, aren't you?"

Julia snorted. "I have a feeling Will Garrett might be just a tad harder to manage than my fifth-grade boys."

"We all have complete faith in you," Sage said.

Before she was quite aware of how they had managed it, they ushered her and Conan out the front door and closed it behind her. She was quite surprised when she didn't hear the click of the door locking behind her. She wouldn't have put anything past them at this point.

Conan strained on his leash to be gone but she stood on the porch steps of Brambleberry House trying to gather her frayed nerves as she listened to the distant crash of the sea and the cool October breeze moaning in the tops of the pines.

Finally she couldn't ignore Conan's urgency and she

followed the walkway around the house to the gate that opened to the beach.

It would probably be a quicker route to just take the road to his house but she wasn't in a huge hurry to face him anyway.

Conan seemed less insistent as they walked along the shoreline, after he had marked just about every single rock and tuft of grass they passed.

It gave her time to remember her last summer on Cannon Beach. She passed the rock where she had been sitting when he kissed her for the *last* time—not counting more recent incidences—the night before she left Cannon Beach when she was fifteen.

She paused and ran her finger along the uneven surface, remembering the thrill of his arms around her and how she had been so very certain she had to be in love with him.

She'd had nothing to compare it to, but she had been quite sure at fifteen that this must be the real thing.

And then the next day her world had shattered and she had been shuttled to Sacramento with her mother, away from everything safe and secure in her life.

Still, even as her parents' marriage had imploded, she had held the memory of a handsome boy close to her heart.

At first she thought the moisture on her cheeks was just sea spray, then she realized it was tears, that she was crying for lost innocence and for the two people they had been, and for all the pain that had come after for both of them.

She wiped at her cheeks as she knelt and hugged Conan to her. The dog licked at her cheeks and she smiled a little at his attempts to comfort her.

"I'm being silly again, aren't I? I'm not fifteen anymore and I'm not that dreamy-eyed girl. I'm thirty-one years old and I need to start acting like it, don't I?"

The dog barked as if he agreed with her.

With renewed resolve, she squared her shoulders and stood again, gathering her courage around her.

She had to do this. Will's life was here in Cannon Beach. It had always been here, and she couldn't ruin that for him.

She swallowed her nerves and headed for the lights she could see flickering in his workshop.

Chapter 13

He would miss this.

Will stood in his father's workshop—his workspace now, at least for another few days—and routered the edge of a shingle while a blues station played on the stereo.

He had always found comfort within these walls, with the air sweet with freshly cut wood shavings and saw-dust motes drifting in the air, catching the light like gold flakes.

He left the door ajar, both for ventilation and to let the cool, moist sea air inside. In the quiet intervals without the whine and hum of his power tools, he could hear the ocean's low murmur just down the beach.

This was his favorite spot in the world, the place where he had learned his craft, where he had forged a connection with his stern, sometimes austere father, where he had figured out many of his own strengths and his weaknesses.

Before Robin and Cara died, he used to come out here so he could have a quiet place to think. Sage probably would have given it some hippy new age name like a transcendental meditation room or something.

He just always considered it the one place where his thoughts seemed more clear and cohesive.

He didn't so much need a place to think these days as he needed an escape on the nights when the house seemed too full of ghosts to hold anyone still breathing.

In a few days when he started working for Eben Spencer's company, everything would be different. He expected his workspaces for the next few months would be any spare corner he could find in whatever hotel around the globe where Eben sent him to work.

Who would have ever expected him to become an itinerant carpenter? *Have tools, will travel.*

His first job was outside of Boston but Eben wanted to send him to Madrid next and then on to Portofino, Italy before he headed to the Pacific Rim. And that was only the first month.

Will shook his head. Italy and Spain and Singapore. What the hell was he going to do in a foreign country where he didn't know a soul and didn't speak the language?

It all seemed wildly exotic for a guy who rarely left his coastal hometown, who only possessed a current passport because he and Robin had gone on a cruise to Mexico the year before Cara came along.

The work would be the same. That was the important thing. He would still be doing the one thing he was good at, the one thing that filled him with satisfaction, whether he was in Portofino or Madrid or wherever else Eben sent him.

Maybe those ghosts might even have a chance to rest if he wasn't here dredging them up every minute.

He sure hoped he was making the right choice.

He set down the finished shingle and picked up another one from the dwindling pile next to him. Only a few more and then he only had to nail them to the roof to be finished. A few more hours of work ought to do it.

Against his will, he shot another glance out the window at the big house on the hill, solid and graceful against the moonlit sky.

The lights were out on the second floor, he noted immediately, then chided himself for even noticing.

He was almost certain he wasn't really trying to outrun any ghosts by taking the job with Spencer Hotels. But he knew he couldn't say the same for the living woman who haunted him.

He sighed as his thoughts inevitably slid back to Julia, as they had done so often the last two weeks. Tonight was Sage's bridal shower, he knew. He had seen cars coming and going all night.

Julia was probably right in the middle of it all, with her sweet smile and the sunshine she seemed to carry with her into every room.

For a man who wanted to push her away, he sure spent a hell of a lot of time thinking about her. He sighed again, and could almost swear he smelled the cherry blossom scent of her on the wind.

But a moment later, when the router was silent as he picked up another shingle, he thought he heard a snuffling kind of noise outside the door, then a dark red nose poked through.

An instant later, Conan was barking a greeting at him and Julia was walking through the doorway behind him.

Will yanked up his safety glasses and could do nothing but stare at her, wondering how his thoughts had possibly conjured her up.

Her cheeks were flushed, her hair tousled a little by the wind, but she was definitely flesh and blood.

"Hi," she murmured, and he was certain her color climbed a little higher on her cheeks.

She looked fragile and lovely and highly uncomfortable. No wonder, after the things he had said to her the last time they had spoken.

"I'm sorry to bother you... I... we..." Her voice trailed off.

"Wasn't tonight Sage's big bridal shower?"

"It was. But it's over now and everyone's gone. After the shower, Conan needed a walk and he picked me to take him and Sage and Anna made me come down here to talk to you."

She finished in a rush, without meeting his gaze.

"They made you?"

Her gaze finally flashed to his and he saw a combination of chagrin and rueful acceptance. "You know what they're like. I have a tough enough time saying no to them individually. When they combine forces, I'm pretty much helpless to resist."

"Why did they want you to talk to me?" he asked, though he had a pretty strong inkling.

She didn't answer him, though, only moved past him into the workshop, her attention suddenly caught by the project he was working on.

Damn it.

He could feel his own cheeks start to flush and wished, more than anything, that he had had the foresight to grab a tarp to cover the thing the minute she walked in.

"Will," she exclaimed. "It's gorgeous!"

He scratched the back of his neck, doing his best to ignore how the breathy excitement in her voice sent a shiver rippling down his spine. "It's not finished. I'm working on the shingles tonight, then I should be ready to take it back up to Brambleberry House."

She moved forward for a closer look and he couldn't seem to wrench his gaze away from her starry-eyed delight at the repaired dollhouse he had agreed to work on the day she moved in.

"It's absolutely stunning!"

She drew her finger along the curve of one of the cupola's with tender care. Will could only watch, grimly aware that he shouldn't have such an instant reaction just from the sight of her soft, delicate hands on his work.

"You fixed it! No, you didn't just fix it. This is beyond a simple repair. It was such a mess, just a pile of broken sticks, when you started! And from that, you've created a work of art!"

"I don't know that I'd go quite that far."

"I would! Oh, Will, it's beautiful. Better than it ever was, even when it was new from my father."

To his horror, tears started to well up in her eyes.

"It's just a dollhouse. Not worth bawling about," he said tersely, trying to keep the sudden panic out of his voice.

She gave a short laugh as she swiped at her cheeks. "They're happy tears. Oh, believe me. Will, it's wonderful. I can't tell you how much this will mean to Maddie. She tried to be brave about it but she was so heartbroken when I told her the dollhouse hadn't survived the move. It was one of her last few ties to her father and she has always cherished it, I think because he gave it to her right after her diagnosis, a few days before he…"

Her voice trailed off for a moment and he thought she wasn't going to complete the sentence, but then she drew in a breath and straightened her shoulders. "Before he left us."

Will stared at her, trying to make sense of her words. "I didn't realize your husband died so soon after Maddie's cancer was discovered."

She sighed. "He didn't," she said slowly. "His car accident was eighteen months after her diagnosis but…we were separated most of that time. We were a few months shy of finalizing our divorce when he died."

She lifted her chin almost defiantly when she spoke the last part of the sentence.

He wondered at it, even as he tried to figure out how the hell a man with a beautiful wife and two kids—one with cancer—could walk away from his family in the middle of a crisis.

He left us, she had said quite plainly. He didn't miss the meaning of that now. The man had a daughter with cancer and he had been the one to walk away from them.

Will had a sudden fierce wish that he could have met her husband just once before he died, to teach the bastard a lesson about what it meant to be a man.

She was waiting for him to answer, he realized.

"I'm sorry," he finally said, wincing at the inane words. "That must have been hard on you and the kids during such a rough time."

She managed a wobbly smile. "You could say that."

"All this time, you never said anything about your marriage. I had no idea it was rocky."

She sighed and leaned against the work table holding the resurrected dollhouse.

"I don't talk about it much, especially when the kids are around. I don't want them thinking less of their father."

He raised an eyebrow at that, but said nothing. He had his own opinions about it but he didn't think she would be eager to hear them.

"Maddie's diagnosis kicked Kevin in the gut. The stark truth is, he just couldn't handle it. His mother died of cancer when he was young, a particularly vicious form that lingered for a long time, and I think he just couldn't bear the thought that he might lose someone else he loved in the same way."

What kind of strength had it taken her to deal with a crumbling marriage at the same time she was fighting for her daughter's life? He couldn't even imagine it.

He studied her there in his workshop and saw shadows in her eyes. There was more to the story, he sensed.

"Was there someone else?" Some instinct prompted him to ask.

She gave him a swift, shocked look. "How did you know that? I haven't told anyone else. Not even Sage and Anna know that part."

"I don't know. Just a guess." He couldn't very well tell her he was becoming better than he ought to be at reading her thoughts in her lovely green eyes.

She sighed, tracing a finger over one of the arched windows on the dollhouse. "A coworker. He swore he only turned to her after we separated—after Maddy's diagnosis—because he was hurting so much inside and so afraid for the future."

"That doesn't take away much of the sting for you, I imagine."

"No. No, it doesn't. I was angry and bitter for a long time. I mean, I was the one dealing with appointments and sitting through Maddie's chemotherapy with her and holding her when she threw up for hours afterward. I was scared, too. Not scared, I was *terrified*. I used to check on her dozens of times a night, just to make sure she was still breathing. I still do when she's having a rough night. It was a miracle I could function, most days. I was just as scared, but I didn't turn to someone else. I toughed it out by myself because I had no choice."

He couldn't imagine such a betrayal—more than that, he couldn't understand why she could seem to be such a happy person now after what she had been through.

Most women he knew would be bitter and angry at the world after surviving such an ordeal but Julia seemed to bubble over with joy, finding delight in everything.

She had been over the moon that he had repaired a dollhouse her bastard of an almost-ex-husband had worked on. He figured most betrayed women would have smashed the dollhouse to pieces themselves out of spite so they wouldn't have one more reminder of their cheating spouse.

"I don't know why I told you all that," she said after a moment, her cheeks slightly pink. "I didn't come here to relive the past."

Since she seemed eager to change the subject, he decided he wouldn't push her.

"That's right," he answered. "Sage and Anna sent you."

"I would have come anyway," she admitted. "They just gave me a push in this direction."

He found that slightly hard to believe, given his rudeness the last time they met.

"Why?" he asked.

She let out a breath, then confirmed his suspicion. "I...Sage just found out from Eben tonight that you're leaving."

He picked up another shingle, stalling for time. He did *not* want to get into this, especially not with her, though he had been half-expecting something like this for two weeks, since he accepted Eben's offer.

"That's right," he finally said. It would have been rude to turn the router on again—not to mention, Conan wouldn't like it—but he was severely tempted, if only to cut her off.

She seemed to have become inordinately fascinated with one of the finials on the dollhouse.

"I know this is presumptuous and I have no real right to ask..."

Her voice trailed off and he sighed, yanking his safety glasses off his head and setting them aside. He had a feeling he wasn't going to be finishing the dollhouse anytime soon.

"Something tells me you're going to ask anyway."

She twisted her hands together, her color still high. "You love Cannon Beach, Will. I know you do."

"Yeah. I do love it here. I always have."

"Help me understand, then, why you would suddenly decide to leave the town you have lived in for thirty-two years. This is your home. You have friends here, a thriving business. Your whole life is here!"

"What life?"

He hadn't meant to say something that raw, that

honest, but his words seemed to hang between them and he couldn't yank them back.

It was the truth, anyway.

He didn't have a life, or at least not much of one. Everything he had known and cared about was gone and he couldn't walk anywhere in Cannon Beach without stumbling over a memory of a time when he thought he had owned the world, when he was certain he had everything he could ever possibly want.

Since Julia came to town, everything seemed so much harder, his world so much emptier—something else he wasn't about to explain to her.

Her eyes were dark with sorrow and something else that looked suspiciously like guilt.

"Maybe I was ready for a change," he finally said. "You just said it yourself, I've lived here my entire life. That's pretty pathetic for a grown man to admit, that he's never been anywhere, never done anything. Eben offered me the job some time ago. I gave it a lot of thought and finally decided the time was right."

She didn't look convinced. After another long, awkward moment, she clenched her hands together and lifted her gaze to his, her mouth trembling slightly.

"Will you tell me the truth? Are you leaving because of me?"

He shifted his gaze away, wishing his hands were busy with the router again. Unfortunately, his gaze collided with Conan's, and the dog gave him an entirely too perceptive look.

"Why would you say that?" he stalled.

She stepped closer, looking again as if she wanted to weep. "I've been sick inside ever since Sage told me you were taking this job with Eben's company."

"You shouldn't be, Julia. This is not on you. Let it go."

She shook her head. "I pushed you too hard the other day. I said terrible things. I had no right, Will. I have a terrible habit of always thinking I know what's best for everyone else."

Her short laugh held no trace of humor. "I don't know why. I mean, I've made a complete mess of my own life, haven't I? So why would I dare think I have any right to tell anyone else what to do with their life? But I was wrong, Will. I shouldn't have said what I did."

"Everything you said was right on the money. I knew it even while I was reacting so strongly. I've thought the same things myself, deep in my subconscious. Robin wouldn't want me to hide away from life, to sit out here in my workshop and brood while the world carries on without me. That wasn't what she was about, what *we* were about. But even though I've thought the same thing, I can't deny that hearing it from you was tough."

"I'm so sorry."

He sighed at the misery in her voice and surrendered to the inevitable. He stepped forward and picked up her knotted fingers, feeling them tremble in his hands.

"I care about you, Julia, more than I thought I could ever care about anyone again. When I'm with you, I feel like I'm sixteen again, sitting on the beach with the prettiest girl I've ever seen. But it scares the hell out of me. I'm not ready. That's the bald, honest truth. I'm not ready and I'm afraid I don't know if I ever will be."

"That's why you're leaving?"

"I'd be lying if I said you had nothing to do with my decision to take the job with Eben. But leaving—trying something new—has been on my mind for some time.

I was considering it long before you showed up again, back when you were just a distant memory of a past that sometimes feels like it should belong to someone else."

He paused, struck by the contrast of her soft, delicate hands in his fingers that were hard and roughened by years of work.

"I guess you could say you're part of the reason I'm leaving, but you're not the only reason. I need a change. If I stay here, buried under the weight of the past, I'm afraid I'll slowly petrify like a piece of driftwood."

She took a long time to answer. Just when he was about to release her hands and step away, she clutched at his fingers with hands that still trembled.

"Would it make any difference if I…if I were the one to leave?"

He stared at her, taken aback. "Where would you go? You love your new job, Brambleberry House. Everything."

Sadness twisted across her lovely features. "I do love it here and the twins are thriving. But I have much less invested in Cannon Beach than you do. I've only been here a short time. We started over here, we can start over somewhere else."

That she would even contemplate making such a sacrifice for his sake completely astounded him.

"You can't do that for me, Julia. I would never ask of it you."

"You didn't ask. I'm offering. I hate the idea that I had anything to do with your decision to leave. I blew into town out of nowhere and ruined everything."

"You ruined nothing, Julia."

Whether he liked it or not, tenderness churned through him and he couldn't bear her distress. He lifted their joined hands and pressed his mouth to the warm skin at the back of her hand.

She shivered at his touch and he couldn't help himself. He pulled her into his arms, where she settled with a soft sigh.

"You ruined nothing," he repeated. "If anything, you made me realize I can't exist in this halflife forever. I have to move forward or I'll suffocate and right now taking this job with Eben feels like the best way to do that."

"I don't want you to leave," she murmured, her arms around his waist and her cheek against his chest.

He closed his eyes, stunned by the soft, contented peace that seemed to swirl through him. Right at this moment, he didn't want to think about leaving. Hell, he didn't want to move a muscle ever again.

They stood together for a long time, in a silence broken only by the sea outside the door and the dog's snuffly breaths as he slept.

When at last she lifted her face to his, he gave a sigh of surrender and lowered his mouth to hers.

Chapter 14

His kiss was slow and gentle, like standing in a torpid stream, and it seemed to push every single thought from her head.

After their last kiss and the words they had flung at each other afterward, she had been certain she wouldn't find herself here in his arms again.

The unexpectedness of it added a poignant beauty to the moment and she leaned into him, savoring his hard strength against her.

He kissed her for long, drugging moments, until her knees were weak and her mind a pleasant muddle.

Through the soft haze that seemed to surround her, she had a vague awareness that there a subtle difference this time, something that had been missing the other times they kissed.

It took her several moments to pinpoint the change. Those other times they had kissed, he had always held part of himself back and she had sensed the reluctance underlying each touch, even when she doubted he was fully aware of it himself.

This time, that hesitancy was gone. All she tasted in his kiss was tenderness and the sweet simmer of desire.

She smiled against his mouth, unable to contain the giddy joy exploding through her.

"What's so funny?" he murmured.

"Nothing," she assured him. "Absolutely nothing. It's just…I've just missed you."

He stared at her for a long moment, his face just inches from hers, then he groaned and kissed her again. This time his mouth was wild, urgent, and she responded eagerly, pouring all the emotions in her heart into their embrace.

She was in love with him.

Even as her body stirred to life, as their mouths tangled together, as she seemed to sink into the hard strength of his arms, the truth seemed to washed over her like the storm-churned sea and she reeled under the unrelenting force of it.

He was leaving in three days and had just made it quite plain he wouldn't change his mind. Nothing but heartache awaited her. She knew it, just as she knew she was powerless to change the inevitable.

But that didn't matter. Right here, right now, she was in his arms and she couldn't waste this moment by worrying about how much she would bleed inside when he walked away.

She tightened her arms around him and he made a low sound in the back of his throat and his arms tightened around her.

"Julia," he murmured. Just her name and nothing else.

"I'm here," she whispered. "Right here."

She brushed a kiss against the skin of his jawline, savoring the scent of sawdust and hard-working male. He made a low sound in his throat that sent an answering shiver rippling down her spine.

"You're cold."

"A little," she admitted, though her reaction was more from the desire spinning wildly through her system.

"I'm sorry. I like to keep it cool out here when I'm working, especially at night to keep me awake."

He paused for a moment, his gaze a murky blue. "We could go inside," he said, with a soberness that told her exactly what he meant by the words—and how much it cost him to make the suggestion.

A hundred doubts and insecurities zinged through her head. It would be tough enough for her to handle his departure. How could she possibly let him walk away after sharing such intimacies without her heart shattering into a million pieces?

But how could she walk away *now,* when he was offering her so much more of himself than she ever thought he would?

"Are you sure?" she asked.

He paused, taking his time before answering. "I'm not sure of anything, Julia. I only know I want you and this feels more right than anything else has in a long, long time."

"Oh, Will." She framed his face with her hands and kissed him again, pouring all her heart into the kiss.

When at last he drew back, both of them were trembling, their breathing ragged.

"I don't know if I can promise you anything," he said, his voice a low rasp in the night. "Hell, I'm almost a hundred percent certain I can't. But right now I can't bear the thought of letting you out of my arms."

"I'm not going anywhere," she said.

"Not even inside, where it's warmer and far more comfortable than my dusty workshop?"

She smiled, aware of the cold seeping through her jacket despite the heat of his embrace. "All right."

He returned her smile with one of his own and she shivered all over again at the unexpectedness of it. "I'm not going to let you freeze to death out here. Come on inside."

Conan was already standing by the door waiting for them, she saw when she managed to wrench her gaze away from Will's, as if the dog had heard and understood their complete conversation.

She shook her head at his spooky omniscience, but didn't have time to ponder it before Will was holding her hand and walking inexorably toward his house.

It had started to rain again while she was inside the workshop, a fine, cold mist that settled in her hair and made her grateful for the warmth that met them inside the house.

She hadn't been inside his home since that last summer so long ago, though she had seem glimpses of it through the window the day they had gone for ice cream, another lifetime ago.

She had the fleeting impression as she followed him inside of a roomy, comfortable place with a vaguely neglected air to it. He slept here but she had the feeling he spent as little time as possible within these walls.

Conan stopped in the kitchen and plopped down on a rug by the door but Will led her to a large family room with two adjoining deep sofas facing a giant plasma television on one wall.

"Are you still cold?" he asked. "I can start a fire. That should take the chill out of the air."

"You don't have to."

"It will only take a moment."

Without waiting for an answer, he moved to the hearth and started laying out kindling. She didn't mind, sensing he needed the time and space, just as she did, to regain a little equilibrium.

She shrugged out of her jacket and settled into one of the plump sofas, nerves careening through her.

It had been a long time for her and she hoped she wasn't unforgivably rusty. She would have been completely terrified if she didn't have the feeling he hadn't been with anyone since his wife's death.

"I imagine you have a spectacular view when it's daylight."

He gave her a rueful smile as he set a match to the kindling. "I guess. I've been looking at it every day of my life. I tend to forget how breathtaking it is. Maybe traveling a little—seeing other sights for a change—will help me appreciate what I've taken for granted all my life."

Somehow she didn't think the reminder of his imminent departure was accidental. She tried to pretend it didn't matter, even as sorrow pinched at her.

"Do you know where Eben's sending you first?"

"Outside of Boston. I'll be there for a few weeks then I guess I'm off to Italy. Quite a change for a guy who's never left the coast."

The tinder was burning brightly now so he added a heavier log. The flames quickly caught hold of it.

Already, the room seemed warmer, though she wasn't sure if that was from the fire or from the nerves shimmering through her.

Will stood for a moment, watching the fire. When he seemed confident the log would burn, he turned back to her, his features impassive.

"Is something wrong?" she finally said, when the silence between them dragged on.

His sigh sounded deep, heartfelt. "You scare the hell out of me."

She tensed. "Do you want me to leave?"

"About as much as I want to take a table saw to my right arm," he admitted. "In other words, absolutely not."

Despite her nerves, she couldn't contain the laughter bubbling through her as he moved toward her and sat on the sofa beside her. He reached for her hand, but didn't seem in a rush to kiss her again.

This was lovely, she thought, sitting here gazing into the flickering firelight with a soft rain sliding against the window and his fingers tracing patterns on hers.

"I don't know if this is any consolation," she said after a moment, "but you're not the only one who's nervous. It's, uh, been a long time for me. I'd be surprised if you couldn't hear my knees knocking from there."

He gave her a careful look. "Do *you* want to leave?"

She mustered a shaky smile. "About as much as I want to *watch* you take a table saw to your right arm. In other words, absolutely not."

"Good," he murmured.

Finally he kissed her and at the delicious heat, the familiar taste and scent of him, her nerves disappeared. She was suddenly filled with the sweet assurance that this was right. She loved Will Garrett, had loved him since she was a stupid, naive girl.

She wanted this, wanted him, and even if this was all they would ever share, she wouldn't allow any regrets.

He kissed her until she was trembling, aching for more. She held him close, pouring all the emotions she couldn't verbalize into her kiss.

By the time he worked the buttons of her blouse, her head was whirling. When he pushed aside the lacy cups of her bra to touch her, she almost shattered apart right there as a torrent of sensations poured through her.

Oh, it had been far too long since she had remembered what it was to be touched with such heat and tenderness. She had forgotten this slow churn of her blood, the restless ache that seemed to fill every cell.

She arched against him, reveling in his hard strength against her curves, in his rough hands against her sensitive skin.

He groaned, low in his throat, and lowered his head to take her in his mouth. She clutched him close, her hands buried in his hair, as he teased and tasted.

His breathing was ragged when he lifted his clever, clever lips from her breast and found her mouth again while he shrugged out of his own shirt.

She couldn't help shivering as his hard strength covered her again.

"Are you still cold?" he murmured.

"Not even close," she answered, framing his face in her hands and kissing him fiercely. He responded with a groan and any tentativeness disappeared in a wild rush of heat.

In moments, they were both naked. Silhouetted in the

dancing firelight, he was gorgeous, hard and muscled, ruggedly male.

"Okay, now I'm nervous again," she admitted.

"We can stop right now if you want," he said gruffly. "It might just kill me to let you out of my arms, but we don't have to go any further."

"No. I don't want to stop. Just kiss me again."

He willingly obeyed and for several long moments, only their mouths connected, then at last he pulled her close, trailing kisses from her mouth to the sensitive skin of her neck.

"Okay now?" he murmured, his body warm and hard against her.

"Oh, much, much better than okay," she breathed, her mouth tangling with his again as he pressed her back against the soft cushions of the sofa.

It was everything she might have dreamed—tender and passionate, sexy and sweet. When he filled her, she cried out, stunned at the emotions pouring through her, and she had to choke back the words of love she knew he wasn't ready to hear.

His mouth was hard and urgent on hers as he began to slowly move inside her and she lifted her hips to meet him.

Oh, she had missed this. She hadn't fully appreciated how much until right this moment.

How was she ever going to be able to go back to her solitary life?

She pushed the grim thought away, unwilling to let anything destroy the beauty of this moment.

He moved more deeply inside her and she gasped his name, feeling as breathless and shaky as the time she and Will had sneaked out to go cliff diving.

He withdrew then pushed inside her again and the contrast between the tenderness of his kiss and the wild urgency of his body sent her spinning and soaring over the edge.

With a groan, he joined her, his hands gripping hers tightly.

As they floated together back to earth, he shifted and pulled her on top of him, tugging a knit throw from the back of the sofa to cover them.

She nestled into his heat and his strength, a delicious lassitude soaking into her muscles, more content than she could ever remember being in her life.

She must have slept for a few moments, tucked into the safe shelter of his arms. When she blinked her eyes open, the grandfather clock in the hallway was tolling midnight.

Like Cinderella, she knew the spell was ending and she would have to slip away home.

She shifted her gaze to Will and found him watching her. Was he regretting what they had shared? To her frustration, she could read nothing in his veiled expression.

She sat up, reaching for her blouse as she went. "I need to go back to Brambleberry House. Sage and Anna are going to be sending a search party out after me."

He sat up and she had to force herself to look away from that broad, enticing expanse of muscles.

"Oh, somehow I doubt that. I have a feeling they know exactly where you are."

"You're probably right," she answered ruefully. "A little on the spooky side, those two."

He raised an eyebrow as he slid into his jeans. "A little?"

She smiled. "Okay. A lot. I should still go, much as I don't want to."

He was quiet for a long moment, watching out of those veiled features as she worked the buttons of her shirt.

"Julia, I can't promise you anything," he finally said.

She met his gaze, doing her best to keep the devastation at bay. "You said that earlier, and I understand, Will. I do. I don't expect anything."

He raked a hand through his hair. "I'm just so damn screwed up right now. I wish things could be otherwise. I'm just…"

She returned to him and cut his words off with a kiss, hoping he didn't taste the desperation in her kiss. This would be the one and only time for them, she knew.

He didn't have to say the words for her to accept the reality that nothing had changed. He was still leaving in a few days, and she would be left here alone with her pain.

"Will, it's okay," she lied. "My eyes were wide open when I walked into your house. No illusions here, I promise."

"I'm so sorry." His voice was tight with genuine regret and she shook her head.

"I'm not. Not for an instant."

She drew in a breath, gathering the last vestiges of courage left inside her for what somehow she suddenly knew she had to say.

"While we're tossing our cards out on the table, I think I should tell you why I'm here."

His expression turned wary. "Why?"

She sighed. "You haven't figured it out? I'm in love with you, Will."

The words hovered between them, raw and naked, and she had to smile a little at the sudden panic in his eyes.

"I know. It was a big shock for me, too. I'm not telling you that as some kind of underhanded tactic to convince you to stay. I know that nothing I say will change your mind and, believe me, I don't expect my feelings to change your decision in any way. I just felt that you should know. I wouldn't be here with you right now if I didn't love you—it's just not the kind of thing I do."

"I think some part of me guessed as much," he admitted.

"You've been in my heart for sixteen years, Will. Through my parents' divorce, through my own difficult teen years, through the breakup of my marriage, some part of me remembered that summer with you as a wonderful, magical time. Maybe the best summer of my life. You were my first love and I've never forgotten you."

"Julia…"

She shook her head, willing herself not to cry. Not now, not yet. "You don't have to say it. I know, we were different people then. And to be honest, the place you held in my heart was precious but only a tiny, dusty little spot, a corner I peeked into once in awhile with a smile and fond memories but then quickly forgot again."

She forced a smile. "And then I came back to Cannon Beach and here you were. As I came to know you all over again, I revisited those memories and realized that the boy I fell in love with back then had become a good, honorable man. A man who takes great pride in a job well done, who talks to dogs, who cares deeply about his neighbors and is kind to children…even when they make him bleed inside."

She touched his cheek, wishing with all her heart that he was ready to accept the precious, healing gift she so wanted to offer him.

Even as she touched him, though, she didn't miss his slight, barely perceptible flinch.

"Don't. Don't love me, Julia." His voice was ragged, anguished. "I'll only hurt you."

"I know you will." She managed a wobbly smile, even though she could swear she heard the sound of her heart cracking apart. "But I'll survive it."

She kissed him again, a soft, sincere benediction, then stepped away to shrug into her jacket. "I have to go."

He didn't argue, just pulled on his own shirt and boots. "I'll walk you back."

"I have Conan. I'll be fine."

"I'll walk you back," he said firmly.

She nodded, realizing that arguing with him would only be a waste of strength and energy, two commodities she had a feeling she would be needing in the days ahead.

In truth, she didn't mind. These were probably her last few moments with him and she wanted to savor every second.

Conan was again waiting expectantly by the back door. He cocked his head, his expression quizzical. She had no idea what he could read in their expressions but he whined a little.

More than anything, she wanted to bury her face in his fur and sob but she managed to keep her composure as Will handed her an umbrella and picked up a flashlight hanging on a hook by the door.

The slow, steady rain perfectly matched her mood. She shivered a little and zipped up her jacket, then headed toward Brambleberry House.

Will didn't share the umbrella—instead, he simply pulled the hood of his Gore-Tex jacket up, which given the dark and the rain effectively obscured his features.

They walked in silence and even Conan seemed subdued, almost sad. Instead of his usual ebullient energy, he plodded along beside her with his head hanging down.

As for Will, he seemed as distant and unreachable as the Cape Meares lighthouse.

She shouldn't have told him her feelings, she thought. He already carried enough burdens. He didn't need that one, too.

He finally spoke when they approached the gates of Brambleberry House, but they weren't words she wanted to hear.

"Julia, I'm sorry," he said.

"Please don't be sorry we made love. I'm not."

"I should be. Sorry about that, I mean. But I'm not. It was…right. That's not what I meant. Mostly, I guess I'm sorry things can't be different, that we have all these years and pain between us."

She touched his cheek. "The years and the pain shaped us, Will. They're part of who we are now."

He turned his head and kissed her fingers, then pulled her into his arms once more. His kiss was tender, gentle, with an underlying note of finality to it. When he drew away, her throat ached with unshed tears.

"You're not leaving until after the wedding, are you?"

He nodded. "Sage would kill me if I missed her big day. My flight leaves the next morning."

"Well, I'll see you then, anyway. Goodbye, Will."

She had a million things she wanted to say but this wasn't the time. None of them would make a difference anyway.

Instead, she managed one last shaky smile and tugged Conan up the stairs and into the entry, forcing herself not to look back as she heard his muffled footsteps on the sidewalk.

Anna's apartment door opened the moment Julia closed the front door behind her, and Sage and Anna both peeked their heads out into the entryway. They had changed into pajamas and she could smell the aroma of popcorn from inside the apartment.

Conan hurried inside as soon as she unclipped his leash, probably looking for any stray kernels that might have been dropped. She would have smiled if she thought she could manage it.

"So?" Sage demanded. "What happened? You were gone *forever*. Did you talk Will into staying?"

As much as she had come to love both the other women in just the few short months she had been in Cannon Beach, she couldn't bear their curiosity right now, not when her emotions had been scraped to the bone.

"No," she said, her voice low. "His mind is made up."

Sage made a sound of disgust but Anna gave her a searching, entirely perceptive look. She was suddenly aware that her hair was probably a mess and she no doubt had whisker burns on her skin.

"It's not your fault, Julia," she said after a moment. "I'm sure you tried your best."

She fought an almost hysterical urge to laugh. To hide it, she yanked off her jacket and hung it back in the closet. "He has his reasons. He didn't take the job with Eben on a whim, I can promise you that."

"That still doesn't make it right!" Sage exclaimed.

"As people who...who care about him, we owe it to Will to respect his decision, even if we don't agree with it or think it's necessarily the best one for him."

Sage looked as if she wanted to argue but Anna silenced her with a long, steady look.

"He won't change his mind?" Anna asked.

"I don't think so," Julia said.

To her surprise, though Sage was usually the demonstrative one, this time Anna was the one who pulled her into her arms for a hug. "Thanks for trying. I know it was hard for you."

You have no idea, she thought, even as Sage hugged her as well. For just a moment, Julia thought she smelled freesia and it was almost as if Abigail herself was there offering understanding and comfort.

"Don't badger him about it, okay?" she said. "It was a hard decision for him to make but I think taking the job is something he...he needs to do right now."

"Are you okay?" Anna murmured.

For one terrible moment, the sympathy in her friend's voice almost made her weep but she blinked away the tears. "Fine. Just fine. Why wouldn't I be?"

Anna didn't look convinced but to her immense relief, she didn't push. "You look exhausted. You'd better get some rest."

She nodded with a grateful look. "It's been a long day," she agreed. "Good night."

She quickly turned and hurried up the stairs, praying she could make it inside before breaking down.

After she closed the door behind her, she checked

on the twins and found them sleeping peacefully, then returned to the darkened living room. Against her will, she moved to the windows overlooking his house and saw lights on again in his workshop.

The thought of him in his solitary workshop by himself, putting the finishing touches on Maddie's spectacular dollhouse was the last straw. Tears slid down her cheeks to match the rain trickling down the window and she stood for a long time in the dark, aching and alone.

Chapter 15

Three days later, he stood on the edge of the dance floor in the elegant reception room of The Sea Urchin, doing his level best not to spend the entire evening staring at Julia like the lovesick teenager he had once been.

He hadn't seen her since the night they had shared together but he was quite certain he hadn't spent more than ten minutes without thinking about her—remembering the softness of her skin, her sweet response to him, the shock that had settled in gut when she told him she loved him.

Just now she was dancing with her son, laughing as she tried to show him the steps of the fox-trot. She looked bright and vibrant and beautiful in a lovely, flowing green dress that matched her eyes. Despite her apparent enjoyment in the evening, he was almost certain he had caught a certain sadness in her eyes whenever their gazes happened to collide, and his heart ached, knowing he had put it there.

He couldn't stay much longer. He was leaving in the morning and still had work to do packing and closing up his house for an indefinite time. Beyond that, it hurt more than he ever would have dreamed to keep his distance from Julia, to stand on the sidelines and watch her, knowing he could never have her.

He needed to at least talk to Sage before he escaped, he knew. When the music ended and she returned to the edge of the dance floor on the arm of ancient Mr. Delarosa, one of Abigail's old friends, he hurried to claim her before anyone else.

"Have any dances left for an old friend?"

Surprise flickered in her eyes, then she gave him a brilliant smile. "Of course!"

He wasn't much of a dancer but he did his best, grateful at least that it was another slow song and he wasn't going to have to make an idiot out of himself by trying to shake and groove.

"You make a stunning bride, kiddo," he said when they fell into a rhythm. "Who ever would have believed it?"

He gave an exaggerated wince when she punched him lightly in the shoulder.

"You know I'm teasing," he said, squeezing the fingers he held. "I'm thrilled for you and Eben, Sage. I really am. You're a beautiful bride and it was a beautiful ceremony."

"It was, wasn't it? I only wish Abigail could have been here."

"I don't doubt she was, in her own way."

She smiled, as he intended. "I think you're probably

right. I was quite sure I smelled freesia at least once while Eben and I were exchanging our vows."

"I'm glad the weather held for you." It had been a gorgeous, sunny day, warm and lovely, a rarity on the coast for October.

"I thought for sure we were going to have to move everything inside for the ceremony but the weather couldn't have been more perfect."

"That's because Mother Nature knows she owes you big-time for all your do-gooder, save-the-world efforts. She wouldn't dare ruin your big day with rain."

She laughed softly then sobered quickly. "I forgot, I'm not supposed to be speaking to you. I'm still mad at you."

"Don't start, Sage. We've been over this. I'm going. But it's not forever—I'll be back."

"It won't be the same."

"Nothing will. Look at you, Mrs. Spencer. You're moving to San Francisco with Eben and Chloe. Things change, Sage."

"I'm going to miss you, darn it. You're the big, annoying, overprotective brother I've always wanted, Will."

He was more touched than he would dare admit. "And since the day you moved in to Brambleberry House, you've been like a bratty little sister to me, always sure you know what's best for everyone."

She made a harumph kind of sound. "That's because I do. For instance, I am quite certain you're making a huge mistake to leave Cannon Beach and a certain resident of Brambleberry House who shall remain nameless."

"Who? Conan?"

She smacked his shoulder again. "You know who I mean. Julia."

He shook his head. "Leave it alone, Sage."

"I won't." She stuck her chin out with a stubbornness he should have expected, knowing Sage. "If Abigail were here, she would tell you the exact same thing. You can't lie to me, you have feelings for Julia, don't you?"

"None of your business. This is a great band, by the way. Where did you find them?"

"I didn't, Jade Wu did. You know perfectly well she handled all the wedding details. And I won't let you change the subject. What kind of idiot walks away from a woman as fabulous as Julia, who just happens to be crazy about him?"

"I'm going to leave you right here in the middle of the dance floor if you don't back off," he warned her. Though he spoke amicably enough, he put enough steel in his voice that he hoped she got the message.

She gave him a piercing look and then her gaze suddenly softened. "You're as miserable as she is! You know you are."

He shifted his gaze to Julia, who was dancing and smiling with the owner of the bike shop—who just happened to be the biggest player in town.

"She doesn't look miserable to me."

They were several couples away from them on the dance floor, but just at that moment, her partner swung her around so she was facing him. They made eye contact and for one sizzling moment, it was as if they were alone in the room.

He caught his breath, snared by those deep green eyes for a long moment, until her partner turned her again.

"She does a pretty good job of hiding it, but she is," Sage said.

She paused, then met his gaze. "Did I ever tell you how I almost lost Eben and Chloe because I was too afraid of being hurt to let them inside my heart?"

"I don't think you did," he said stiffly.

"It's a long story but look at the happy ending, just because I decided Eben's love was worth far more to me than my pride. You're the most courageous man I know, Will. You've walked through hell these last few years. I know that, know that you've endured more than anyone should have to—a pain that most of us probably couldn't even guess at. Don't you think you've been through enough? You deserve happiness. Do you really think you're going to find it traveling around the world, leaving behind your home and everyone who loves you?"

"I don't know," he said, more struck by her words than he cared to admit. "But I'm going anyway. This is your wedding day. I don't want to fight with you about this. I appreciate your concern for me, but everything will be fine."

She sighed and probably would have said more but Eben came up behind them at that moment.

"What does a guy have to do to get a dance with his bride?"

"Just ask," Will said. "She's all yours."

He kissed Sage on the cheek and released her. "Thanks for the dance and the advice," he said. "Congratulations again to both of you."

Much as he loved her, he was relieved to walk away and leave her to Eben. He didn't need more of her lectures about how he was making a mistake to leave or her not-so-subtle hints about Julia.

What he needed was to get out of here, and soon. He couldn't take much more.

He made it almost to the door when he felt a sharp tug on his jacket. He turned around and found Maddie Blair standing beside him wearing a frilly blue party dress and a blazing smile.

His heart caught just a little but he probed around and realized he no longer had the piercing pain he used to whenever he saw Julia's dark-haired daughter.

"Hi," she said.

He forced himself to smile back. "Hi yourself."

"I had to tell you how much I love, love, *love* my doll-house. It's the best dollhouse in the whole world! Thank you so much!"

"I'm glad you like it."

"Did you know it has a doorbell that really works? And it even has a secret closet in the bedroom that you open a special way."

"I believe I did know that."

He had finally finished the dollhouse late into the night two days before and had dropped it off at Brambleberry House, leaving it covered with a tarp on the porch for Julia to find. He knew it was cowardly to drop it off in the middle of the night. He should have picked a time when he could help carry it up the stairs for her, but he hadn't been able to face her.

"I would like to dance with you," Maddie announced, leaving him no room for arguments.

"Um, sure," he said, not knowing how to wiggle out of it. "I'd like that."

It wasn't even a lie, he realized to his surprise. He held out his arm in a formal kind of gesture and she grinned and slipped her hand into the crook of his elbow.

Together they worked their way through the crowd to the dance floor.

While they danced, Maddie kept up an endless stream of conversation during the dance—about her dolls, about how she was going to go visit Chloe in San Francisco some time, about some mischief her brother had been up to.

He listened to her light chatter while the music poured around him, making appropriate comments whenever she stopped to take a breath.

"You're the best dancer I've danced with tonight," she said when the song was almost at an end. "Simon stepped on my toes a million times and I think he even broke one. And Chloe's dad wouldn't stop looking at Sage the whole time we danced. I think that's rude, don't you, even if they did just get married. Grown-ups are weird."

Will couldn't help it, he looked down at Maddie's animated little face and laughed out loud.

"You have a nice laugh," she observed, watching him through her wise little eyes that had endured too much. "I like it."

"Thanks," he answered, a little taken aback.

"You know what?" she whispered, as if confiding state secrets, and he had to bend his head a little lower to hear her, until their faces were almost touching.

"What?" he whispered back.

"I like you, too." She smiled at him, then before he realized what she intended, she stood on her tiptoes and kissed his cheek.

He stared at her as her words seemed to curl through him, squeezing the air from his lungs and sending all the careful barriers he thought he had built around his heart tumbling with one big, hard shove.

"Thanks," he finally said around the golf ball-size lump in his throat. "I, uh, like you, too."

It wasn't quite true, he realized with shock. His feelings for this little girl and her brother ran deeper than simple affection.

He had tried so hard to keep them all at bay but somehow when he wasn't looking, Julia's twins had sneaked into his heart. He cared about them—Simon, with his inquisitive mind and his eagerness to please, and Maddie with her unrelenting courage and the simple joy she seized from life.

How the hell had he let such a thing happen? He thought he had been so careful around them to keep his distance but something had gone terribly wrong.

He remembered Maddie offering to eat her ice cream slowly so he could have a taste if he wanted, Simon talking about baseball and inviting him to watch a Mariners' game, budding hero worship in his eyes.

He loved Julia's children.

Just as he loved their mother.

He stopped stockstill on the dance floor. It *couldn't* be true. It couldn't. His gaze found Julia, standing at the refreshment table talking to Anna. She looked graceful and lovely. When she felt his gaze, she turned and gave him a tentative smile and he suddenly wanted nothing more than he wanted to yank her into his arms and carry her out of here.

"Are you okay, Mr. Garrett?" Maddie asked.

"I…yes. Thank you for the dance," he said, his voice stiff.

"You're welcome. Will you come play Barbies with me sometime?"

He had to get out of there, right now. The noise and the crowd were pressing in on him, suffocating him.

"Maybe. I'll see you later, okay?"

She nodded and smiled, then slipped away. On his way out the door, his gaze caught Julia's one more time and he hoped to hell the shock of his newfound feelings didn't show in his expression.

She gave him another tentative smile, which he acknowledged with a jerky nod, then he slipped out the door.

He climbed into his pickup in a kind of daze and pulled out of The Sea Urchin's parking lot in the pale twilight, not knowing where he was heading, only that he had to get away. He thought he was driving aimlessly, following the curve of the ocean, but before he quite realized it, he found himself at the small cemetery at twilight, just as the sunset turned the waves a soft, pale blue.

He parked outside the gates, knowing he didn't have long since the cemetery was supposed to be closed after dark. Leaves crunched underfoot as he followed the familiar path, listening to the quiet reverence of the place.

He stopped at his father's grave first, under the spreading boughs of a huge, majestic oak tree. It was a fitting resting place for a man who could work such magic with his hands and a piece of wood. He stopped, head bowed, remembering the many lessons he had learned from his father. Work hard, play hard, cherish your family.

Not a bad mantra for a man to follow.

After long moments, he let out a breath and walked over a small hill to Abigail's grave, decorated with many tokens of affection. Sage had left her a wedding invitation, he saw, and a flower from her bouquet, and Will couldn't help smiling.

He saved the toughest for last. With emotion churning through him, he followed the trail around another curve, almost to the edge by the fence, where two simple headstones marked Robin and Cara's graves.

He hadn't been here in a few months, he realized with some shock. Right after the accident he used to come here every day, sometimes twice a day. He had hated it, but he had come. Those visits had dwindled but he had always tried to come at least once a week to bring his wife whatever flowers were in season.

Like Abigail, Robin had loved flowers.

Guilt coursed through him as he realized how he had neglected his responsibilities.

He rounded the last corner and there they were, silhouetted in the dying sun. Two simple markers—Robin Cramer Garrett, beloved wife. Cara Robin Garrett, cherished daughter.

Emotions clogged his throat. Oh, he missed them. He walked closer, then he blinked in shock, certain the dusky twilight must be playing tricks with his eyesight.

A few weeks after the accident, Abigail had asked him if she could plant a rosebush between Robin and Cara's graves. He had been wild with grief, inconsolable, and wouldn't have cared whether she planted a whole damn flower garden, so he had given his consent.

He hadn't paid it much attention, other than to note a few times in the summer that if she had still been alive, Abigail would have been devastated to know she must have planted a sterile bush. He hadn't seen a single bloom on it in two years.

Now, though, as he stood in the cool October air, he stared in shock at the rosebush. It was covered in flowers—hundreds of them, in a rich, vibrant yellow.

This couldn't be right. He didn't know a hell of a lot about horticulture but he was fairly certain roses bloomed in summer. It was mid-October now, and had been colder than usual the last few weeks, rainy and dank.

It made absolutely no sense but he couldn't ignore the evidence in front of him. Abigail's roses were sending their lush, sweet fragrance into the air, stirring gently in a soft breeze.

Let go, Will. Life moves on.

He could almost swear he heard Abigail's words on the breeze, her voice as brisk and no-nonsense as always.

He sank down onto the wooden bench he had built and stared at the flower-heavy boughs, softly caressing the marble markers.

Let go.

His breathing ragged, he gazed at the flowers, stunned by the emotion pouring through him like a cleansing, healing rainstorm, something he hadn't known since his family was taken from him with such sudden cruelty.

Hope.

It was hope.

These roses seemed a perfect symbol of it, a precious gift Abigail had left behind just for him, as if she knew that somehow he would need to see those blossoms at exactly this moment in his life to remind him of things he had lost along the way.

Hope, faith. Love.

Life moves on.

Whether he was ready for it or not, he loved Julia Blair and her children. They had showed him that his life was not over, that if he could only find the courage, his future didn't have to be this grim, empty existence.

She had roared back into his life like a hurricane, blowing away all the shadows and darkness, the bone-deep misery that had been his companion for two years.

He couldn't say the idea of loving her and her kids still didn't scare the hell out of him. He had already lost more than he could bear. But the idea of living without them—of going back to his gray and cheerless life—scared him more.

He sat on the bench for a long time while the cemetery darkened and the roses danced and swayed in the breeze, surrounding him with their sweet perfume.

When at last he stood up, his cheeks were wet but his heart felt a million times lighter. He headed for the cemetery gates, with only one destination in mind.

Chapter 16

"Mama, I just love weddings." Though she was drooping with fatigue, Maddie's eyes were bright as Julia helped her out of her organza dress.

"It was lovely, wasn't it?"

"Sage was so pretty in her dress. She looked like an angel. And Chloe did a good job throwing the flower petals, didn't she? She didn't even look one bit nervous!"

Julia smiled at Maddie's enthusiasm. "She was the best flower girl I've ever seen."

"Do you think when you get married, I could wear a dress like Chloe's and throw flower petals, too?"

She winced, not at all sure how to answer. "Um, honey, I've already been married, to your dad," she finally said.

"But you could get married again, couldn't you? Chloe said you could because her dad was already married before, too, to her mom. Then her mom died just like Daddy and now her dad is married again to Sage."

Julia forced a smile. "Isn't it lucky he found Sage?"

She, on the other hand, had given her heart to Will Garrett, wholly and completely, and somehow she knew she would never be able to love anyone else. Will wasn't ready for it. For all she knew, he would *never* be ready. If Will couldn't bring himself to love her back, she was afraid she would spend the rest of her life alone.

But she wasn't about to confide her heartache to her daughter. "You need to get to sleep, kiddo. It's been a big day and I know you're tired. Simon's already in his bed, sound asleep."

She helped Maddie into her nightgown and was tucking her under the covers when Maddie touched her hand.

"Mama, I think you should marry Mr. Garrett."

Julia nearly tripped over Maddie's slippers in her astonishment. "Wh…why would you say that?"

"Well, lots of reasons. He smells nice and I just love the dollhouse he made me."

Not the worst reasons for a seven-year-old girl to come up with to marry a man, she supposed.

"And maybe if you married him, he wouldn't be so sad all the time. You make him smile, Mama. I know you do."

Tears burned in her eyelids at Maddie's confident statement and she knelt down to fold her daughter into her arms.

"Go to sleep, pumpkin," she said through the emotions clogging her throat. "I'll see you in the morning."

She turned off the light and closed her door, then moved to Simon's room to check on him. He was sleeping soundly, his blankets already a tangle at his waist.

She tucked them back over his shoulders then returned to the living room, lit only by a small lamp next to her Stickley rocking chair.

Though she tried to fight the impulse, she finally gave in and moved to the window overlooking Will's house. No lights were on there, she saw. Was he asleep already?

He was leaving in the morning. Maybe he intended to get a solid night's rest for traveling across the country.

The emotions Maddie had stirred in her finally broke free and she felt tears trickling down her cheeks. He hadn't said a word to her all day. She had felt his gaze several times, both during the ceremony and then after at the reception, but he hadn't approached her.

After his dance with Maddie, she had intended to track him down—if only to tell him goodbye before he left for his new job—but he had rushed out of The Sea Urchin so fast she hadn't had the chance.

She didn't need a pile of two-by-fours to fall on her head to figure out he didn't want to talk to her again.

She swiped at her tears with her palm. He hadn't even left town yet and she already missed him like crazy. Despite her determined claims to him that she wouldn't regret making love, she couldn't deny that the tender intimacy they had shared had only ratcheted up her pain to a near-unbearable level.

Sage's joy today had only served to reinforce to Julia that she was unlikely ever to know that kind of happiness with Will. He might have opened up his emotions to her a few nights ago but now they were as tightly locked and shoved away as they had been since she returned to town. If she needed proof, she only had to look at the careful distance he maintained at the wedding.

What a strange journey she had traveled since making the decision to return to Cannon Beach. She never would have guessed when she took that teaching job several months ago that she would find love and heartbreak all in one convenient package.

He was leaving in the morning and she could do nothing to stop him.

She sobbed, just a little, then the sound caught in her throat when she suddenly thought she smelled freesia.

"Oh, Abigail," she murmured. "I wish you were here to tell me what to do, how I can reach Will. I don't think I can bear this."

Silence met her impassioned plea, but an instant later she jumped a mile when she felt something wet brush her hand.

"Conan! You scared the life out of me! Where were you?"

The dog had followed her and the twins upstairs when they returned to Brambleberry House from the wedding, apparently needing company since Anna was still busy cleaning up at the reception and Sage and Eben were staying at The Sea Urchin for the night until they left for their honeymoon in the Galapagos in the morning.

He must have gone into her room to lie down, since she hadn't seen him when she came out of Simon's room and had forgotten he was even there. Still, she had to admit she was grateful for the company. The dog leaned against her leg, offering his own unique kind of support and sympathy.

"Thanks," she whispered, as they sat together in her dim apartment looking out at the lights of town.

But his steady comfort didn't last long. After a moment, his ears pricked up and he suddenly barked and rushed for the door, his tail wagging.

She sighed. "You want to go out *again?* We let you out when we came home!"

He whined a little and watched her out of those curiously intelligent eyes. With a sigh, she abandoned any fleeting hope she might have briefly entertained about sinking into a hot bubble bath to soak away her misery, for a while anyway.

"All right, you crazy dog. Just let me find some shoes first."

She had changed after the reception into worn jeans and her oldest, most comfortable sweater. Now she grabbed tennis shoes and headed down the stairs.

The moment she opened the outside door, Conan rocketed down the porch steps and toward the front gate, then disappeared from sight.

Oh rats. She forgot to check that the gate was still closed. Conan usually stuck close to home, preferring his own territory, but if he smelled a cat anywhere in the vicinity, all bets were off.

What was she supposed to do now? No one else was home, the twins were sleeping upstairs and the dog was loose. She couldn't let him wander free, though.

"Conan," she called. "Get back here."

He barked from what sounded like just the other side of the ironwork fence, but she couldn't see him in the darkness.

"Here, boy. Come on."

He didn't respond to the command and with a sigh, she headed down the sidewalk, hoping he wasn't in the mood for a playful game of tag. She wasn't at all in the mood to chase him.

"Come on, Conan. It's cold." She walked through the gate, then froze when she saw in the moonlight just why the dog hadn't answered her summons.

He was busy greeting a man who stood silent and watchful on the other side of the fence.

Will.

She stared at him, stunned to find him here, tonight, and wondering if she had left any evidence of the tears she had just shed for him. All those emotions just under the surface threatened to break through again—sorrow and regret, doubt, sadness.

Love.

Especially love.

She wanted to go to him, throw her arms around his waist and beg him not to leave.

"I didn't see you there," she said instead, hoping her emotional tumult didn't show up in her voice.

He said nothing, just continued to pet the dog and watch her. She walked a little closer.

"Is everything okay?"

"No." His voice sounded hoarse, ragged. "I don't think it is."

He stepped closer to her, so near she could smell the scent of his aftershave, sexy and male. Her heart, already pounding hard since the instant she saw him standing in the darkness, picked up a pace.

"What is it?"

He was quiet for a long time—so long she was beginning to worry something was seriously wrong. Finally, to her immense shock he reached out and grasped her fingers and pulled her even closer.

"I had to come. Had to see you."

"Why?"

His slow sigh stirred her hair. "I love you, Julia."

"Wh-what did you say?" She jerked her hand away and scrambled back. Her heartbeat accelerated and she couldn't seem to catch her breath as shock rippled through her.

He raked a hand through his hair. "I didn't mean to just blurt it out like that. I must sound like an idiot."

"I'm…I'm sorry. You don't sound like an idiot. I just…I wasn't expecting that. You're leaving tomorrow. Aren't you leaving?"

A tiny flutter of joy started in her heart but she was afraid to let it free, afraid he would only crush it and leave her feeling worse than ever.

"Yes. I'm leaving."

She expected his words but they still scored her heart. He said he loved her, but he was leaving anyway?

"I wish I didn't have to go but I gave my word to Eben and I'm committed, at least for a few weeks, until he can find someone else to take my place."

He reached for her hand again and she could feel her fingers trembling in his hard, callused palm. "And then I'd like to come back. To Cannon Beach and to you."

While she was still reeling from his words, he paused, then touched her cheek softly. "You were so right about everything you've said to me. I need to move forward, to give myself the freedom to taste all life has to offer again. It's time. I've known it's time, but I've been so afraid. That's a tough thing for a man to admit, but it's the truth. I was afraid to let myself love you, afraid I was somehow…betraying Robin and Cara by all the feelings I was starting to have for you."

She squeezed his fingers. "Oh, Will. You'll never stop loving them. I would never ask that of you. That's exactly the way it should be. But the heart is a magical thing. Abigail taught me that. When you're ready, when you need it to, it can miraculously expand to make room."

He studied her for a long moment and then suddenly he smiled. Only when she saw his mouth tilt, saw the genuine happiness in his expression, did she realize he truly meant what he said. *He loved her.* She still couldn't quite absorb it, but his eyes in the soft moonlight were free of any lingering grief and sorrow.

He loved her.

He cupped his hands around her face and kissed her then, soft and gentle in the cool October air. She wrapped her arms around his waist as a sweet, cleansing joy exploded through her.

"My heart has made room for you, Julia. For you and your beautiful children. How could it help but find a place? You already had your own corner there sixteen years ago. I think some part of me was just waiting for you to return and move back in."

His mouth found hers again, and in his kiss she tasted joy and healing and the promise of a sweet, beautiful future.

Not far away, a huge mongrel dog sat on his haunches watching them both with satisfaction in his eyes while the soft, flowery scent of freesia floated in the autumn air.

* * * * *

SPECIAL EDITION

Life, Love and Family

Look for a charming new holiday tale from
USA TODAY bestselling author

RaeAnne Thayne

It's Trace Bowman's job as police chief to be
protective of his town and the good people who
live there. So when Becca Parsons moves into town
to work at the local diner, all of Trace's warning
bells go off. She's mysterious, cautious and a
temptation he can't let himself indulge in.
Becca has a secret—and Trace won't rest until
he finds out what it is.

THE COWBOYS OF COLD CREEK

CHRISTMAS IN COLD CREEK
Available October 25 wherever books are sold!

*If you enjoyed these stories from RaeAnne Thayne,
here's a sneak peek of CHRISTMAS IN COLD CREEK,
her brand-new tale from Harlequin® Special Edition™,
available November 2011!*

*Join the excitement as we meet the Bowmans—four
siblings who lost their parents but keep family ties alive
in Pine Gulch. First up is Trace—only two things get
under this rugged lawman's skin: beautiful women and
secrets. And in Rebecca Parsons, he finds both!*

On impulse, he unfolded himself from the bar stool. "Need a hand?"

"Thank you! I…" She lifted her gaze from the floor to his jeans and then raised her eyes. When she identified him, her hazel eyes turned from grateful to unfriendly and cold, as if he'd somehow thrown the broken glasses at her head.

He also thought he saw a glimmer of panic in those interesting depths, which instantly stirred his curiosity like cream swirling through coffee.

"I've got it, Officer. Thank you." Her voice was several degrees colder than the whirl of sleet outside the windows.

Despite her protests, he knelt down beside her and began to pick up shards of broken glass. "No problem. Those trays can be slippery."

This close, he picked up the scent of her, something fresh and flowery that made him think of a mountain meadow on a July afternoon. She had a soft, lush mouth and for one brief, insane moment, he wanted to push aside that stray lock of hair slipping from her ponytail and taste her. Apparently he needed to spend a lot less time working and a great deal *more* time recreating with the opposite sex if he could have sudden random fantasies about a woman he wasn't even inclined to like, pretty or not.

"I'm Trace Bowman. You must be new in town."

She didn't answer immediately and he could almost see the wheels turning in her head. Why the hesitancy? And why that little hint of unease he could see clouding the edge of her gaze? His presence was obviously making her uncomfortable.

"Yes. We've been here a few weeks."

"Well, I'm just up the road about four lots, in the white house with the cedar shake roof, if you or your daughter need anything." He smiled at her as he picked up the last shard of glass and set it on her tray.

Definitely a story there, he thought as she hurried away. He just might need to dig a little into her background to find out why someone with fine clothes and nice jewelry, who so obviously didn't have experience as a waitress, would be here slinging hash at The Gulch. Was she running away from someone? A bad marriage?

So…Rebecca Parsons. Not Becky. An intriguing woman. It had been a long time since one of those had crossed his path here in Pine Gulch.

Trace won't rest until he finds out Rebecca's secret, but would he still have that same attraction to her once he does? Find out in
CHRISTMAS IN COLD CREEK.
Available November 2011
from Harlequin® Special Edition™.

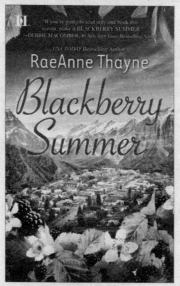

Harlequin Super Romance

*Discover a fresh, heartfelt new romance
from acclaimed author*

Sarah Mayberry

Businessman Flynn Randall's life is
complicated. So he doesn't need the
distraction of fun, spontaneous Mel Porter.
But he can't stop thinking about her. Maybe
he can handle one more complication....

All They Need

LONGER
BOOK
Same Price!

*Available November 8, 2011,
wherever books are sold!*